I0831472

THE DISAPPEARANCE OF OLIVER KIPMAN

KEONA MISTISSHEN

Cover art: Miblart

www.keonamistsshen.com

ISBN:979-8-9993907-0-7

For Mom and Dad,
for always supporting and encouraging me.

PROLOGUE

Gianna didn't know why she kept going back to it. It wasn't as if she didn't have a million better things to do than reread five-year-old news reports. She had a math assignment due in two days, a new episode of her favorite podcast to catch up on, and an Agatha Christie paperback collecting dust on her shelf. Then there was the long-dreaded talk with Anthony about the criminology camp flier collecting dust in the back of her drawer.

Every one of them—even the last—were a bit productive. And yet, she couldn't stop her fingers from typing his name in the search engine.

Whoever had snapped the photo had caught Ollie as he was looking up. The flash caused a red flare in his eyes, making the simple action come off as menacing. No one could tell what Ollie was doing when the photo was taken. He could've been watching a movie or texting a friend.

How many photos did they go through before choosing this one? How many smiles and goofy moments of a teenage boy did they swipe by so they could paint him as a monster?

There had to be a lot of them. Oliver Kipman always wore a smile on his face.

But that was the problem.

Monsters didn't smile.

They certainly didn't if their face was to be plastered on the front of every television screen in the state. If their nickname began with "Killer".

In the end, it didn't matter what photo they chose. It wouldn't change the outcome, the undeniable truth. No one had laid eyes on Oliver Kipman in five years. The last anyone saw of him was his car pulling into a bus station ten miles outside of Echo Falls, New Hampshire.

And that was the last time anyone wanted to see him. At least, that was the case for the citizens of Echo Falls. The town now known as the home of Killer Oliver, the boy who murdered his best friend and got away with it. They'd prefer to forget him entirely; if not that, then scowl every time his name was mentioned. *So what if he vanished into the wind and never returned?* they said. *What do we care about as long as a cold-blooded murderer is anywhere but here?*

Everyone had given up on finding him—but for a reason she couldn't place, Gianna hadn't. Perhaps it was because the murder took place in her hometown and she'd grown up for five years hearing about it. Or perhaps the mystery of it all intrigued her. People didn't vanish into thin air—yet Oliver Kipman managed to do just that.

She glanced at his picture again, the same question worming its way to the front of her mind: *Where are you?*

And like the past five years, there was no answer—just Ollie's red eyes staring back at her.

ONE

The boyfriend is the killer."

"But isn't he the most obvious choice? I thought the killer was never the most obvious."

Gianna poked at the half-eaten waffle on her plate, drowned in Lori's famous homemade maple syrup. "Not really. Eighty percent of homicide victims know their murderers. Besides, Cole had no alibi, a key to Rachel's apartment, and according to his own mother, the two were having problems. Rachel's own sister, Riley, even backed her up on that one."

"Huh." Valarie propped her chin onto her hands, her blonde hair brushing against her elbows. "So is he the killer?"

"I don't know," Gianna admitted. "I haven't finished the episode yet."

"How many episodes are in this podcast again?"

"A hundred."

One Hundred Days of Crime became one of her favorite podcasts immediately. But then again, anything with the words *crime* or *mystery* in it drew her attention. Such as the criminology program in Boston. The flyer in her desk flashed through her mind.

"By the way," Valarie said, noticing the direction Gianna's thoughts went, "you still haven't told me how the talk with your uncle went."

Her shoulders slumped at the thought of the night before. After weeks of staring at the crumpled flyer, Gianna finally gathered up the courage to ask Anthony about the criminology spring program. Two weeks of examining mock crime scenes, listening to lectures from real-life investigators, and even getting to work in a crime lab. Two weeks of complete and utter bliss.

Or so she hoped.

Anthony hadn't said no—he completely brushed off the program like it was nothing more than a fleck of dust on his jacket.

Valarie frowned. "Why not? Is it because of the cost?"

Gianna shook her head. Money wasn't the issue. Even if it had been, Gianna still worked part-time over at The Retro, the local corner coffee shop. She'd saved up enough over the summer to cover the fees for the camp and the expenses for travel.

No, the issue had everything to do with Anthony, or rather his overprotectiveness.

Being a detective isn't as easy as it sounds, he told her the night before. *It's tough work. You have people breathing down your neck, relying on you. And the cases aren't anything like the movies make it. They're worse.*

He believed being a detective was too dangerous. And while she admired Anthony's protective nature, she couldn't help but feel it was holding her back.

"So that's it?" Valarie folded her arms across her chest. "You're giving up? You?"

"Not exactly." She sighed, running a hand over her face. "I don't know. I guess? I mean, what else can I do, Val? He's made up his mind."

"Oh, I don't know … how about you convince him to let you go?"

Gianna laughed. If only it were that simple. Once Anthony made up his mind, there was no changing it.

"What's so funny?" Valarie asked. "It's a good idea. Anthony adores you. You're practically his daughter. Remember that Christmas he got you all the special editions of Sherlock Holmes?"

"That's different. There's no life-threatening danger in getting lost in a fictional world."

"You'd been begging for those books all year. You used to cry yourself to sleep for months."

Gianna tilted her head to the side. "I don't remember any crying."

"Okay, so you didn't cry, but that's beside the point." Valarie leaned into the table. "You have to show him that missing this opportunity would absolutely crush you. Destroy your soul, kill your spirit."

Gianna considered Valarie's words. It wasn't the worst idea, but no amount of tears would convince Anthony to change his answer. No, if she were to get him to change his mind, she would have to do something big. Something that would show Anthony she was capable of being a detective and all that came with it. That she could handle it.

But how?

As they traded ideas on how to convince Anthony, her friend's gaze lingered out the window. The fifth time it happened, Gianna finally said, "What are you looking at?"

"Nothing!" Valarie squeaked.

"Okay. Keep your secrets." Gianna had meant it as a joke, but Valarie's face flashed with panic. Gianna's smile faded when her best friend's eyes darted to the window. It was like she was waiting for something.

Or someone.

Of course. How could she not have seen it before? The way not a single strand of Valarie's hair was out of place, her makeup nothing short of perfection. Plus the overwhelming cloud of perfume Gianna noticed when Valarie first walked in. All of those together could only mean one thing.

"No. No," she groaned. "Please don't tell me you invited him."

Gianna covered her face with her hands. This was the first brunch she and Valarie had in weeks, and now Valarie's latest boyfriend was about to ruin it. She eyed the parking lot for his hideous white van and felt relief when she didn't see it.

"Why would you do this to me?" she said. "Are you trying to torture me?"

Valarie rolled her eyes. "You're overreacting. There is nothing wrong with wanting my best friend and my boyfriend to find common ground."

"Oh, is that the new name for being deceitful?"

"It wasn't lying; it was more like … withholding information."

"That's still lying."

"Look, I just want you two to get along. And you can't do that if you keep disappearing every time he shows his face." Valarie gave her a knowing look. Darn. Gianna thought she was being discreet when it came to avoiding Liam. The headache excuse four times a week was too obvious.

"It's not his face that's the problem," Gianna said. "Maybe if he didn't try selling me his CD every time he saw me … and if it weren't for the fact that you are way too good for him."

"I'll be the judge of who's good enough for me or not. As for his band, I told him not to try selling his CD for a few hours, and he agreed. Just give him a chance? For me?" Her lips tugged into a pout, her eyes widening.

"That's not fair!" Gianna exclaimed. "You're making that face."

"What face?" Valarie said, feigning innocence.

"That face." Gianna groaned, but even as she said it, her resolve weakened. Valarie hated when the people in her life didn't get along. Once she saw something broken, she aimed to fix it. For most of their friendship, the broken thing in question had been Mr. and Mrs. Springfield's marriage. Nothing could fix that. However, Valarie was convinced she could get Liam and Gianna on the same page.

"Fine," she relented. "But if he calls me that nickname again, I can't promise that I won't dump this syrup over his head."

"Deal."

Tires squealing against the pavement reached her ears, announcing Liam's arrival. The bell jingled as Liam walked into the diner. He headed straight for their table. Before Gianna could blink, he had his arms wrapped around Valarie, pulling her in for a kiss.

After what seemed like an eternity, they finally pulled away so Liam could slide into the booth. She braced herself as his gaze fell on her, lips pulling into a razor-sharp smile. "Drew," he said.

She raised her chin. "Liam."

"Fancy seeing you here." He leaned back in the booth, stretching his arm along the back of the booth. "How's it going?"

Gianna's lips pulled into a sharp smile, a snarky retort already on the tip of her tongue. She felt Valarie's gaze on her. She didn't have to see her friend's eyes to know what she was trying to communicate. *Be nice, for my sake.* She swallowed back her words.

"Fine." Remembering that she was supposed to be civil, she added, "How are you, Liam?"

"Stellar."

"Oh, I'm sure."

Tension hummed in the air around them, sharp as a knife's edge. The clatter of dishes and chatter from nearby tables grew louder as the two glared at each other. Sensing the crackling hostility, Valarie cleared her throat. "So, uh, what does everyone have going on today?" Her green eyes turned to Gianna. "Gianna?"

"Homework," she muttered.

"I've got practice with the band later," Liam volunteered. "We've got this sick demo we're working on. There's this new song that we've been …"

And here we go. Gianna tuned out of the conversation as she glanced out the window. A boy riding his bike came to a stop outside the diner. She caught a glimpse of his face, and a chill ran down her spine. Her eyes followed him to the door until he stepped inside. He was younger than they were—Gianna guessed around fourteen or fifteen. That would make him a freshman at Echo Falls High, but Gianna knew for a fact she had never seen him before.

So why did he seem so familiar?

He made his way to the counter, murmuring a name she couldn't hear to the waitress. The waitress nodded and disappeared into the back. The boy, left to his own devices, scanned the room for a place to sit. His eyes widened as they fell on her table. His back was to them in a heartbeat. Before Gianna could gauge the reason for his reaction, Liam answered her question for her.

"Yo, Nathan!" he hollered. "Is that you?"

The boy—Nathan—looked as if he wanted to melt into the black-and-white checkered tile floor. She couldn't blame him. Liam had that effect on people.

Liam nudged Valarie's shoulder. "Remember the tutor I was talking about? The one that Mr. C assigned me?"

"That's him?" Valarie whispered. "I thought your tutor would've been someone older."

"Yeah, you'd figure, but this kid's practically a genius. Hey, Nathan!"

Nathan's fists clenched the countertop. He glanced in the direction the waitress went, but there was no sign of her. Liam either couldn't take a hint or didn't care.

"Maybe he thinks I'm talking to another Nathan," Liam said to Valarie. *Can't take a hint it is, then.* He cupped his hands around his mouth, yelling, "Nathan Kipman!"

The chatter in the diner came to a halt around them. It hadn't been until Liam had said his name that it struck Gianna why Nathan looked so familiar. Why he had pegged her interest the second he walked through the door.

This was Nathaniel Kipman.

Oliver Kipman's younger brother was standing right in front of her.

TWO

People tended to notice the similarities between siblings, but their differences drew her attention. There were the obvious traits—Nathan was taller, his hair two shades lighter and shorter than Ollie's ever was—and there were the subtle differences you wouldn't notice unless you knew Ollie. While Ollie often stood slouched and relaxed, Nathan was the opposite. His back was straight, and a look in his eye held suspicion and distrust.

He approached their table slowly, as if he were approaching a den of lions.

"Hey, man, what's up?" Liam held up a hand casually as if he hadn't yelled Nathan's name across the diner a minute ago. "This is my girlfriend, Val. Oh, and this is Gianna."

"Hey, Nathan, it's nice to meet you." Valarie held out her hand, but Nathan stared at it as if it were a different creature entirely. She withdrew her hand, her smile wavering slightly before she replaced it with a cheerful one. "Did you want to sit with us? The diner gets pretty crowded around this time. It might be a while before your order is ready."

Nathan glanced around the room, sighing reluctantly. "Uh, sure."

The only available seat was the spot in Gianna's booth. She scooted closer to the window, pulling her plate and phone with her. From the corner of her eye, she watched him sit down, shoulders tense, making sure to put space between anything near him.

Gianna hadn't realized she'd been staring until Liam said her name.

She tore her gaze from Nathan. "What?"

Liam gestured to her headphones on the table. "I said, are you still listening to those creepy murder stories?"

"True crime," she said.

"Same difference. Hey, Nate, did you know Gianna here is our town's very own Nancy Drew?"

"Liam," Valarie hissed.

"What?" Liam frowned at Valarie while Nathan's gaze slid to Gianna. It was the first time he'd looked at her, and an eerie chill went down Gianna's back as she met his eyes. At that moment, he looked so much like Ollie, it was like staring at a ghost.

"Is that true?" he asked. "You solve mysteries and stuff?"

"Yeah," she said, fingers drifting to her cup, to something solid to keep her from drifting back to the past. "That's the plan at least."

"Have you solved anything yet?"

Gianna's fingers stiffened around her mug. It was a harmless question, and yet all she heard were Anthony's words. *I know I make it look easy, but it really isn't, kiddo. My line of work takes something out of you. You'll see and know things you wish you could forget. It's not for everyone.*

"Not yet," she replied.

"She's going to, though," Valarie said, sending Gianna an encouraging smile. Gianna returned the smile, but doubt filled her eyes. "She's already got the grades to get into some of the best schools in the state."

"Val." Gianna's face heated but Valarie continued as if she hadn't heard her.

"She's one of the smartest kids at school, and I bet if Theodore Rodriguez wasn't running for valedictorian this year, it would've easily gone to her. They're practically rivals."

"Not this again! Me and Theodore Rodriguez are not rivals, we are not anything," Gianna protested. "We've never even met."

It was true. She never had set eyes on Theodore Rodriguez, but she had heard the stories that swirled around school in the beginning of the year. Rumor was Theo was top of the class and a reckless daredevil.

Before Valarie could continue, Gianna turned to Nathan and asked, "How come we've never seen you around school before?"

"I do most of my classes online, and when I'm not in class, I usually stick to the library," Nathan explained, tapping his fingers on the table. "It's quieter there. That or the robotics classroom."

"You're a freshman, right?" Valarie asked.

Nathan shook his head. "Sophomore."

Another question sat on the tip of Gianna's tongue when the waitress called out, "Order for Angela!"

"Um, that's me—well, my mom," Nathan stammered.

The couple at the table beside them watched Nathan with narrowed eyes as he stood. Judging by the way his head ducked between his shoulders, Nathan had noticed their stares as well.

A bitter taste filled her mouth. Gianna glared at the couple from across the room, until the woman's head turned. The woman raised her chin stiffly and dropped the stare. *Good,* Gianna thought as Nathan returned to their table, a greasy paper bag in his hand.

"It was … uh … nice meeting you guys." He glanced at Gianna. "Good luck with your mysteries."

"He's a little odd," Liam told Valarie as Nathan left. "But the dude's like wicked smart. He even skipped a grade."

"Why does his name sound so familiar?" Valarie asked.

"Oh, you might've heard about his brother—Killer Oliver. Dude was a psycho. Story goes that he went crazy and killed his own best friend and then left town before the police could nab him."

Gianna's concentration wavered at the chatter at the table beside them. The man at the table had waved over the waitress to complain about the omelet missing from his plate.

"Hey, there's a case for you, Nancy Drew. The Case of the Missing Omelet." Liam snickered, amused by his own joke.

Valarie nudged him in the ribs and sent Gianna an apologetic look, but it did little to settle the red Gianna saw.

Her knuckles turned white as her fingers clenched the napkin in her lap. She bit back all the words she wanted to spew at Liam. She wasn't going to be the petty person in this scenario. She was going to be the better person, and she wasn't going to ruin this brunch for Valarie. Taking a deep breath, she let go of the napkin and glanced out the window at the empty spot where Nathan's bike had been.

Anthony's voice trickled into her mind. *Until you solve a case for yourself,* he said, regarding her with that stern look of his, *you won't understand.*

And that was when it clicked.

Like a piece of a puzzle finally coming together. She could laugh. All along the solution was right there beneath her nose. A way to pique the mystery nagging at her brain for five years and convince Anthony she had what it took.

"As it turns out, I do have a case," Gianna said.

She relished the shocked look on Liam's face. It lasted for a second before he shrugged it off. "Yeah, sure," he scoffed.

"You do?" Valarie said.

"Yes. I'm going to solve the Kipman case." Her spirit returned, along with a newfound sense of determination. Because now she had a plan. "I'm going to find Oliver Kipman."

Log #1, Nov. 15th, 2023

Echo Falls Times

Body of Missing Teen Discovered; Search Efforts Continue for Second Missing Teen

July 8th, 2019

Written by Kyle Jenkins

Earlier this morning, the body of a young male with multiple gunshot wounds was discovered by the police off of Topsfield Road. The deceased has now been identified as seventeen-year-old Grant Hayes, who was reported missing by his parents in the early hours of July 5th.

Search efforts have been underway this past week for Hayes and Oliver Kipman. Both were last seen driving away from Hayes's house at approximately 8:20 p.m.

The police declared Hayes's death as a homicide and are opening an investigation. It is still unclear whether Kipman played a part in Hayes's death.

"As far as we can see, this has been an isolated event and the public is in no danger," Police Chief Goodeman said. "At the moment we have no suspects, but we are working diligently to get to the bottom of this. Our priority is locating Oliver Kipman."

Echo Falls police will be leading a search party tomorrow morning to continue the search for Oliver Kipman. The department asks that anyone who can, join the search to help with the efforts of locating the missing teen.

Kipman is 5'8", 150 lbs with dark hair and brown eyes. He was last seen wearing an orange hoodie, black sweatpants, and red-and-white checkered Vans. If anyone has any information about Kipman's whereabouts or has seen him in the past week, you can contact the number(s) listed below or call the police department.

THREE

The low fluorescent lights of The Retro flickered overhead as Gianna felt for the outlet by the table with her hands. The smell of coffee grounds and burnt croissants wafted through the air, causing her stomach to grumble. She had been too nervous to eat at school and didn't have time before her shift started. However, she did take whatever was left in the coffee pot, just enough to fill two mugs.

Gianna glanced at her watch. It was only five minutes past three. There was a good chance she wouldn't show, but that didn't stop Gianna from hoping.

With each tick of the clock, her stomach twisted with disappointment. Five minutes turned into ten, into fifteen, and then twenty. She glanced at her now cold coffee mugs and sighed. Reluctantly, she began packing her things, when the bell attached to the front door rang. Her head snapped up.

A woman walked through, shoulders hunched, tucking the stray hair that fell out of her bun. Even if Gianna hadn't spoken to her a few days prior, she would have recognized her. She had seen her around the neighborhood, stapling flyers to the light poles and leaving them in mailboxes.

"Hi," Gianna greeted as the woman approached the table. "I'm Gianna Reyes. We spoke over the phone. Thanks again for coming on such short notice. I ordered you a coffee. I hope black is okay."

"Black is fine." Angela's gaze wandered to the cup before it traveled back up to Gianna's face. "I'm sorry I'm so late. I couldn't find my keys."

"It's okay," Gianna said.

Angela slid into the empty seat across from Gianna, smoothing out her dress. She regarded Gianna with warm brown eyes—Ollie's eyes. "You sounded older on the phone," she said. "But you can't be much older than my youngest son."

"I'll be eighteen in July." Gianna opened her laptop and typed in her password with record speed. When she looked back up, she found Angela surveying her setup. Gianna's laptop, tape recorder, and microphone were all laid out in an orderly fashion. Not one of the cords was tangled—just how Gianna preferred it. She even made sure to get one of the tables in the back, far away from the front counter, so the microphone wouldn't pick up any unwanted noise. But luckily for them, the café was practically empty around this time.

"Did you want anything before we start?" Gianna asked. "They make the best croissants in town."

Angela blinked, as if snapping out of a daze, and shook her head. "No, thank you. I think … I think I'm ready to start now, if that's alright."

"Okay." Gianna tried not to look too eager as she reached for her laptop and hit the record button on all her devices. "The date is November 20th, 2023, and I am here with Angela Kipman, Oliver Kipman's mother."

Log #2, Nov. 20th, 2023

Transcript of Interview with Angela Kipman

Gianna: I want to start off this interview by saying this entire conversation will be recorded. Is that okay with you, Mrs. Kipman?

Angela: Yes, dear, I don't mind. And please, call me Angie. Everyone does.

Gianna: Alright, then. Angie it is. I guess we can start at the beginning, the day that your son went missing: July 4th, 2019. What do you remember about that day?

Angela: It was our neighborhood's Fourth of July cookout. Every year everyone comes together to celebrate. I spent most of the morning and afternoon setting up tables, chairs, and tents with my husband. Some of our neighbors were already there, also helping. Ollie was in the backyard playing tag with his brother and the younger children. All the kids loved Ollie. He had this aura around him. Nathaniel—my youngest son—looked up to him.

Gianna: Do you recall what time Ollie left the cookout?

Angela: Yes. It was the same time I gave to the police. Seven-thirty. It was around the time we started lighting up sparklers and handing out firecrackers to the kids. Ollie came up asking me for my car keys so he could drive to Grant's. I told him to be careful and keep an eye out for people on the street. That was the last time I saw him.

Gianna: And at what point did you realize he was missing?

Angela: Not until the next morning. There was so much going on that day. We ran out of chips and Dave had to run to the grocery store, and then Nathan's ears started hurting from the fireworks. By the time everyone went home and I finished cleaning, I was so exhausted I fell straight into bed without even brushing my teeth. I woke up later that night when I heard a noise—well, I thought I heard a noise.

Gianna: What did you think you heard?

Angela: It's silly to think about now, but I could've sworn it was Ollie coming inside through the back door. I looked over at my phone and was a little more awake when I saw the time—it was a quarter past two in the morning. Ollie was good at telling us when he would be staying over at Grant's or if he'd be coming home late, but I hadn't heard anything from him that night.

Angela: I thought it was odd he'd come inside through the back of the house. He has the keys to the front door. I went to his room to ask why he was home so late, but he wasn't there. And then I checked outside the window and saw my car wasn't in the driveway either. After that, I realized I must've dreamt the noise altogether.

Gianna: What did you do when you realized he wasn't in his room?

Angela: I woke up my husband to see if he had heard from Ollie, and when he said he hadn't, he got up to check Nathan's room. I called Ollie's phone, but it went straight to voicemail. I figured it must have died—Ollie had a bad habit of not charging his phone.

Angela: I knew he was going to Grant's, so I called Grant's mother. I hadn't known that she and Mr. Hayes were out of town that day. They said they hadn't heard from Grant either.

Angela: That's when I called the police. They had me fill out a missing persons report, and I told them the same thing I'm telling you now. And then later that day, they found my car at that bus station, and then a few days later, that's when they … when they found Grant. [sniffles]

Gianna: I'm sorry. If this is too much, we can stop—

Angela: No! [sniffles] I'm sorry, I don't mean to shout. I promised myself I would come here today. That I would at least try. For Ollie. Please, go on.

Gianna: Are there any places you can think of that Ollie would go to?

Angela: No. We don't have any other family in the state. I gave the police a list of my husband's closest relatives and their addresses, but if Ollie showed up there, they would have called me.

Gianna: Do you think Mr. Kipman would be open to an interview?

Angela: Why would you need to speak to him?

Gianna: To get another perspective on that night. It's good to hear many points of view, just in case a detail is forgotten or there's something the police might have missed the first time.

Angela: I haven't forgotten a single thing about that night. It was the worst night of my life. And to answer your first question, no. Even if Dave were, I wouldn't know how to contact him in the first place, honestly. I haven't seen my husband in over a year.

Gianna: Oh. I'm sorry.

Angela: Don't be. It was nothing more than differing opinions.

Gianna: What about your other son? Nathan? Would he be open to talking?

Angela: I'd prefer it if we left Nathan out of this. He's only fourteen and he just started high school. He's already had such a hard time with everything and I … I don't want to give him any false hopes.

Gianna: I understand. Well, that wraps this interview up.

FOUR

Gianna shut her laptop and slipped it into her bag. Angela sipped her coffee, watching as Gianna gathered her belongings.

"If you don't mind," Angela said, resting her cup on the table. "Can I ask you a question?"

"Sure."

"Why reach out to me? Why ask about Ollie in the first place? You couldn't have been a teenager when he went missing. No one else in this town cares much."

She sighed, wearily. "And I know what people say about him. What they say about *me.* No mother wants to think their child is capable of ruthless murder, but I know in my heart that my son isn't. Ollie is a giver, not a taker. And he is a *good kid.* If he killed Grant, he would've turned himself in right away. No. I know he didn't do it. Something else happened and I—"

Her voice cracked and she stopped, turning away to gather herself. Gianna offered her a napkin.

"Thank you." She sniffled, crumpling it in her hand. "I'm sorry. I don't—I'm not normally like this. I haven't spoken to anyone about Ollie in so long. To someone who believes he's innocent as well."

Gianna waited before speaking. "You said that something else happened that night. What do you think happened?"

"I don't know, I just know that it did. I know that my son did not kill his best friend. You can say I'm crazy for believing it, but I'm not sorry about it."

"I don't think that," Gianna reassured her. "And to answer your first question, I reached out because I know a little about what you're going through."

Surprise lit her eyes. "Has someone you love gone missing, as well?"

"Um … not exactly." Gianna shifted in her seat, forcing herself to meet Angela's eyes. "My mother passed away when I was little. I don't have any memories of her. Just the ones I created in my head from what others tell me. There's so many things I wondered about her: what her laugh sounded like, if she liked true crime TV shows, too, or did I inherit my love of ranch and fries from her?" A strange sensation rose in the back of her throat. "I guess you could say she was a mystery of her own—to me, at least."

Angela's hand covered hers. "Oh, I'm so sorry. I can't imagine what that must be like for you. How old were you when she passed away?"

"Four. But I wasn't alone. My mother's older brother took me in and raised me."

"That's good that you weren't alone."

"Yeah. Look, I know my situation is a lot different than yours, and there's no way to compare the two, but I meant what I said before—I want to find Ollie. Regardless of whether he's guilty or not. I want you to know that I'm one hundred percent serious about this."

Angela was quiet for a few moments, considering her words. "Do you truly believe that you can find him?"

"I can't make any guarantees that I will. But I can promise you, Angie, that I will do everything I can to find Ollie. And promises are something I don't take lightly."

"Well, that's one thing we have in common, dear," Angela said, "because neither do I."

***

Gianna's shoes slapped against the sidewalk as she hurried home from the café. It began to pour as soon as she left the coffee shop, and she missed the bus by five minutes. Luckily, she'd had the foresight to check the forecast for the day and bring an umbrella.

Anthony's car was in the driveway when she got home.

"There's my favorite niece!" he hollered as Gianna walked in.

"I'm your only niece." She peeled off her wet shoes and found Anthony in the kitchen putting away groceries. "I thought you were working the graveyard shift today."

"Yeah, well, Dennis was asking for extra hours, so I let him cover my shift." He held up a plastic grocery bag in his hand. "I thought after I stopped by Lori's and got some dinner, I'd go by the store and get some more mint chip and pistachio—your favorite."

Gianna grimaced. "I'll stick with my mint chip, thank you very much."

He barked out a laugh as she grabbed the ice cream from the bag. "Dessert before dinner? Who raised you?"

They sat down in the living room, eating their burgers and fries as the evening news played on the TV. But Gianna's mind was far from the weather forecast for the week. She was back in the low-lit room of The Retro with Angela Kipman across the table, who wondered why a teenage girl wanted to find her son.

What else did she see? A girl not much younger than her oldest son when he disappeared? A girl desperate to prove herself?

A girl without a mother?

At the thought of her mom, Gianna's eyes drifted to the fireplace mantle. Her chest constricted as she caught her reflection in her mother's photo. Everything she told Angela about her mom was the truth. The only thing she knew about Elena Reyes was the sprinkles of things she heard over the years. Stories from some of the people her mom cared for.

Her favorite story was the one where she saved a little boy from drowning in a lake. News of Elena's bravery spread across town and made headlines in the *Echo Falls Times*. Gianna had the newspaper clipping pinned to her bulletin board in her bedroom. Whenever she felt sad or hopeless, she looked up at it, reminding herself why she wanted to be a detective in the first place. She wanted to do something good in the world, like her.

She wasn't embarrassed to talk about her mother; she was proud to be Elena Reyes's daughter. But Gianna learned early on about pity, and she hated being on the receiving end of it. Hated that people treated her differently because of it. *You poor thing. It's so sad that you never knew her. No child should have to go through life without knowing their mother.* What made it worse was that everything they all said was true. Apart from the few stories she knew, Elena Reyes was a mystery.

Even to her own daughter.

"How was everything today, kiddo?" Anthony asked, drawing her out of her thoughts. "School go okay?"

"Same as usual," she replied, picking at the pickles on her burger. "Nothing too special."

"Well, I'm glad to know that our talk didn't hit you too hard the other day," Anthony said. "I know I may have come off harsh, but—"

"But you're just trying to protect me," Gianna finished for him. "I know."

Anthony had always looked after her, ever since her mom died and her father was nowhere to be seen. Anthony quit his high-paying job and moved back to his hometown. It hadn't been Royce who taught her to tie her shoelaces into bunny ears or how to kick a soccer ball, who took her to all her doctor appointments and showed up at her award ceremonies. Anthony filled the gaps her father left behind.

And it was because of him and her mom that Gianna wanted to do better in the world. And her way of doing that was the thing she wanted to do more than anything. The thing Anthony disapproved of the most—solving mysteries.

The corners of Anthony's eyes wrinkled. "When did you become so old and wise?"

"I'm not so sure I'm the old one here." She gestured to the white hairs forming at his temples.

"Thirty-nine is not old."

"That's not what Mr. Delgado said the other day," Gianna teased.

"That man is twenty years older and forgets his glasses hourly. He is the last one to be talking about age." Anthony leaned back as Gianna laughed. "Also, Irene's coming down this weekend."

"What's the occasion?"

Her aunt rarely left New York and her law business except for when she flew up to visit them for Christmas.

"No occasion," Anthony said. "She just has a few weeks off of work and decided to spend it here. Her flight lands on Saturday. After the airport, we're going to head over to the Delgados' for Andrew's birthday dinner. The big six-o. Now *that's* old."

Normally, Gianna would've laughed at Anthony's failed attempts at humor, but she was too busy wondering whether Irene's visit was good or bad: good news because she only saw Irene a few times a year; bad news because her aunt had a nose for trouble. If she discovered what Gianna was doing, then Anthony wouldn't be far behind. Her investigation would be over before it began.

The weight of her promise to Angela hung in the air like a thick fog. *I can't make any guarantees that I will. But I can promise you, Angie, that I will do everything I can to find Ollie. And promises are something I don't take lightly.*

She would have to be more careful.

Log #3, Nov. 21st, 2023

Transcript of Interview with Molly Goldstein (Grant's girlfriend)

Gianna: What can you tell me about Ollie and Grant?

Molly: Oh boy. [Laughs] That's a loaded question. Where do I even start?

Gianna: From the beginning. How did Ollie and Grant first meet?

Molly: Oh, that's an easy one. I've been told the story at least a dozen times. Ollie and Grant had been best friends since before they could walk. Their dads were best friends in college. They were out of their minds ecstatic when they discovered they were having kids at the same time—with boys, nonetheless. They did everything together: birthdays, graduation parties, summer vacations, you name it.

Gianna: I'm assuming you saw Ollie around a lot, then?

Molly: You'd be right. Wherever one went, the other followed. Ollie's the reason I met Grant in the first place. I saw him around at school, but I didn't get to know him until I started going over to Ollie's house for a school project. Grant was always hanging out there and one day we got to talking. The rest is history.

Gianna: I heard that you were the last one to see Ollie and Grant that night. Is that true?

Molly: The night Grant died? Yeah. His parents were out of town for some business dinner, so we hung out.

Gianna: Can you go over what you remember from that day? I know it was five years ago, and memories can get all muddled.

Molly: Uh, yeah, actually, I remember it all. I used to go over every detail about that day in the early years, and it all sort of stuck with me. Like I told you, I was with Grant most of the day at his house, hanging out. Ollie showed up to pick up Grant. Grant told me they were going to head back to the Kipmans' for the fireworks. It was getting late and I had to get home, so I didn't go. Ollie stayed for like twenty minutes before we all left. I only live a few blocks away, so I walked back home.

Gianna: Did Ollie say where they planned to go after the fireworks?
Molly: No, actually. I assumed he'd stay over at the Kipmans'. Most of the time, he was either at their house or Ollie was at his, so I didn't think it was too big of a leap. But then later that night, I texted Grant goodnight and he never responded. I figured he'd fallen asleep. It never occurred to me that the reason he didn't reply was because he was … was because he was dead.

Anyway, Mrs. Hayes called me in the middle of the night asking if Grant was at my house. She told me that no one had heard from him or Ollie for hours. I tried Grant's phone, but no answer. I wanted to go out and help look, but my parents told me it was best for me to stay home and let the police do their job.

All day I was sick with worry calling Grant's phone. My mom kept saying that he would show up, that Grant probably went to a party and passed out in the woods somewhere. [Laughs dryly] She wasn't much help. And then we heard … we heard that Grant was dead and Ollie was still missing and I don't think I left my room for a whole week. The next time I turned on the TV, they started saying that Ollie could have had something to do with Grant's murder. I didn't want to believe it.
Gianna: Is there any reason you can think of why Ollie would hurt Grant?
Molly: Absolutely not. Ollie was the closest thing to a brother that Grant had, and Grant was practically Ollie's second brother. He'd hurt himself before he hurt Grant. All that stuff about him having a breakdown … well, I knew a load of bull. But everyone always thought otherwise because … well, you know.
Gianna: I don't, actually. Could you elaborate?
Molly: The reason everyone believed he had a breakdown was because of his depression.
Gianna: Ollie was depressed?
Molly: Yeah. Stuff to do with his parents, I think. Grant told me Ollie was taking medication, that he was getting better.
Gianna: Wow, I had no idea. Um, was there anything off about Ollie's behavior on July 4th?
Molly: No. He was calm and relaxed, as usual.
Gianna: What about before that night? It could be weeks or months in the making. Even if it's the smallest thing you might have noticed.

Molly: Actually … now that I think about it, there was something off. I didn't think much of it at the time. It was a week before the fourth, at this party some of our friends from school threw for Ollie for his 18th birthday. I noticed some weird tension between Grant and Ollie.
Gianna: What was weird about it?
Molly: The fact that there was tension. Grant and Ollie hardly fought, but that night there was something that was upsetting Grant. At some point I went to the restroom, and when I came back, I heard Grant whisper to Ollie, "We need to tell her."
Gianna: Those were his exact words? "We need to tell her"?
Molly: Yep.
Gianna: What did he mean by that?
Molly: I don't know. Ollie stopped talking when he saw me and switched the subject. They didn't bring it up again for the rest of the night.
Gianna: Huh. Well, I think that's about all the questions I had to ask you. Thank you again for agreeing to talk. I know it can't be easy.
Molly: No, it never is. But for the record, I really appreciate you doing this. I'd be lying if I said I wasn't grateful that there's someone out there who cares enough to still find Ollie. I would've tried myself, but I went through a rough patch after Grant died. I won't go into the details, but there were a couple of times I thought I'd never get to where I am now. It took a lot for me to get here. I used to feel so guilty after leaving for college. It felt wrong, like I was trying to leave Grant behind, like I was dishonoring his memory by not searching for Ollie.

My first two years of university, I barely left my dorm. It didn't feel right for me to have fun and meet people at the time. For being alive, when Grant's life was taken from him. Do you know what I used to tell myself on the nights I felt like I was drowning in my own guilt? I used to tell myself that Grant would want me to keep going, to keep moving forward. But if I'm being completely honest, if I go back, I don't think I'll make it out again. That's why I stopped searching for answers. That probably makes me sound heartless, doesn't it?
Gianna: No, I think that just makes you human.

Timeline of July 4th, 2019

7:30 p.m. *- Ollie leaves to go to Grant's house*

7:40 p.m. *- Ollie arrives at Grant's*
8:20 p.m. *- Grant and Ollie leave Grant's house to head to the Kipmans'.*
9:00 p.m.–9:30 p.m. *- Grant's estimated time of death (Did the math and it would take at least thirty minutes for Ollie to drive from Topsfield Road to the bus station)*
10:05 p.m. *- Ollie's car is seen pulling into the parking lot of a bus station via CCTV footage*

***

Ollie's case only got stranger as Gianna dug. Based on Angela's and Molly's accounts, Ollie never returned to his house for fireworks. Why lie to Molly about where they were going?

She searched up the street where Grant was shot. It was a long road, with nothing but woods and the old settlement ruins nearby, which begged the question: what were Ollie and Grant doing there that time of night?

And more importantly, what went down in the time between Ollie driving away from the Hayes's house to Grant's death? Had Ollie murdered Grant and chosen the place as a random location? Or were they lured there? They weren't at Grant's or the Kipmans' house, so where were they?

She had also stumbled upon something else noteworthy. The official police report stated that Grant was missing his phone and wallet from his person. Did Ollie take them? Was it someone else? Or was Grant missing his personal belongings before he left?

She couldn't get what Molly told her out of her mind—about what Grant said to Ollie on the day of Ollie's birthday dinner. *We need to tell her.* Who was *her*? Molly? Angela?

Gianna released a frustrated breath. The more she searched, the more questions she had than answers. She was still missing so much more about that night.

But one person who was there on July 4th might be able to provide more insight into Ollie's case. She couldn't put it off anymore. She needed to speak to Nathan. Even if it was against Angela's wishes, Nathan might know something his mother didn't. And that was a chance Gianna couldn't pass up.

FIVE

She didn't hear the footsteps until it was too late.

Valarie peered over her shoulder. "If you weren't my best friend, I'd be seriously concerned about your hobbies. Or lack thereof."

"I have hobbies," Gianna scoffed, shutting off her phone. The black screen swallowed up the MISSING picture of Ollie with it.

"Reading articles from five years ago doesn't count." Valarie hooked an arm around Gianna's shoulder as they squeezed through the crowded hallway. Kids and teachers scurried about, eager for Thanksgiving break to finally begin.

"You know I'm reading it because—"

"Because you want to find Ollie, so you can prove to Anthony that you can handle a case," Valarie finished for her. "I know. But how about a break from mystery-solving? You know I was thinking—"

"If you're going to say what I think you're going to say …"

"—we should go shopping!"

Gianna bit back a groan. Valarie could spend hours in a single aisle. Gianna would know—Valarie often dragged her along with her.

"Cool. Anthony mentioned we were running low on tomato sauce."

Valarie flicked her ear in annoyance. "Not that kind of shopping. I'm talking about dress shopping. Prom is a few months away, remember?"

Remember? Gianna wished she could forget. Even though prom wasn't until the spring, the school strung up posters on every wall. Giant, sparkly letters shouted at students to get their tickets before they sold out. Unease crept onto her as she glanced at them now.

"Val ..." she began.

But Valarie wasn't having any of it. Her eyes sparkled, excitement spilling over as she leaned into Gianna. "No way. You are not backing out of this. It's our last year of high school. We've already had our last first day, our last first brunch, our last homecoming. You can't miss the prom!"

"Prom? Val, I can't even think about dances right now. Besides, I don't have anyone to go with."

But Valarie was one step ahead of her. "You can come with me and Liam."

"And be the third wheel for the entire night?" she snorted. "I'd rather swallow a bucket full of nails."

Valarie huffed. "Okay, but you still have to come with me to go dress shopping. You know I need your opinion on which dress looks best."

And there it was. The real reason why Gianna wanted to avoid this talk of prom and dresses and *lasts*. All the mothers and daughters would be out together, trying on dresses and going to get overpriced coffee after. Styling their hair for the big night, putting on makeup, singing music together.

Gianna swallowed. Valarie was right—this year was full of lasts. And Gianna hadn't gotten to experience any of it with her own mother. She figured she would've gotten used to it. Especially after all the Mother's Days when she had no mom to give the card she made in class, or when she got her first period in middle school, or started her first day of high school. But she hadn't. Every first was a painful reminder of what she never got to experience. A reminder of what she never would.

Whenever she tried to talk to Valarie about her mom, she found her throat tightening and a weird sensation in her chest. It was ridiculous. It wasn't like Valarie didn't already know about Gianna's mom from day one. The Mother's Day Picnic in kindergarten. Valarie and Gianna had been the only two kids whose mothers didn't show up that day. While all the other students in their grade ate with their moms, Valarie and Gianna sat at a separate table, poking at their pies.

Six-year-old Valarie had turned to Gianna with bright eyes and said with absolutely no hesitation, "I think my mom forgot about the picnic.

She and my dad got into a fight last night and she doesn't sleep well after fights. Did your mom forget, too?"

"My mom's dead," Gianna had replied sullenly. She was sure that Valarie would stop talking to her then, but to her surprise, the other girl wrapped her in a hug. She held her tight and didn't let go.

From that day on, they'd been each other's other half, their crutch. Gianna stood by Valarie through her parents' nasty divorce in middle school and the aftermath. Work took up all of Valarie's mother's energy, leaving little time for Valarie. Mr. Springfield was too busy with his new family to answer a phone call from his daughter. And Gianna was there a year later when Mrs. Springfield married Boring Bob and became Mrs. Duncan.

They'd stood together through it all.

And Valarie had seen it through for Gianna. She'd been there on Elena's birthdays when Gianna went to the cemetery to lay flowers at her grave. Valarie even went as far as scolding any of the kids at school who made *Yo Momma* jokes around Gianna.

Telling Valarie how she felt should have been easy, yet it was impossible to put into words.

"You'll look great in any dress you pick," Gianna managed to say, not meeting her eyes.

"Nice try." Valarie tapped her nose, oblivious to Gianna's inner turmoil. "You're just trying to weasel your way out of going dress shopping, but I applaud the effort. Liam's band is performing at The Retro this Thursday, and I have to babysit Vivian on Friday. How does Saturday sound?"

Gianna froze, her shoes squealing against the tile. "I can't make it on Saturday."

"Homework doesn't qualify as an excuse. It's the weekend." Valarie gave her a pointed look. "You can't weasel your way out of this, you know."

"I really can't," she insisted. "Irene's coming up to visit."

"What's the occasion?"

She shrugged. "It's as much of a mystery to you as it is to me."

"Hm. Do you think she and Jim broke up?"

Gianna pictured Irene's fiancé with his red hair and freckles. Irene brought him a few times during the years at Christmas. He was a little shy, and his jokes had room for improvement, but he was a nice guy. "No way. They've been together for like a decade."

"Yeah, but I mean, when has your aunt ever stopped her workaholic streak for anything?"

She wasn't wrong there. Irene was a workaholic to her core.

"It can only mean one thing," Valarie concluded. "Trouble in paradise. That, or Irene had a stroke."

Gianna rolled her eyes, and they snagged on a bulletin board on the wall. Or rather, the orange flyer that hung from it. ROBOTICS CLUB SIGN UP SHEET. *Mrs. Delgado's Classroom 42B. Monday, Tuesday, and Thursday afternoons from 2:00–5:30.*

Her feet skidded to a halt. *I do most of my classes online, and when I'm not in class, I usually stick to the library. It's quieter there. That or the robotics classroom.*

Of course. The one place she hadn't checked for Nathan.

Valarie was still rambling on about prom when Gianna turned to her. "Hey, you go on without me," she said. "I've got to check up on something real quick."

"Okay. Call me later?"

Gianna gave her a thumbs-up. She waited until Valarie disappeared down the hall before opening the door to Mrs. Delgado's classroom. The first thing she noticed was that there were more people in the room than she was expecting. There had to be at least three people at every science table. The second thing she took note of, with utter disappointment, was that Nathan wasn't among any of them.

The hum of machinery filled her ears. Her gaze lingered on the metal projects on tables as she slid into the crowded room and steered herself to the closest table. A boy she didn't recognize was constructing something with a box of LEGO bricks.

She cleared her throat to get his attention. "Hi. Is Nathan here?"

"Which Nathan?" he asked without glancing up. "There's three."

"Um … Nathan Kipman."

He shrugged. "I don't know anyone named Kipman. What does he look like?"

"Fourteen, glasses, light brown hair. Ring any bells?"

"Nope."

Gianna restrained a frustrated sigh. "I know he's usually here. You must have seen him."

"Sorry chump," he said, not sounding an ounce of sorry at all. "Can't help. You're welcome to give Theo a try. He knows all the freshmen."

"But he's not a—"

"What's this about a freshman?" another voice piped, and Gianna's chest retracted with relief at one familiar face.

"Hey, Marcus," she breathed, greeting the other boy from her Spanish class. "I didn't know you were in robotics."

"I think what you meant to say was *No sabía que te dedicabas a la robótica.*" Marcus smiled, leaning against the table. "It's extra credit and colleges eat this stuff up on applications." He stopped in front of her. "Are you interested in joining the team?"

"No. I'm looking for someone, but your friend seems to have no idea who he is."

"Don't mind Tim. He's like that with everyone."

Gianna raised an eyebrow. "Incredibly unhelpful?"

"Yep. By the way, my grandma was asking—did you finish that one podcast?"

"*One Hundred Days of Crime*?" At his nod, Gianna added, "Not yet. I've been kind of busy lately."

"Well, she loved it and wanted me to ask if you had any more recommendations. Oh, and can you do me a solid and recommend something a little less gory? I had to hear about this one guy in South Dakota who severed off his victim's feet and kept them in a lockbox. It took her a week to finish that episode."

"Severed feet?" a voice from behind them said. "Now my interest is piqued. What's the name of this book?"

Gianna turned around to face the table behind them, catching the eye of the taller boy.

He lifted the safety goggles off his face and onto his curly black hair. He held out a green-gloved hand in her direction, a wide grin on his face. "Theodore Hugo Rodriguez, at your service. But that's typically a mouthful so everyone calls me Theo."

Two thoughts occurred to her in that moment: that this was the Theodore Rodriguez Valarie had labeled as Gianna's rival; and that he was the one Tim was referring to.

His smile didn't once let up as her gaze narrowed on him, slowly putting a face to all the stories she'd heard about him. A whisper of shame rushed through her when he let the green glove drop, but she pushed it aside.

"Have you seen Nathan Kipman around here?" she asked him.

"You know, most people say 'Hi' or 'Nice to meet you' when they meet someone new," Theo said, messing with the wires on the table. "Or introduce themselves. But yeah, to answer your question, I know Nate. You just missed him. He came to see me a few minutes ago before he left."

She narrowed her eyes. "Why did he come to see you?"

If Theo had heard the disdain in her tone, he didn't show it. "I'm the team leader of the club. Nathan's our programmer. He wasn't feeling too good and said he wouldn't be able to come after school today. We've got our very first competition in two weeks, and we've all been cramming."

She frowned. "But didn't you guys form a team less than a month ago?"

"Yeah, but Mrs. Delgado got us in the door. She's great." Light brown eyes met hers. "Are you interested in joining robotics? You should give it a try sometime. If you're not too busy with your murder podcasts, that is."

Marcus let out a chuckle at that. A red flush rose up her neck. Theo met her stare, unabashed, leaning against the table. While she had been putting a face to the rumors, he had been sizing her up as well. All her guilt about her rudeness disappeared in an instant.

"As it turns out, I am too busy with—what was the word you used? Ah, yes, my *murder podcasts*. So, no thank you." She turned away from him to Marcus. "Tell your grandmother I said hello and that I'll pop by the diner later this week."

"Sure. See you around, Gianna," Marcus said.

As she left, she felt a gaze on her, and she glanced over her shoulder once more at his table. But Theo was no longer looking at her, instead lost in concentration at whatever it was he was assembling on the table.

Gianna pulled her coat tighter around her and walked out, thankful that was the first and last time she would ever have to do anything with Theodore Rodriguez.

SIX

Everybody say 'cheese!"

"Cheddar!" they cried in unison. The flash went off and no one dared to move until Irene gave the thumbs-up. She lowered the camera to examine the pictures. "Wait, one more!"

"I think that's enough photos, Irene," Anthony said, giving his sister a pointed look.

"Don't be a party pooper, Pescelli," Dale guffawed. Anthony's boss patted him on the shoulder, a smile lighting his face as he faced the camera again.

The flash went off four more times before Irene finally lowered the camera for good. Gianna plucked the party hat from her head and set it on the table as Mrs. Delgado started cutting the cake. She handed a slice to Gianna and offered one to Anthony.

"No thanks, Christine." He waved away the plate. "I'm good."

She set a hand on her hip. "You say that every year. When are you going to finally relax and let go?"

"Take the damn cake, Pescelli," Mr. Delgado bellowed. Orange frosting was stuck in the bottom of his mustache. "Put the poor woman out of her misery."

Anthony reluctantly took the cake with a forced smile. Mr. Delgado gave him a thumbs-up. He'd been Anthony's closest friend since the beginning of his career, and his wife, who taught at the high school, was just as close. For as long as Gianna could remember, the Delgados came over to the house every weekend. Anthony and Mr. Delgado would lounge around on the couch watching whatever sports game was on. Gianna would help Mrs. Delgado make cookies and play Go Fish while they baked in the oven.

"I remember when you signed up for the police academy," Mr. Delgado said, eyes shining with nostalgia. "I took him under my wing, I did, and he's been stuck there ever since."

"I don't know why," Anthony muttered. "You're more of a pain in the ass than anything. I don't know how you put up with him, Chris."

"A lifetime's worth of patience," Mrs. Delgado muttered.

Mr. Delgado let out a belching burp. "What was that, Christine?"

"Nothing, hon!" She winked at Gianna, who hid her smile behind a forkful of cake.

A phone rang out, interrupting the easy mood. Dale swiped his phone off the table, standing. From his posture and the way he was speaking, Gianna gathered it was work-related.

"Goodeman speaking," he said, his voice fading as he walked down the hallway.

Gianna felt a tap on her shoulder.

"Hey," Anthony whispered. "You've got something right there." He proceeded to tap her nose, leaving behind a dollop of icing.

"Ugh, really?" She wiped it away with the sleeve of her shirt, only half-annoyed as she was pretending to be. "I'm way too old for that."

"You thought it was funny when you were eight."

"I also believed unicorns and fairies were real when I was eight."

"Lies," Irene said. "You used to call unicorns demonic horses."

Point Irene.

Dale returned to the living room, running a hand through his salt-and-pepper hair. "There's a problem at the office. I'm going to go and check on it."

"Do you need someone to go with?" Anthony asked, already standing on his feet before Dale could reply.

"Can you believe my brother?" Irene said to Mrs. Delgado. "Can't even take a day off from work, let alone a couple of hours."

Anthony pulled an arm through his coat. "Crime doesn't stop—not even for chocolate cake."

Irene made a sound like *pfft*. "What crime? You live in a town with less than five percent crime. The last exciting thing that happened in this town was when the Hurley's cat got stuck in a tree. Admit it; you sit in your little cubicle all day getting fat on donuts and overpriced coffee."

Mr. Delgado, still lounging on the couch, sucked in a breath through his teeth and slurred, "She's got a point, Tony."

Ignoring his comment, Anthony stuck a finger out at Irene. "You are the last person to bring up my diet with your five-dollar avocado toast."

Irene opened her mouth right as Mr. Delgado waved his hand. "It's all right, Irene. It's getting late anyway. I'm not as young as I used to be and my pillow is calling my name."

"Happy Birthday. Don't party too hard." Anthony slapped Mr. Delgado on the shoulder as he followed Dale out. To Gianna, he called, "See you later, gator."

"In a while, crocodile," Gianna replied.

Anthony smiled before closing the front door.

Mr. Delgado sighed, sinking into the couch. A sad smile touched his lips as he glanced at Irene. "Some things never change, do they?"

"Oh, I'm sorry, Andrew," Irene whispered. "I tried to get him to stay, but you know how he is with parties. He's been that way ever since . . ."

Since Gabriel died, Gianna finished in her head. She'd never met Anthony's twin before he died, but she knew all too well the effects his death had on Anthony, who was uncomfortable at parties and hated his photo being taken.

"It's okay," Mr. Delgado said. "I know it's nothing personal."

Despite his reassurances, a troubled look plagued Irene's face.

Mrs. Delgado swooped into the room, clasping her hands together. "So, now that all the riff-raff are gone, what's everyone doing this week?"

The question pulled Irene out of her worries. She tucked a strand of silky black hair behind her ear. "I was thinking of taking a trip around town."

Gianna exchanged a concerned glance with Mrs. Delgado. "A trip?" they chorused.

"Yes." Irene lifted her chin, eyes flaring. "What's so wrong with that?"

"Nothing's wrong," Mrs. Delgado said, quickly. "It's just . . . you've never been interested in trips before."

Irene frowned, as if she'd never considered it before. "Oh. Well, I am now."

"I have a lot of papers to catch up on during break," Mrs. Delgado said. "But if you really want to find something to keep you busy, you and Gianna should check out the new theater."

"They built a new theater?"

"Yes, and thank goodness. I remember Andrew and I drove thirty minutes just to watch *Little Women* in Dennisport."

"I don't remember watching *Little Women*," Mr. Delgado remarked.

"Oh. It must've been me and some of the other teachers." Mrs. Delgado coughed into her elbow before gathering the plates from the table. "It's been quite a night. My memory's not what it used to be."

Irene nudged Gianna's shoulder. "What about you? Any grand plans for this weekend?"

She scraped the frosting off her cake with her fork. "Valarie wants to go dress shopping."

"Does that mean you've changed your mind about going to prom?"

"No. She just needs help picking out a dress. I don't think we're going this week anyway."

Her mind drifted to Nathan, who she still needed to talk to.

"Hm. Well, luckily I still have a few more days here to change your mind." Irene placed her hands on her hips. "Do you mind helping Christine clean up? I need to use the bathroom."

"Sure," Gianna yawned, strolling over to where Mrs. Delgado was sweeping the confetti underneath the coffee table. As Gianna scooped up the confetti from under the rug, an idea occurred to her.

"Hey, Mrs. Delgado," she said, "Do you know Nathan Kipman in your robotics club?"

Mrs. Delgado placed a finger on her chin, as if putting a name to a face. "Yes, I do believe I remember seeing the name on the sign-up sheet. Why?"

"Kipman," Mr. Delgado grumbled from the couch. "As in Oliver Kipman? I remember that case." Mr. Delgado yawned. "Kipman went crazy, had a psychotic break … lured his friend to the woods and shot him. His prints were all over his father's gun."

"Were there any symptoms?" Gianna asked.

"Of what?"

"Of his breakdown."

Mr. Delgado scoffed. "You mean, besides killing his best friend?"

"So there was nothing—wait." Gianna's thoughts stuttered to a stop. "The gun belonged to Mr. Kipman?"

"Yep. His father reported the gun stolen a few weeks before. We did a second search and found the gun in the bushes. Mr. Kipman … identified it … himself." Mr. Delgado yawned once more before his head slumped against the arm of the couch.

Gianna processed his words. Ollie had stolen his father's gun weeks before Grant's murder and held onto it. If Grant's death was a result of Ollie's sudden breakdown, he wouldn't have had the foresight to hold onto the gun weeks prior.

So why did he steal the gun?

Gianna hesitated, glancing over at the bathroom door to make sure it was still closed, before turning to Mrs. Delgado. "Did you ever teach Ollie?"

She noted the way Mrs. Delgado's fingers stiffened around the broom. Her eyes darted to her husband, passed out on the couch. "Why are you asking about Oliver, Gianna?"

"I want to ask you a few questions about him, if that's alright?"

"I … I don't know."

"Just a few questions," Gianna urged. "Please."

Mrs. Delgado chewed her lip. "I suppose it couldn't hurt."

Gianna rushed toward the couch for her bag, and in her haste, knocked her knee against the coffee table. She barely felt the pain as she took out her notebook and tape recorder. Mrs. Delgado sunk into the couch across from her. Gianna hit record.

"Just to set the record straight, you've taught at Echo Falls High School for how long again?"

"Twenty-two years," Mrs. Delgado answered. "I taught Ollie during his senior year."

"What was he like as a student?"

"He was a good kid. Always had a smile on his face when he came into class and a joke in his back pocket. He was quite the prankster, as I recall. He'd leave those little fart pouches on chairs." Mrs. Delgado smiled. "One morning, he even managed to sneak into my classroom before I got there. He glued everything upside down. Even the desks. His grades, on the other hand, were … less than what I would've liked for someone with so much potential."

"Potential?"

"All I mean is that he could've made some better decisions academically. Ollie was smart, I never doubted that, but he focused all that potential on the wrong things, like video games, skating, etcetera."

"What about Grant?"

"I knew Grant a bit better. He came to me personally one day after class to talk about college. It must've been that November, right before Thanksgiving break. He wanted to get into one of the Ivy League schools, but because he neglected his grades in the past, he was worried he wouldn't be able to. I told him he'd have to work hard to bring his grade up. And he did. By the time the year wrapped up, he had a B-plus in my class."

Pride filled her voice. "I hardly saw them apart. Oh, the mischief between those two. They'd get up to all sorts of shenanigans. It came as a shock to me to learn what happened in the end. It still makes me sad to think about it. I've taught my fair share of students throughout the years, but none had a bond that compared to those two."

"So there was no indication or reason for you to believe Ollie wanted to hurt Grant?"

She shook her head. "No signs that I ever saw. But the thing with being a teacher is you can only see so much. I only saw Ollie and Grant for fifty minutes a day, five days a week for nine months out of the year. I can't account for their behavior outside of school or at home." She glanced at her lap. "But I wish I had. Maybe then … well … you know."

Gianna understood what she was trying to say. "When was the last time you saw either of them?"

"The last day of school. We had a half-day and I spent the day with my sixth period. I remember we had a pizza party and watched a movie. The class talked about their plans for the summer. Ollie mentioned learning some new tricks on his skateboard and going on a cruise for his birthday, I believe. Grant's family was going camping. They were excited for the summer."

Gianna tapped her pen against her chin. "Mrs. Delgado," she began. "Did you know that Ollie was taking medication to treat his depression?"

"Um, I—I was aware he was being treated for depression, but that was the extent of it," she stammered. "I don't think that's appropriate for this conversation."

"I'm just trying to set the facts straight. You said that Ollie was talking about skating and all the fun things he was planning to do in the summer. School let out the second week of June. That meant this was two weeks before Ollie and Grant went missing. It's hard to believe that a teenager who was looking forward to the summer, with no symptoms at all, could have a breakdown out of the blue and murder his best friend."

"You can never really know what's going on in a person's mind," Mrs. Delgado said. "Some manage to hide their feelings really well. Anything could've happened between that time to trigger a breakdown. We may never know the real reason."

"Or the police got it wrong," Gianna countered. "Perhaps Ollie never suffered a psychotic breakdown."

"Perhaps he didn't. It's just another one of life's mysteries. And some mysteries can be quite sensitive, especially if they occurred here and not that long ago. Is Anthony aware you're looking into this case? Because if he isn't—"

"I know what I'm doing, Mrs. Delgado," Gianna said.

"I'm sure you do. But Anthony worked on this case himself. Don't you think that if he had the slightest ounce of proof that the boy was innocent, he'd stop fighting?"

That was the one part Mrs. Delgado didn't grasp. Anthony was a police officer. He had rules he had to go by. Once a case closed, he couldn't do anything about it. But Gianna *could.*

"Just … promise me you'll be careful," Mrs. Delgado continued. "This tragedy is very sensitive for a lot of people."

Gianna nodded. "I will. Thanks, Mrs. Delgado."

Log #4, Nov. 25th, 2023

Ollie did not suffer a psychotic breakdown. Reasons:

A) Two witnesses stated they saw Grant and Ollie behaving normally in the weeks leading up to Grant's death. (Exception: strange tension between the boys at Ollie's birthday dinner. Still don't know who her is yet.)
B) Mr. Kipman reported his firearm stolen on June 10th, 2019. A little less than a month before Ollie's disappearance. Unless Ollie was planning Grant's murder, there was no reason he needed the gun, at least none to be sure of.

Open Questions:
Why did Ollie steal father's gun in the first place?
Where did he keep it hidden?
Was Ollie in danger and that was the reason he stole it?
If so, then from who?

SEVEN

The following Sunday afternoon, Gianna made her way to the Kipmans' house. It wasn't a long walk. Only a block separated their houses, but Gianna took her time getting there. She practiced the words she planned to say to Nathan. What was the easiest way to break it to someone that you were looking for their missing brother who you didn't believe was guilty of murder?

She thought she'd have until she reached the door to practice her speech, but to her dismay, Nathan was sitting on the front porch. A math textbook lay by his feet, and he had a pair of white headphones over his ears as he tapped his pencil to the rhythm of whatever song was playing.

Her feet froze at the end of the driveway; her thoughts evaporating into thin air.

Be honest with him, she told herself. The thought was enough to spur her into action and close the distance in the driveway. The wooden step groaned beneath her weight. Her shadow fell over Nathan, causing him to look up. He pulled his headphones down to his neck.

"Hey," she said, feeling like she hadn't used her voice for days. "You probably don't remember me, but we met a few weeks ago at Lori's. I'm—"

"I remember you," he interrupted. "How'd you know where I lived? Did you Google it along with everything else there is to know about my brother?"

"Actually, I only live one street away—" Her words stumbled to a screeching halt as the realization of what he said came crashing down on her. He wasn't looking at her anymore; instead, he was back to scribbling in his math textbook.

She shut her eyes, the words falling from her mouth in a whisper. "You know."

"Yeah, I know." Nathan's voice was flat. When she opened her eyes again, he was standing, his fist clenched by his side. "I accidentally saw the text you sent to my mom's phone about meeting her at The Retro. I recognized your name from the diner and put two and two together. Then I remembered what Liam said about you and mysteries."

He met her gaze. "Let me make one thing clear for you: my brother isn't going to be that for you. So if it's some big mystery you're looking for, then you can forget it."

His jaw tensed as he turned to the door.

"Nathan, that's not what I'm trying to do, I promise." Her throat was dry. "Look, I know what it's like to lose someone and—"

"Ollie's not dead!" he snapped. "He's missing. He's not—" His voice cracked, hand flexing on the door handle. "He's missing."

"I know that," she said softly. "I want to find out where he is. I don't think he did what the police say—"

He cut her off. "Why not? It's not like you knew him anyway. What makes you so different from everyone else in this town?"

Stunned, she took a step back. Nathan was more than upset; he was *livid.*

Despite the heat of his words, Gianna stepped closer. "Look, you don't have any reason to believe me, and I understand that. But you should know that I am serious about finding Ollie, and I don't take his being missing or Grant's death as a joke. I want to find him. I don't care about the press or if he's guilty or not. I just want to find him, and I think we can help each other do that."

Nathan was quiet for a long time. Gianna shifted her weight onto her other foot as she waited for his verdict.

He paused, his jaw tightening, before finally meeting her gaze. "If you're as serious as you say about finding him, tell me the truth about how you know my brother."

Gianna's heart skipped two beats. "What makes you think that I—"

"The only people who call my brother Ollie are the people close enough to him to know he prefers being called Ollie to Oliver. The rest of the world and the town call him Killer Oliver." He took a step toward her and stopped. "You called him Ollie. So tell me, how did you know my brother?"

Gianna refrained from picking at the loose thread of her sweater. This was not the conversation she had planned on having when she came here, but it was the one she was going to have. Nathan wouldn't trust her otherwise.

Besides, it was about time she told someone else. And out of everyone, Nathan was the one who deserved to know.

She leaned against the porch railing. "You're right. I do know Ollie."

Nathan's stare pinned her in place. "How?"

"We met ten years ago," she said. "When Ollie saved my life."

EIGHT

The day Gianna nearly met her fate with death happened to be the first day of spring break. Anthony was at work and Valarie was out of town, leaving Gianna alone in the house, bored out of her mind. That was, until she looked out the window and spotted some of the neighborhood kids playing a game of tag.

She was eight years old, without a care in the world, all her focus put into the game. She ended up running away from the tagger and crossed the street. So lost in the game, she didn't see the truck speeding in her direction until it was too late.

She thought she was a goner when she saw the headlights in front of her, but when she opened her eyes, she was on the opposite side of the street. Her knees and hands were messed up, but she was alive. And there he was beside her.

Her saving angel.

"It was Ollie who pulled me out of the way." She cleared her throat, clearing out the daze from the memories. She could still feel everything from that day—the heat of the sun on the back of her neck, the tires squealing, the burning on her palms and knees. "He had been riding around on his skateboard nearby and was able to push me out of the way before the truck hit me. He took me here afterwards."

She gestured to the porch. "He had me wait on the bench while he grabbed some Band-Aids and stuff to clean up my knees. I remember crying so hard from the sting of the peroxide."

She cried for more than the pain. Even as a young girl, she knew that if she had died, Anthony would be left with no one. She had been seconds away from being hit by the truck.

"It was quite a horrible experience. But Ollie talked me through it. He started talking about skateboarding. Asked if I'd ever ridden one. He showed me some tricks. I remember him saying 'This trick's called an Ollie, named after me.'"

Nathan's lips tugged upward. It wasn't quite a smile, but the closest to one she'd seen on him since they met. "He used to say that all the time."

"After that, I poorly attempted to start skateboarding. I was convinced once I'd get the basics down I'd be the next Tony Hawk. Jokes on me because I didn't even get past the basics."

Nathan nodded, like he understood exactly what she meant. "Ollie has a way of making people feel like they could do anything."

"I'm going to find out where he is," she said. "I have to. Not because it's a mystery I can solve, but because Ollie and Grant deserve to have some justice. I owe it to Ollie. And while I'm at it, I want to prove that he's innocent."

"You don't think he did it?" Nathan asked.

"Of course not. I thought it was ridiculous when I first heard it. That he did it because of his …"

"His depression," Nathan finished for her. His jaw tensed with unspoken anger. "They don't understand. Ollie's a happy person who just gets really sad sometimes. But it doesn't cause him to lash out. And I knew he'd been taking that medication for years and it never caused him to change. Grant knew it, too. They use it as an excuse to hide behind because the police don't have a real reason. But if you think my brother is innocent, you must have an idea about what went down that night."

As it turned out, she did have a few. She held up a finger. "First, there's the story everyone knows. Ollie had a psychotic breakdown and lured his best friend in the woods to murder him. The second explanation is that Ollie had no intentions of killing Grant, but the two of them got into a nasty argument that ended up taking the wrong turn. They get into a fight that results in Ollie shooting him and leaving him to die."

Nathan shook his head. "Ollie isn't a violent guy. And he wouldn't have hurt Grant, no matter what the police said."

"I agree. Which leads me to my last and final explanation: that a third party was involved, someone with a personal vendetta against Ollie or Grant, or both. They somehow pull off framing Ollie for Grant's death, and Ollie, who can't very well prove his innocence, runs away."

"They'd have to really hate my brother to go through all that." Nathan tapped his knuckles against the porch railing. "Do you have any theories as to where Ollie might be?"

"No," she said softly. "Your mom told me the same list of places he could've gone that she gave to the police five years ago. I checked, of course, but no Ollie. I think our best bet of finding him is retracing his steps."

"You think there's something the police might have missed."

"I know there is."

"Have you told anyone else about my brother?"

Gianna hesitated. "I've spoken to a few other people who knew him." She gave him a brief description of her talk with Molly and Mrs. Delgado.

Nathan considered this. He rolled his neck and cracked his knuckles. "Okay," he finally said. "But I want to help you. Ollie's my brother. There's no one who wants to find him more than I do."

Gianna wanted to agree with him, but one thing stood in the way. "Ang—your mom. She told me she didn't want me to involve you in your brother's case."

"She thinks she's protecting me," he murmured. "But she's wrong."

Gianna glanced at her lap. She already disobeyed Angela's wishes by talking to Nathan. Actively working with him would break her trust in Gianna indefinitely.

Nathan must've seen the battle in her face, because he turned to her. "Look, you don't have to decide right now. But there's something you should see. It's in Ollie's room."

Interest piqued, she followed him inside. Nathan took a step back, allowing Gianna to enter the room first. She turned the handle and pushed. She peered inside, but didn't dare take a step over the threshold. Not yet. Her eyes roamed from the Tony Hawk posters on the wall, to Ollie's undisturbed bed, and then to the carpet, or specifically, the indent marks of a vacuum cleaner. Angela must've cleaned in here recently.

"It wasn't always this organized," Nathan said, interrupting the flow of her thoughts. "The TV was always crooked and Ollie left clothes out everywhere. You couldn't take a step into this room without slipping on a sock. Mom used to yell at him to clean it all the time."

His lips were curled into a sad smile. She could see the memories playing behind his eyes. Gianna's shoe still hovered at the threshold, and she willed it to move.

"You can look around," Nathan said, as if sensing her hesitance. Or maybe she wore her thoughts plainly on her face. "After all that is what you came to do, right?"

He was right. She couldn't get distracted now. But even as she stepped inside, Gianna was seeing a part of Ollie the media refused to tell. Out there he was nothing more than a cold-blooded killer, but his room suggested otherwise. Ollie was only a teenage boy. Posters of famous skaters hung from the wall. A few books on skateboarding techniques lined the space underneath the TV. Gianna ran a finger along the spines—not a speck of dust came off of them. Her heart panged at the thought of Angela cleaning her son's room, not knowing when or if he'd be back.

She stepped away from the bookcase and walked over to Ollie's desk. Nathan appeared by her side, staring down somewhere to her right. She looked to where his gaze had fallen—a picture taped to the monitor. A young Ollie smiled at the camera, his arm slung around the shoulders of another boy his age. Even though this picture was taken years before he ended up on the front page of every newspaper in New Hampshire, Gianna recognized the smile that spread across the face; the crinkle at the corner of his eyes and the shaggy blond hair that fell in them. Grant Hayes. He and Ollie couldn't have been older than ten in this photo.

"I don't know how anyone can think he killed him," Nathan murmured.

Neither did she.

She cleared her throat. "What is it that you wanted to show me?"

He pointed to the desk. "It's in the top drawer."

Gianna found the handle and pulled it open to find it filled with random junk. Paper clips, broken pencils, batteries, bolts and screwdrivers of various sizes rolled around inside. Yet nothing caught her interest.

"What exactly am I supposed to be looking for?" she asked.

"In the back left corner of the drawer."

The only thing in that corner was a bubblegum wrapper. When she picked it up she noticed the faint writing on one side. *116203.*

"He must've written it down in a hurry," she said, running her fingers over the streak of ink that went over the corner of the wrapper.

"It looks like a license plate, doesn't it?" Nathan fidgeted with a loose thread on his pants. "I tried googling the numbers before, but nothing ever came of it. And it's not on any of our cars. Why would Ollie have a license plate number written down?"

"I don't know," Gianna admitted, pulling out her phone to snap a picture of the wrapper. "Did you show this to the police?"

"Them and my parents."

"What did the police say?"

"What do you think?" he deadpanned.

She set the bubblegum wrapper back into the desk and slid it closed. "What did your mom say when she saw it?"

"Nothing." Nathan let out a breathless laugh. "Mom doesn't say much these days. I have to admit, I was a little surprised she agreed to meet with you in the first place. She doesn't talk about Ollie much."

"It surprised me, too," she confessed.

Nathan was quiet for a moment, fidgeting with a skateboard figurine from Ollie's dresser. "I'm guessing you asked about that night. Did she tell you about the back sliding door? How she thought Ollie came through it?"

"She mentioned it. But she said it was just a dream."

"She didn't always think so. For the longest time she thought Ollie did come back. She swore to the police and my dad she heard him come through that door that night. None of them listened."

"Do you think he came back?" she asked.

"I don't know." He shrugged. "On one hand, my mom insists she heard he did, but on the other I can't think of a reason why Ollie would come back here only to leave."

"I asked your mom if she thought your dad might know where Ollie went," Gianna told him.

He snorted. "Considering Ollie's disappearance is the reason he left in the first place, I highly doubt it."

"Did he know Ollie stole his gun?"

"Not until the rest of us knew." He sighed. "He used to keep the guns in a safe in his room."

"And I'm guessing Ollie knew the passcode."

Nathan nodded. "Ollie and Dad used to go hunting. Ollie must've seen him punch in the passcode one time."

That made sense. "Any reason you can think of that he'd steal your dad's gun?"

"No clue. Dad was convinced Ollie had gotten himself into some trouble, and if he came back that night, it was only for money. My mom threw a wine glass at his head." He hesitated, looking at her before his gaze lingered on the ground. "He left not long after that."

Gianna grimaced. "I'm sorry."

"It's not your fault." Nathan set the skateboard figurine back on Ollie's dresser. "It's not even Ollie's." His lips pulled into a wry smile. "Fathers, right?"

A similar smile worked its way onto her face. "I know a thing or two about that."

"Really?" His head tilted in surprise. "It's just … I've seen you around town. You were grocery shopping with a man—"

"That's Anthony," she clarified. "My mother's brother. He was a detective, once, too."

"Wait, your uncle is a detective?" His eyes lit up. "Is he interested in my brother's case?"

"He has no idea I'm looking into Ollie's disappearance. And if he did, he'd probably ground me until I'm thirty."

"Oh." His shoulders sagged. "I take it he thinks my brother's guilty then."

"It doesn't matter what he thinks. The police department closed the case and he can't open it up. At least, not until we come up with concrete proof." She stood, walking over to the door, when she noticed a pair of keys on the corner of the dresser. "Are those Ollie's car keys?"

"Yep," Nathan said, grabbing the keys and tossing them to her. "His house and car keys."

Car keys. That was right—Ollie had his own car. But he had taken Angela's car to Grant's house that night.

"How come Ollie didn't take his own car to Grant's house that night?" she asked.

"It was at the shop. He took it in to get an oil change at first. At least that's what he claimed."

"You don't think he was telling the truth?"

"Three hundred dollars for an oil change he could've done himself? He was definitely lying."

Gianna filed this information away for later. "What about this one?" She held up the key. "What does this open?"

Nathan frowned and walked over to her, examining the keys as if he never noticed before. "I don't know. It's not for the front door or his car."

"What about the other doors in the house?"

"Only my mom's room locks from the outside," he said. "Don't know what he'd be doing with a key to their door, though."

"Only one way to find out," Gianna walked into the hallway. "Which room's your mom's?"

Nathan led her down the hall. Gianna inserted the key, but the door didn't budge. She huffed, retreating a few steps. What did the key unlock?

"It's probably nothing," Nathan said, shrugging. "Ollie has a lock for his bike. It's probably what it is."

Gianna handed him back the keys. That was the most likely solution, but the third key still nagged at the back of her mind. Nathan was right. They were probably nothing.

"So." He clasped his hands together. "What do you say about working together?"

"Your mom will kill me," she stated.

He shook his head. "No, she won't. But she'll definitely kill me. But that's only if she finds out I'm helping you."

She'd be going against Angela's wishes … but wouldn't it be better if she had help to find Ollie quicker?

"Alright," Gianna said. "We work together."

"Great." He smiled. "Tell me more about Operation Find Ollie."

NINE

Molly Goldstein's voice filled her ears as she walked. *Actually … now that I think about it, there was something that was off. I noticed some weird tension between Grant and Ollie.*

Stop. Fast-forward.

At some point during dinner, I went to the restroom, and when I came back, I heard Grant whisper to Ollie, "We need to tell her."

Those were his exact words? Gianna blinked, still unused to the gravelly sound of her own voice on tape. "*We need to tell her*"?

Stop. Rewind.

Is there any reason you can think of why Ollie would hurt Grant?

Absolutely not. Ollie was the closest thing to a brother that Grant had, and Grant was practically Ollie's second brother. He'd hurt himself before he hurt Grant.

Gianna pressed the rewind button again. *He'd hurt himself before he'd hurt Grant.* Rewind. *Ollie was the closest thing to a brother—*

"Watch out!"

Gianna registered the tires squealing a second too late before she was thrown off her feet. Her body slammed onto the ground. Hard. Coughing out a mouthful of dirt, she looked up in time to see the red Mustang whizzing by. The revving engine and laughter roared in her ears as she struggled to catch her breath. Why did it feel like an elephant had decided to sit on her chest?

Her answer came in the form of a pained groan above her.

No, not above her—*on* her.

She pushed the weight pressing down on her, earning an *oomph* from the other person. She trembled as she stood, taking in her current state. Her shirt and pants were caked in dirt, her white Converse no longer visible beneath the mud that covered them. She tried wiping it off, but it was no use. The dirt only sank lower into her shirt, creating a giant stain in the center.

Face flushed, she whipped around to face the person who had pushed her. "What was that for?" she demanded hotly.

"I think I'm the one who should be asking that, seeing how you punched me," he ground out. He propped himself up on his knees with a grunt. He looked up, and that was when a flare of recognition passed through her. Her stomach sank, and the urge to laugh overwhelmed her. Why, out of all the people to shove her into a ditch, did it have to be him?

Theodore Rodriguez stood, equally as covered with mud as her. Strands of straw and grass stuck out of his hair, and he brushed a hand through them, missing all but one of them.

"You missed one," she said flatly.

"You know, most people just say 'thank you' for saving their lives." He plucked the straw from his hair and let it fall to the ground. "Did you not hear that car speeding down the road?"

She stifled a sigh. *Of all people.*

"I heard it," she said through gritted teeth, "and I would've been perfectly fine without you throwing me into a ditch."

She gave him what Valarie deemed her murderous glare at the word *throwing*.

"This is a new version of gratitude, but I'll take it." He rubbed the back of his neck. "You … er … might not remember, but we met the other day. I'm—"

"Theodore Hugo Rodriguez," she interrupted, "but everyone calls you Theo."

His lips parted in surprise before they twisted into an easy smile. "And you're the girl who likes murder podcasts. I, uh, never caught your name before."

She didn't know what surprised her more: that he remembered their brief interaction in the robotics club or that he was asking for her name.

"It's Gianna. Reyes," she added as an afterthought. Her fingers slid into her pocket, in search of her tape recorder. "And I really need to get going or Val's going to kill me and—"

Gianna frowned. Her pocket was empty. She shoved down the panic rising in her chest as she fumbled through her jacket. The recorder wasn't there. Her eyes snapped to the grass. She must've dropped it during the tumble in the ditch.

"Looking for this?" Theo's arm outstretched toward her, revealing her tape recorder and headphones in his hand. "I was worried I might've crushed it during the fall, but it looks in good shape."

It was. Not a single dent in it. She couldn't stop the breath of relief that left her at the sight of it. She forced herself not to snatch the recorder from Theo's hands, politely plucking them from his grasp and back to the safe place in her pocket.

"Thanks." She took a step back. "I'll, uh … see you around." She started walking, but Theo remained by her side.

"I can walk you home," he offered. "In case those guys in that car decide to come back this way."

"It's fine," she said quickly. Theo glanced over at her. "I mean, I walk down this road often. Those guys drive by here all the time."

He raised his eyebrows. "You walk on this road with full knowledge that there are drivers going fifty miles an hour down here every day?"

She shrugged. "What can I say? I live for the danger."

He snorted, a faint line of amusement in his eyes.

"Seriously, I'm fine. I'm not heading home anyway."

"Oh." A pause. Surely he was leaving any second now. "Where are you going, then?"

"The Retro."

"So we're heading to the same place then."

She stopped dead in her tracks. "You're not heading to the Retro," she blurted.

His lips tugged into an amused smile, which confused her. Nothing was amusing about the situation. "I'm pretty sure I am … hence why I'm walking instead of driving. I usually take my car to school, but I'm heading up there to meet a friend, and I've got a thing after that's not too far away. Who are you meeting?"

"A friend," she said curtly. "Her boyfriend's band is playing there. If you could even call it that."

Why am I still talking to him, again?

"I take it you're not a fan of your friend's boyfriend?" Theo asked as they resumed walking.

"You'd be right."

He gestured to her jacket. "So, what's the tape recorder for?"

Gianna shoved the recorder further into her pocket and continued walking. "It's for a project I'm working on."

"What kind of project is it?" he pressed. "Is it for school?"

"Why?" She fixed her sharp gaze on him. "Worried I'll take your spot as the future valedictorian? Beat you for the highest grade in class?"

Theo simply shrugged. "It looks like you've got me all figured out. So, what kind of project are we talking about?"

"Does anyone ever tell you that you ask a lot of questions?"

"I can't help but be a little curious. You're quite infamous yourself, Gianna Reyes."

She tilted her head to the side. "Whatever you say."

"I'm serious," Theo insisted. "I mean, everyone kept telling me you were top of the classes before I showed up, that you were the one to beat."

"Well, whoever told you that has greatly exaggerated."

"Still, it's strange that we haven't crossed paths until now, isn't it?"

She glanced at him. The same thought had crossed her mind on several occasions. But that would mean acknowledging that she knew who he was before they met.

"Echo Falls is a big school," she said. It wasn't, and thankfully he didn't call her out on her lie. "The project I'm working on, though, is not for school. It's an old case that happened right here in Echo Falls. Although I doubt it'll interest you."

"Yeah?" he said. "Why's that?"

Did he have a short memory? How could he forget the last time they spoke? He mocked her mysteries in front of the entire robotics club.

"Come on," he urged. "The suspense is killing me. What's the case about?"

She whirled around to face him. The question *You don't know?* was on the tip of her tongue, until she remembered that he was still fairly new to Echo Falls. The town's greatest tragedy probably hadn't even reached his ears yet.

And it was lucky for him that he had stumbled on one of her favorite topics—mysteries.

She told him everything from the top of her head about Ollie's case. Theo proved to be a good listener. If he was this attentive with his lessons, no wonder he quickly rose to the top of the class.

"Everyone thinks he ran to Canada," she explained. "You really haven't heard about this until now?"

Theo shook his head. "No one's ever mentioned it to me. Then again, I haven't lived here that long—or in New Hampshire for that matter."

"Where did you live before here?" she asked, and mentally kicked herself in the knee for giving in to the conversation.

He kicked a pebble into the grass with his shoe. "Florida, in a much bigger area than this. Bigger neighborhood, bigger school."

"You must miss it." Her house with Anthony in Echo Falls was the only home she had ever known. Moving a thousand miles away to a new place—the thought was enough to shatter her heart in two.

"I do. But I think this place is growing on me. I could get used to it—the quiet." He glanced up at the trees towering above them before looking at her.

"The quiet is the best part," she agreed.

He smiled. "Well, look at that. We already agree on something."

Gianna had no response to that. He made it sound as if he wanted to agree more with her, but of course that would be ridiculous.

They walked in silence the rest of the way to The Retro. Unlike the beginning of their walk, it wasn't filled with the tension of two strangers. Not friends, but not strangers either.

Inside, Gianna found Valarie at one of the tables in front of the small stage where the crew was still setting up. Liam was beside her, one leg propped up on the chair and a guitar slung over his shoulder.

"Hey, you made it!" Valarie exclaimed when she noticed Gianna approaching the table. Her eyes widened as she took in her mud-stained clothes. "Oh my God, what happened?"

"Long story," she mumbled, slipping into the seat beside her.

Valarie's eyes flew to Theo, widening with interest, before returning to Gianna with an entirely different question: *Who's this?*

"Sup, Nancy Drew," Liam said. His gaze swung behind her, where Theo was standing. He walked over to him and held out a fist to which Theo bumped. "What's up, cous?"

"Cous?" The girls exclaimed in unison. The word swirled around in Gianna's mind as her eyes darted between the two boys.

"You never told me you two are related," Valarie said, no doubt recalling their conversation in the diner.

Theo rubbed the back of his neck. "We're not exactly related."

Liam chuckled, coming up behind Theo and landing a hand on his shoulder. "I think what Theo's trying to say is that we're not cousins *yet*. Theo's dad is marrying my Aunt June. That's why they moved here in the first place."

Gianna glanced at Theo, but he refused to meet her gaze. And then it hit her. When Gianna had told Theo about the band, he knew she was talking about Liam. Liam most likely told him about her; his girlfriend's insufferable best friend he couldn't stand. Betrayal she had no right to feel seeped its way into her bones, and she tore her gaze from him.

He knew who she was this entire time, and he hadn't said a word about it, pretending from the get-go. And she told him all about her case, which he would no doubt laugh over with Liam later.

One of the baristas stood at the front of the café and announced that Eternal Flame was about to perform. Liam gave Valarie a quick peck on the cheek before dashing toward the stage, guitar in hand. The lights dimmed and the chatter quieted.

Gianna let out a breath of relief when Theo slid into the seat beside Valarie. If he sat next to her, she might have been tempted to punch him in the arm again.

As the first song began, she felt eyes on her. She turned her head slightly, catching Theo's gaze. He looked at her as if he were trying to tell her something, but she turned away, breaking the stare.

Halfway through the band's first song, Gianna's phone vibrated in her pocket. She reached for it and saw that it was Nathan calling and that he had texted her three times already.

"I'll be right back," she said, ignoring Theo's curious stare as she headed back outside for some quiet. She lifted the phone to her ear. "Nathan, hey. What's up?"

"Gianna, finally," he breathed. "I've been trying to reach you—"

"What's going on? Is something wrong?" Worry flooded her. But it wasn't trembling from fear in his tone—it was exhilaration.

"No, you couldn't be more wrong," Nathan said. "I figured out what the third key unlocks.

TEN

Gianna moved aside just before the boys in roller skates flew past her, nearly knocking her to the floor. She clutched her bag closer to her body as she made her way through the dark parking lot. The flickering neon SKATING MOOSE sign above the building cast an orangish-green glow on the sidewalk. Her nose wrinkled as she was welcomed with a smell mixed of pizza, musk, and Lysol.

She scanned the rink for Nathan. Finally, she found him in the corner of the room, engrossed in a game on his phone.

"Hey!" She nudged his shoulder, and he startled. Alarm ran over his face before he realized it was her, and he let out a huff.

"Don't do that!" he shouted over the thuds of wheels hitting the ground. "You never interrupt a gamer in the middle of a game."

"Sorry. What game were you playing?" She peered over his shoulder to get a look at his phone, but he shut it off before she could see.

"It's nothing," he muttered, pocketing his phone. "What was so important that you couldn't get here two hours ago?"

"Hey, I'm not happy about it either," she grumbled. She couldn't have gotten out of hanging out with Valarie and Liam at The Retro. Halfway through Liam's second song, Theo suddenly left, presumably to do whatever he had going on after Liam's performance, since he never returned to the table. Not that Gianna was keeping track or anything.

By the time Gianna had left the coffee shop, two hours had passed.

"Why do you think the key unlocks something here?" she asked.

"Ollie used to work here. He only had the job for a few months," Nathan explained. "When you asked about the third key the other day, it got me thinking. I went to the garage to test out the bike lock, but that didn't work. Then I remembered something. A few days before Ollie went missing, he asked my mom to borrow her car to go to work. He needed it to grab something from his locker. When he got back, I asked him if he got what he needed. He told me he did, but he didn't bring anything inside, and he sounded upset."

That was definitely weird. "So you think that whatever Ollie went to get might still be in the locker?"

"I'm sure of it. But we have two problems. I don't know which locker was Ollie's, and the staff's locker room is completely off-limits to customers. That guy"—he pointed to the employee at the front counter—"is like a hawk. I've been here for two hours and he hasn't once left that counter. And he's had two slushies. *Two.*" He held up two fingers for emphasis.

Gianna eyed the locker room and the employee, a plan forming in her mind. She pulled Nathan aside.

"Okay, here's the plan: you distract the guy at the counter," she said, "and when he's not looking, I'll slip into the back room."

"But what if he tries to go into the back room? How do I warn you?"

She tapped her phone. "That's what these are for."

But Nathan was still stammering. "What do I even talk about?"

"Anything. Talk to him about that game you were playing earlier."

"But that's not—"

She pushed him in the direction of the counter. He looked back at her. The meaning was clear on his face: *Please don't make me do this.* But she made a motion by tapping her wrist. *Time's ticking,* she mouthed. *For Ollie.* At those words, he relented, shoving his shoulders back as he marched toward the counter.

"Can I help you?" the guy asked flatly.

"Um, yes," Nathan replied. "As a matter of fact, you can. Uh … how much do you know about video games?"

The man's face twisted into confusion, and then blatant annoyance as Nathan rambled on. He put a hand up. "Listen, man …"

Gianna took her chance and sprinted to the door. The clatter of skates matched her racing heart as she pressed herself against the wall. Without taking her eyes off the counter, she twisted the knob. Right as she was about to push the door, a shadow fell over her. She gasped, spinning around until she came face to face with the Skating Moose mascot.

"Go away," she hissed, gaze flying back to the counter. The employee was becoming more irritated by the second with Nathan's rambling. Her distraction was about to disappear. Her fingers squeezed around the door, only to find it locked. She swore.

A noncommittal noise like a snort came from the moose. "You do realize I'm not an actual moose, right?"

Even though the voice was partly muffled by the costume, it sounded familiar. She was scrutinizing who it could be when they saved her time and took off the head of the costume. Her eyes widened, and she couldn't help the incredulous laugh that followed. Why was he always there when she didn't want him to be?

Black curls stuck to his forehead, a shiny sweat running over Theo's face, but even so, he still smiled. Always smiling. *So this was the thing he had to do after The Retro.*

"Why are you—you know what, I'm not even going to ask."

Theo had no qualms about asking himself. "Why are you trying to get into the staff room?"

"I'm not."

"Doesn't look like it to me." His brow furrowed. "Oh, does this have something to do with that case you told me about earlier?"

"Do me a favor and forget I ever told you about that. In fact, forget that this day happened at all," she spat. Her mind wandered to the moment she learned he was Liam's cousin. The sting of betrayal.

She wouldn't let it happen again.

"Ah, you're still angry, I take it," Theo concluded.

"Who said I was angry?"

"You did, just now. With your face."

Gianna sighed. "Could you please go away?"

Theo tilted his head to the side. "Has anyone ever told you you're incredibly hostile?"

"Has anyone ever told you you're incredibly annoying?"

"Plenty of times." He leaned against the wall. "Look, I'll gladly get you into the staff locker for whatever mysterious reason you need to get in there so badly."

Gianna blinked. Had she heard him right? "You will?"

"Sure. On one condition." He held up a finger. "You let me explain what happened back at the coffee shop."

She frowned. It wasn't the condition she'd expected. *Who cares what it is? You have an opportunity to get into the staff room. Take it.*

"You've got yourself a deal," she decided. "Now, open the door."

His lips tilted upward in wry amusement as he murmured, "Hostile and demanding."

He pulled a key hanging off a chain around his neck and unlocked the door. Her retort fell short as her eyes fell on the rows and rows of lockers surrounding the room. The confidence she'd felt earlier whittled away at rapid speed. This was going to take longer than she had expected.

Shuffling noises erupted from behind her. Gianna turned enough to see that Theo was shedding the moose costume.

"Do I need to turn around?" she asked dryly. "I don't want to see something that will traumatize me for life."

"You're not that lucky, Reyes." Theo winked and removed the costume, revealing the Skating Moose uniform he was wearing beneath. She rolled her eyes and walked over to one of the lockers.

"God, I hate wearing that thing. You can barely breathe in it." Theo threw the costume onto one of the benches. "Speaking of, why are there so many moose-themed places around here? We live right next to a Moose-mart and there's a Moose Milkshake Shack a mile down the road."

"It's not like you live in the middle of New Hampshire or anything," she said, as she moved on to the next locker. The door was already ajar. She opened it and found a bag full of empty soda bottles. "Ugh." She wrinkled her nose and slammed the locker shut. "When's the last time anyone went through these? The 1900s?"

Theo blew out a breath. "Try 1986. According to Norman—the cheerful guy at the skate counter—after the original owners died, the place went downhill. It's a miracle they even have one employee at this rate."

"Don't you mean two?" she countered, eyes running over his red polo shirt.

He hesitated. "I wouldn't exactly consider myself an employee. I help out from time to time. June's good friends with the owner of the place and asked me to come help on some of the busier nights. That's why I had to leave The Retro early."

Huh. June—his dad's fiancée. And Liam's aunt. Gianna moved to the next locker and inserted the key.

Theo slid his hands in his pocket. "So, about earlier—" he began.

"We don't have to talk about that," she said briskly, moving on to the next locker.

"I got the impression you were a little upset with me."

She turned away from the locker. "Of course I was. You made me look like a fool. You knew exactly who I was when I walked into the robotics club but pretended otherwise."

Theo didn't bother denying it. "Yes, Liam mentioned you."

"I'm sure he's told you plenty of stories."

He sighed. "Look, I've known Liam for almost two years now and have come to understand three major things about him. One: his obsession with his band supersedes almost everything in his life. Two"—Theo held up a second finger—"he has a tendency to exaggerate."

She raised an eyebrow. "And the third?"

"The guy loves bacon."

Gianna let out a little laugh. *Understatement of the year.* "I don't get it. Why didn't you just tell me you were Liam's cousin in the first place?"

He shrugged. "Maybe I didn't want you to judge me based on who I'm related to."

And that was exactly what she had been doing.

She tried to think of the words to apologize, but Theo held out his hand. "What do you say we start over?"

Gianna stared at his hand, at a loss. He was nothing like the stories she had heard of him. Far from them. Most of the time, she was able to figure a person out ahead of time—how likely it was they would leave or stay, laugh or cry in certain situations—but it was different with Theo. One moment he was all sly grins and jokes, and the next he was helping her sneak into a locker room expecting nothing in return but for her to listen. He was an anomaly of his own. She had no idea what to make of him. And she hated how much he intrigued her.

His hand was surprisingly warm in hers.

"Now that's settled," he said, pulling his arm away, "what exactly are we doing in here?"

She held up the key. "I'm looking to see which locker this unlocks."

"What are you hoping to find inside?"

Nothing. Anything. A hint of where Ollie went, of what he had been up to before he disappeared.

"I don't know," she admitted. She moved to the next locker, expecting the same result as her last few attempts, but this time the key fit into the slot. The faint click echoed through the room. Her breath escaped her. She pulled, only for the door to not budge.

"Here. Let me try." Theo leaned forward as Gianna stepped to the side, his arm brushing against hers, leaving a trail of goosebumps in its wake. "There."

He stepped back, waiting for her to say something, but words evaded her. He smiled as if he knew the effect he had on her. Now it was her turn to feel warm because the stupid part of her had noticed the dimple on his cheek.

"Thanks," she mumbled, opening the locker door all the way. "I—"

Her words stumbled to a halt in her throat.

Inside the locker lay a black backpack. Beside her, Theo went still, gaping at the bag.

Gianna unzipped the bag and flipped up the tag on the inside. *O. Kipman.*

"This is Ollie's," she whispered, but she barely heard herself over her blood rushing. They'd found something. And when she looked at the contents of the bags, it was enough to send a rush of dizziness to her head, along with confusion and exhilaration through her. "I've—I've got to go," she said, throwing the strap of the bag on her shoulder. She looked up at Theo. "Thank you."

His mouth opened to speak, but she didn't hear what he said. She was already out of the door, her heartbeat drumming against the walls of her mind.

***

They took a step back to observe the contents of the bag scattered over the bed. Gianna placed a hand on her chin, trying to make sense of it. What would Ollie need with three burner phones, one hundred eighty dollars, a handful of photos, and a gold watch?

"Remember when I told you Ollie withdrew three hundred dollars for an oil change and I thought it was a lie?" Nathan asked. "There's about one hundred and eighty here. If each of these burner phones were about forty dollars each …"

As Nathan listed off numbers and estimates, Gianna cradled the watch in her hands. It was a nice watch. More than nice. Far beyond the salary you'd make in ten years at the Skating Moose. It felt odd in her hands—out of place—like a piece of glass too precious for her to hold. She ran her fingers along the smooth edges, pausing when she came across an uneven surface on the bottom of the watch.

She flipped the watch over. It wasn't any uneven surface, but a set of initials engraved: P.R.B.

Interesting.

"There was no way Ollie could afford it." Nathan stopped his rant to look at her. "He barely made a hundred here on a good week."

"Maybe someone gave it to him," Gianna suggested. She set the watch back down on the bed, trading it for the Polaroids she found in the front pocket of the bag. "Does Ollie own a Polaroid camera?"

"Not that I know of. Grant might have, though. He was into photography."

Huh. Gianna flipped through the photos. They were shot all over Echo Falls: the library, the high school, Lori's, the skatepark. They switched between Ollie and Grant posing with their skateboards, flipping off the camera. A lot of photos flipping off the camera, on second thought. One photo didn't fit in with the rest. The one taken of a girl looking toward the sunset, her face obscured by her blonde hair.

"Who is she?" Gianna asked.

Nathan came to her side and peered down at the photo. "I don't know. I've never seen her before. A random photo that Grant took, maybe?"

It could have been that, or …

Gianna went back through the other photos, lying face up. Grant flipping off the camera, Ollie halfway through a water bottle flip, and then one of them both skating down an empty road. She gasped.

"What is it?" Nathan asked.

"It's not a random picture. See?" She pointed at the photo farthest to the left. "This one is of Ollie and Nathan skating ahead."

"Yeah, so?"

"So," she said, meeting his eyes, "who took the picture?"

Nathan was quiet for a moment. "Can I see it again?" She handed him the picture. A line formed between his eyebrows as he studied the photo. "I recognize that wall. See the graffiti? There's a skatepark right outside of town that has that type of wall. Grant and Ollie liked to go down there because of the dips and ramps."

She clasped her hands together. "Well, that's a start."

Nathan ran a hand through his hair. "I don't see how this matters," he snapped. "He was obviously planning on running away, and the photos don't tell us why he had all this stuff and where he planned on going!" Nathan tossed the photo on the bed and let out a frustrated sigh. "I'm sorry. I just … I thought …"

"You thought we would have found him by now," Gianna said, understanding. "If it were that easy, I wouldn't be here."

"I know."

"Let's try to look on the bright side. We don't know where he was going or why, but we know he was planning on going somewhere." She glanced at the three burner phones. "And that he wasn't planning on going alone."

Nathan's head snapped up. "How do you know that?"

"Remember how I told you I spoke with Molly? She mentioned how Ollie and Grant were acting strangely at Ollie's birthday dinner, whispering about how they needed to tell some *her*?"

"Yeah." His face lit up with realization. "You think the girl in the photo is her."

She nodded. "Three burner phones. Three people: Ollie, Grant, and whoever the girl is. Grant and Ollie might not be around to tell us where they planned on going—"

"But maybe she can," Nathan finished.

"We'll go to that skatepark from the photo tomorrow," she decided. "Did you want to keep Ollie's stuff here?"

Nathan thought about it, before shaking his head. "It's better if you take it. I don't want to risk my mom finding it."

"Where is she anyway?" Gianna hadn't seen Angela's car in the driveway. It was the only reason she agreed to come inside.

"Another late-night shift at the hospital," Nathan replied. "She won't be back until the morning. I'll give her an excuse tomorrow."

Gianna nodded. All they had to do was find the girl from the photo. And fingers crossed, they would finally get some answers this time.

ELEVEN

Gianna raced down the stairs, time working against her favor. She dashed through the kitchen, stopping long enough to grab a waffle off the plate and sip a little bit of the drink Irene left out for her. She gagged, setting the cup down. She wiped away the juice from her lips.

"Orange juice? Ew."

"That was meant for me," Anthony said dryly. He lowered the newspaper he was reading at the table to look at her. "Where are you off to in such a hurry?"

"Just meeting up with a friend and I'm late."

The page crinkled as he turned to the next one. "What friend is this? Valarie?"

Irene whirled around from the stove, poking him with the spatula. "Since when are you so nosy?"

"I was just curious," Anthony said, which was code for *making sure she wasn't hanging around any boys and doing drugs.*

"Don't worry," Gianna said, bemused, "Nathan's harmless."

"What's a Nathan?"

Gianna laughed, giving them each a peck on the cheek on her way out.

"Oh, ask him if he wants to come over for dinner," Irene called out after her. "I'm going to attempt to make a turkey."

"Key word—*attempt*," Anthony whispered from behind his newspaper.

Gianna held back a laugh as Irene shot him a death stare. "See you guys later."

The good news was that the skatepark wasn't a far drive. She was able to pick up Nathan on the way and get there at their planned time. He had been playing that same game on his phone when she arrived, but she couldn't tell what it was, and it irked her. The bad news was that, in her rush, she forgot her tape recorder was in the pocket of her other jacket.

"You look like someone just ran over your cat," Nathan stated upon noticing her expression when they got out of the car.

"I forgot my tape recorder. I spent all night cataloging everything we found."

"Oh." Nathan mustered up what she assumed was meant to be a sympathetic face, but it ended up looking more like someone had run over *his* cat. "Why do you use a tape recorder? Wouldn't a phone work just as well?"

"My uncle gave me the tape recorder as a gift," she explained. Anthony knew how much she was obsessed with mysteries and got her one as a surprise. Even though her phone would be the more practical choice to use for recording, she preferred her tape recorder over it. However, it would have to work for today. At least she wouldn't have to spend more time tonight typing up everything she recorded.

She turned to Nathan. "Ready for this?"

"No," Nathan admitted. "I haven't been here in almost five years."

Since Ollie went missing.

"If you don't want to," she began, but he interrupted her.

"I do. I'm just being weird about it." He straightened his shoulders. "I want to find Ollie, and in order for us to do that, we need to find the girl from the photo."

The two of them walked toward the park. The crisp autumn leaves crunched beneath their feet. Gianna made sure to watch her step and avoid tripping over any of the dips and getting in the way of people riding past. The sounds of laughter and wheels surrounded them on all sides. They came upon a giant hole in the ground shaped like a swimming pool that people were diving in and out with their skateboards and scooters. A guy on a scooter whizzed past them, disappearing into the pool-like hole up ahead.

"They call it the Fishbowl," Nathan explained, following her stare to the swimming pool.

Her gaze snagged on a flash of blonde hair inside the bowl and paused. She inhaled deeply as the girl turned around. Disappointment washed over her. This girl was too young to match the girl in the photo.

A blank expression twisted her face as she turned to Nathan. "I don't see her anyway."

"Me neither," he mumbled.

"Maybe someone else has seen her. We could ask around," she said. When he didn't respond to her suggestion, Gianna lifted her head. He was looking somewhere to their left. She traced his gaze to two guys standing on the deck, skateboards propped beside them. They looked to be in their early twenties.

"Do you know them?" she asked.

Nathan swallowed before nodding. "They used to hang around with Ollie. The guy on the left's name is Roger."

"Perfect. Let's go talk to them." She could hear his blubbering protests from behind her, but Gianna held her head up high as they crossed the park to them.

Both men turned to look at them as they approached. Gianna glanced at the man with the red beanie, the one Nathan said was Roger.

"Roger?" she asked.

"Yeah, that's me." His brows furrowed. "Have we met?"

"No, but you might know my friend's brother. He used to hang around here a lot. His name is Ollie."

Both men's eyes lit with recognition. Their demeanor shifted from distrust to friendliness in an instant.

"No way!" said the guy on the right. "You're Ollie's little bro? Holy shit. The last time I saw you, you were like five feet shorter. You tried skating one time and fell clean off right over there." He pointed at one of the smaller ramps.

Nathan scratched the back of his head, a red flush rising on his neck. "Yeah, that was me. So, you guys know my brother?"

"Yeah, dude was cool. I'm Dexter, by the way," the boy on the right said. "For the record, we never thought for a second that your brother killed Grant. I mean, him vanishing into thin air wasn't the best look, but those two were two peas in a pod."

"So you guys hung around here often about five years ago?" she asked.

"Yep," Dexter said.

"Great. Then you might be able to help us." She stepped forward to show them the Polaroid. "We're looking for this girl."

Dexter squinted at the photo, scratching his jaw. "I'm not one hundred percent sure, but it looks like Emmaline. Right, Rog?"

"Yeah, it kind of does look like her," Roger agreed.

"Emmaline," Gianna repeated the name, imprinting it in her memory. "Have you seen her around here lately?"

"She hangs around here every now and then. The last I saw her was a few weeks ago, but she didn't stay long." Dexter handed her the photo. "Why are you looking for her?"

"We think she can help us find my brother," Nathan said. "Do you have her phone number or a way we can contact her?"

Dexter and Roger shared an amused look.

"Hell no," Roger said. "Emmaline's … well, you'd have to meet her."

"What's that supposed to mean?" Nathan asked.

"Let me put it this way: the last time a guy tried to hit on Emmaline, he couldn't skate for a whole month. The girl's nuts. Trust me, you don't want to mess with her."

If one of them used phrases like *hitting on her*, Gianna couldn't blame Emmaline for putting them in their place. Nathan seemed to agree.

A sly smile tugged at Nathan's lips as he pointed to Roger. "Wasn't your wrist sprained the last time I saw you?"

"Shut up," Roger snapped, the red in his cheeks rising as Dexter coughed to hide his laughter.

Gianna cleared her throat. "Back to the subject: Emmaline. Did you guys ever see her hanging out with Ollie or Grant?"

"We saw them together a couple of times, yeah. We even had a bet going," Dexter said.

"A bet?" Nathan asked.

"If she and Ollie were together."

Gianna and Nathan exchanged wide-eyed glances. "And were they?"

"We never knew. They hung out a lot that summer."

"Yeah," Roger piped. "Dude, remember that fight between Ollie and Michael? Wasn't that over her?"

"A fight?" Gianna's eyes darted between them. "What fight?"

"It happened sometime in the summer. Wait, I might have a video of it."

Dexter fished through his pocket for his phone. As his fingers swiped through photos, he said, "It was crazy, man. I don't think I'd ever seen Ollie like that. Your brother was usually pretty chill. Here, I found it."

He thrust his phone in the center of them and hit play.

The video was blurry, but Gianna could make out two figures near the ramp. One skinny and tall—unmistakably Ollie—and the other older and brawny. He had to be in his mid-forties to fifties. The two of them stood inches apart. Ollie's mouth was moving, but whatever he said was lost in the gust of wind. And then it all happened so fast: Michael's fist collided with Ollie's face. Ollie fell back, clutching his bleeding nose before letting out a roar of anger and throwing himself at Michael.

Beside her, Nathan watched the video with a pained expression on his face.

"Yeah, get him, Ollie!" Roger in the video yelled. "Holy shit. Dex, are you getting this?"

"Yeah," Video Dexter replied, zooming the camera in on them. The video lasted no more than thirty seconds, ending with Michael delivering a swift kick to Ollie's side. Michael stormed away off-camera. Right as the video ended, Grant ran up to Ollie's side, helping his friend up.

The four of them stared at the picture of the two best friends frozen in time.

"That hoodie," Nathan said, a slight tremor in his voice. "Ollie got that hoodie for his eighteenth birthday from our mom. This had to be a few weeks before he went missing."

Dexter tapped the screen. "June 30th, 2019," he read the timestamp out loud.

Gianna and Nathan let out a breath of disbelief at the same time.

June 30th.

Five days before Ollie went missing.

Nathan turned to Dexter, fists clenched by his side. "Who was that guy? Why was he assaulting my brother?"

"Beats me," Dexter said, pocketing his phone and leaning against his skateboard. "Although I did hear Ollie say Emmaline's name when it all went down. Honestly, at first I thought it might've been about …" He trailed off, looking uncertain. "Look, you didn't hear this from me, but the burly guy in the video? He hangs around here sometimes selling … stuff."

"Stuff?" Gianna's brows furrowed before she understood his meaning. "You mean he sells drugs?"

Dexter coughed into his fist. "Yeah. But nothing like … too serious."

"Yeah," Roger piped. "Like marijuana."

Gianna pulled her notepad from her pocket and began writing down notes. "This dealer—did Ollie buy from him?"

"Sometimes. Wait, you're not writing this down, are you?"

"The man in this video," she insisted, ignoring his question. "What's his full name, and where can we find him?"

"He goes by Michael Price. But a piece of advice: this is not the type of guy you go up to and ask questions about."

"She didn't ask for your advice," Nathan snapped, still shaken by the video of his brother getting beaten up. "She asked where we could find him."

Roger raised his hands in a surrendering position. "Hey—I'm only trying to help you guys out. It's your funeral, man."

Dexter nudged Roger with his elbow, giving his friend a look of disdain before turning to him. "He lives on the outskirts of town, down by the lake in some broken-down shack. That's all we know."

Gianna and Nathan exchanged looks. *Do you think he's lying?* Nathan seemed to ask. She gave a slight shake of her head. As far as she could see, neither of them had any reason to lie.

"One last question. Where can we find Emmaline?" Gianna asked.

"No clue. Emmaline comes and goes as she pleases. And she doesn't like anyone getting into her business." He gave them a pointed look.

"Girl's a mystery," Roger hummed.

Well, that was lucky for them.

Gianna had Dexter send her the video. Once that was done, she and Nathan headed back to the car.

"None of this makes sense," Nathan said as Gianna opened the driver's door of the car. "Ollie doesn't do drugs."

"That you know of," she pointed out.

Nathan stopped and Gianna's hand stilled on the door. "You really think my brother bought drugs from a drug dealer? Ollie, the same guy who saved your life and patched up your knees as a kid? Is that what you're saying?"

Gianna sighed. "I'm saying that it's possible. You were just a little kid when he went missing. Ollie's smart—he would've made sure that you never caught on. And it makes sense that he bought from the same drug dealer he got into a fight with."

"I remember that day," he said quietly. "I was sitting at the kitchen table doing homework when he came in. He got an ice pack from the freezer, and I asked him what happened to his nose. He said he broke it while skating and I believed him."

Something in her heart softened. "You couldn't have known he was lying."

"I'm his brother," he said. "Of course I could have."

Gianna wanted to say something to comfort him, but she had a feeling that no matter what she said, Nathan would still blame himself.

"Look, we can't keep going over what-ifs. We need to get our facts straight." She set her notebook on the front of the car. Uncapping the pen with her teeth, she flipped to an empty page. "So it's possible that, at some point before Grant's death, he, Ollie, and Emmaline were planning on going somewhere. At Ollie's birthday dinner, there was some tension between him and Grant."

Over Emmaline? She scribbled beneath the last bullet point.

"My brother goes missing, gets his nose broken by a drug dealer," Nathan added. "Which could also be about Emmaline."

"Or possibly drug-related or both." Gianna chewed on a nail. "If only we had Ollie's phone. He could have contacted her through it." A thought occurred to her, and she looked up. "What if the watch we found in the bag belongs to her?"

Nathan tilted his head to the side. "It could be possible. But I don't see how P.R.B could be her initials. Then again, it could be a family heirloom."

She turned the page. That left them with two things on the to-do list: Finding Emmaline and having a talk with Michael Price. If they found Emmaline, they would get answers about what Ollie was up to in the weeks leading to his disappearance. Why he stole the gun, why he lied about his car needing an oil change. And Michael Price could fill in some of those gaps.

"My aunt asked if you wanted to stop by for dinner," she told him after they settled on a day to visit Michael. "She's making turkey. She wants to do this big family dinner before she leaves this week."

"I better not," Nathan said. "I can't be late coming home again or my mom will start to be suspicious. I've been feeding her excuses but there's only so many driving lessons I can have a week. She'd lose her shit if she knew what I was really doing." Gianna looked up at him. "Don't think I'm giving up," he said. "I'm not. I want to find my brother."

"We will," Gianna said. "Especially now that we have our first lead."

Log #5, Dec. 2nd, 2023

Clues

License plate bubblegum wrapper

3 burner phones (unused)

Ten polaroids

$180

Gold watch. (Who is P.R.B.??)

Tension between Ollie and Grant (Over Emmaline?)

Fight with Michael Price (Drugs/Emmaline related or both?)

To Do List:

Find Emmaline

Talk to Michael Price

TWELVE

Knock-tap-knock-tap. Gianna recognized Irene's signature knocking pattern. She swiveled around in her chair as Irene poked her head through the door.

"Knock-knock," she sang. "Mind if I come in?"

"No." Gianna closed the tabs she had been using to research Michael Price and whirled around in her chair. "What's up?"

Irene helped herself to the edge of Gianna's bed. "Nothing. I thought I'd make sure you're not suffocating yourself with homework."

"No suffocating to be seen here." Gianna tilted her head, surveying Irene's pink sweats and fuzzy slippers. "Shouldn't you be getting ready for your flight?"

Irene would rather catch the flu than be caught dead outside the house without red lipstick and heels, even at the airport.

"Oh, yes. That. I canceled the flight." Her smile widened. "I've decided to stay in town a little longer."

"A little longer," Gianna echoed.

"Until your spring break!" Irene exclaimed, clasping her hands together. Her smile dimmed when she saw Gianna didn't share the same enthusiasm. "Well, I had hoped you'd be more excited than that."

"It's not that. I am happy. So, so happy," she insisted. Spring break was months away. This would be the longest Irene ever stayed. But Valarie's words bounced around in her mind. *It can only mean one thing. Trouble in paradise.* "It's just … is everything alright in New York? The business? Work?" She noted the way Irene spun her engagement ring on her finger. "Jim?"

"Of course." Irene cleared her throat. "Why wouldn't it be?"

Gianna shrugged. "You've never stayed this long in Echo Falls before."

Irene rested her chin on her hand. "I suppose I've been feeling pretty nostalgic lately. Even a little homesick. This town does that to you. It's like a warm embrace, the smell of pie on a fall evening. It makes it harder for you to leave each time."

The question was on the tip of Gianna's tongue. *Why would you want to leave?* But she already knew the answer. The memories were too unbearable.

Even so, there was more to what Irene wasn't saying, but before she could think more about it, her phone buzzed on the desk.

"Did you need to get that?" Irene asked.

Gianna shook her head, silencing the phone. "It's probably Val. She wants to set a date for us to go dress shopping."

"Does this mean you've changed your mind about going?"

"No. Sorry to disappoint," she said.

"Oh, you could never disappoint me." Irene smiled. "You know, if you want, I can go with you girls. I promise I won't be too embarrassing."

Gianna fought to keep the surprise out of her tone. "You want to go with me?"

"Of course I do," Irene said, and this time it was her phone that buzzed. "Oh, that's Christine. I promised to go over and help her out with some school stuff, and then we'd go out for drinks."

"So you'll have the car for the whole day?" Gianna asked.

"Considering the bar is halfway across town, yes. Why?" She paused in the doorway. "Did you want me to drop you off anywhere on my way?"

"No. I'll walk over to The Retro and meet Valarie there."

"Suit yourself."

Once Irene was gone, Gianna faced back toward her desk and picked up the phone. The text was from Nathan about what time they were going to see Michael. One problem: Irene would have the car for the whole day and Nathan didn't have a license. She laid her head down on the desk, closing her eyes. She was going to have to find another way to get to Michael Price's house.

While searching for bus routes out of town, her phone buzzed on the desk again. Only the text wasn't from Nathan.

do u like robots?

Gianna's eyebrows pulled into a frown as she stared at the screen. She didn't recognize the number displayed on her screen, but she had an idea who it was. Her suspicions were proven correct by a follow-up text: *this is theo from robotics club btw*

Gianna texted back a reply. *Your grammar is atrocious. Who gave you my number?*

I thought u were supposed to be sherlock holmes

Liam had used the term Nancy Drew back at the Retro, but there was no way Gianna was going to correct him. *It was Valarie, wasn't it?*

yeah, he replied. *she seems to think you fancy me.*

Before she could even think of a response to that, another text bubble appeared beneath it. *don't worry holmes, ur secrets safe with me :) also u never answered my question.*

Holmes? She sent. *And for the record, Yes, I guess I like robots as long as they're not the apocalyptic-take-over-the-world kind. Why?*

just curious. and yeah holmes. ur solving a mystery and who solves mysteries?

Ah, I see. Also, you texted me out of the blue because you were curious? She didn't know what to make of this, of him. Gianna pressed a hand to her mouth as she waited for him to text back, a thread of anxiety in her stomach.

is that a crime? uh, oh, am i in trouble, holmes?

She scoffed. If this was his idea of flirting, he was in for a real surprise.

As Gianna texted back a reply, a thought occurred to her. She erased the text she was going to send and replaced it with another one. *Where are you right now?*

just getting off my shift at work. why?

Can you meet me at The Retro in twenty minutes? It's about what happened at the skating rink.

His response came back in twenty seconds. *i'll be there in fifteen.*

A triumphant smile overcame her face. She might've found her solution to getting to Michael Price's house.

***

True to his words, Theo arrived at The Retro fifteen minutes on the dot. Gianna had already found a table near the back, not far from the booth where she interviewed Mrs. Kipman weeks before. Theo strolled inside, his dark hair wet as if he'd just gotten out of the shower.

"Thanks for meeting me here last minute," Gianna said as he settled himself in the seat across from her.

"Well, I admit I was too curious not to. When Gianna Reyes asks you to meet her for coffee, you can't really say no, can you?" He grinned. "While we're on the subject, why am I here?"

"Remember the other day when you—"

"Which event are we referring to? When I saved your life? Or when I snuck you into the skating rink staff locker room like a thief in the night?" he mused.

"You mean when you bruised my ribs and nearly squashed my tape recorder," she corrected, "And the second one. I told you about the case I was working on."

"Right. I remember." He snapped his fingers. "You're trying to find the guy who allegedly killed his best friend."

"Yep. That's the one."

"So what did you need from me?"

Gianna glanced out the window. "That's your truck parked out there, right?"

"Uh … yeah."

"I need to borrow it."

"Come again?"

Gianna stifled a sigh and gave him a brief description of her trip to the skatepark. Once Theo was caught up to speed, he took a moment to process her words.

"Let me get this straight," he said. "You want to borrow my truck to drive all the way across town to the middle of nowhere to talk to a felon at his own house?"

She swirled her straw in her drink. "Technically, he lives in a shack and he's an ex-felon."

Gianna was glad to learn that one fact before Irene had interrupted her research.

"That's not helping." Theo took a deep breath, scratching the side of his jaw.

She sighed, grabbing her bag. "Look, I don't know why I even asked. It's fine if you don't want to. I'll find someone else—"

"Whoa, I never said no." Theo put his hands up, and she sank into her chair. "When do we leave?"

She raised an eyebrow. "We?"

"Yeah, *we*. Did you think I was going to let you go to a drug dealer's house alone? The guy's a criminal. He could be dangerous. You said it yourself that you were looking into him because he has a violent past."

"I never said I was going alone."

He frowned. "Then who's going with you?"

"Hey, guys." Nathan appeared beside the table.

Theo jumped, startled. Gianna smiled inside with glee at catching him off guard. "See? I'm not going alone."

Theo held up a fist that Nathan bumped with his, wiping the smirk off Gianna's face. "Hey, man."

"Wait, you two know each other?" she asked.

"Theo's my driving instructor," Nathan said. *He* was the driving instructor? Future valedictorian, moose mascot, robotics club captain, and now driving instructor, apparently. She studied Theo, attempting to figure him out. *What other surprises do you have hidden up your sleeve?*

"So, you're our ticket to Michael Price's house?" Nathan asked.

"Sure am," Theo replied, much to Gianna's dismay. "After all, it's not every day you get to interrogate an ex-felon in his own home.

THIRTEEN

"Wow. Dexter wasn't exaggerating when he said that Michael literally lived in a shack," Nathan said as Theo pulled into the driveway.

If it could be called that. The so-called driveway was more of a dirt road that led to the water. The shack wasn't any better; part of the roof had a gaping hole in it, and the color of the wooden planks had faded with age.

"Maybe we should rethink how we go about this," Theo suggested as they exited the car. "Who says the guy will tell us anything?"

Gianna scoffed. He already insisted on accompanying them—she wasn't about to let him call the shots now.

"I have a plan." She held up her phone.

"You're going to get the drug dealer to talk with your phone?" Theo retorted, raising an eyebrow.

"It's not about the phone itself, but what's on it." She swung around, facing forward as she walked. Gianna knocked twice on the door. Theo sucked in a breath beside her, tapping his hands on his legs, whistling some tune under his breath.

"Can you stop that?" she snapped, and the tune died a slow, painful death.

Despite the display of confidence on the way up there, her palms were slick with sweat. When no one answered, she knocked again, louder. Coughing erupted from the other side of the door, followed by a string of curses before it swung open. She wrinkled her nose, unable to tell if it was him or the shack that smelled of smoke, liquor, and mold. Perhaps both.

"Hi," Gianna greeted, more cheerfully than she felt, pushing her way past the open door and the man that stood in it. "Michael Price, isn't it?"

The Michael standing in front of her looked different from the one she witnessed in the video. His skin had taken on a waxy yellow, and he had grown a scraggly beard. His stomach hung out from his shirt, and there was an orangish-brown stain on the corner of his jacket. From the bleariness in his eyes, her knocking had woken him up.

Gianna surveyed the inside of the shack. It wasn't any better than the outside. She had to tiptoe over crushed beer cans and empty bottles. A large bucket sat beneath the hole in the roof, right next to the ragged couch. A black flip phone poked out between the cushions. She tore her stare from it to Michael, who looked seconds away from losing his temper.

"Who the hell are you, and what are you doing in my house?"

They didn't have time for this. She showed him Ollie's missing picture on her phone. "Five years ago, you were seen in a fight with this boy, Oliver Kipman. I'd like to know why you were fighting."

"I don't have to answer to some little girl," he growled.

"Actually, you do." She swiped and played the video. Michael's jaw slackened as he watched it. "Did you know Ollie was seventeen when this video was taken? That makes him a minor, and that not only makes you the man who not only assaulted a minor, but also initiated the first punch."

She stared at him, waiting to see if he would buy the lie.

"That was years ago," he grumbled. "Besides, it's not like he's around to press charges."

The smile on his face was cruel and mirthless, but Gianna spotted the droplets of sweat beaded on his forehead. She'd put him in a corner he couldn't escape, and something told her Michael didn't like feeling trapped.

"You're right," she admitted. His eyes widened slightly with shock, then confusion. "Ollie isn't here to press charges, but his family is. And they won't stop looking for answers. Everyone knows that he's missing, and this video shows you having a disagreement with him just days before he disappeared. Who do you think will be the first suspect the police think of after they see this video? Maybe Ollie wasn't responsible for Grant's death after all. Maybe it was someone else, someone with a violent past and a long criminal history."

Michael took a menacing step forward at the same time Theo did. "I wouldn't do that," Theo warned, moving in front of Gianna.

Facing each other, Theo had a good head over Michael. Judging by the reluctance on Michael's face as he took a step back, she wasn't the only one who noticed.

His gaze dragged from Theo back to Gianna, who stepped away from the couch. The tension skyrocketed in the five seconds it took Michael to answer. "Yeah, I hit the kid. But I ain't had nothing to do with him going missing or that other dead boy." In her peripheral vision, she saw Nathan flinch at Michael's callous use of words.

"What was the fight about then?" Gianna questioned.

Michael grinned, revealing a set of yellow teeth. "Kid didn't know when to shut up. I taught him a valuable lesson."

Nathan shuddered behind her.

"What did he say to you?"

"Hell if I remember. That was years ago." He scratched his beard. "How many people have that video?"

"Enough that if anything happens to any of us, it'll be blasted all over the news outlets along with your mugshot," she answered with a smile, turning her back to the couch. "Now, please try to remember what it was that made you punch him, or my finger might slip and send this to the police."

"He was spewing lies. Insisting that I owed him and his friends money, threatening to expose me to the cops." His head tilted to the side slowly as his eyes ran over them. "Much like you're doing now."

She held up the watch they'd found in Ollie's bag. "Have you ever seen this before?" He looked over it with disinterest before grunting out a no. She slid the watch into her bag.

"What about Emmaline?" she pressed. "People overheard you two speaking about her. Who is she?"

Michael's gaze narrowed. "Nobody important."

"She asked you a question," Theo said.

Michael glared at him. "Emmaline owed me. Not the other way around, and that little punk knew it. If he's missing, it's because he has it coming to him."

"Hey!" Nathan took a step forward.

Michael looked at Nathan the way someone would look at a piece of gum stuck to their shoe. His eyes lit with recognition. "You," he said, raising a finger. "You look like him. You must be his brother. You know what everyone says, don't you? That he killed that boy and ran off."

"That's a lie!" Gianna shouted.

Theo gripped Gianna's forearm, but she tore her arm out of his hold. Michael leered at her hostility and Nathan's red face. "Oh, so that's what this is. You want to find your brother? Good luck. Because the way I see it, with how long it's been, that boy is either out of the country or someone else got to him before the cops did."

Both Gianna and Nathan burst out with protest, but Michael waved a hand.

"Get out of my house!" he hissed. "I answered your questions. I held up my end of the bargain and you will do the same. I know who you are"—he pointed a beefy finger at Nathan—"and don't think a measly prison cell will be enough to hold me."

"Message received. We're leaving," Theo said, pushing Nathan and Gianna out the door. He didn't take his eyes off of Michael until the front door slammed shut. None of them let out a breath until they were in the car and back on the road.

"Well, all in all, not too bad for my first interrogation and blackmail. Checking all the boxes. He was friendly," Theo rambled, fingers shaking on the wheel from adrenaline. "We should bring him over for lunch sometime, maybe catch a movie. I was thinking something light and comedic; hey, maybe even a rom-com. What do you think, Nate?"

"I hate rom-coms," Nate replied, his face green. From Theo's hasty driving or from their conversation with Michael, Gianna didn't know.

Theo glanced at Gianna. "Happy now? We're officially on a drug dealer's radar. Was it worth it?"

Gianna tilted her head to the side, pretending to consider it. "I don't know . . ." she said, pulling the black flip phone from her bag. "I'd say that it was pretty darn worth it."

The tires squealed as the truck came to a sudden halt. Theo's eyes went comically wide as Nathan let out a laugh from the back seat.

"Tell me you didn't," Theo groaned. "Please, please, for the love of God, please tell me you didn't steal a drug dealer's phone."

"I'm no liar, Theodore Rodriguez," she said. "And besides, I couldn't steal if it weren't for you."

While Theo had been facing off against Michael, Gianna had taken the opportunity to snatch the phone she had spotted when she first walked in.

Theo was still rambling. "What if he wrote down my plate? What if he tracks us down and shows up at my house with a loaded rifle?"

"He won't. You were there. The room reeked of beer. Worst case scenario, he'll think he misplaced the phone or lost it somewhere."

He had misplaced it—wedged between the couch cushions, but by the time Michael reached that conclusion, they would be long gone.

"You're insane," Theo said, but he didn't make it sound like anything bad, but as if he were impressed by the notion.

"Careful," she warned. "That almost sounded like a compliment. Anyone want to take a crack at guessing Michael's passcode? It's four digits."

"Let me see." Nathan tapped a finger on his chin. "If I were an airhead drug dealer like Michael Price, what would I put my phone passcode as?"

"Something easy enough to remember," Theo said. "Something predictable. Try all 1s."

Gianna typed it in. *Incorrect password* flashed on the screen.

"What about 1-2-3-4?" Nathan suggested.

She typed the numbers in, and the phone screen unlocked. She gasped.

Theo raised an eyebrow. "Wow. That actually worked?"

"Check the contacts," Nathan said.

She swiped through the contact list until she reached the E section. One name was listed under it.

Emma.

Nathan shrugged. "It could be her."

Gianna pressed the call button. "There's only one way to find out."

They waited for what felt like a century. After a while, it seemed she was never going to answer, and then the line went silent. Gianna sucked in a breath.

"Hello?" a girl's voice.

Theo's eyes widened.

"Uh, hi." Gianna's voice was hoarse, as if she hadn't used it for days. "Um, is this Emmaline?"

"Who is this?" the girl demanded. A long moment of silence went by before she said, "You're not Michael."

The line went dead; the dial tone echoed through the car.

Log #6, Dec. 4th, 2023

Text Message Thread with Molly Goldstein

Gianna: Hey, it's Gianna. Sorry to bother you again, but I had a question about Ollie. Do you know if he ever hung out with a girl named Emmaline?
Molly: No problem. I remember hearing him and Grant talk abt her. Ollie knew her from summer camp from when they were younger.
Gianna: Do you know any way I can contact her?
Molly: No, never met her, sorry! I'm pretty sure she went to the high school outside of town, if that helps.
Gianna: It does. Thanks!
Molly: No probs. Also, if you do find a way to contact her, will you let me know if she and Ollie were a thing? I kind of had a hunch they were by the way Grant spoke of them, but I never knew for sure.
Gianna: I'll keep you posted if I hear anything. Thanks again.

FOURTEEN

"Flour, mozzarella, pepperoni … why do I get the feeling I'm missing something?" Irene looked at her shopping list, puzzled.

Gianna pointed at the last item scribbled down. "Tomato sauce. Anthony was right. You do need those glasses."

Irene slapped her arm with the list, and Gianna laughed. Her laughter trailed off when she noticed a familiar head of hair standing outside the window.

"I'll be right back," she said, heading outside where Theo stood. They hadn't had a chance to speak since their visit to Michael Price's house.

"Hey," she said, breathless. She glanced down at the dog running circles around Theo's legs, tangling the leash around his knees. "Who's this?"

"This fluffball of infinite energy," Theo drawled, untangling the leash from around his legs, "is Bagel. You can pet her if you want. Be careful though—she's more than friendly."

As soon as Gianna crouched down to pet the small dog, she understood what Theo had meant by *more than friendly*. The dog all but jumped into her arms, licking her face, tail wagging behind her.

"Wow," she managed, between dog kisses. "She's definitely friendly."

Theo grinned and leaned against the wall. "Do you have any pets?"

Gianna shook her head, ruffling the sides of Bagel's ears. "I did, once, though. A pit bull. He was the sweetest thing. His name was Horns because you know … bulls, they have … anyway, we had him for a while until he died."

A heavy weight settled in her chest. She didn't recall how he died, but she remembered the way he jumped when he was excited, how he barked at everything that walked. The clearest memory she had of him was walking him on the road by their old house. He had a green leash and blue collar. She couldn't have been older than four. How was it that she had such vivid memories of her dog from a decade ago, while she had none of her mother?

Gianna realized she had gone quiet and cleared her throat, shaking off the memories. "Bagel is an interesting name," she said, eyes flying up to Theo.

Theo smirked. "So is Horns. But as you can see, Bagel is a beagle. And if you switch around those letters, you get—"

"Bagel," she finished. "Without an added 'e.'"

"Typically we just drop the 'e.'" He scratched the back of his neck. "So, about the other day. We didn't get much of a chance to talk about what happened."

Right. That was what she came over to talk to him about.

"About that. Thank you for driving us there. I know it was risky and you didn't have to," she said. "I'll pay you back for the gas."

Theo shook his head. "You don't have to. But if you're so earnest about paying debts, maybe I can help."

Gianna didn't expect that answer. "Why?" she asked. "Especially after the other day …"

"Nate's my friend," Theo said. "You know, during all our lessons, he never once mentioned having an older brother. And I get it. Missing older brother wanted for murder. It's a hard pill to swallow, especially for a newbie like me. Still, I wish he would've told me …" Theo sighed, shaking his head. "Never mind. The point is I can tell how much finding his brother means to him, and I want to help. Besides, I'm an accomplice to blackmail now. I'm a critical piece of this investigation."

"Critical?"

"Yes, critical. If it weren't for me, you wouldn't have found the bag in the locker, leading you to Michael Price in the first place. Whose shack I also gave you a ride to."

She crossed her arms over her chest. "I would've gotten there eventually."

"But not nearly as quick and efficient," Theo quipped. "Face it, Holmes—I have useful attributes."

She rolled her eyes. She couldn't help but agree it was convenient that he had his own truck. And that he did help in his own way to find their next clues.

"Come on, Holmes," he coaxed, voice as sweet as sugar. "You know I can help. Besides, solving a mystery is on my bucket list."

Bucket list? she thought as a voice called from behind Theo.

"There you are." A woman with fair skin and bright blue eyes walked up to them, grocery bags hanging off her arms. "I was beginning to think Bagel ran off again and you went to catch her. But I can see now it's the other way around." She pushed aside a red lock of hair, turning to Gianna with a bright smile. "Who's this, Theodore?"

Theo visibly winced at the use of his full name but recovered with a smile. The red-haired woman didn't seem to notice.

"Gianna, this is June, my dad's fiancée."

"It's so nice to meet you!" June gushed. "And here I thought I had met all Theodore's friends. I'd hug you if my hands weren't full."

"A little warning in advance: June's a hugger," Theo whispered behind his hand.

"I'm going to throw these in the car. You two keep talking. I need to stop over by the pharmacy real quick and grab my medicine. It was nice meeting you, Gianna! Theo never brings any of his friends over by the house." She paused as an idea sprang to her mind. "You should stop for dinner sometime."

"June," Theo huffed. "Maybe give her a chance to talk?"

Gianna smiled. "Dinner sounds nice."

June sent them one more smile before disappearing into the parking lot.

Gianna turned to Theo, whose cheeks had flushed red. "She's nice."

"Yeah, June's great," Theo said.

"Is it weird? Her marrying your dad?" The question clawed its way out of her before she had the chance to keep it inside. "Sorry," she blurted. "You don't have to answer that if you don't want to."

Theo shrugged. "It's cool. And no, not really. My dad and June have been together for two years, so it's not like he's marrying a total stranger. She makes my dad happy, he makes her happy, it's a win-win. It's one of the reasons why we moved, so she could be closer to her family. She's from here."

"Is your mom back in Florida?" she asked.

"Uh, no." Theo let out a light chuckle. "She, um … she died when I was three."

Her heart sank. "Please tell me you're joking," she pleaded.

Theo kneeled beside Bagel, petting her fur. "I'm afraid I couldn't even if I wanted to. She passed away from cancer. Doctors didn't catch it until it was too late, so there was nothing to be done."

Theo's face was somber. Thoughtful. Meanwhile, Gianna's mind was whirling with questions. *Did he share the same thoughts about his mother as she did hers?*

"Dad doesn't talk about her much," Theo lifted his gaze. "So, if you're worried about dredging up any bad memories, don't. I don't have any."

She didn't know what caused her to say her next words. Or maybe she did; she recognized the look that passed over Theo's face—that hollowness in your chest, waiting to be filled by the person you never knew and never would know.

"I don't remember my mom either," she admitted.

Theo's face twisted with genuine surprise. A sad smile tugged on his lips. "Look at the club we make. Sorry, if I joke a lot, I find it's better to laugh at it than be sad, you know? Better for the other person and less awkward for both of us."

Gianna nodded. In a way, she understood. She could only wish to have Theo's easygoing and charismatic self while growing up. It would have made her life at school easier, and she might have made more than one friend.

Theo tapped the side of his knee, hesitant. "If you don't mind me asking … um … your mom, how did she …?"

"Car accident." Her fingers ran absently over her tape recorder in her pocket. "She was coming back from a late shift, fell asleep at the wheel, and swerved into a nearby tree."

Irene used to say that her mother's death was almost the end of

Anthony. After losing his twin a few years before, Irene didn't think he could handle losing another sibling.

What was different? Gianna had asked, peering up at her aunt.

The corners of Irene's eyes had wrinkled as she ran a hand over Gianna's hair. *He had you.*

"I'm sorry," Theo apologized, pulling her back from the memories.

She sniffled. "I'm sorry about your mom."

Silence hung between them as heavy as the losses they both carried. Theo spoke first. "So your dad raised you, too?"

"My uncle. But he's the closest thing I have to a dad."

Theo stood. "He's the detective, right? Nate mentioned it."

"Ex-detective. He's a small-town cop now. Not much mystery solving to be done here," she said dryly.

"Says the Sherlock Holmes in question." A grin lit up his face and suddenly the sun was shining again. "What does he think about Ollie's case?"

She scratched her jaw. "He doesn't exactly know I'm looking into it. He doesn't think I can handle being a detective one day. I'm going to prove him wrong."

"You will."

She tilted her head to the side, looking over at him. "How would you know? You don't even know me."

"No?" Theo raised his eyebrows. "We just had a somber conversation about our dead moms and family issues. I can count on one hand how many people I've told that to—and believe me, it's not something I enjoy talking about."

Something that Theodore Rodriguez didn't like. Color her surprised.

"Then how come you talked about it with me?"

He frowned, as if unsure of the answer himself. After a few moments, he said, "I don't know. I guess … it feels different with you than with other people." He scoffed, rubbing the back of his neck. "That probably sounds ridiculous."

"It doesn't," she said.

Their gazes locked and Gianna's breath hitched. Every time she thought she had him figured out, he proved her wrong. There was more to Theodore Rodriguez than meets the eye.

"Alright, I think I've got every—"

Gianna whirled around to see Irene pushing the cart. She paused upon seeing Theo. It was Gianna's turn to make the introductions.

"Nice to meet you," Theo said, shaking Irene's hand.

"I can't say I've seen you around town before," Irene said. "Then again, I'm only here for a short amount of time throughout the year."

"Oh, I only moved here a few months ago," Theo answered. "My dad bought the old mechanic's shop down the road. I work there when I'm not parading around in a moose costume."

Irene's eyebrows perked in interest. "The shop that used to belong to Gary Ryder?"

"Yeah, that's the one," he said. "You know it?"

"More than know it. I used to spend hours at that shop after school. I used to go out with Gary Ryder's son back in the day. He taught me everything I knew about cars, and between you and me, a little more," she said in a conspiratorial whisper.

Gianna gagged, her face flushing red while Theo laughed into the back of his hand. "Oh God," she said, mortified. "No one wants to hear about your ex-boyfriends, Irene."

"You've been hanging around Anthony too much." Irene gave her stern look. "Anyway, I'm glad the shop is back up and running again. It feels like the town is finally coming back to life."

Irene and Theo chatted a little more about the town and Theo's move before it was time for them to leave. "We should get going. I've got ice cream in the bags. It was nice meeting you, Theo!"

"You, too," Theo said, and then to Gianna, "See you around, Holmes."

As they walked back to the car, Irene leaned over to whisper in Gianna's ear, "Holmes?"

"Stop it," Gianna insisted, pushing past her into the car, ending the conversation right there and then. But Irene was still smiling the entire drive back to the house.

"He seems like a very nice boy," Irene said as they unloaded the groceries.

Anthony rounded the counter, coffee cup in hand. "Who does?" he asked, taking a sip from his mug.

"Oh, no one." Irene winked in Gianna's direction.

"Not another word," Gianna hissed, her cheeks flaming.

She raced upstairs before Anthony could see, Irene's laughter chasing her all the way to her room.

She tossed her bag on her desk chair and went to lie on the bed when she heard paper falling onto the floor. She sat up and found a neatly folded paper by the legs of her chair. Frowning, she went over and picked it up. It must have been an assignment she threw in her bag the other day.

The paper crinkled as she unfolded it all the way. She was wrong. This was no school assignment. It was a clean piece of notebook paper, and the red words seemed to shout at her.

STOP LOOKING OR YOU'LL BE NEXT.

Every bone in her body went rigid, her blood as cold as ice. Her fingers clutched the edges, wrinkling the smooth paper as her eyes skimmed the words, her mind trying to make sense of it.

Anthony's laughter boomed up the stairs, startling Gianna out of her stunned state. Her hands trembled as she crumpled the note up as small as she could and threw it in her wastebin. *It's just a joke*, she told herself, grabbing her phone off her bed and rushing downstairs, no longer wanting to be alone.

But the red words still followed her the rest of the night.

STOP LOOKING OR YOU'LL BE NEXT.

FIFTEEN

Gianna's fingers toyed with the loose green fabric, hoping Valarie was too busy admiring her reflection to notice her quietness.

"Is everything alright? That's the third time you've picked up that dress," Valarie said, a hint of accusation in her tone. So she *had* noticed.

Gianna turned away from the breathtaking dress to see the dress Valarie was donning. A periwinkle dress with ruffles on the end that stopped short of her knees.

"That one," Gianna said, "that's the dress."

The smile on Valarie's face could light up a room. "I know. I knew the moment I saw it."

"Then what's with all the other ones?" Gianna gestured to the handful of dresses strewn over the chair that Valarie made her carry across the store.

"I wanted to see which one looked best on you, and that green one over there is calling your name." She stepped away from the mirror, turning her studious gaze onto Gianna. "Are you sure everything is okay? You seemed kind of out of the loop on the car ride here."

Gianna's mind flashed to the other day, to the note she found in her backpack. She told herself that the note was nothing, that it was somebody's cruel idea of a prank, and that she should forget it. But her mind refused to cooperate, instead doing what it did best by asking more questions. She had pulled the note from the trash, uncrumpling it and allowing herself to analyze and study what she was too shocked to see before.

Such as the letters—they had been scratched with the red pen over and over. The left side of the paper was ragged and uneven, as if someone had ripped it out of their notebook. Whoever put the note in her bag wanted their message to get across in the simplest way possible.

If it was a joke, who was the jokester? How did they get it into her bag without her noticing?

And then there was the matter of the message itself. *STOP LOOKING OR YOU'LL BE NEXT*. Stop looking for who? Emmaline? Ollie?

Another thought, insistent, crept into her mind. What if the note wasn't a harmless prank? What if someone really was trying to stop her because they had something to lose from her continuing her case?

It wasn't as if she was being discreet about finding Ollie. She'd already spoken to a handful of people, and there was no telling who could have left the note in her bag. She took it everywhere with her. They would have had any opportunity to slip it inside; it could have been there for weeks, and she never noticed.

For a moment, she considered showing Valarie the note and getting her thoughts on it. Then she thought about it. Valarie would worry the note was a threat and tell her to call the whole thing off, which was the last thing Gianna wanted to do. It was better to keep this to herself. Including from Nathan and Theo. She couldn't risk them stopping their investigation. Not when it was clear that they were getting closer to piecing together the events of July 4th.

Besides, it wouldn't be forever. Just until they were closer to finding Ollie.

"I was thinking about the dance," Gianna said, which wasn't a lie exactly.

"Does this mean you've changed your mind about going?"

She snorted. "No."

Valarie groaned. "Why not?"

"What is with you and this dance?" Gianna asked.

"I just don't want you missing out on any more lasts," Valarie said. "Senior year is going to fly by and you'd rather spend all your free time mystery-solving with Nathaniel Kipman."

"You know that's not true." She grabbed a dress and held it up in front of her body. Valarie gave it a thumbs-down, and she tossed it back onto the chair. "Also, no one calls him Nathaniel. He goes by Nathan."

Valarie wrinkled her nose. "He's just … awfully odd."

"You're starting to sound a lot like Liam." Gianna crossed her arms, studying her friend. "You didn't have a problem with Nathan at the diner."

Valarie turned away from her, gathering her clothes and disappearing back into the changing room. "That was before you teamed up to find his brother. What if he's lying to you? Maybe he knows exactly where his brother is and is trying to mislead you."

"Who sounds like a conspiracy theorist now?" Gianna retorted.

"What's this about conspiracy theorists?" Irene strutted toward them, Barnes & Noble bags hanging off her arms.

"Done book shopping already?" Gianna asked.

"Not even close. I was thinking of getting some coffee. Do any of you girls want anything?"

Valarie poked her head out from behind the curtain. "Just something with caramel in it."

"You got it. Gianna?"

"Black is fine."

Irene hummed and walked back out. Gianna waited as Valarie changed back into her normal clothes. She bided her time counting the tiles on the ceiling when her phone buzzed with a text from Theo. *we have a dilemma.*

Valarie poked her head out of the door. "Who's that?"

Gianna glanced at her phone, ignoring the little skip her heart made in her chest. "Just Theo," she replied coolly.

"Oh, 'Just Theo?'" Even though Gianna wasn't looking at her, she could hear the smirk in her friend's voice. "I knew giving him your number was a good idea."

"One, I'm still not over you doing that, and two, it's not like that. Theo's just helping with the case."

The door whipped open and Valarie stepped out, holding the periwinkle dress by the hanger. She set a hand on her hip. "Mhm. And why, pray tell, would Theodore Rodriguez take an interest in a five-year-old investigation other than the girl trying to solve it?"

"Because Nathan is his friend," Gianna said. "And something about a bucket list."

"What?" Valarie asked, but Gianna was preoccupied with replying. *Yes, we already went over your lack of grammar skills.*

not that, Theo sent. *june told my dad about you and now we're having taco night tmrw*

I'm not seeing the issue? Gianna responded.

they want you to come by for dinner. tacos = guests. its a simple equation, holmes

No, it isn't. And I like tacos.

good. but just so you know june's chipper. real CHIPPER. she'll probably talk your ears off.

Gianna grinned at her phone. *I think I'll manage.*

dont worry i invited nate too so you wont have to suffer alone. anything on Emmaline?

Nothing yet, she replied.

youll find something.

Gianna hoped so. But it had almost been a week since she searched, and it was dead end after dead end. She attempted the number from Michael's phone again, but it was no longer in service. She asked some of the kids that would have graduated around the same time as Emmaline, reached out to teachers, but nobody at any of the schools outside of town could recall her. If Gianna believed in the supernatural, she would say Emmaline was a ghost.

But she had heard her voice. She had the picture from Ollie's bag. Why would she go through all the trouble of deleting her number from a random call? *What do you know, Emmaline?*

Her phone vibrated with another text. *taco night will be commencing at five o' clock.*

Feeling eyes boring into the side of her head, Gianna looked up. A smirk played its way across Valarie's face.

"'We're just working together, that's all,'" Valarie mocked, in a high-pitched impersonation of her.

"Shut up," Gianna said.

"Do you smile like that when you get texts from me?"

Gianna pretended to think about it for three seconds before reaching out and snatching Valarie's phone from her hands.

"Hey!" Valarie squealed, chasing after her.

The other customers in the store shot them weird looks, but Gianna was too busy laughing to care.

***

Later that night, Irene knocked on her door.

"Do you have a moment?" she asked, poking her head through the door.

"Yeah." Gianna's eyes flew to the box in her hands. "What's with the box?"

A secretive smile spread across her lips. "I'm getting there. But first, I wanted to talk to you. I couldn't help but notice you looked a little down at the mall earlier."

Gianna shrugged. "Dress shopping isn't my thing I guess."

"Is that the only reason?"

"Is visiting us the only reason you came back to Echo Falls?" she countered.

"Touché." Irene clicked her tongue, gazing at the wall thoughtfully. "Alright, I'll make you a deal. We'll play a little game. A question for a question. You answer my question and I'll answer yours."

"Any question?" Gianna asked. Irene nodded. "Okay. I'll go first. Why are you staying with us until the spring?"

"I needed to get out of New York for a while."

"Because you and Jim are no longer together?"

Irene's brows rose to the ceiling in question.

Gianna lifted a shoulder. "You stopped wearing your ring four days ago."

Irene glanced at her left hand on the wheel, flexing her bare fingers. "Right." She sighed. "Should've known you would have noticed it."

"The wine, the new clothes, and the dramatic haircut were also a dead giveaway."

"That makes me feel so much better. Also, that was two questions. My turn. Does you not wanting to go to prom have anything to do with your mom?"

"Maybe." Gianna looked down at her lap. "It just feels wrong not being able to do any of it with her."

"Elena would want you to be happy," Irene said. "She wouldn't want her not being here to hold you back. You know that."

"Do I? I didn't know her. At least there's nothing I remember from the time I did. And you and Anthony hate talking about her, so where does that leave me?" She said more than she was supposed to, but she didn't care. Years of pent-up emotions weighing on her rushed free. It was all out in the open now.

Irene's mouth opened and closed and opened again. "We talk about her."

Gianna scoffed. She remembered nothing of her mother's death, only the aftermath. Being held in Anthony's arms, nuzzling her face in his coat that smelled like him. Him taking her to his home in Echo Falls. Her calling out for her father at night, wondering why he hadn't taken her home.

For three years, she waited for her father to come and whisk her away. Her four-year-old mind couldn't comprehend where her dad had gone, why he hadn't come back to her. She would continue to be disappointed for another year, until suddenly one day, Royce showed up on the doorstep. She had squealed as he swung her in his arms, his laughter ricocheting through her ears. She didn't notice the glassiness of his eyes, the bitter smell of alcohol on his breath, or the weird crackle of tension in the room when Anthony stepped inside. All she knew was that her dad was here. Life would be normal.

Then, not even three hours of being back, Irene realized she was missing three hundred dollars from her purse. Royce left as quickly as he reentered her life, three hundred dollars richer.

She convinced herself that she didn't care that her dad left. She didn't need him. She had Anthony, the Delgados, and the memory of her mother. That was more than enough family. But she would soon learn that the memory of her mother was not enough. The older she got, the more questions came with it. *What was my mother like? What was her favorite color? Did she like to read, too?* At the time, Gianna didn't understand why Anthony's eyes dimmed whenever she mentioned Elena. Why he'd abruptly change the subject or distract her with a game.

The longer her questions went unanswered, the more her curiosity grew.

As did her frustration.

She started lashing out.

She needed someone who knew Elena, who didn't shut down every time her name was uttered. She needed her father. She did something she would regret to this day. It wasn't until she returned home that she would understand why. Irene had pulled her off to the side and showed her a picture she'd never seen before. One of her mother and all her siblings. But there were two boys with Anthony's face.

Gianna came to learn the tragedy of her family's past. Anthony was a twin—growing up, he and Gabriel were inseparable, until the day Gabriel died of a heart attack. Everything changed after that. Gianna's grandparents became cold and distant, and Anthony was a shell of the boy he used to be. It wouldn't be for a long time that he would smile again. And then, Elena died a few years later. It had been hard on him.

And Gianna *understood.* She really did. But she had so many questions, so much wonder, that would never get answered.

And she wasn't sure if she could accept that.

"It's impossible to truly know a person one hundred percent." Irene seemed to consider her next words carefully. "Elena was … quiet. Ever since she was a baby. My mother—your nonna—used to say she was the quietest out of all four of us kids. And she wasn't the type of quiet you didn't notice when she walked into a room, but more of a quiet one when you felt at peace. When one of us was in pain, she felt it ten times more."

Irene glanced at her sadly. "And she loved you with everything she had. Did you know I was there with her when she found out she was pregnant with you?"

Gianna shook her head. She had never known that.

"She was terrified, but she was so excited at the same time."

Gianna's heart warmed a little at the thought. Sniffling, she sat up. "That counts as a question. What's in the box?"

That same smile tugged at her lips. "When we were younger, your mother and I kept photo boxes like these where we kept important stuff. When Elena died, most of her stuff went into storage. I found this in the closet of her bedroom. It's old stuff from high school. I told myself I was saving it for her, but I think I was saving it for you."

Gianna felt like she was holding something dearly precious and fragile. "Are you sure?"

"She would have wanted you to have them. You're her daughter." Her voice choked up a bit at the end, and Irene sniffled, straightening her shoulders. Forever the strong face of the family. "Now, I'm going to go and start dinner."

"Irene," Gianna called before she could leave. "I'm really glad you're here."

She smiled. "Me too."

There were pictures of her mom—some she'd seen before and some she hadn't. Her sitting at a table in the school library poring over a bunch of textbooks, smiling at the camera with another girl who was in a lot of other photos. The last one made Gianna's breath hitch. It was a photo of all four siblings in front of the school. She flipped it over and read the ink on the back: *First Day of Sophomore Year! 8/20/02*

The school year Gabriel died. Gianna laid the photo on the bed carefully with the others and continued to go through the rest of the contents. Friendship bracelets, notes she passed around in class. The sight of her mother's handwriting nearly brought tears to her eyes. These were hers. She finally had a peek at who her mother was.

Gianna went through everything until she saw what was at the bottom of the box. A stack of wrinkled envelopes. Gianna pulled them out, surprised to find a different handwriting than her mother's.

Dear E,
I don't think I've ever laughed that hard in my entire life. Thank you for yesterday. I really needed that.
Love,
R.

Dear E,
Roses are red,
Violets are blue,
You look beautiful
Happy birthday to you
Yours truly,
R.

P.S (And before you go and say it, yes, I know it's cheesy and unoriginal. You can scold me about it later)

Dear E,

Do you ever wish you had wings? Or that you could teleport to anywhere in the world you wanted to go? Because for the longest time I did. But now I don't think I would want to go without you.

Love,

R.

Dear E,

Still think about running away someday?

Love,

R.

There were many similar letters to the ones she read, all addressed to her mother from her dad. Gianna read each one until one last envelope remained in the box. She picked it up.

Dear Gianna,

A jolt of surprise and exhilaration went through her as she read the first two words. *Mom wrote this one for me.* Her heartbeat picked up. It wasn't a full letter like the others, but two words that felt like a bucket of cold water had been dumped over her head.

I'm sorry.

SIXTEEN

Gianna balanced the pan of cinnamon rolls in her arms as she made her way up the road. The sound of a shovel hitting dirt echoed throughout the street. The source of the noise came from next door. A woman with gray hair and bright yellow boots stepped out of the greenhouse. Dirt covered her pants. In one arm, she held the shovel, and in the other, a potted plant. She set the pot down and resumed digging. She looked up as the shovel hit the dirt, meeting Gianna's eyes, and lifted her free arm to wave. Gianna smiled back at her before venturing up the driveway.

She was used to the clamor of her neighbors, the occasional dog barking, car door slamming—but besides the old woman gardening and the wind chimes coaxing her to the porch, the street was silent.

Someone must have spotted her walking toward the house because the door swung open before her foot touched the first step. A man with salt-and-pepper hair and tanned skin stepped out, greeting Gianna with a warm smile akin to Theo's.

"Ah, you must be Gianna," he said, with a slight Southern drawl. "Come on in. Name's Mitchell, but all my friends call me Mitch."

"It's nice to meet you." She stepped inside, taking in the eccentric carpets, oversized plants, and paintings that covered the walls. Although she'd only met her once before, Gianna had the feeling the living room was June's doing. "You have a lovely home."

"I can't take the credit for it. June did all this when we got the place. It was her father's home before he passed away last year. These same walls used to be covered with mounted deer heads before he left it and everything in here to June. I'm sure Theo's already told you all that, though."

She nodded. "He also said that you bought the old auto repair building."

"Sure did," Mitch replied. "It was the perfect place to start my new business."

"How long have you been a mechanic?"

"My entire life. My father owned his own garage, and so did his father, and so on. You could say it's a family business. And if Theo chooses to settle here, too, he will as well." Pride coated his voice—Mitch was a legacy and proud of it.

He led her to the kitchen, where June was dicing a tomato. Or trying to.

"Gianna!" she exclaimed, dropping the knife and rounding the counter to embrace her in a hug. The hug was unexpected, and Gianna, still holding the pan, felt a rush of warmth, but also awkwardness.

Another shadow moved into the kitchen. Theo walked in, Bagel yapping at his heels. Her heart did an irrational little skip when she saw him, his hair mussed as if he'd just jumped out of bed.

"See? What did I tell you?" he smirked. "Hugger."

June ignored him, pointing to the pan of cinnamon rolls. "Are those for us?"

Gianna handed her the pan. "My aunt helped with them. I'm afraid I'm not that good of a cook."

"Well, if we're being completely honest, neither am I. Mitch cooked the ground beef and Theo chopped up the onions. There's a reason I became a hairdresser instead of a personal chef." June smiled and set the tray on the counter. "Theodore, be a dear and set the table? Food's almost ready."

He barely concealed a grimace as he grabbed a stack of plates. "On it," he said, ignoring Gianna's questioning stare. He always went by Theo. Everyone called him that at school, even his own dad did. So why didn't he tell June that?

She tried to concentrate on what June was saying. Maybe she was thinking too much into it. Perhaps Theo didn't mind being called by his first name.

Once the table was set, they all took their seats at the table, leaving one plate empty beside Gianna.

"Where's your other friend?" June glanced at Nathan's empty plate.

"He's running a little late. He said we could go ahead without him," Theo replied.

"Remind me, is Nathan one of your basketball teammates?" June asked.

Gianna smothered her laugh with her napkin. Nathan playing basketball—he'd faint from the simple notion.

Theo bit back a smile as if the same thought crossed his mind. "No, he's one of the kids I'm teaching to drive," he said. "Although, he'd probably be flattered that you thought of him as an athlete."

Doubtful, Gianna thought. Theo winked.

"Is he planning on going to college?" Mitch asked. "An athletic scholarship is the best way to go."

The words were directed at Theo, who stiffened in his chair.

"I didn't have a scholarship when I went to school," June said, meeting Mitch's eyes. "And I graduated debt-free."

"Well, that worked out for you, but if Theo wants a higher chance of getting into a good school, he'll need a scholarship. And the only way to get that is by playing basketball. Isn't that right, Theo?"

Theo nodded, staring at his plate, silent as the dead.

"So Gianna," Mitch said casually, either unaware of or ignoring the tension that seized the room, "are you heading to college next fall?"

"I'm hoping to," she answered, spooning some beans onto her plate.

"Any schools in mind?"

"I'm still deciding. There's a few schools with good criminology programs to choose from."

"Criminology!" June's eyes widened. "What made you want to study that?"

"My uncle used to be a detective," she said. "I guess I picked it up from him."

"I can see it now," Theo grinned, as if staring at an imaginary headline. "One day the whole world will know the infamous detective Gianna Reyes."

June's fork clattered onto the plate. "You didn't tell me her last name was Reyes! I knew there was something about you when we met. You're Elena Reyes's daughter."

Gianna caught her fork before it could fall. "You knew my mom?"

"Yes, but back then she was still Elena Pescelli. I was a year above her in school. Your mom was pretty smart, so she was in a lot of the advanced classes back in the day. One time she helped me out by giving me the answers to a pop quiz I didn't study for. I never forgot that." June smiled. "Then again, the Pescellis were quite infamous in Echo Falls."

Gianna had never heard about this. Her heart raced in her chest as she said, "Really?"

June folded her arms on the table and leaned forward. "Your aunt won so many academic awards, and your uncles were Echo Falls' troublemakers. I can't tell you how many days we missed school because of the pranks they pulled. One time, they glued all the tables and chairs in the teacher's lounge upside down. It took the school three days to remove them."

"Anthony?" Gianna could hardly believe her ears. She shook her head, scoffing under her breath as she imagined the stoic look on Anthony's face. "No way."

"Well, I'm sure he's told you stories," June said.

"No." Gianna glanced down at her lap. "He doesn't really talk about that time in his life that much."

June nodded. "I suppose it's difficult remembering that year. Gabriel's death shocked everyone. Oh God, he was so young, so full of life, and then the next day … gone. We lost two of our own that year, and there were the Lily Killer murders …" She shook her head, reaching across the table to squeeze Gianna's hand. "I was sorry to hear about your mom passing, too. Your family has been through so much. No one should have to grow up without a mother."

Gianna's heart panged.

"June," Mitch whispered.

"Sorry." She jerked her hands back and blinked away the unshed tears. "No crying at the dinner table. I'm sorry, Gianna. It's probably such a hard topic for you."

"Yes, but I like hearing about my mom from other people," Gianna said. "It feels like every time I do, I have another part of her that I can construct in my mind. Kind of like putting all the puzzle pieces together."

June looked like she wanted to bawl for Gianna at the sound of that, but she settled for a watery smile. "Well, I'm glad I was able to give you a piece."

The rest of the dinner went fairly smoothly. They talked about June's work at the hair salon, Mitch's shop, and the latest book series Gianna was reading. Soon it was time to clear the table. It had begun to rain while they were eating, storm clouds hovering over the sky. Nathan still hadn't showed up.

"I'll make him a plate just in case," June said, as Theo led Gianna to the living room.

She took her time scanning the spines of the books on the shelves, and Theo let her. There was a mix of fantasy books along with yoga and breathing guides. Most likely June's. On the top shelf, she noticed a basketball trophy she hadn't seen when she first walked in; Mitch's name was engraved on the bottom of it.

She glanced at him. "Your dad was a basketball player too?"

"Yep. He went pro for a little while before my grandpa died, and he took over the shop." Theo slid his hands into his pockets, leaning against the bookshelf. "As he likes to remind us every chance he gets. Believe it or not, what you heard back there isn't even close to his actual lectures."

He strummed his fingers against his knee, a common habit she noticed he did whenever the silence got too loud. "Sorry if June got a little personal there. She's been a little emotional lately, with the wedding coming up and all the planning, plus being back in her hometown without her dad. They were close."

"I don't mind." Gianna turned away from the books to look at him. "I meant what I said. I like hearing about my mom from other people. I know I should feel sad every time I hear about her, but I don't. If anything, it's the lack of memories that makes me mournful." She scoffed. "Sorry. That sounds silly."

Oh God, she really was in a sorrowful mood today. She blamed the letter she found in her mother's box. All day all she did was think about it, what it could've possibly meant. When her mother wrote it, *why* she wrote it. Another mystery, and frankly, one that was beginning to aggravate her.

"It doesn't," Theo said, pulling her from her thoughts.

Right. Theo never knew his mother, either. If anyone in the world knew what she was feeling, it was Theo.

Aware of his gaze on her, Gianna ran her fingers along the bookshelves. "How did you get into playing basketball?"

"I was eleven and ran into some kids from my neighborhood, asking me if I wanted to shoot some hoops. I didn't realize I had been out there for hours until my dad came outside the house to get me. He hollered my name, and we went inside, and all he said was, 'That was a good shot.' He had me enrolled in basketball camp the next day." He paused, a thoughtful look on his face. "It was the first time I ever felt like I had done something to make him proud."

"Is that why you play basketball?" she asked. "Because it makes your dad happy, or because you like it?"

Theo looked up at her. "You know, no one has ever asked me that question before."

"Really?"

"Never."

She waited for him to say more, but his lips pressed into a line. "Well?" she prompted. "Are you going to tell me the answer or what?"

His lips curled into a smile. "What would be the fun in that?"

She rolled her eyes, pushing away from the bookshelves and walking across the room. "Your dad said you were going to run the family business after you were done with basketball."

"Yep." Theo clasped his hands together in front of him. "Us Rodriguezes are from a long line of mechanics. Dad's been planning out my stuff since I was born."

"And you work at the shop when you're not at school," she said, recalling their conversation ages ago. "Didn't you tell Nathan the other day that you were planning on captaining the robotics team next semester?"

He tilted his head to the side. "Who says I can't do both?"

"Logic. You can't run the shop, play basketball, and do robotics all at the same time."

His smile promised nothing she'd like. "We'll see. On to more pressing matters, any luck with tracking down our mysterious Emmaline since yesterday?"

The mention of her name was enough to put a damper on Gianna's mood. "Don't even get me started," she warned.

"We'll find her," Theo insisted. "We just have to keep looking."

Looking. All Gianna had been doing for the past few days was look. She was hitting dead ends, both with Emmaline and with her mother's strange letter addressed to her.

Except for one thing.

"I did some digging on the watch we found in Ollie's locker. It's a vintage Rolex and it's a hefty amount of money."

"Define hefty."

"Fifteen thousand."

Theo swore under his breath. "And he had that watch in his locker the entire time. Where is it now anyway?"

"Somewhere no one will find it," she said. She couldn't say how she knew, but she had the feeling the watch was more important than just its monetary worth. P.R.B was obviously someone's initials—the original owner. She was still figuring out how they were connected to Ollie, why he had the watch in the first place, and what it had to do with his disappearance.

She was in the middle of her thoughts when Theo dashed into the hallway. He returned a moment later with his laptop in hand and plopped on the couch.

"What are you doing?" she asked, leaning against the couch to peer over his shoulder.

"I was thinking if this watch is worth as much money as you say, surely somebody's looking for it, right?" He typed in his password and unlocked the computer. He moved the cursor to exit out of the tab he'd been in, but before he could, she spotted bold words on the article he'd been reading: FREDDY ATWATER TRIAL TODAY!

"What's that?" she said.

"Oh. That." He lifted the laptop so she could get a better look. "I thought I'd go ahead and do my homework on the town. Figured it would be helpful in the long run—seeing how I'm living here and all for the foreseeable future. I was reading up on Ollie's case, but I found this while doing some research."

She looked up at him, a thoughtful expression on her face. "You really are serious about this, aren't you?"

"I told you the other day I was."

"I remember. I just … didn't expect you to be so thorough about it."

He slapped a hand over his heart. "I'm always thorough."

She resisted the urge to slap him over the head. "Tell me what this is all about. Who's this Freddy Atwater guy?"

"Remember when June was talking about your uncle and she mentioned two kids died that year? Well, that second kid? Turns out he was murdered by this guy." He pointed to the picture of the red-headed man wearing an orange jumpsuit. "And get this—the kid Freddy murdered was the son of Echo Falls' mayor at the time."

"The plot thickens," she murmured. "Can I read it?"

Theo handed her the laptop and she skimmed over the article. *Freddy Atwater's trial will conclude the town's worst tragedy to be seen. Back in May of 2003, Paul Beckett was reported missing from his family home when his mother found his room empty in the morning before school. No one had heard or seen Paul since the night before. Deputy Dale Goodeman led search parties all over Echo Falls for Paul. On the second day since his disappearance, an anonymous call was made to the police department regarding Paul's whereabouts. Police discovered the young man's body near the old settlement ruins and his car just off of Topsfield Road.*

Gianna frowned at the screen. The name of the street nagged at her. She opened a new tab and typed in Paul's full name. The first result was a link to a eulogy posted online ten years ago. Gianna clicked on it, and then on the picture. And when she saw the picture of Paul, she gasped.

"Theo," she breathed.

He went still beside her. "I see it, too."

The first picture of Paul was of him posing for the photo in front of a tree. He wore a blue polo shirt and khakis, his light brown hair mussed from the wind, cheeks round as he smiled.

And on his left wrist was a gold watch.

The watch in the locker.

P.R.B.

They'd been wondering whose initials they were, and now they knew who they stood for. Paul Rowan Beckett. A boy who had lived in Echo Falls.

A boy who died on the same street as Grant Hayes twenty years ago.

SEVENTEEN

"It says here Paul was missing for two days before authorities found him," she read. "A civilian reported an abandoned car by the side of the road but no signs of any driver. Two officers checked it out and found Paul's body a half-mile from the car by the woods."

She stood. This changed *everything*. They had thought the watch might have been a gift or something Ollie wanted to hold on to, but it was much more than that. So much more.

Theo tapped the screen. "It says here that the Becketts put out a ten thousand–dollar reward for the watch. That's a lot of money."

Gianna scoffed. A lot? That was enough money to change someone's life. *So why didn't Ollie turn in the watch and get the prize money?* She stared at the screen, willing the answers to come to mind.

Theo slumped on the couch, as lost in thought as she was, until he snapped his fingers. "What if he was working with Emmaline and Grant? They had to know, right? After all, there were three burner phones. Maybe they planned on splitting the prize."

"Yes, but why try to run away? There's no need to run unless—"

The answer hit her the moment the words left her mouth. The note in her bag flashed through her mind, the threatening red words glaring at her. Gianna paced the length of the room, mind abuzz. The answer had been in front of her all along.

"Someone was after them," she concluded.

Theo's head whirled to her. "How do you know that?"

"Why else would they run?" she countered. It made sense. The burner phones, the unexpected withdrawal from Ollie's bank account, his odd behavior in the weeks leading up to Grant's death. "According to that article, Paul's watch has been missing for almost twenty-one years. No one has been able to find it, not even the police, but somehow Ollie did. How does a teenage boy suddenly find a watch linked to a decades-old murder case?"

"From the murderer himself," Theo said.

She could sense the gears turning around in his head the same as hers. "We have to tell Nathan."

"Tell Nathan what?" Droplets of rainwater dripped onto the floor as Nathan walked into the room, shaking out his sandy-brown hair. His eyes bounced between the two of them. "What did I miss?"

***

"Son of Mayor Found Dead; Killer Still At Large," Theo read aloud, in a deep sports announcer's voice. He set the paper on the table along with the other newspapers related to Freddy Atwater. Gianna picked up another newspaper from the same year. *Search for Missing Echo Falls Teen Continues,* it read.

"Where did you get all these?" Gianna asked Theo, who was rummaging through his backpack.

"The library archives—ah, got another one." A triumphant grin broke out on his face as he held out the paper to Gianna. "Told you I was thorough."

She sniffed. "I'm more shocked that the librarians let you take anything out of the archives." They certainly never let *her*.

"Must have something to do with my irresistible charm—*oomph*." Gianna shoved the paper back into his hands.

"Make yourself useful and start taking notes," she demanded.

Nathan cracked his neck, fixing his glasses on his face. "What exactly are we supposed to be looking for in all this? How is this going to help find my brother?"

"We need to look for clues related to Paul's watch," she said. "It's what links Freddy's case to Ollie, and figuring out the slightest idea of where it's been all these years can help us. If we find out what Ollie was up to before he disappeared, it could help us figure out where he went."

"Uh, Theo," Nathan said, chewing down on his taco, "What do we say when your dad or his fiancée comes in and asks what we're doing?"

"They won't. June's been on the phone with her bridesmaids for the past hour and Dad won't move from the couch until the game is over. We're looking at least two hours before someone bothers us."

That was all they needed. For nearly an hour, all that could be heard were the occasional sighs, the click of the keyboard, and flipping of pages and scribbling. Gianna suspected Theo was doing more doodling than note-taking. Storm clouds hovered outside, rain still pouring down while they'd been researching, and Gianna stifled a yawn. She rubbed away the bleariness in her eyes as she read Paul's obituary.

Paul Rowan Beckett, a lifelong resident of Echo Falls, died tragically on May 30th, 2003. He was 18 years old.

Paul was born on February 9th, 1985, to proud parents, Magnolia Jane (Hall) Beckett and Richard James Beckett. Paul was quick-witted, charming, and a joy to have in the community. He was a rising senior at Echo Falls High and a hard worker who looked forward to college in the fall.

Paul was a talented athlete who played sports all through his childhood. His favorite sport was football, which he continued to play in high school, and hoped to play professionally one day.

Paul is remembered as a kind soul and an irreplaceable teammate by his friends and family. He was a loving son, a devoted teammate, and a friend to all. He will be missed by everyone who had the pleasure of knowing him.

Paul is survived by his parents, Magnolia Beckett and Richard Beckett; his grandmother, Caroline Beckett; and many dear friends. Paul was preceded in death by his grandparents, Georgianna Hall and Adam Hall, as well as his cousin, Emilia Hall.

She glanced at Paul's obituary photo. Under it was another picture of Paul standing on a podium, holding up a trophy. To his left were two other boys with medals around their necks. *Paul and his best friend, Mason, winning first and second place at their first swim meet of senior year.* The boy closest to him—Mason—held his medal up for the camera, while the boy in third place was glancing somewhere off to the side, his face and dark hair blurred together.

"Hey." Theo cleared his throat, distracting her from the photo. "It's not about the watch, but it says here that it took the police over forty-eight hours to find him until they got an anonymous tip to look through the old settlement ruins."

Nathan's head jerked up. "Grant's body was found not far from the ruins."

"I wonder how far apart the murder sites were," Gianna murmured, staring at the blue walls of the room. *The walls.* These same walls used to be covered with mounted deer heads. She turned to Theo. "June's dad used to hunt, right?"

"He did. He used to hang those creepy deer trophies everywhere." Theo shivered. "Why?"

"Hunters use maps to figure out which land is private and public property."

"A map of Echo Falls," Nathan said.

"Some of his stuff is still boxed up in his old office. I'll go check." Theo left the room and returned with a map shortly after. "Good thinking, Holmes."

Nathan tilted his head to the side. "Holmes? What does that make you—Watson?"

Uncapping a red pen with her teeth, Gianna drew a circle around the grassy area near Topsfield Road. "This is where Grant's body was discovered by police in 2019." She drew a red line across the paper before ending it in another circle. "And this is where Paul's body was found in 2003."

The three of them stared in stunned silence at the map.

Three miles. That was all that separated the sites of two murders spanning two decades. It was too close to be a coincidence.

Unsurprisingly, Theo was the one to break the silence. "Well, this is getting weird." He looked up from the map. "How can two people from two different decades both die on the same street *and* have the same watch?"

Gianna tapped the newspaper. "It says here that Paul was missing his wallet and watch. Grant was missing his wallet and phone." She grabbed the papers, flipping through them until she landed on a page. "When the police discovered Paul's body, he wasn't wearing the watch. His parents went on live television the day after he went missing, asking whoever killed their son to turn themselves in with Paul's watch. That same day, a witness came forward, saying they saw Freddy walking the same road on the same night Paul was murdered. But when the police finally searched Freddy's car and house two days later, they didn't find the watch but found Paul's wallet in the glovebox."

"Doesn't seem like a smart place to hide critical evidence of a crime," Theo remarked.

"But the watch," Nathan insisted. "Freddy never told the police where he hid it or who he gave it to, and yet Ollie had it stashed away in a locker for safekeeping. So how did it end up with my brother?"

Theo let out a breath. "I bet this guy might have an idea."

He pulled up the video on his phone and set it in the center of the table. It was a forty-second clip of Freddy Atwater being escorted into the courthouse. "Freddy! Freddy!" A man in a hoodie and jeans approached with a microphone. "Why did you do it, Freddy? Is it true that Mayor Beckett was going to evict you from your home? Is that why you killed his son?"

The man escorting Freddy turned to the reporter and briefly said, "My client will not be answering any questions today," and turned to walk back into the courthouse.

Gianna paused the video there.

"I recognize the guy with the microphone," she said. "He's a reporter for the *Echo Falls Times*."

"Former reporter," Nathan corrected, a strange look on his face. "I've heard of him. Kyle Jenkins. He used to work for the *Echo Falls Times*, but he's been an independent journalist for a few years now." He swallowed. "He wrote some stuff about my brother's case."

"He also wrote a lot about Freddy Atwater's case, too," Theo mentioned. "Half the stuff here was written by him, and according to his blog, he followed it closely for the first few months before the trial."

"Wow," Nathan said. "You found all of this out in only an hour of research?"

Theo hesitated for a second before shrugging. "What can I say? Once I'm interested in something, I can't help but go all in."

Gianna glanced at him, noting his hesitation before saying, "We should go after school tomorrow to talk to him."

"Who says we have to wait until then?" Theo held up his keys, a mischievous gleam in his eyes. "Let's go now."

"And leave when we're guests?" Gianna retorted.

"Dad's probably already asleep and June's talks on the phone last hours. They won't mind," he said.

While part of her agreed now would be a good time to go, the other part told her to stop and think. How convenient was it that Theo had all those newspapers on Paul Beckett's murder? That he had been researching the murder that was connected to Ollie? Coincidence? She didn't think so.

Why do you really want to solve this case? The words were on the tip of her tongue, but she swallowed them back. She met Theo's hopeful expression, Nathan's blank face, and reluctantly nodded. "Okay. Let's go."

EIGHTEEN

Kyle Jenkins, last to Gianna's knowledge, lived alone in his three-story house on the other side of Echo Falls.

Theo parked the truck on the side of the road. The three of them looked up at the house.

"This big house for one guy?" Theo said.

Nathan glared at the house. "The guy's an asshole."

Gianna turned to look in the back seat. "You've met him?"

Nathan didn't answer her, opening his door. "Let's just get this over with."

They rang the doorbell and waited. When two minutes passed with no answer, Theo reached for the bell again. But before he could press it, the door swung open, revealing an older and grayer version of the Kyle Jenkins in the video.

"Can I help you?" He peered down at them over his large nose, his thin lips curled in a condescending smile. His eyes went to Gianna's bag, and he held up a hand. "Oh, no, I'm not interested in whatever you're selling."

"We're not selling anything," Gianna rushed to reply. Kyle's hand paused on the door. "We were hoping to speak with you. We have some questions about a few articles you wrote."

"Most of everything I've written is posted on my blog. I'm sure you can find the answers to your questions there. As it so happens, I am quite busy at the moment—"

"But we—"

"It won't take long," Nathan interrupted. "Just five minutes."

"I don't have five—" Kyle's words seemed to escape him as he did a double take at Nathan. "You're—no, you're not him."

"We haven't met," Nathan said flatly.

"No, but I know who you are—Nathaniel Kipman. I've had dozens of your brother's photos plastered on the front of each of my newspapers five years back. You, kid, are the spitting image of him. I'd be a deadbeat reporter if I couldn't see that."

Theo leaned over to whisper to Gianna, "I bet he doesn't know who I am."

"Your father is engaged to Cory Wilkin's youngest daughter," Kyle said. He turned his head to the side. "June, was it? Heard she moved back to town a few months ago and brought along her fiancé and his prodigious son."

Theo cringed at the word *prodigious*. Or perhaps it was the way Kyle said it, in the way he said all things, with a certain smugness that overreached confidence and became arrogance.

"How do you know who we are?" Nathan asked. "Is it really called journalism or an excuse for stalking and prying into the business of people who are just trying to live their lives?"

"I make it my business to know everything and everyone in this town. It's my job. If someone slips and falls and breaks their neck, I know it. Any whiff of illegal activity happening right under our noses, I'm the first to know. Like I said, it's just business, kid. However, you—" His finger stopped right in front of Gianna. "I'm afraid I don't know who you are, but you do seem quite familiar, Miss …"

"Gianna Reyes," she answered.

"Reyes." He lowered his finger. "And what did you say brought you and your friends to my humble home?"

"We wanted to talk to you about a case you followed twenty years ago."

"I've followed a lot of cases, sweetheart."

Gianna tensed at the word *sweetheart*. "This one happened here. You may know it. The Freddy Atwater case."

"Ah, yes. That was long before your time. Everything I've ever written or discovered about the case is on my blog, which is free, and if you want, add a small donation." He glanced at his watch. "Now, I have a meeting in half an hour and time's ticking."

"The thing is, we were really hoping to talk to you personally about it, seeing how you followed it so closely," Theo said, moving in front of them.

Gianna looked over at him and mouthed, *What are you doing?*

Play along, he mouthed back before turning to Kyle. "The three of us are actually journalists." Kyle raised an eyebrow. "Well, at least, that's what we want to be. We asked around, but we were told you were the best person to go to for advice. You've been an independent journalist for some time now. I heard a rumor that the *Times* fought to keep you from leaving."

"They sure did," Kyle cackled. "And they lost, too. No, my day in the *Times* is over. I'm my own boss now."

Seeing her opening, Gianna followed through. "So you can see why we'd prefer to talk to you in person. Someone who managed to become as great a reporter as you—you're practically a legend."

"Yeah," Theo echoed, with a sly grin directed at her. "A legend."

Kyle considered the three of them for what felt like an eternity. Gianna fought to keep from squirming beneath his gaze. Finally, he said, "I think we can work something out. Follow me."

He led them inside to the living room, where they all squished together onto the bright orange sofa.

"Nice couch," Nathan said, but the sour expression he wore said otherwise.

"It is, isn't it? Bought it after I moved out of the old house—my ex-wife got that one. This place is all mine." He walked over to a mini-fridge in the corner of the room. "Did you kids want something to drink? I think I've got some Diet Coke."

They all shook their heads no.

"Suit yourself." He sat on the couch opposite them, arms resting lazily on the armrest. "Alright, I'll tell ya what, kid. I'll tell you everything I know about the Freddy Atwater case—which more than any other person in this entire world can—and you'll do something for me in return. A little quid pro quo, if you will."

"We don't have any money," Gianna said.

Kyle's loud laugh echoed around the room. "Does it look like I need the money, kid?" He gestured to the room with wide arms. "No, I don't want your money. What I want," he said, elbows propped on his knees as he leaned forward, turning his gaze to Nathan, "is an exclusive interview with you."

"No," Theo said, at the same time Gianna shouted, "Absolutely not!"

"That's my deal—take it or leave it." Kyle leaned back in his chair.

Gianna was seconds away from giving him a piece of her mind when Nathan asked, "Why would you want an interview with me?"

"The five-year anniversary of your brother's disappearance is coming up next year. Five years since Oliver Kipman murdered his best friend and proceeded to fall off the face of the Earth, without so much as an indication of where he was going. And you"—he tipped his drink toward Nathan—"are the only member of your family that I haven't spoken to."

Nathan cocked his head to the side. "That's not exactly true now, is it?"

Kyle's smile tensed. "Look, kid, you want information about Freddy's case? That's my offer. Take it or get out."

Nathan was quiet, considering Kyle's ultimatum. Gianna stood. "Forget this," she said. "Come on, Nathan, let's just—"

"No," Nathan said, meeting her eyes. "I'll do it. I'll do the interview with him. But he's going to answer any question we ask."

"Smart kid," Kyle remarked, scratching his large nose. Gianna lowered back down onto the sofa. "What do you want to know? Anything you want to know about it I can tell ya. There is no one on this Earth that knows more about this case than me."

That was what they were counting on.

"Do you mind if I record the conversation for research purposes?" she asked.

Kyle waved a hand, crossing his leg over his knee and leaning back on the couch.

She hit start on her tape recorder and set it on the coffee table. "What was it like when Paul first went missing?"

"Chaos. Paul went missing around the time the Lily Killer murders were happening. I'm sure you already know about those."

She and Nathan nodded while Theo exchanged a quizzical look

between them. Everyone who was born in Echo Falls was aware of the Lily Killer, a serial killer who stalked the area and kidnapped and killed young women for years. Five women died before the killings suddenly stopped. No one knew what happened to the Lily Killer—if he had given up, gone somewhere else, or died—only that his identity was still unknown to this day.

"The Lily Killer targeted young women, not teenage boys," Gianna said.

"My point exactly. The town was already shaken up from the serial killings. Not a lot of people go missing from Echo Falls, and Paul was your typical Echo Falls kid. Smart kid, great at sports, bright future ahead of him, and his family was a big part of the community. His father, as you probably know if you had any sense to look it up, was mayor at the time, and before that, he worked for the town council, and his mother volunteered at the school fundraisers and charities in town."

"You talk as if you know the family," Theo said.

"Well, if you must know, I didn't know the Becketts personally, but when you spend a good few years writing about people and interviewing them, you can't help but feel like you know them, too."

"Right." Gianna shifted in her spot. "What did they think happened to Paul when he didn't show up at home?"

"They thought his car might have broken down somewhere, or worse. Of course, that paled in comparison to the truth. Everyone wanted to help find Paul when word got out he was missing. I think the search party contained over two hundred people. Made it a lot easier to scour the town. I guarantee you if that anonymous tip didn't come in, we wouldn't have found the culprit sooner."

"Anonymous tip?" Gianna echoed. "I thought the tip just mentioned Paul's whereabouts, not who his murderer was."

Kyle's mouth fell open and shut in a long pause. She tilted her head to the side, as the realization slowly came to her. She had unknowingly tricked Kyle into saying something he wasn't supposed to. Theo used his hand to cover his smile.

"Unless there was another tip," she said.

"Yes—there was," Kyle stammered. "I—I mean no."

"It wasn't mentioned in any of your articles."

Kyle shifted slightly on the couch. "Of course it wasn't. I was specifically asked not to write it in by the police department. At the time, they didn't want anyone writing it in because Paul's murderer hadn't been found, and they didn't want to cause any more panic that the suspect was living among them."

"You were asked," Nathan repeated. "Asked by whom?"

"Deputy Goodeman. Well, he was deputy at the time, but he's come a long way since then, old Dale."

"You know him?" Gianna tilted her head to the side, picturing Anthony's boss being friends with someone as slimy as Kyle Jenkins. She couldn't see it.

"Oh, yeah," Kyle drawled. "Old Dale's been here almost as long as I have. We're Echo Falls bred, he and I."

"How come he was in charge of the case?" Nathan asked. "Wouldn't that responsibility go to … I don't know … the sheriff?"

"The sheriff was out of the country at the time. That duty passed on to Dale, and he was glad to do it. He had the most motivation out of anyone to find Paul, seeing how Paul was practically the closest thing he had to a son. Dale's his godfather. He and Richard were best buds growing up. Dale was his best man at his wedding and stayed the longest at Paul's funeral, then eventually Richard's when he died a few years back. Who better to find the bastard who beat Paul's face until he was unrecognizable."

Godfather. Best man. Gianna mentally filed this information away for later. "Why would Dale ask you to keep a second anonymous tip a secret?"

"Well, at that point in the case, news was spreading about Paul's murder. People were worried whether they would be next; there was a killer on the loose, and we didn't want to spread panic by suggesting one of our citizens could have done this to one of their own. At least, until the authorities had concrete proof.

"Someone called the station, saying they knew of a man who was out on that road that night and to check his car. They wished to remain anonymous. Then, the next day, there was also a witness who came forth who saw Freddy walking on that road around the same time the coroner placed Paul's time of death."

"What witness?" Gianna asked.

"An old woman who lived out in one of the houses on that street," Kyle said offhandedly. "Anyway, after they found Freddy and connected him to the Beckett family, it was a clean case. Especially when they learned of Freddy's connection to the Becketts."

"What was Freddy's motive?" Gianna asked.

"Freddy used to work at the mayor's office. He was let go a few weeks before Paul's death. A little context: Freddy Atwater had accrued over five thousand dollars in debt and was at risk for being evicted from his house. Too many missed mortgage payments. So there was a lot of anger and hostility building up before Paul's murder. When he saw Paul's car broken down on the road, Freddy saw an opportunity to get revenge on the man who fired him and blamed for everything going wrong in his life. He killed Paul mercilessly. An innocent boy with a bright future ahead of him who had nothing to do with Freddy Atwater losing his job, who hadn't even met the guy once in his life."

They all had gone quiet to listen to Kyle speak. "So there's no one else the police thought of?" Gianna asked. "No other suspects, nobody else with the motive to kill Paul?"

"There was no one else who would do such a thing," Kyle said. "Paul was popular, had plenty of friends, and two loving parents who doted on him. He was the star quarterback of Echo Falls High. Who else would do such a thing to him?"

He had a point, but something was still nagging at her. "If the goal was to take revenge on the mayor, then why steal Paul's wallet and watch?"

He shrugged. "Atwater was broke. He needed the money. He probably planned on pawning the watch once the whole case blew over. Of course, he got caught. They searched his home and interrogated his family, but there was no sign of it."

"Was it true they were going to lessen his sentence if he gave back the watch?" Theo asked.

He nodded. "Yes, that deal was offered to him. Of course, Freddy denied ever knowing where the watch was."

"Why?" Gianna pressed. "If he knew there was no chance of him getting out of prison?"

Kyle shrugged. "Who knows. There's sadistic people out there, those who take the joy out of everything we love. They do things because they're twisted in the head. Did you know that Freddy killed his own father when he was sixteen years old? Pushed him down the stairs in the middle of the night. Of course, they said the dad fell, but it was public knowledge that Freddy and his dad didn't get along. And Freddy was the only one in the house when it happened.

"So don't get any ridiculous notions that Freddy's innocent." Kyle leaned back in his chair. "The man's been a killer his entire life, no matter what his wife and daughter claim. And mark my words, Freddy Atwater is the most sadistic one of them all, right next to Killer Oli—"

Nathan jumped to his feet. "Don't you dare call my brother that," he seethed. "Don't. You. Dare."

"Hey—I didn't give him the name. It was the one he earned," Kyle said. "If he hadn't killed his best friend, then maybe—"

"He didn't do it," Nathan spat. "You have no proof! There was never a trial. My brother is innocent, and it's people like you who go around ruining other people's lives by—"

"I ruin lives?" Kyle retorted. "You've got it backwards, kid. I'm not a killer. I don't shoot my friends and leave them to die. I only state the truth and the facts and give them to the public."

"Your truth," Nathan hissed. "You don't care about *the* truth. You twist words around and paint a picture with it that's anything but the truth, and you don't care whose lives you destroy in the process to do it. But you know what? I'm not going to let you ruin mine any longer. You can take your truth and your picture of my brother, and while you're at it, your interview, and shove it up your ass."

He stormed out of the room.

"Thanks for the talk," Theo said, his glare burning a hole into the side of Kyle's head. He followed after Nathan, calling for him to wait up.

Gianna grabbed her tape recorder off the table and her belongings. As she headed after them, Kyle's voice stopped her in her tracks: "When you come back with more questions, you know where to find me."

She should have kept walking, should've pushed herself through that door after Theo, but then she thought of Nathan and anger stirred in her chest. She turned around to face a smug-faced Kyle.

"You didn't have to provoke him like that," she said.

"You seem like a sensible girl. You look at the facts, at the evidence. You know I'm right about his brother. I'm doing that kid a favor. The longer he believes his brother is innocent, the harder it will be for him to accept the truth."

She considered his words. After a moment, she said, "You're wrong. I'm not sensible at all."

***

She left Kyle behind in his lonely living room. The wind bit at her cheeks as she looked for the boys. Eventually, she spotted Theo's truck parked by the lake a street away. Nathan was throwing stones into the water while Theo stood off to the side, his arms crossed against his chest. He looked up when she approached, his nose pink from the cold.

"Sorry we left you behind," he said in a low voice. "I needed to get Nathan away from there before he started throwing rocks at Kyle's house."

A cold laugh ripped from Nathan's throat as he swung his arm. Another poor rock landed in the water. "I'd like to throw a rock at his face."

Theo made a face that seemed to say *See?*

Gianna sighed, brushing past Theo. "What happened back there?" she demanded. "We didn't even make it to all our questions."

"Screw the questions," Nathan said. *Plink*. Another rock in the water. "And screw him." *Plink*. "The guy can rot in that place he calls home." He picked up another rock from the creek bed. "He can take that interview and shove it up his—"

"Hey!" Gianna said. "Whatever's going on right now, you can talk to us. We're your friends. You've been acting strange all day, even before Kyle said that stuff about Ollie. What's going on?"

"Yeah," Theo said, coming to his side. "We're here for you, man."

Nathan's arm braced to throw the rock, and he held it there for a while before he let his arm drop. "I thought I could handle him. It's just … I guess I didn't realize how angry I was until we spoke to him. No—

no, that's a lie." His fists clenched around the rock. "I knew how angry I was. I've been angry."

"Why have you been angry?" Theo asked.

"Because Kyle Jenkins ruined my family's life." Nathan looked up at them. "Not long after Ollie went missing, my parents thought all the news and eyes on us would affect me. So they took me to see a therapist. They told me I could trust her, and I told her things. Stuff I couldn't talk to my parents about because I didn't want them to worry. She asked me during one of our talks if I thought my brother was capable of violence like that. I told her about going hunting with my dad and Ollie, how they were better at killing animals than I was. How they did it so easily.

"I knew I shouldn't have said any of it. I was worried about Ollie, but I was also angry. Angry that he had left and that Mom and Dad were fighting because of him, like they always were."

He shuddered. "My parents … they didn't know she was related to Kyle, at least not until his latest article about my brother came out a few weeks later, with information that I told her during our sessions. My parents couldn't leave the house without being harassed for weeks. And then not long after Dad left and it …" His voice cracked and Gianna felt something give out inside of her. "You want to know who really gave my brother the name Killer Oliver? It wasn't Kyle Jenkins; it was me."

"Please tell me that the therapist lost her license." Theo's voice was dangerously low.

Nathan nodded. "But it was too late. The damage was already done. And it was my—it was my—it was all my—"

"Oh, Nathan." Gianna reached forward to wrap him in a hug. She wasn't sure if she was doing it right, but Nathan didn't tell her otherwise, holding on tightly as he cried into her shoulder. She couldn't imagine how long he had been carrying this guilt with him, without anyone to tell it to.

"It wasn't your fault," she whispered. "You were just a kid. They were adults. They were supposed to protect you, but they let you down. It wasn't your fault."

When they finally stepped apart, Nathan's eyes were puffy and red, but no more tears fell. He couldn't meet their eyes.

"Thanks," he sniffled.

"Hey, that guy isn't worth a moment of your time," Theo said.

Nathan swallowed, quiet for a moment. "I told him I'd do the interview."

"Forget the interview," Gianna said. "Forget him. We don't need him to find Ollie. Besides, we got all the information from him that we needed. We know Freddy's motive and that his family believes he's innocent. They might know something about the watch."

"And if they don't?" Nathan asked.

Theo answered, "What's the saying? If you keep failing, try, try again?"

"Something like that," Gianna murmured.

"And we'll keep trying," Theo said, meeting their eyes. "Together."

Nathan sniffed. "Together."

Their heads turned to her, but Gianna's gaze was aimed at Theo. She still wasn't sure what he was keeping from them, but she was certain of one thing: Theo cared about Nathan. She saw the way his jaw clenched when Nathan mentioned his therapist. He cared, and for now that would have to do.

"Together," she swore.

Log #7, Dec. 9th, 2023

Email Thread with Carrie Atwater

New Message
To: carrieatwater03@gmail.com
From: giannar3yes@gmail.com
Subject: Common Interests

Hello Carrie,

We've never met, but my name is Gianna Reyes. I'm a senior at Echo Falls High and I've been researching criminology. I've been investigating a case of mine when I came across an article about your father. This is going to sound strange—and I wouldn't blame you for leaving this email in your junk bin forever—but I believe your father's case might be connected to mine. I believe we can help each other.

If you're interested in discussing it, I'd love to arrange a time and a place to talk. You can contact me by this email.

From,
Gianna Reyes.

NINETEEN

Gianna was torn between taking the pencil tucked behind her ear and stabbing her eye with it, or walking into one of the various open lockers. Either option would be preferable to listening to Liam speak one more word about his band.

"We've also got a few more gigs lined up," he was telling a few of the freshmen that wandered beside them. "Ash put out some more ads, and Conrad's got his grandma promoting us on Facebook and stuff."

"That's great, Lee," Valarie said, ever supportive. "Hey Gianna, The Retro is still looking for more band performances, right?"

"Yeah, speaking of." *Click.* Liam looked over in her direction for the first time during their lunch period. "How's the case going, Nancy Drew? Any luck finding Killer Oliver yet?"

"Don't call him that," she snapped, glaring in Liam's direction. He chuckled, clicking his pen. *Click. Click. Click.* He twirled it in his left hand, and Gianna's eyes snagged onto it, noticing its color for the first time.

Red.

STOP LOOKING OR YOU'LL BE NEXT.

"Nice pen," she remarked.

His eyebrows furrowed at the strange compliment. "Uh, thanks?"

The foreboding note in her bag flashed through her mind. Wasn't Liam one of the first people who knew Gianna was looking for Ollie? Gianna found the note in her bag, which she carried around school and brought to The Retro. Any of those times, he could have slipped it in there.

But why? To sabotage her investigation? To scare her away so he could say that he was right and she was wrong? As she watched him twirl the pen in his hand, another thought crossed her mind. What if it was something more? Another reason that Liam would want to stop her investigation. He was a few years younger than Ollie now. She did the math in her head. He failed a year twice, so he was older than most of the students. That would make Liam a freshman when Ollie was a senior. It was possible they crossed paths at least once.

But surely Liam would have mentioned knowing Ollie. He had no problem with boasting. *Not unless he has something to hide.* Gianna sighed, uncertain. She would have to keep a close eye on Liam in the meantime.

She pulled out her phone, pretending not to be listening, when she noticed an email notification and opened it. She stared at the phone, dumbstruck. "Oh my God."

"What?" Valarie looked over at her, alarmed. "Did something happen?"

Something did happen. The words *I just got an email from Carrie Atwater* were on the tip of her tongue, when she noticed Liam had also stopped mid-conversation to glance over at her. The words felt like sawdust on her tongue as she bit them back.

"It's uh, nothing," she stammered.

"It didn't sound like nothing." Valarie's gaze narrowed as Gianna slowly retreated down the hallway. "Where are you going?"

"I'm uh, not feeling good. I think I'm coming down with something." She coughed into her arm. "Must be the flu going around."

Gianna turned away, avoiding Valarie's gaze. "You guys go ahead without me. I'm going to head down to the nurse's office."

Before Valarie could protest, Gianna was halfway down the hall. She turned the hallway, running into the Delgados.

"Gianna!" Mrs. Delgado scolded, holding her coffee away from her navy blue top. "No running in the halls! You know that!"

"Sorry, Mrs. Delgado! Is that a new shirt?"

Gianna was down the hall before she could reply.

***

"You know, I was a bit hesitant when I saw your email," Carrie said, closing the door behind Gianna. "I mean, having Freddy as a dad was tough. Mom was lucky enough to enroll us in a school far away from Echo Falls where no one had even heard of our last name before. But even then, you had to deal with the questions. Like, 'What does your dad do for a living?' or 'How come he's never at any of the graduations?' Questions like that. I can't exactly say that he's in jail for murder; one, because our mother forbade us from ever telling the truth, and two—because I know that he's innocent."

"Oh." Gianna couldn't keep the shock off her face if she tried. She wiped away the look in an instant, but it was too late.

Carrie cocked her head to the side, a brown curl falling in front of her face. "That is … that's why you emailed me, right? You said you were a detective. I assumed you wanted to prove his innocence." Carrie played with her fingers. "Unless I was wrong?"

"Actually, I reached out because I believe your dad's case might be connected to one I'm working on now. I was hoping that you could shed some light on that. But I'm willing to hear how you think he's innocent."

Carrie let out a shaky breath as she poured herself a cup of water. "I know I wasn't even born when he was arrested, but I've looked over everything and I know what the evidence says, but I know he's innocent. I've gone over everything there is about his case. The police interrogations, coroner's reports, the trial." Carrie's eyes took on a familiar shine as she spoke, her hands lighting the way she spoke. "But I'm curious. How do you think my dad's case connects to yours?"

"I don't know. That's what I was hoping to find out today by speaking to you."

Carrie opened her mouth to speak, but the front door opened. A man with the same light brown skin and freckles on his cheeks walked in, carrying an array of bags on his arms. His face turned sour when he spotted Gianna at the table.

"So that's why you weren't answering my calls," he said, kicking the door shut with the back of his foot. "Who's this, Care?"

"Uh, Gianna, this is my older brother Tanner," Carrie said. "Tanner, this is Gianna Reyes. She just stopped by to ask some questions." A long pause. "About Dad."

At the mention of his father, Tanner's expression darkened. He slammed the bags on the counter with unnecessary force. "You mean she's poking around in a business that isn't her own?" He glanced at her, lip curling. "Is this some sort of joke? She's just a kid."

"Don't be an asshole, Tanner. Ignore him. He doesn't like it when I talk about Dad."

"No, I don't like it when *you* talk to other *people* about Dad." He crossed his arms over his chest, leaning back against the refrigerator and looking at Gianna. "Let me guess, Care's convinced you that dear old dad is innocent?"

"Our dad was framed," Carried insisted, raising her voice over her brother's. "My mom believed it until she died of a stroke two years ago. She never stopped loving him, never stopped looking for a way to prove he was innocent."

"Yeah, and she played detective more than she played the role of a mother," Tanner said.

"She wouldn't have had to do that if the police had done their job," Carrie shot back.

Tanner snapped his fingers. "There. Right there. That's the part you fail to recognize. The police did their job and you know what they found? They found the boy's wallet in his car, Carrie! The evidence was right there for everyone to see."

"Someone could've planted that there—"

"Who, Carrie? Who could've framed him? Santa Claus? The Easter Bunny? Oh no, let me guess. *Richard Beckett.*" He laughed, mirthlessly, as if this was not the first time they had had this conversation.

"Paul's father?" Gianna glanced between them. "What does he have to do with any of this?"

To her surprise, Tanner answered. "There were rumors that the mayor wasn't as righteous as the people claimed he was. And that he was involved in some scandals. Theft, fraud, even drugs. Of course, Mom bought into it, started digging deep into it and convinced herself that he killed his own son. *Because*"—he pointed a look at Carrie—"she was grieving her husband and needed someone to blame for it—anyone except for the man himself."

When he spoke again, his voice was quieter: "The guy had bruises on his fists. The wallet was in his car. He confessed. You don't do that if you're not guilty of something."

Carrie inhaled a shaky breath, looking at Gianna. "It's called the Reid Technique. A tactic police sometimes use to extract a confession from a suspect."

"Oh, for the love of—"

"He's your own father!" Carrie cried, turning around to face Tanner. "I'll never understand how you can't defend him."

"Because unlike you, I actually knew him." Tanner's features hardened. "And let me tell you, Dad was not a nice man after he lost his job. He started drinking, and he got irritated easily. Mom would tiptoe on eggshells around him when he got home after a long shift because she knew he had been drinking. I wouldn't be shocked if he'd been drunk that night as well."

She scoffed. "You paint him out to be some deadbeat."

"Yeah, because he was like that those last few months before his arrest." Tanner ran a hand over his face, exhausted. He looked at Gianna. "Look, I don't know what you think you're trying to find, but you're not going to find it here. Our dad killed someone. He was given a fair trial, prosecuted, and convicted. He's guilty. And his family paid the price."

"But there was one piece of evidence they didn't find," Carrie said.

He swore. "Not this again—"

"The watch, Tanner." Gianna's head snapped to Carrie. "It's the one piece of evidence that could prove that Dad didn't kill Paul. They never found it on him or at the old house."

"Probably because he tossed it before it ever came to that. Or wasted it all at a bar. We can argue in circles all day about Dad's innocence, but it won't change the fact that he's still behind bars and Mom spent her last years trying to free a guy who didn't deserve it."

He headed toward the front door, slamming it shut behind him.

Carrie stared in the direction her brother went. "I'm sorry about him. Our dad being in jail … it caused a lot of problems for him. Tanner always thinks it's his responsibility to take care of me. He's been that way for as long as I remember."

"I get it," Gianna said, thinking of Anthony, who had stepped in when she was a kid to take care of her. "Do you two ever speak with your dad?"

"We visit him about once a month. At least, I do. Tanner stopped going to the prison years ago. Mom used to come with me, but now … it's just me." Carrie leaned across the table, her voice barely above a whisper. "I know my dad is innocent. And I know who framed him."

"Richard Beckett," Gianna guessed.

Carrie nodded. "One time when I was five, my mother took me to visit my dad—it was one of the earliest memories I have of visiting the jail. But I remember hearing everything. How upset they were. My mom asked him, 'Why would you confess to murdering that boy when we both know you didn't do it?' And my dad said, 'You can't know that.' And then my mom told him that she knew in her heart that he had lied, and she couldn't figure out for the life of her why he would want to leave his family behind.

"My dad broke down crying right there at that table. And the worst thing is? We couldn't even comfort him. No touching, no hugs. I had to sit there and watch my father cry as my mother was helpless to do anything about it." Her fists turned white as they clenched the tablecloth. "Even though she wasn't allowed to, she took his hand in hers and made him look at her, and she vowed that she wouldn't stop until Richard Beckett paid the price."

A tear had slipped from Carrie's eye, and she wiped it away and stood up. Without another word, she vanished into the hall. When she returned from the hallway, she had a brown box in her hands.

"These are the tapes of my father's confession. His interrogation, the trial—everything she could find about it." She took a shuddering breath. "And everything she could find on Richard Beckett."

"How did you get these?" Gianna asked, wonder in her voice. She had requested days ago for the same transcripts but hadn't heard back.

"One of my friend's dad works for the state police. He was able to pull some strings and get these for me."

The boxes felt like glass in her hands. "Are you sure you want to give this to me?"

Carrie nodded. "I trust that you'll take care of it. You seem like the type. And maybe you can do what I haven't been able to—finish what my mother started."

Gianna paused. "I just have one more question—about the watch."

"What about it?"

"This is going to sound crazy, but I came here today thinking that your dad might have given it to you or your brother. The police never found it."

"It's not the craziest thing I've heard," Carrie said. "And it's not the first time I've been accused of that. Some cocky reporter thought Tanner and I might've had the watch, but Tanner sent him on his way. He was a real piece of work. Anyway, no, my dad never told us what happened with the watch. I don't know where it is. My dad never had it, and even if he had, he didn't tell any of us." She straightened her shoulders. "But good luck with your case. I hope you find whatever you're looking for."

Ollie's face flashed through her mind. Gianna's fingers tightened around the box. "Me too."

Log #8, Dec. 12th, 2023

Transcript of Freddy Atwater's Police Interview

Date: June 2nd, 2003

Duration: 55 minutes

Location: Echo Falls Police Department

Conducted by Officers of New Hampshire State Police

OFFICER: Could you please state your full name?
FA: Frederick Atwater.
OFFICER: Date of birth?
FA: April 14th, 1972.
OFFICER: Alright. Can you describe your relationship for us with the Beckett family?
FA: I worked at the town hall for about two years as a secretary, where Richard Beckett worked, but that was about it.
OFFICER: So during those two years you never had any arguments or altercations with any members of the family?
FA: None that I can think of. What's all this about anyway? Does this have to do with Richard's missing son? Has he been found?
OFFICER: Let's stick to the conversation at hand, first, and then we'll get to that. Where were you on May 30th of this year between 8:00 and 9:00 p.m.?
FA: Was that Thursday? I, uh … I was at work until 8:30 and then I walked home.
OFFICER: What time did you get home?
FA: Around 10:15.
OFFICER: How long does it take for you to walk from your job to your home?
FA: Around an hour and a half, usually.
OFFICER: Do you always walk to and from work?
FA: Not usually. My car's transmission was wrecked, so I had to take it to the shop. It's been there for the past few days.
OFFICER: Alright, I want to go back to the statement you made earlier.

I asked you if you ever had any altercations or arguments with anyone in the Beckett family. You told me no. However, I have multiple witness statements from the day of May 6th that allege they saw you in the town hall courtyard yelling for Richard Beckett to—and I quote—'Come out and face me like a man.' What do you have to say about that?

FA: That wasn't an argument. Richard never stepped foot out of his office. It was a protest and I wasn't the only one there in that courtyard that day.

OFFICER: But you were the only one yelling for Richard specifically.

FA: The guy fired over half of us without so much as a notice. I was angry and rightfully so. I've got a family at home, mouths to feed, and a roof to keep over our heads. I said some heated things in the moment, but that was all.

OFFICER: Heated things, such as 'You'll get what's coming to you, Richard?' Did you say that?

FA: I did.

OFFICER: Sounds sort of like a threat.

FA: I only meant that people are realizing what a crook he is and that he has no chance of winning the mayoral election again. It wasn't meant as a threat.

OFFICER: Still, out of everyone that showed up for that protest that afternoon, your face was one most witnesses remembered. It's said that you made quite the ruckus. There was damaged property involved, even a few arrests made if I recall correctly.

FA: We were exercising our right to the first amendment. I'll admit that some people took it a bit too far, but the majority of us were peacefully protesting.

OFFICER: Then what about the protest made at Richard Beckett's home? According to some, you led the protest yourself.

FA: I wanted our voices to be heard.

OFFICER: Bit extreme, is it? Protesting at a man's own home?

FA: We didn't step foot on the property. We protested from the sidewalk, which is one part of this town that Richard Beckett doesn't own. Like I said before, a lot of us were angry that we were let go. I'm sorry, is there a point to this? This all happened weeks ago.

OFFICER: I'm getting there. How did you know Paul Beckett?

FA: Richard's son? I don't. At least, nothing apart from the news I've seen lately about him missing.
OFFICER: He's not missing. Not anymore. Paul's body was found near the old settlement ruins right off Topsfield Road.
FA: I … shit. Sorry, excuse my language. I haven't heard about that yet. How did that happen?
OFFICER: I was hoping you could tell me that.
FA: Wait … you guys don't think I had something to do with this, do you?
OFFICER: I don't know, Freddy. That depends on you. Where were you the evening of May 30th?
FA: I told you before. I was at work for most of the day and I walked home.
OFFICER: Is there anyone who can verify the time you left work and arrived home?
FA: My … my boss can tell you when I left and my wife always stays up until I get back.
OFFICER: You won't mind if we speak to the mechanics and search your car, just to verify you're indeed telling the truth?
FA: No. I told you before—I have nothing to hide.

Transcript of Freddy Atwater's Post-Arrest Interview

Date: June 3rd, 2003
Duration: 210 minutes
Location: Echo Falls Sheriff's Department
Conducted by officers of New Hampshire State Police
[Cut some of the stuff from the beginning. For the first two hours of the interview, Freddy refused to speak.]

OFFICER 1: Come on, Freddy. We've been here a while. Might as well confess now and get this over with.
FA: I have nothing to confess.
OFFICER 2: No? You have nothing to say about the wallet we found in the glove box of your car?
FA: I don't know how that got there.
OFFICER 1: Sure you do. You put it there. Right after you stole it off

Paul Beckett's cold body.

FA: If you already know, then why am I here? Why all of this?

OFFICER 2: Paul's family needs an explanation. They want to understand why someone would take their only son from them. You were angry with Richard Beckett for losing your job and that's understandable—

FA: Yes, I was angry, but I didn't kill his son!

OFFICER 1: The evidence disagrees with you. Unless you have proof that someone else committed this crime.

OFFICER 2: Where is it, Freddy?

FA: Where's what?

OFFICER 1: You know what. You stole it from Paul after you murdered him.

FA: I don't know how his wallet got in my car I swear. I didn't, I didn't do this.

OFFICER 2: All you have to do is tell us where the watch is, Freddy. Tell us where you put it and this will all be over.

FA: You're not listening to me! [slams table] I don't know where it is! I didn't kill Richard's son, and I didn't steal anything!

OFFICER 1: Then how do you explain the wallet we found in your car?

FA: How many times do I need to say it? I didn't put it there.

OFFICER 2: If you didn't, then who did?

FA: [whispers something unintelligible]

OFFICER 1: Speak up.

FA: Voices. I heard—there were voices that night.

OFFICER 1: Were these voices in your head, Freddy? Were they telling you to kill Paul? Are these the same voices that told you to kill your father?

FA: No! That was an accident. I didn't—I didn't kill him. You're not listening.

OFFICER 2: We're listening, Freddy.

FA: The voices.

OFFICER 1: But you didn't hear voices. Admit it, Freddy: there were no voices. There was no one else that night but you and Paul. His wallet was found in your car at the shop. The evidence is there.

OFFICER 1: I'll tell you what happened. You were on your way home from a long day of work. You took your usual route home, and on the way there, you noticed a car broken down on the side of the road. You go over to see if the driver needs any help. You recognize the driver as Paul Beckett and an idea begins to form in your head. This is the son of the man who cost you your job. You want to make him hurt just as much as you're hurting, but you take it too far. You cross a line. You kill him. Beat his face in until it's unrecognizable. You can't get caught—so you steal his wallet and his watch to make it look like a random robbery. Am I on the right track, Freddy?

FA: No! That never—that didn't happen. That's not how any of that happened.

OFFICER 2: Where is it, Freddy?

FA: Where's what?

OFFICER 1: You know what. You stole it from Paul's body after you murdered him.

FA: I didn't murder anyone. I don't know how that wallet got in my car, I swear. I didn't—I didn't do this.

OFFICER 1: Enough with the squabbling. Where's the watch?

FA: I don't know.

OFFICER 1: We can stay here all night, Freddy. All night until we get a confession from you.

OFFICER 2: All you have to do is confess, Freddy. Confess, and it's all over.

FA: I confess and we're done here?

OFFICER 2: Yes.

FA: Yes. I confess. I did it.

OFFICER 1: Did what, Freddy?

FA: I killed him. I killed Paul Beckett.

OFFICER 1: Was that so hard?

TWENTY

Gianna was in the middle of cutting carrots for the chicken soup when the doorbell rang.

"I'll get it." Gianna set the knife down on the cutting board. She swung the door open to find Theo and Nathan. "What are you guys doing here?"

"We have something to tell you," Theo said. "And you weren't at school earlier."

"I have something to tell you guys, too."

Gianna ushered them inside. "Wait here." She walked over to the kitchen, poking her head in. "Is it okay if I take a break for fifteen minutes? Nathan and Theo are here."

Irene turned from the stove. "Yeah. I've got it from here."

Gianna led them up the stairs to her room and pulled out the tapes. When they were done listening to them, Gianna pressed the off button. Nathan's face rested in his hands, and Theo was tapping the side of his knee. "Well?" she said.

"Whoever that Officer 1 guy is sounds like a real asshole." Nathan picked up one of the tapes and examined it. "Where did you get these?"

"I spoke to Carrie Atwater today. Freddy's daughter." She told them all about their conversation.

"That's why you weren't in class," Theo said. "Valarie mentioned you left early."

She shoved down the sliver of guilt that passed through her. "It was a last-minute thing. Carrie could only meet today, and after listening to her and these, I don't think our guy is Freddy Atwater." She hesitated. "He's been in prison since 2003."

"Which means he couldn't have anything to do with my brother," Nathan said, disappointment flashing over his features. "Which means we're back to square one."

"Maybe not. Carrie claims someone framed her dad for murder."

Theo raised his eyebrows. "And you believe her?"

"I believe that she believes it. Let's say Freddy Atwater is innocent; it means that Paul's true killer is still out there."

Nathan sat up. "And the watch is the only thing that can prove Freddy's innocence."

She nodded. "Ollie somehow finds the watch. He tells Grant about it, and both of them learn the history of it. They start digging into Paul's case, and they find something they shouldn't. Freddy Atwater was working with a second party, or Carrie and her mother were right, and Freddy was innocent and only confessed because he felt there was no other choice but to."

"The second party slash real killer finds out that someone took the watch," Theo continued. "And that they're onto him, which isn't so good for him."

"And he can't let that happen, so he stops them," Nathan finished. "He kills Grant and goes after my brother."

A long pause of silence passed over them as they drew their conclusions.

"But Kyle said there were no other suspects," Theo said.

She turned in her chair. "Carrie and her mother suspected Richard Beckett."

"Paul's own dad?" Theo swore. "That's cold."

Gianna nodded in agreement. "I want to see what I can find about him. Finding the second party slash killer is our way of finding Ollie. If we find the killer and reveal it to them, it will make statewide news."

If Ollie were in hiding because of the killer, he'd see it would be okay to come back. He wouldn't be in any more danger.

"We find the killer, and we get my brother back." Excitement filled Nathan's voice.

Gianna turned to them. "Okay, you guys said you had news."

Theo smiled. "I think I'll let Nate tell you."

"Oh, yes, that," Nathan said. "We found Emmaline."

She all but shouted the word, *"How?"*

Nathan smiled triumphantly. "While you were occupied with Paul Beckett's case, I started my own search for Emmaline. First, I gave the school yearbooks a try, but that was a deader than dead end. Did you know the school keeps digital copies of the books going back forty years?"

"Nathan," Gianna urged. "You were getting to the part about how you found Emmaline." The girl they'd been searching for weeks.

"It was Ollie."

"Come again?"

"Not *Ollie* Ollie, of course, but it was him that led me halfway there. I found Dad's old tablet we used to play games with when we were younger. I turned it on and noticed another app downloaded: Instagram. Ollie had another account. It was for skateboarding stuff only. You know when you sign up for an account and it asks if you want to connect to your contacts? Well, I did that and this account showed up." He clicked on his phone to show the username_o11ie.sk8ter.

Her brows furrowed. "But I looked at his account already."

"You saw his main account that our parents and everyone else saw. This one is mainly videos of tricks and stunts. If my mom saw this … let's just say Ollie wouldn't have had a chance to disappear. Mom would've done it herself."

Gianna understood what he meant as soon as she watched the videos. The stunts Ollie performed were dangerous, to say the least. There were videos of him skating down an eight-foot ramp and zooming fast across a narrow street without any helmet or body protection. Grant was in a few of them too, right beside Ollie.

"I went into the comments and saw he tagged some people. There's Grant's account, Roger's, and a few other guys from the skatepark. And then this handle: emmylime_01."

"That's her," Gianna breathed as the profile popped up. Gianna looked at the one photo posted of the blonde-haired girl posed by her skateboard, holding up a peace sign at the camera, with a sunset behind her. She also noticed another thing. "She's not in any of the videos."

"No, but she liked most of them. Both her and Ollie followed each other."

"Please tell me you were able to hack his account."

Nathan let out a long, wistful sigh. "It hurts that you doubt me. I tried every passcode I could think of. My birthday, Dad's, Mom's, and Grant's. Even Grandpa's and he's been dead for ten years. Then I remembered good old verification codes. I sent the link to the email on the tablet, and I was able to set up a new password from there. I found this."

He showed them a thread of messages from five years ago. A video of a skateboarding stunt by Grant. And the second recent message was from emmylime_01. Gianna held her breath as Nathan clicked on the thread of messages. The timestamp showed under the text at 6:02 p.m. on Tuesday, June 21st, 2019.

Can you meet me at the spot? It's important.

From Ollie, *OMW*.

"That was underwhelming," Theo stated. "What do you think about the place where they were meeting?"

"Dunno. But I was able to find Emmaline through the picture she posted. I went into Photoshop and zoomed in and cleared up the photo. I figured the card hanging up was important. It was Emmaline's school ID. Her full name is Emmaline Renee Pearson and she went to Portsmith High, about a half hour outside of Echo Falls. Apparently, she dropped out halfway through her senior year to do online classes."

"That explains why she wasn't in any of the school's yearbooks." Gianna leaned closer to the computer. "Where is she now?"

"She's going to a community college about a half hour from here. I went through her recent posts, and it turns out that Emmaline signed up back in the fall for a ceramics club at her college."

"Ah, so that would explain the photos of mugs and oddly shaped vases," Theo remarked.

"When does the ceramics club meet next?" Gianna asked.

Nathan's eyes shined with excitement. "In two hours."

TWENTY-ONE

Are you sure she's going to show up here tonight?" Theo asked. He had parked the blue truck beneath a set of trees. The branches poked through the window slit, reaching out to them. The college building was dark against the yellow and pink hue of the sky.

As immaculate as the view was, it wasn't the only reason he parked there. From their spot, they had a clear view of everyone entering and exiting the building. So far, Emmaline had been a no-show, and Nathan had resorted to biting his nails.

Gianna pulled out her phone and showed him the picture Emmaline uploaded to her social media profile ten minutes ago, of a view of her baby-blue top and a heart emoji, captioned: *On the way to Cc <3*

Nathan peered at the screen over her shoulder. "Who would've thought that the addiction to sharing every waking moment of people's lives would come in handy?"

Theo snorted. "You're one weird kid, Nathaniel Kipman."

Nathan wrinkled his nose at the mention of his full name.

"I could say the same about you, Theodore," Gianna retorted.

Theo winced. "Please don't."

She rested her elbow on the center console and propped her chin with her hands. "You know you never said why you don't like being called by your full name."

Theo smiled secretively, tearing his gaze from hers.

"What?" she said when she couldn't take the silence any longer.

"It's killing you, not knowing, isn't it?" That same smile was still on his face, and Gianna's fingers itched to wipe it clean off. She was about to make a witty remark when Nathan sighed.

"Will you two please refrain from flirting until we're out of the car? Just because I wear glasses doesn't mean I'm one hundred percent blind."

Gianna and Theo fell back into their seats faster than a rubber band snapping.

"That is not—"

"We're *not*—"

Nathan smirked, sitting back in his seat. "Whatever you guys say."

Gianna avoided Theo's gaze as her neck flushed hot. They were not flirting. At least, she wasn't. Theo was like that with everyone—she wasn't any different. Besides, they were just friends, working together for a common cause.

So why did her heart pang at the thought?

Before she could dissect her whirlwind of emotions further, her gaze latched onto someone walking toward the art building wearing a baby-blue shirt.

"That's her," she said.

Nathan sprang up, his head hitting the roof of the truck, knocking his glasses askew. When no one else had moved, he said, "Well, what are we waiting for?"

Theo met Gianna's eyes before looking at Nathan. "Maybe it's best if Holmes does this alone first."

"What? Why?"

"Yeah," Gianna said, narrowing her eyes at Theo. "Why?"

"Imagine three strange kids bombarding you and asking questions about your past," Theo said. "Not exactly the best first impression. Also, this girl literally deleted her entire number after one phone call." She hated to say it, but Theo had a point. "Besides, out of us, she can convince her."

Nathan slumped into his seat. He didn't look happy about it, but he reluctantly nodded his head. Gianna exited the car and hurried to the door of the art building that was wheezing as it closed. Her hand barely brushed the handle before it shut completely. She opened the door and glanced one last time at the parking lot.

She was in.

She followed the low chatter and smell of clay to a classroom down the hall. The door was propped open with a large sign that read CERAMICS CLUB. She spotted Emmaline at one of the tables near the back, tying an apron around her waist. Uncertainty washed over her. Now what?

Emmaline's head snapped up, meeting her gaze.

"Aren't you going to get an apron?" she asked. "They're hanging up over there."

"Oh … right." Gianna grabbed one off the hook and walked back toward the table.

Emmaline smiled. "First time doing ceramics?"

"Yeah."

"What do you major in?"

She blurted the first thing that came to mind, which happened to be Valarie's major that she chose for college in the fall. She darted a look at Emmaline. She hoped she didn't have the same major because chemistry was *not* something she specialized in.

"I come here strictly for classes and end up spending my Friday nights making pottery," Emmaline snorted.

"Everyone has their ideas of fun," Gianna said.

"What's yours?" Emmaline set her phone down, and Gianna caught a glimpse of her lock screen—two small children; the girl was Emmaline, and she had her arm wrapped around a boy not much older with the same blond hair.

Gianna tore her eyes from the phone. "I like mysteries."

"Oh. Like TV shows and books about them?"

"Yeah, I like those." She set to mixing the clay and water, like Emmaline was doing. "But I like solving them, to be more precise."

"Oh?" The word came out strained. "That's … nice. It's certainly a hobby."

"Yeah. There's this mystery in my town I'm actually trying to solve."

"Where are you from?"

"Echo Falls." Emmaline's fingers stilled on the clay. "You see, five years ago, a boy was allegedly killed by his friend. The friend disappeared without a trace and his family is worried about him. They want him back, but the police aren't doing anything because, as far as they're concerned, he's gone."

Emmaline's face had gone pale as a sheet, the lump of clay in her hand long forgotten. "Oh. I … um … I forgot something."

She abruptly stood, walking to the sink. She moved so fast that Gianna barely got a word in before she left the room. Her phone lay forgotten on the table. Gianna snatched it and dashed after her.

"Wait!" she called out, breathless. If she couldn't get Emmaline to talk, they would be left without answers. She couldn't return to the boys empty handed. "Emmaline!"

Emmaline froze and turned around slowly. "I never told you my name." The iciness in her eyes was enough to freeze the entire school over. "Who are you?"

"Someone who wants to find the truth." Gianna held out the phone. "I believe this is yours."

Emmaline reluctantly took the phone. Her eyes went to it and then back up to Gianna, slowly calculating. "It was you," she said. "You're the one who called from Michael's phone." She swallowed, glancing at the door before looking back at Gianna. "Look, I don't know how you found me, but I can't help you."

"Actually," Gianna said, holding the Polaroid of Emmaline between them, "I think you can. Unless you're not the girl in that photo."

Emmaline plucked the photo from her hands. Her jaw went slack as if the picture in her hand was lost treasure. "Where did you find this?"

"A locker at Skating Moose skating rink. And it's not the only thing I found there." Emmaline's head snapped up. "I can tell you more if you want."

Emmaline hesitated, staring at the photo. Then her fingers curled around it, before she handed it back. "No, thanks."

She started down the hall.

"Wait!" Gianna ran after her. "I know about you, Ollie, and Grant working together."

Emmaline's stride remained unbroken. "I have no idea what you're talking about. Now leave me alone."

"If you don't want to tell me everything, that's fine," she panted. "I just need to know one thing: Was Ollie looking into Paul Beckett's case?"

"I don't know." Her face was blank, impossible for Gianna to read.

"Then tell me about Michael Price. How do you know him?"

Emmaline sighed, annoyed. "He was my foster dad."

"Why did he get into a fight with Ollie?"

Emmaline stopped. "How do you know about that?"

"There's a video," Gianna said. Her eyes narrowed. "So you *did* know Ollie."

"No." Emmaline sighed, folding her arms across her chest. "I mean, I did, but I didn't really know him that well. We went to the same summer camp one year, and we saw each other around at the skatepark, but nothing more than that."

Gianna wasn't sure she believed her yet. "But you knew him. Have you heard from him in all these past years?"

"No." Emmaline's gaze was somewhere off to the side. "If I had, I would've gone to the police."

"What about Grant? I assume he was the one who took the picture I found in the locker. Did you know him?"

"No better than Ollie. He probably took that photo when we were at the park one time without me knowing. I can't tell you how it ended up in that locker."

Emmaline's eyes darted to the side, away from Gianna. She was lying—but Gianna didn't know about which part, or why. "So Michael's your foster father. Were you aware—"

"That he's a drug dealer?" Emmaline raised an eyebrow. "I'm not an idiot. And before you ask, I haven't spoken to him in years. I don't know why his number's still on my phone."

"I wasn't accusing you of being anything," Gianna insisted. "It's just that he got into that fight five days before Ollie went missing."

"And you think Michael had something to do with it?" Emmaline snorted. "Michael had nothing to do with Ollie; trust me."

"How can you be so sure?"

"Because I know Michael. He doesn't like getting involved with the police or drawing attention from them and getting his hands dirty. Such as murdering kids in cold blood in the middle of the woods. He's not your guy. But."

Gianna glanced at her. "But?"

She shrugged. "There was this shady guy who used to hang around the skatepark. He drove a van and listened to horrible music. Probably knew Michael, and even worked for or bought from him."

"A van?" Gianna's heart thumped in her chest. "Did he have blond hair? Wore a beanie and had terrible taste in music?"

"Uh, yeah, that sounds about right."

Wait, Gianna had to be certain. She pulled her phone from her pocket and went to Valarie's Instagram account and clicked on the most recent picture of her and Liam.

"Is this Michael's partner? The guy you saw around the skatepark?"

Emmaline glanced at the picture and then back at Gianna. She nodded slowly. "That's him."

Gianna went over everything she knew about Liam from what Valarie told her. He had failed a grade twice, wasn't close to his family, and she mentioned he had a sordid past with drugs. Something about Liam bugged Gianna from the start. He knew she was looking into Ollie's disappearance and probably asked Valarie about it. He knew they went dress shopping and when they hung out.

Yet the last thing she felt was satisfaction. Because if Liam had something to do with Grant's death and Ollie's disappearance, that meant her best friend's boyfriend was possibly a murderer and implicated in a boy's disappearance. And that would hurt Valarie more than anything.

"One more thing." She pulled the watch from her bag. Emmaline's eyes widened—and then narrowed into slits. "Get that away from me!" she hissed venomously, taking a step away as if the watch had electrocuted her. Her chest heaved with deep breaths, and she clutched her phone in the hand that wasn't pointed at Gianna. "If you come near me again with that," she said in a low voice, "I'll make you regret it."

"I'm sorry," Gianna whispered, stuffing the watch back in her bag, out of sight.

"I mean it." Emmaline gave her an icy glare that could freeze over the hallway. "Stay the fuck away from me."

She stormed down the hall, and this time, Gianna didn't stop her.

***

"Theo?" Nathan said. "You're freaking us out, man."

Gianna toyed with the string of her hoodie. Theo had been quiet ever since she got back and told them about her conversation with Emmaline.

"Theo?" she whispered.

He looked over at her in the passenger seat. "You're sure it was Liam that Emmaline described?"

"I showed her a picture and she said it was him."

Theo slumped back in the driver's seat and stared out the window. Gianna exchanged a worried glance with Nathan. She had never seen Theo so quiet.

"Theo?" Nathan repeated, nudging his shoulder. "Is everything all right, man?"

"I don't know. You just told me that my future cousin might be a murderer." A nervous laugh spilled from him. "So no, I'm not."

"We don't know that for sure," Gianna said.

"But we suspect him."

"Yeah," Gianna said quietly. "We do. He worked with Michael. Emmaline said herself that Michael hated getting his hands dirty. But that doesn't necessarily apply to anyone else."

"What happened to suspecting Richard Beckett? Nathan asked. "Liam would've been around my age when Ollie went missing. Do you really think he could've murdered Grant?"

"Okay, maybe murder is a bit extreme," she admitted. "But he has to know something. Emmaline said so herself that she saw him with Michael. If Liam knows anything at all, it could help us narrow down our options. Maybe Michael and Liam found out about the reward for the watch and tried to take it from them."

Theo let out a heavy breath, running a hand through his hair. "Let's just say Liam does know something. It's unlikely he'll even tell us."

"Then we'll prove he didn't have anything to do with it, and we can cross him off the list."

Right now, Liam was their best lead, followed by Richard.

"How are we going to do that?" Nathan asked.

"I have an idea," Theo said. He locked eyes with her. "But you might not like it."

Log #9, Dec. 13th, 2023

Transcript of Interview with Mrs. Delgado

Gianna: Thanks for agreeing to an interview, Mrs. Delgado. Refresh my memory—you've taught math all your career?

Mrs. Delgado: Yes, I have.

Gianna: Do you recall having a student in your class by the name of Paul Beckett? He would have been a senior back in 2003.

Mrs. Delgado: Now that is a name I haven't heard in a long time. Yes, I remember Paul. I taught him in his sophomore and senior years.

Gianna: So you're aware he was murdered then.

Mrs. Delgado: Yes. I don't think there was a person in town who wasn't aware at that time. I remember I was grading tests when Andrew—my husband—called me and said that he had received a call that Paul was missing. A lot of people knew him and were worried about him.

Gianna: What was Paul like as a student?

Mrs. Delgado: I'd say he was a fairly popular student. He was well-liked by a lot of his classmates. When word that he passed reached the school, his friends and teammates organized the vigil for him. It was a very sad day for us all, and losing a student is never a good feeling for anyone.

Gianna: What about his parents? I think it was Paul's father who initially reported him missing.

Mrs. Delgado: No. Actually, it was Paul's mother. But there's no surprise there.

Gianna: What do you mean by "no surprise"?

Mrs. Delgado: I'm sorry. [sighs] I shouldn't have said that.

Gianna: Are you implying that Paul and his father had a strained relationship?

Mrs. Delgado: I really never should have said anything, Gianna.

Gianna: Mrs. Delgado, please. If it's anything you think of as noteworthy, it could be important, even the most insignificant detail.

Mrs. Delgado: [sighs] You know how I feel about spreading rumors. But I suppose, well, it's not entirely a rumor.

Gianna: So I'm right? Paul and his father had a strained relationship.
Mrs. Delgado: In a manner of speaking, yes. When you're a teacher, you tend to pick up things from other students. Tidbits of conversations, certain sayings and expressions, etcetera. And you also hear things as well. One afternoon, I was on lunch duty when I passed a table and overheard a couple of students talking. I heard one of them say that the bruise on Paul's cheek was put there by the mayor.
Gianna: His own father?
Mrs. Delgado: Mhm. Obviously, I was concerned. I tried to push it out of my mind—kids tended to come up with all sorts of things, and words can get twisted—but no matter what, I couldn't stop thinking about it.
Mrs. Delgado: Later that same afternoon, I had Paul stay after class. I asked him about the bruise on his face. He claimed he got it during football practice. He didn't seem to be happy about me asking, so I dropped the subject there. I never reported it; I thought he was telling the truth, but now … I was a new teacher back then. It's no excuse, I know, but I regret not telling someone. At least then maybe he wouldn't have … I don't know what I'm talking about anymore. But there was always something off about that family.
Gianna: Off how?
Mrs. Delgado: It's silly, really. It could be nothing but … It was a few weeks after I asked Paul about his bruise. The whole school had gathered in the auditorium for a pep rally. Richard Beckett came out to give a speech before the big game that night. Paul and Mrs. Beckett stood off to the side of the podium, and I saw Paul's mother grasping his arm tight. They were listening to the mayor's speech. Mrs. Beckett leaned over and whispered something in Paul's ear, and whatever she said made him visibly tense. And it wasn't just him. She also seemed rather on edge. As if she were bracing herself for the worst.
Gianna: That's odd. I've only ever heard good things about Mayor Beckett.
Mrs. Delgado: That's exactly why I found it hard to believe what those kids were saying about Paul and his father. Richard Beckett was well liked by the town. He was planning on running again. I never heard anything about Paul or his dad again after that. I thought it all had been in my mind.

Gianna: So, correct me if I'm wrong, but you're saying that it's possible that Richard was abusive towards his family?
Mrs. Delgado: Well, I can't say for sure—but based on my observations and my conversation with Paul and my career working with kids, yes, I could say that it's possible that Paul was a victim of some form of abuse.

***

Gianna should've asked for the interview earlier. Who would've thought that behind the curtain and shiny windows and fancy cars, something sinister shadowed the Beckett family? But was Richard Beckett sinister enough to lure his son into the woods and murder him there? She didn't know. But until she got more, Echo Falls' former mayor was on her list.

And not only that—Richard was rerunning for Mayor of Echo Falls at the time of his son's murder. A son brutally murdered could earn him sympathy, of course; this was only speculation. But the events were all close together that it was hard not to think of it as a noncoincidence. It was a possible motive. It would explain the bruise on Paul's face and the weird tension Mrs. Delgado noticed between Mrs. Beckett and her husband.

It only got worse for Richard as Gianna looked deeper. While he was rerunning for mayor, Richard seemed to find himself in many scandals. Accusations of infidelity, corruption, and not making good on his promises to help end the opioid crisis—the list went on.

If Richard Beckett were really a power-hungry, abusive maniac, then murdering his son would be nothing to him.

And with help from the police department, he could cover his tracks.

She couldn't say that she knew Dale that well. He was Anthony's boss and his friend, but that was way before Anthony joined the police department. Dale was close friends with Richard before he died. Surely he suspected something?

Either way, they were both going on her list. She also found a classmate of Paul's who was still living in town. Hopefully, she could interview him before next week.

TWENTY-TWO

Gianna was seconds away from shoving Valarie's arm out of her face and ditching this idea altogether.

"It's not a big deal," Gianna said, for what felt like the hundredth time that afternoon.

"Of course it's a big deal," Irene insisted, as Valarie fussed over Gianna's makeup. She took another pile of hair and curled it with the iron. "It's your first date."

Gianna silently cursed Valarie and herself. She hadn't been planning on making this an announcement. She planned on dressing normally for the lunch, but Valarie, in her excitement, had told Liam about the double date on Friday, who told Mrs. Duncan, who told Irene, who told Anthony, and suddenly everyone in her household knew she was going on a double date with Theodore Rodriguez.

She winced as Irene pulled another strand of hair through the curling iron a tad too hard. "It's not a date," she said, flippantly cursing herself for going along with Theo's ridiculous plan. "It's *lunch.*"

"Yeah, lunch with Theodore Rodriguez." Valarie wagged her eyebrows suggestively.

"It's not like he's Tom Cruise."

Valarie placed a hand on her hip. "Well, if you don't like him, then why did you agree to go with him on a double date?"

Gianna hesitated. She couldn't tell Valarie the truth—that the whole date was a façade so she could corner Liam and pick his brain about Ollie and Grant.

She shrugged. "Like you said, I needed to try new things. Plus, I owe you for ditching last week."

"Oh, this more than makes up for it," Valarie squealed, switching out the eyeliner in her makeup bag for some blush. "Hold still."

"Are you sure this isn't too much?" Gianna couldn't see her face at the moment, but she could feel the makeup on her face like an unwelcome second skin. "It's just lunch."

"You know, my first boyfriend and my date was lunch," Irene piped, her voice taking on a dreamlike quality. "He worked at an auto shop."

"Didn't you two break up when you left for college?" Gianna inquired.

Irene whacked her shoulder. "That's not the point. He was my first love, and our relationship started out with something as simple as a meal. Plus, I learned everything I know about cars from him. I've never had to pay for tire changes in all my forty years."

Gianna snorted as Valarie's brush left her face.

"Okay," Valarie declared. "All done. Look."

Gianna opened her eyes and glanced at herself in the mirror and tried her best not to feel weird. The purple dress was something she found shoved in the back of her closet and far from what she usually wore, except for the cardigan that belonged to her mom.

"Oh, you look gorgeous," Irene gushed, her voice thick with emotion.

Gianna's gaze narrowed in the mirror. "Irene Pescelli, are you crying?"

"No." She sniffed, unplugging the curling iron and turning away. But Gianna noticed her hands wipe at her face. "Nope, not at all. Now, enough of that, let's get you downstairs before Anthony scares off your date."

That had Gianna moving down the stairs. Fake date or not, Gianna wouldn't subject Anthony's wrath to her worst enemy.

"I'm so excited for this," Valarie whispered.

The smile on her face was enough to send a pang of guilt running through Gianna. *You're helping her*, she told herself. *If Liam really was involved in Ollie's disappearance, then you're doing Valarie a favor by exposing who he really is.*

Gianna linked her arm through Valarie's. "Me too."

They found Anthony pacing across the floor of the kitchen, no doubt waiting for Theo's truck to pull into the driveway. His steps came to a halt when he saw Gianna. His eyes softened.

Irene placed her hands on Gianna's shoulders. "She looks just like Elena, doesn't she?"

He bobbed his head, swallowing. "Yes."

A flutter of warmth ran through her chest. Anthony wrapped Gianna in a hug, his shirt smelling of tobacco and pistachios. "Your mom would be so proud if she could see you," he said, low enough for the two of them to hear.

For a brief moment, she forgot all about the reasons for the date, content to stay in Anthony's arms a little while longer. She sniffled, blinking back the tears welling up in her eyes.

"I hate to ruin this moment," Valarie interrupted, "but no tears! It'll ruin your makeup."

They all let out a laugh at that as the doorbell echoed throughout the house. Gianna bolted toward the door but it was too late. Anthony was already there, swinging it open. Theo stood on the doorstep, a bouquet of flowers in his hand. What was he doing? She specifically told him to wait in the truck.

"You must be Mr. Pescelli," Theo held out a hand.

Anthony shook his hand. "And you must be Theo. Gianna's told me a lot about you."

Gianna rolled her eyes. She hadn't, but he was just saying it to make Theo sweat.

"She's said a lot about you, too, sir," Theo replied.

"Oh?" Anthony raised an eyebrow. "Did she also mention I'm a cop?"

Theo swallowed, having the gall to look nervous. "Yes, sir."

"Good. Then you know that I own a gun," Anthony crossed his arms. "Several, in fact."

"Anthony," Irene scolded, shouldering past him to the doorway. "Hi Theo, it's so good to see you again. Please excuse my brother. It's not every day he gets to scare off Gianna's date." Her gaze dropped to his hands. "Those are beautiful flowers."

Theo's gaze went to the flowers in his hand like he'd forgotten they were there. He cleared his throat and held them out. "They're for you."

"Oh, that's so thoughtful of you. And look, Anthony—they're irises." Irene took the bouquet gingerly, glancing up at her brother. "Wasn't that sweet of him, Anthony?"

"I've dealt with a lot of hardened criminals in my time," Anthony continued, ignoring his sister. "I used to be a detective years ago. These eyes"—He pointed to his eyes—"have seen things. Terrible atrocities."

Valarie shook with silent laughter while Gianna's face burned hotter than a pot of boiling water.

"I've also seen how people get away with it," Anthony went on. "How and where to bury a body so that no one finds it. At least not for thirty years."

"Okay," Gianna announced loudly, moving between them. "That's enough of the talk. I think Theo gets your point. We'll be back before dinner. Promise." She kissed Anthony on the cheek and went to pull Theo away, but he stopped.

"I'll have her home by six-thirty, Mr. Pescelli," he promised.

"Six o'clock," Anthony said.

Gianna gave him a look.

"Six-fifteen," he amended. "On the dot."

Thank you, she mouthed before pulling Theo to the truck.

"Oh, I forgot my bag. I'll be right back," Valarie called, disappearing back into the house. As Gianna glanced back at Anthony and Irene in the doorway, she was reminded of why she agreed to this in the first place. *I'll make them proud, Mom,* she promised as Theo opened the door for her. Gianna didn't waste a second getting into the truck.

As soon as the doors closed, Theo turned to her. "So much for charming your uncle."

"Oh, you charmed him, alright," she said. "He didn't tell you the story about the serial killer who sawed off his victim's hands."

"And …?"

She smoothed out the ruffles of her dress. "He knows which prison he is in."

Theo swallowed, rubbing the back of his neck. "That's … comforting."

"I did tell you to wait in the car. What happened to that?"

"I'm not going to take you out on a date without meeting your family first!" he exclaimed. She would have laughed if he hadn't sounded so earnest.

"It's not a date," she reminded him. "We're undercover, remember?"

"So you mean I showed up at your house in my best shirt for nothing?"

Despite her best efforts, the ends of her lips tilted upward. How did he always do that? Make her turn into a smiling idiot at the least expected times? She turned her head to the side but not before it escaped Theo's notice. "Was that a smile, Holmes?"

"Shut up," she said.

"Yes, ma'am." The silence lasted all of two seconds before he glanced at her again, whispering, "You look beautiful, by the way."

She didn't have a chance to respond. The back door swung open and Valarie slid inside, face flushed from running. She pushed a blonde curl from her face and looked at them. Her eyes darted from Gianna's reddened cheeks to Theo's smirk, and a smile spread across her face. "Okay, so what did I miss?"

***

As planned, Liam met up with them at the Chinese restaurant.

"Here's the plan," Gianna had whispered as they walked in. "You distract Valarie and I'll talk to Liam."

"Shouldn't I talk to him?" Theo suggested. "I don't know if you noticed, but he doesn't really like you."

The feeling was decidedly mutual. "Just leave it to me," she said, a finality in her tone that Theo didn't push against.

Gianna bided her time as the waiter checked them in, taking them to their table and serving the drinks. After the first serving, Liam stood up to get seconds, and Gianna saw her opening.

She stood. "I think I'll go get some seconds, too."

"But you haven't finished your first plate," Valarie pointed out.

"Is that sweet-and-sour chicken they just brought out?" Gianna squinted somewhere to the right. "I'll be right back."

Theo gave her a slight nod, leaning over the table to talk to Valarie. Gianna grabbed a plate from the stack and maneuvered her way over to Liam. She made a show of looking over the food, before placing some noodles onto her plate.

"Chinese food," she said, as she placed the tongs back on the tray. "An interesting take for lunch."

Liam shrugged. "Chinese is Val's favorite."

"So you wanted to impress her. Because impressing people—it's what you do."

"Whatever you say, Nancy Drew." Liam gave her a smile, but it didn't quite reach his eyes. When he went to scoop out a spoonful of rice, some of it fell to the floor. Her eyes landed on the shiny new Vans he was wearing.

"Those are nice shoes. Are they new?" she asked casually.

"Yeah, I got them last week. Fifty dollars at the store on sale."

"How'd you get the money or that?"

"Work." He said work like someone would say *duh*. "How else?"

"Well, plenty of people make money from all types of work. Illegal and legal otherwise. You know, selling drugs and that kind of thing, for example."

He swallowed. "Right …"

"Speaking of," she continued, placing her plate in front of him to block him from moving. "Where does one go if they want to buy?"

"Buy what?"

"You know …" she said, searching for the right word. What was it Dexter had called it? "*Stuff.*"

"Um, I'm not sure I'm the right person to talk to about that. Excuse me."

Liam took his plate and made a beeline back toward the table. Gianna swore. That was her chance. She hurried back to the table. Liam didn't look in her direction as she sat.

"Did they run out of sweet-and-sour chicken?" Valarie teased.

"Huh?"

Valarie pierced a piece of broccoli with her fork. "You said you saw someone bring out more chicken. That's why you went back up there …"

Oh.

She shrugged. "Yeah, it was something else they brought. I thought it was chicken."

Valarie laughed at that. From across the table, she could feel Theo's stare boring into her and the worry flowing off him in waves. She could read the question in his eyes. *What happened?*

What happened was she let her chance slip right out of her grasp. She couldn't let it happen a second time. Valarie pierced her broccoli with her fork again, and an idea occurred to her. She turned to Valarie, covered her mouth with her hand, and whispered, "Val, you've got some in your teeth."

Valarie's eyes went wide with horror. Her hand flew to her mouth. "I'll, uh … be right back. Uh, restroom," she stammered, rushing off in the other direction.

As soon as she was out of earshot, Gianna's gaze flew to Liam. "So, Liam, do you hang around the skatepark often?" she asked, straight to the point.

"No." He shifted in his seat. He grabbed his Mountain Dew off the table and took a sip, breaking eye contact.

Come on, you're obviously feeling guilty about something.

Gianna folded her hands on the table. "What about five years ago?"

"Maybe. What's it to you?"

From the corner of her eye, she saw Theo make a face at her, but she ignored whatever he was trying to tell her. "What about Michael Price? When was the last time you talked to him? July 4th, 2019, perhaps?"

"Theo, what the hell is your date going on about?" Liam demanded, turning to Theo, who seemed at a loss for words.

"I'm not just his date, I'm Valarie's friend," she snapped. "And if you care for her a little bit at all, you'll tell us the truth."

"Us?" Liam's eyes flew to Theo. "You're part of this, too? You know what, never mind. I don't care because I have no idea what the fuck you two are going on about."

"Are you sure about that?"

"Positive," he declared.

She scoffed. "Cut the crap, Liam. You know what I think? I think you know more than you're letting on."

"For the last time, I don't—"

She didn't give him a chance to finish. "Ever heard of Freddy Atwater?"

"How many times do I have to say it? I have no idea what the fuck you're talking about," Liam spat.

"For someone who doesn't know anything, you sound defensive."

He leaned across the table and snarled, "Maybe it's because you keep fucking interrogating me."

"What's going on?" Valarie came up to them, her eyes flying between the two. Heads were now looking at them, couples murmuring words behind their spoons.

Liam dropped the plate with a clatter and stood to his feet. "What's wrong is your friend's a psycho. I'm out of here."

Oh, no you don't. Gianna hurried after him out of the restaurant, Valarie at her heels. He made it to the road before she ran in front of him.

"What?" Gianna shouted. "Can't handle your girlfriend hearing the truth?"

"Get out of my way," Liam spat.

"Holmes." Theo reached for her arm, but she pulled away from his reach at the last moment.

Liam went to walk around her, but she blocked his path. "Why can't you just admit it?" She stepped closer, lowering her voice so only he could hear. "I know it was you who left the note in my bag. Why do you want to stop my investigation so badly? What do you lose from me finding Ollie?"

"Stop!" Valarie pushed herself between the two of them, her chest heaving. "One of you needs to tell me what the hell is going on."

"Your boyfriend knows something about Ollie." Gianna kept her eyes trained on Liam. "He used to hang around the skatepark, around the time Ollie went missing. I bet he was best pals with Michael Price, the guy who assaulted him."

Valarie frowned. "Around 2019?"

"Yes." Gianna looked at her. Did she not hear a word Gianna said?

"If I didn't know any better, he might've been the one who made Ollie go missing, who—"

"That's enough!" Valarie yelled. Gianna's jaw snapped shut as her eyes stayed on her best friend. Valarie, in all their years of friendship, had never yelled like that. Never at her. "Liam couldn't have been around the skatepark then. He couldn't have known Ollie, at least not then. He was in rehab five years ago."

Gianna blinked, the sound whooshing in and out of her ears. "What?"

"His aunt convinced him to go to rehab that summer. He was there from June to August. He wasn't even in town when Ollie went missing."

"You … you never mentioned that to me," Gianna said slowly.

"Because it wasn't any of your business!" Valarie cried. "None of it was. I can't believe you right now. First you cancel on me many times to go mystery-solving, and then you lie to my face saying you're sick when I know for a fact you're not. I thought when you agreed to go on the double date you'd get over whatever grudge you have against Liam, but you were never planning that were you? This entire lunch was just a way for you to interrogate Liam, to finally push whatever vendetta you have against him. Did you even give him the benefit of the doubt before agreeing to go out for lunch?"

Gianna's mouth opened and closed.

Valarie scoffed. "Of course you didn't. Because you choose to see the bad in everyone before anything else. You don't bother to try to look at the good parts of people. Are you even interested in Theo, or was that a lie too?"

"Val," she said.

"No, I'm not finished. You know you can't just go around accusing everyone you don't like. Are you that eager to prove yourself to your uncle? That you'll just toss the blame on everyone else? Who's next on your list? Me?"

"No, of course not. Val, I honestly thought it was him. I … she told me it was him."

But Emmaline had been mistaken.

"That's not the point, Gianna. You never bothered to ask. Instead, you went straight into the accusations without getting the facts first, knowing who Liam is to me, what he *means* to me." She shook her head. "You know I've been by your side from day one. Every Mother's Day. Every birthday. Your thirteenth birthday when you …" She swallowed, cutting herself off there, and Gianna wanted to cry. Even now, Valarie was still protecting her, still unable to use that horrible day against her.

When she finally spoke, her voice was flat and tired, "You know, you try so hard not to end up like your dad that you can't see that you're already heading right there. I thought you'd be by my side when the time came. I guess I was wrong."

I am on your side, she wanted to say, but no words came out. It was like she'd been shot in the heart, the bullet wound ripping through her chest. She grasped at it, expecting to see blood, but her fingers came away spotless.

When Valarie realized she wasn't going to say anything, she took Liam's hand, and they walked away.

She left without looking back, and Gianna felt a pain in her chest akin to being stabbed with a knife. She wasn't breathing; she wasn't—

"Hey." She was surrounded by warmth. "Hey, Holmes, sorry I had to pay the bill, what's—ah shit. Holmes—Gianna, look at me."

She met Theo's brown eyes—like the bark of the oak trees that surrounded her home. It was as if her air supply was being cut off. She clawed at her chest as the panic rose.

Not again … She squeezed her eyes shut. Why now?

Theo guided Gianna to the curb, helping her sit down. "Take deep breaths. In and out. Like me. See?" He instructed her, gesturing to his own breaths. Gianna focused on what he was doing, unaware of her clammy hand crushing his. She focused on the mint smell coming off him, and the heat of his breath on her neck as he counted breaths with her.

When her breathing finally went back to normal and the pain in her chest eased, she said, "Th-thanks."

"No problem," Theo whispered. "Does … does that happen often?"

Gianna felt her head shaking. "No. It hasn't happened since …"

She closed her eyes, as if she could force the terrible memory from five years ago out of her mind. She didn't want to go back there—not ever. Anywhere but there.

"Not in a while," she managed. "That's the second time it's happened." She peered up at him to find him already looking at her. "How did you know what to do?"

"I used to get them," he confessed. "Back in middle school. There was this group of kids who'd pick on me and, well … I was a lot smaller back then. Still entirely good-looking, of course, but sadly a few inches shorter." His attempt at humor failed at the thaw in his voice.

"Jerks," Gianna muttered, feeling a burning sensation toward the kids. "I hope you slashed their parents' tires."

"More like I waited two years for my growth spurt to kick in and kick their asses." Theo smiled. "Kidding. I beat all of them for the captain of our basketball team. Geez, not everyone can be as ruthless as you, Holmes."

A smile tugged at her lips. And then Valarie's words echoed in her mind. *You choose to see the bad in everyone before anything else. You don't bother to try and look at the good parts of people.*

That wiped the smile clean off her face.

Theo cleared his throat. "She'll come around," he said. "You're her best friend."

Gianna appreciated the kind words, but that's all they were—kind words. He didn't know Valarie like she did. Valarie, who still hadn't forgiven her parents for being too wrapped up in their divorce to remember their daughter; Valarie, who treasured loyalty and friendship more than anything else, and wanted nothing but to be happy. A happiness that Gianna stomped all over.

"I went too far. Valarie was right. I should've just asked Liam; I should've gotten all the facts first. But when Emmaline said she saw Liam, I just pounced."

"We all make mistakes," he reassured her. "But while we're on that topic, what exactly did Emmaline tell you?"

Gianna paused, playing back her conversation with Emmaline. "She mentioned someone shady hanging around the skatepark and mentioned him driving a van. I asked what he looked like and she said …" She blinked as the conversation with Emmaline appeared back in her mind. She hadn't given any description until Gianna showed her Liam's picture.

"It wasn't until I started listing off Liam's description that Emmaline gave me a straight answer. She probably saw how desperate I was to think it was Liam and said what I wanted to hear."

Emmaline never saw Liam at the park, probably never had before, and Gianna allowed her bias to cloud her judgment.

"It's okay, Holmes. Even detectives such as yourself make mistakes. I'm more concerned about why she lied to you," Theo said.

"She's hiding something. When I brought up the watch, her face changed. Less like she was defensive but almost like she was … scared."

Get that away from me! If you come near me again with that, I'll make you regret it.

She had it all wrong. Emmaline had been talking with her fine before she showed her the watch. No, Emmaline wasn't just scared—she was terrified.

And they needed to find out why.

TWENTY-THREE

It took three knocks before the door opened. Emmaline's face appeared, her eyes widening.

Gianna forced a smile on her face. "Hey Emmaline, remember me?"

"Gianna," she breathed. "Um, what are you doing here? How are you—"

"That doesn't matter now. I'm more interested in why you lied to me." Emmaline sucked in a nervous breath. "There was never a shady guy around the skatepark. You didn't see Liam there or anywhere else for that matter. Why did you lie to me?"

Emmaline's mouth opened and closed, shell-shocked. A second figure appeared behind her in the doorway, one that she recognized.

"Nathan?" Gianna and Theo exclaimed at the same time.

"It's okay," Nathan told Emmaline. "They're with me."

"What are you doing here?" Gianna asked.

"I wanted answers, so I came here myself."

"How?" He couldn't drive.

"I took the bus."

"Well, good on you, junior detective," Theo said, patting Nathan on the shoulder.

Gianna's gaze darted between Emmaline and Nathan. "And she answered your questions?"

"*She* is right in front of you," Emmaline bristled. "And you failed to mention that you were working with Ollie's brother the last time we spoke."

"I didn't think it mattered, seeing how you didn't know Ollie," Gianna retorted. "Of course, that was a lie, too."

Nathan stepped between them. "Why don't you guys come inside? We'll explain everything."

Gianna looked at Emmaline, expecting her to argue and banish them from her doorstep altogether. But to her surprise, Emmaline opened the door wider.

Gianna brushed past her, following Nathan to the living room. "Why didn't you tell us you were coming here?"

"You were interrogating Liam. I couldn't help there, so I thought I could try to be useful and get some answers."

"And did you?"

Nathan grinned. "Emmaline was just explaining to me how she knew my brother when you knocked." He looked over at Emmaline. "Do you want to tell them what you told me?"

Emmaline hesitated, her gaze bouncing between Gianna and Theo.

"It's alright," Nathan reassured. "You can trust them."

Emmaline swallowed, glancing at the wall behind their heads. "I first met Ollie and Grant at summer camp when we were twelve. They were as close then as they were when we were eighteen. We hung out a lot that summer at the skatepark. We got close. Ollie and I … grew closer." She glanced down at her hands. "We talked about finding a place together after the summer. You were right." Emmaline looked up at Gianna. "I know Ollie. We were more than acquaintances. He and Grant … they were my friends."

"Then why lie?" she asked. "Why tell me it was Liam? Was there even a guy at the skatepark?"

Emmaline sniffed. "No. I said that to throw you off the truth."

Theo beat her to her next question. "Why?"

"Because it isn't safe for you to know. For anyone to know." She scoffed. "You're just kids. You're the same age we were when …" She faltered for a moment before shaking her head. "It isn't safe."

Gianna folded her arms. "How do you really know Michael?"

"I didn't lie about that. Michael was my dad's friend. He became my guardian after my dad died. It was either him or foster care, and as horrible as he is, Michael was better than the latter. I planned to leave once I was eighteen, but Michael had this notion that I owed him for the money my dad borrowed when he was still alive. I told him to go to hell. And then he showed me the video of my brother along with some of his friends breaking into a jewelry store with a gun. The police hadn't been able to identify any of the robbers yet, but Michael knew it was Eddie. He threatened to turn him in if I didn't pay back my dad's debt."

A memory resurfaced. *Emmaline owed me. Not the other way around, and that little punk knew it.*

"Ollie knew about the video," Gianna guessed. "That's what the fight was about."

Emmaline nodded. "He wanted to help me. Eddie ran away from home when he was fifteen. I didn't know if he was even alive until Michael showed me that video. Ollie and I were going to find him, and then we got caught up in all of that mess."

"And what mess would that be?"

Emmaline sighed. "I already told you. It isn't safe for you to know."

"We know Ollie was looking into Paul's death," Theo said. "We're already close enough to the truth."

"He's right," Nathan added.

Emmaline stared at the three of them, sizing them up. "How do you know that you can even find him?"

A small stretch of silence passed. Did she? It felt like Gianna did nothing but grasp at straws, and she wasn't anywhere close to locating him. She saw the same hope in Emmaline's eyes that she saw in Nathan's and Angela's. The desperation that lay there, the need for answers. Answers she wasn't certain she could provide.

To her surprise, Nathan spoke. "Listen, I know my brother isn't here right now, but if there was a chance we could find him, he'd want us to. There hasn't been a night where my mother hasn't cried herself to sleep because her son is missing and everyone thinks he's a murderer. If there's something you know, then *help us*. Help us find him. Because I'll never stop searching. One way or another, whatever you're trying to hide will come out. I'll find out the truth—either from you or somewhere else."

Emmaline considered his words for a long while. Gianna knew she had made her decision when she looked at them. "I first noticed something was off when summer break started. Ollie had been acting strange all week, not like his usual self, and Grant was MIA. I confronted Ollie about it and demanded that he tell me what was going on.

"According to Ollie, he and Grant were walking out of the store when some guy pulled them to the side. He accused Grant of stealing and demanded he show him the stuff. Grant said he hadn't stolen anything and wouldn't do a single thing the guy asked him. I don't know the full details of what happened, only that when they left, Grant had a bruised eye and some other guy had to pull Grant's assaulter off him."

"What happened after that?" Gianna asked.

"Ollie did something stupid. You know he was when it came to Grant." The words were directed at Nathan. "He saw the same guy's car in the parking lot the next day, and he snapped. He broke into the guy's car and stole the bag inside. Only the car didn't belong to the man who assaulted Grant. It was a similar make but by the time they realized it, it was too late." She swore, rubbing at her temples. "That stupid watch. It caused so many problems."

Gianna looked up. "So Ollie knew who the watch belonged to."

"Paul Beckett," Emmaline confirmed. "Grant figured it out. When we found out how much it was worth, we were going to turn it in and split the reward money. That was until we discovered it was part of a murder case, and then things got weird."

"Weird how?" Theo asked.

"I don't know how to describe it. It's like …" She huffed, struggling to find the words. "It's like a feeling you get when there's someone watching you, but when you turn around, no one is there. That your every movement is being tracked. Then the notes started appearing. First in mailboxes, then on our front doors, on our cars. Threatening messages."

The room swayed around her; Gianna gripped the arm of her chair to keep her grounded. Her words felt like sludge in her throat, her voice barely above a whisper. "What did the notes say?"

Emmaline blinked. "What?"

"The notes," Gianna persisted, her heartbeat a drum in her chest. "What did they say?"

"It was different each time. 'I know who you are' or 'Stop looking.'

Stuff like that. We dismissed the first one as a joke, but after the second one, Grant wanted to take it to the police. Ollie told him we couldn't; that if the police couldn't catch a victim's real murderer, then they wouldn't be able to help us. And since Ollie broke into the car, he could get in trouble. It was more trouble than it was worth."

"So you decided to get rid of it," Nathan supplied.

Emmaline clasped her hands together. "We agreed that Ollie would hide it far away from any of us so we wouldn't be in any danger. We thought that would be the end of the notes, but then a few days later, Ollie got a call from an unknown number. The person knew we had the watch and told Ollie he was willing to trade for it. No police, no authorities involved."

"Sounds like a trap," Theo said.

"Ollie thought so too. We knew someone couldn't be that desperate for the watch unless—"

"Unless they had something to lose by you guys possibly turning it in," Gianna finished.

Unless they were Paul Beckett's true killer.

Emmaline nodded. "We made a plan. We were going to lure the guy in with the watch, get him to confess how he got it, and then tape it and hand it over to the police. If it went sideways, we'd make a run for it so our families would be safe." She choked on a sob. "We had a plan. We were going to do it on the night of the fifth. I should have known what they were going to do when they came to see me that night."

"Wait." Gianna frowned. "Ollie and Grant saw you on July 4th?"

"I was at work," she said hoarsely. "Ollie and Grant came by and brought me dinner. I was still shaken from all the notes. Ollie pulled me to the side and told me that everything was going to be alright. That he was going to fix all of this." She sniffed. "I should've known then what he was planning. But they went ahead without me and that guy killed Grant." More sobs poured out of her, racking her shoulders.

"That explains the hour between Ollie leaving the Hayes and Grant's time of death," Gianna whispered to Theo.

"If all that you're telling us is true, why didn't you go to the police?" Nathan asked. "Your story can clear Ollie's name."

Emmaline sniffled. "I wanted to. I was going to tell them

everything. But two days after Grant died, I got a message on my phone. It was from Unknown. They told me to keep quiet about the watch."

Her gaze flitted to the side, and Gianna followed it to the frame on the entryway table. Gianna recognized the picture—it was the same one on Emmaline's lockscreen.

"The boy on the mantelpiece," Gianna said. "He's the reason you stayed quiet." Emmaline's gaze fell to the ground. "He's your brother? The one who robbed that jewelry store?"

Lips drawn into a straight line, Emmaline nodded. "They didn't just send me a message to keep quiet. They also sent a picture of Eddie sleeping on a bench. Whoever had that watch before us found my brother." Her shiny eyes met Nathan's. "I knew Ollie didn't kill Grant, but I couldn't lose my brother. So I made you lose yours. I'm so sorry."

"It wasn't your fault," Nathan said softly.

No, Gianna agreed silently. It wasn't anyone's.

Gianna slowly approached Emmaline, as one would a skittish horse. "Have you gotten any more messages from this unknown number?"

"At first, I'd get them nearly every day. Then it turned into every few weeks, then every few months, and then once a year. The last time I got a text was six months ago until … until a few weeks ago when I got another text."

A few weeks.

A few weeks ago, when Gianna received her first note.

"Did you guys figure out who the bag belonged to?" Nathan asked.

Emmaline shook her head. "No. All I know is that he drove a blue Chevy."

"Where were Ollie and Grant supposed to meet this unknown person?" Gianna asked. "The night of the fourth?"

"The ruins."

Gianna locked eyes with the others. *Hollow Hill.* That was why Ollie and Grant were out on Topsfield Road that night. It was no coincidence that the place where the killer had them meet was the same place Paul Beckett drew his final breath.

When they were finished, Emmaline saw them out. Gianna was the last to the door, but Emmaline's hand on her arm stopped her in her tracks.

She pulled Gianna back inside, her voice too low for the boys to hear on the other side of the door. "I saw the look on your face when I mentioned the notes. You've been getting them, too." Emmaline must have seen the answer in her face because she didn't give Gianna a chance to speak. Her nails dug into the skin of her arm, pulling her closer so that she couldn't mistake the fear in Emmaline's eyes. "Don't make the same mistake I did; tell your friends what you're going through—before it's too late."

Log #10, Dec. 15th, 2023

Transcript of Interview with Benjamin Taylor (Former Classmate of Paul Beckett)

Gianna: So, I wanted to ask you about Paul's family. What was his relationship with his parents like?
Benjamin: I'm not sure I'm the best person to ask about that. I've only been over to the Becketts once, I think for a team dinner eons ago, before Paul died.
Gianna: Is there anything from that night that stood out to you?
Benjamin: I mean, not really. It was years ago. I showed up to Paul's house with a couple of other guys from the team. We tossed around the football in the backyard for a little while. Paul's mom was probably cooking dinner.
Gianna: Where was Mr. Beckett while all of this was going on?
Benjamin: Uh, if I were to guess, he was probably at his office. He was at dinner, though.
Gianna: And how was Paul after his dad showed up?
Benjamin: Pretty normal. A little quieter, I guess, but then again some kid at our school had just died of an overdose. Everyone was a little on edge.
Gianna: So you didn't notice anything out of the ordinary between Paul and his parents?
Benjamin: Not that I can remember. Like I said, I was only at their house once and only saw them when they came to Paul's games. I didn't know Paul like that. We played at practice and football, and yeah, we saw each other at parties, but we weren't like close friends or anything.
Gianna: Do you know anybody who was close enough to Paul that would know something like that?
Benjamin: Mason Ramsay's the guy you want to talk to. He and Paul were really close.
Gianna: Yes, I searched him up but couldn't find much. Do you have a way to contact him?

Benjamin: Nope. He went off the grid a few years back, full on living in the wilderness, if you can believe it. Then again, his old man was known to be a recluse. Mason grew up in those woods for a lot of his life.
Gianna: Okay, just a few more questions and I'll get out of your hair. While you were at Echo Falls High, did you ever hear any rumors of Paul's father hitting him or abusing him in any way?
Benjamin: What? Where did you hear that?
Gianna: Just a rumor I heard.
Benjamin: Huh. Well, no, I never heard anything about that. I do remember hearing about something else, though. It didn't have anything to do with Paul's dad, but word on the street was that Paul had a relationship with a teacher.
Gianna: An intimate relationship?
Benjamin: Physical, yeah. That's what people were saying. And before you ask, I have no clue who the teacher was, and I highly doubt it was real.
Gianna: Really? How come?
Benjamin: Because it was just bullshit. Anyone who spent five minutes with the guy knew he wouldn't do something so stupid when he was working hard to get into a good school. When he wasn't practicing, he was studying. I doubt he slept at all that year. Plus, his dad was on his tail all the time about getting good grades.
Gianna: I thought Paul had already been accepted into several colleges.
Benjamin: Yeah, he got offers but that was only half of it. He had to have the GPA for it, and in order to stay on the team, it's a requirement we have to keep our grades a B or above, and from my understanding Paul was struggling in a few classes. The coach gave him a warning to get his grades up or else he'd have to be kicked off the team.
Benjamin: And then on top of that, he said his dad was pressuring him to apply to some of the Ivy Leagues, even though Paul was planning to go to a university in New Hampshire. He said something about how he wanted to say his son had gotten accepted into an Ivy League. Bragging rights, you know? Kind of wish my dad was like Paul's dad. At least Paul's dad wanted a future for him. My dad could care less if I ended up working at a gas station for the rest of my life, but you know, that's life. It's unfair.

Gianna: Going back to the rumor about Paul having a relationship with a teacher—
Benjamin: I already told you the rumor was bullshit.
Gianna: Right, but saying hypothetically that it is real, do you recall the subject the teacher taught?
Benjamin: The rumor wasn't true, but if you really want to know, she taught math..
Gianna: Math? Y-you're absolutely sure it was math?
Benjamin: Uh, yeah. Paul used to complain about the class all the time. But like I said, it was just a rumor that some kids started.

TWENTY-FOUR

The rumor wasn't true, but if you really want to know, it was a math teacher.

Gianna stood on the doorstep, her mind whirling. It couldn't be true. It just couldn't. She could hear voices shouting from inside the house before knocking.

The voices fell silent. A few moments went by before she heard footsteps on the other side of the door. It swung open and Mr. Delgado stood on the other side. The normal cheerfulness in his eyes was gone, replaced with heavy exhaustion.

"Oh, Gianna," he said. "I … er … wasn't expecting you. Did Anthony send you?"

"Uh, no. I wanted to talk to Mrs. Delgado about a project I'm working on." She met Mrs. Delgado's gaze over Mr. Delgado's shoulder.

"It's Saturday. Surely this can wait until Monday?" Mr. Delgado suggested.

"It's a really important grade," she insisted. "I just have a few more questions."

Understanding flashed in Mrs. Delgado's eyes. She came up behind her husband, setting a hand on his shoulder. "Andrew, why don't you go pick up that list I gave you for the grocery store while Gianna and I chat?"

Mr. Delgado sighed heavily, snatching his keys off the hook before heading out the door. Mrs. Delgado smiled warmly at Gianna as she closed the door behind her.

"Did you want some tea?" she asked. "I just put a pot on."

"Sure."

The kettle whistled loudly. Mrs. Delgado strode over to the stove, lifting it up. As she grabbed two mugs from the cupboard, Gianna asked, "Is everything okay with you and Mr. Delgado? It seemed a little tense when I showed up."

Mrs. Delgado's hands faltered on the cup she was reaching for before turning to Gianna. "A marriage is a lot like a river." Steam rose when she poured the water in the mugs. "Filled with twists and rocky bends. But at the end of the day, it keeps on flowing."

She slid the mug across the table. "So, what questions does Detective Gianna have for me today?"

Gianna hesitated, her fingers stilling around her cup. The question was at the tip of her tongue. *Were you having an affair with Paul Beckett?* This was Mrs. Delgado. The woman who taught Gianna how to knit, who played tea-parties with her when she was little, and stroked her hair to help her fall asleep. Could she be the same woman who cheated on her husband and possibly committed murder?

Mrs. Delgado looked expectantly at Gianna, who leaned against the table, tipping the mug over with her elbow. "I—*ow*."

She hissed, shooting to her feet as the hot liquid burned through her pants.

"Oh, dear," Mrs. Delgado gasped.

"I'm fine," Gianna squeaked, running over to the sink.

As she ran her hands under the water, her eyes fell out of the window toward the shed. A car she'd never seen before rested by it, a gray tarp covering the top.

"Is that a new car?" she asked.

Mrs. Delgado followed her gaze outside. "Oh, no, I've had that car for about a decade now. I haven't driven it in years. I keep telling Andrew we should sell it, but he insists he can fix it."

Gianna studied the car from the window. The tarp fell short of the license plate, and from here she could make out the numbers. *116203.*

Her breath stalled.

The same numbers Ollie had written down on a bubblegum wrapper in his desk.

She slowly turned to Mrs. Delgado. "Why does Oliver Kipman have your license plate number written down?"

"I, uh, I—I don't know." Mrs. Delgado's face had gone pale as a sheet, her knuckles white where they clenched the ends of her cardigan.

"Mrs. Delgado, I'm going to ask you a question and I want you to be honest with me." Gianna looked at her former teacher. "Were you having an affair with Paul Beckett?"

"What?" Mrs. Delgado stiffened, her hands clenching around her mug as she sputtered, "Of course not! Paul was my student."

Gianna let out a sigh of relief. She was telling the truth—about that at least.

"What would cause you to ask such a thing?" she demanded.

"I spoke to one of Paul's classmates and he said there was a rumor that in Paul's senior year, he was having an affair with one of his teachers." She looked down at her hands as shame washed over her. "I was so eager to find out more, I just believed him. He was wrong."

"He wasn't wrong." Gianna looked up at her. "There was a rumor, although there was no truth to it." Mrs. Delgado rubbed her temples. "Paul was falling behind in my class. Missing assignments, failing tests. Even if by some miracle he managed to pass his final exams, he wouldn't be able to bring his grade up enough to pass. I knew this—and so did Paul. One afternoon after school, he came to see me. He asked—no, he *demanded* that I change his grade. When I told him I wouldn't be doing that, he threatened to go to his father. I told him to go ahead and try. The shock couldn't be clearer on his face. He actually expected me to be intimidated by his threat. He left without another word.

"The next morning, when I came into work, my boss pulled me into his office. Imagine my surprise when he asked me to clear up a story he heard—that I was involved with one of my students."

"Paul started the rumor," Gianna murmured.

She nodded. "I don't have proof he ever did, but I know deep down it was him. He was angry at me for not giving in. Luckily, there was no proof to back up his claims, and I didn't lose my job."

Gianna sat, processing this information. Mrs. Delgado had answered her question—she wasn't having an affair with Paul Beckett. She could rule Mrs. Delgado out as a potential suspect in his murder.

But she was still hiding something.

"That still doesn't explain why Ollie would have your license plate written down."

Mrs. Delgado squirmed in her seat. "I don't know anything about that."

"I don't believe you." She leaned forward on the table. "Ollie was looking into Paul Beckett's murder. The only reason he would bother writing down your plates is that he suspected you or suspected someone you knew."

Her lip trembled. She clasped her hands together, gaze cast downward on the table. A long time passed before she spoke. "I told you before that I wasn't having an affair with Paul, and I was telling you the truth. Paul was not the person I was having an affair with."

It took Gianna a moment to understand what she was saying. She blinked. "You were having an affair with someone else."

She waited for the denial, but it never came. Mrs. Delgado's hands were shaking, but her gaze didn't waver from Gianna's face.

"Yes," she whispered hoarsely.

Mr. Delgado flashed in Gianna's mind, cheerful and round-cheeked, smiling as he held his wife close to him. The love and adoration in his eyes. "Does Mr. Delgado—"

"Andrew doesn't know," she cut Gianna off. "Although, I believe he suspects."

Gianna thought back to when she stumbled into them in the hallway. Mr. Delgado's forced smile and Mrs. Delgado's lowered gaze.

Mrs. Delgado exhaled a shaky breath. "It started back in April of 2019. Andrew and I had gotten into another argument about his work. At that time, all we did was argue. He'd been picking up more hours, staying late at the office. I felt like I was the only one holding up our end of the marriage. After the argument, I stormed out and went to my car. At first, I wasn't really driving anywhere, and then I found myself at a bar outside of town. All the bartenders in Echo Falls knew Andrew, so I figured this one would be safe, where no one knew me.

"I was at the counter for ten minutes before he showed up. I didn't recognize him at first. He started talking with me, flirting, really, and I … I liked the attention. Andrew hadn't flirted with me in a long time at that point. Some days it felt like we didn't even acknowledge each other. So, I . . . kept talking to the man. I thought he looked familiar at the time, and then when he told me his name was Mason, I realized why."

"Mason," Gianna echoed, picturing the 2003 yearbook, realizing she had heard that name before. "Mason Ramsay? Paul's best friend?"

Mrs. Delgado slowly nodded. "I started to tell him who I was, but he said he already knew. I never taught him, but Paul was in my class. Mason and I started talking, and one thing led to another. I regretted it the moment I woke up. But a few weeks later, I went back. I told myself it was just to talk because of how I'd left without any explanation, and he at least deserved that.

"But then it happened again. And soon enough we were planning it out. It wasn't difficult—Andrew was always working. Aside from weekends, our schedules barely coincided. Mason and I saw each other for months. We met up at places far outside of town. Restaurants, theaters, places that no one would recognize us. Until one day in the summer we saw a car across the road from his apartment.

"Mason didn't recognize it. At the time, I thought it was Andrew. That he finally figured out that I was cheating and sent someone over to follow me. I panicked. I told Mason that it was over and then I left. When I got home, Andrew was acting strange, but not for the reasons that I thought. He'd made dinner and set up the table for me, waiting until I got home. He'd never sent that car. He'd never suspected me, not once. I broke down right there at the table, and even though he didn't know the real reason why I was crying, he still comforted me. And that's when I knew I couldn't do it anymore. I couldn't continue to ruin our marriage. So I ended things with Mason."

Mrs. Delgado looked up, eyes glistening. "I didn't put two and two together that it was the Kipmans' car until he went missing and Andrew said they'd found the car near the bus station—the same one I saw outside Mason's cabin that day."

Her mind spun. Ollie must've sought out Mason to speak to him about Paul. But then he saw an unfamiliar car and wrote it down. Did he suspect Mason?

"Did Mason ever mention Paul?" Gianna asked.

"No. We never spoke of him. But Gianna," Mrs. Delgado said,

taking her warm hands in hers. "You cannot mention what I told you to anyone. Please. Andrew—Andrew can't know."

"I won't." Mrs. Delgado sighed a breath of relief. "But only because I'm not the one who should tell him."

A pained expression flickered across her face. "He wouldn't forgive me. And I—I love him."

Gianna had seen the love in Mr. Delgado's eyes that he had for his wife. *How could you?* she wanted to ask, but she bit her tongue. Whatever she had to say, it was clear Mrs. Delgado already thought it about herself. So instead, she asked, "Where can I find Mason?"

She sniffed. "I don't know. I haven't spoken to him since that day. I cut off all ties with him. I'm not so sure he's even in town anymore. He always spoke of moving away again, getting a cabin in the middle of the woods."

"Could you think of any reason that Mason might want to hurt Paul?"

Confusion flashed on her face. "Why would he want to hurt Paul?"

Gianna shrugged. "Jealousy? Paul was the star athlete. Mason was his best friend, his shadow." She thought of the picture in the yearbook, of Paul and Mason standing side by side, showing off their prizes. Paul on top with his first-place trophy and Mason to the side, holding his second-place medal. Jealousy could be a motive. People killed for less.

Mrs. Delgado reached across the table, covering Gianna's hand. "Thank you, Gianna," she said in a hoarse whisper. "For keeping my secret."

"I'm not keeping it for you," Gianna said coldly, pulling her hand from under hers.

She stood up and showed herself out, with the knowledge of another heavy secret on her shoulders. *And one more person in her life that wasn't who she thought she was.*

Log #11, Dec. 16th, 2023

Suspect List

~~Freddy Atwater~~
Richard Beckett
Dale Goodeman
~~Liam Davenport~~
~~Mrs. Delgado~~
Mason Ramsay

TWENTY-FIVE

Gianna stared at the bulletin board she had spent the last hour assembling. Her desk was a mess of cut-out paper, thumbtacks, red twine, and photos scattered over it. She needed something to keep her mind busy for the time being, and the murder board was the perfect distraction.

Paul smiled back at her from where his photo was pinned—all white teeth and shiny hair that he inherited from his father. She had placed his photo in the center of the board. It felt appropriate. His watch connected Ollie's disappearance to his, and Gianna made sure to link a piece of red thread between the two photos to visualize that.

On the other side of the board was Freddy Atwater's mugshot with a giant question mark scribbled in dry erase marker on top of it. And on the opposite side of the board was Richard Beckett.

Despite her last conversation with Mrs. Delgado, Richard was still her number one suspect. There was more to Echo Falls' esteemed former mayor than met the eye. The information Mrs. Delgado told her went hand in hand with Carrie Atwater's theory that Freddy was framed. Freddy was the perfect fall guy. He had the motive and the means. And if Richard was as bad as Gianna thought he was, then he wouldn't bat an eye at a man going to jail for something he was to blame for.

The only problem was that nothing on paper could solidify his part in his son's murder. It also didn't help that Richard Beckett died two years ago. His death should have deterred her—but it only made her more determined.

She was so enwrapped in her project that she almost didn't hear the doorbell ringing downstairs. She waited for Irene to answer it, but then she remembered—Irene was out at a yoga class she had signed up for. Sighing, Gianna laid down the scissors and went downstairs.

Swinging the door open, she was face to face with the last person she expected to see—Theo. He held a plastic bag from Lori's in one hand and a green leash in the other.

"Morning, Holmes," he greeted with a grin, as if his appearance on her doorstep were a normal occurrence. "Brought you some waffles."

Before she could utter a word, Bagel was brushing against her legs, tail wagging.

"I hope you don't mind," Theo said, trying to soothe the excited beagle as she jumped up and down. "I had to get her out of the house for a while, and I was already on my way over here."

Gianna reached for the puppy, cradling her in her arms. "What's going on at your house?"

"Wedding planning. The whole house is overrun with bridesmaids. Bagel started chewing on shoes, and June was practically hysterical. So I thought I'd take a walk."

She raised an eyebrow. "A walk across town?"

"Okay, I drove here. But I bought a peace offering." He raised the plastic bag in his hand. She still stared at him, skeptical. He let out a long sigh. "Alright, you caught me. It's Sunday and I know that Sunday mornings are your brunch with Valarie. Since you two aren't on talking terms, I thought I'd come and bring you some Lori's."

Her chest tightened first with gratitude until she realized what this really was. She snatched her hand away from the bag, her voice hardening. "I don't need your pity."

"It's not pity. It's waffles with extra maple syrup." Theo's lips lifted into a soft smile.

She eyed him warily, trying to figure out the aim of his game. He'd unknowingly found the connection between Paul's murder and Ollie's disappearance. He claimed he wanted in on the case to help Nathan, but Gianna couldn't help but feel the story was bigger than he let on. She could understand if Nathan were here, but he wasn't. It was just her.

As she determined Theo's ulterior motives for coming here, a voice broke through. *You choose to see the bad in everyone before anything else. You don't bother to try to look at the good parts of people.* Valarie's words were a vicious slam to her heart because they were true. Here Theo was bringing her breakfast because he felt bad, and she was searching for an ulterior motive.

"Do you want to come inside?" she asked.

"When your uncle isn't here? I don't know, Holmes. I like my body well enough without a bunch of bullet holes in it."

"Anthony won't shoot you, I promise," she said. "I'd be too heartbroken."

"I'd be pretty heartbroken too," Theo replied, matching her sarcasm.

She rolled her eyes and walked inside. "You can leave the bag on the counter. I want to show you something."

He followed her upstairs. When they crossed into her room, Theo paused.

"Your bedroom?" He made a scandalized face and raised an eyebrow. "Don't you think it's a bit too early in our relationship to be moving this fast?"

She huffed, throwing the door open. Theo stepped in behind her, but instead of joining her by the desk, he was observing her bookshelves. He stood in front of her collection of Nancy Drew books and pointed at one of the spines. "You're missing the third book."

"Theo, focus." She motioned him over to her desk, where she was still in the process of putting the board together.

"Wow." Theo picked up a stray thread of yarn. "You're really serious about this board."

"I never joke about murder boards." She watched from her peripheral vision as Theo's eyes took in the words she'd written. The tick of his eyebrow revealed he was impressed, and a little bubble of pride swelled in Gianna's chest. She'd spent a lot more time than she cared to admit.

He tapped the picture of Richard Beckett and the list of reasons she suspected him of below it. "Seems like you're stuck."

"A little," she admitted. "Emmaline said that she received her last warning from Unknown a few weeks ago, but Richard Beckett died two years ago. Richard can't be unknown."

"Maybe he had a partner." At her silence, he glanced over at her. "You already have somebody in mind."

She showed him the picture she was yet to pin up. "Dale Goodeman. Echo Falls' current Sheriff, but back then he was Deputy."

"Richard's best friend. Do you think he might have covered it up?"

She shrugged. "I don't know. Okay, I hope he didn't. He's Anthony's friend. It would crush him if Dale had anything to do with it."

"Why not ask him about it?"

She raised an eyebrow. "You want me to go up to the sheriff and ask him if he covered up one of the town's most devastating murders?"

"Why not? You already confronted a drug dealer. Might as well take it up to the next level and confront the law."

He set the photo of Richard back on the desk, his gaze roaming around her room until it settled on the top of her dresser. Theo pointed at the photo of her mother and her siblings. "Is that—"

"Mhm. That one's Anthony." She pointed to him on the right.

"He's a twin?"

"His name was Gabriel. I never met him, though. He died of a heart attack when they were eighteen."

Theo sucked in an audible breath through his teeth. "That's …"

"Terribly tragic?" Gianna answered for him. "I know. I wish I could tell you more about him, but Anthony doesn't really like to talk about his family …" She frowned as an idea occurred to her. "His family."

"Yeah, you said that already," Theo teased.

"No. *The* family. Paul's family. His mother's still alive. She could know something that could help us, or at least cross her husband off the list."

She turned to her mess of notes on her desk. "I think I have an address here somewhere—ah, here it is." She whirled around, victorious, the address in hand.

Theo plucked it from her fingers, and an expression she couldn't read pinched his face.

"What is it?" she asked.

"Paul's mother's first name wouldn't happen to be Magnolia, would it?"

"Her full name is Magnolia Beckett," Gianna said, slowly frowning. "How did you know that?"

Theo scratched at his jaw. "Well, because she's my neighbor."

TWENTY-SIX

The house looked like it had in the pictures. White house, perfectly trimmed lawn, the green hedges, and the blue front door. She spotted the giant oak tree that Paul had stood in front of in the picture she had of him. Most of the leaves had fallen to the ground, covered by a thin layer of frost. They crunched beneath their feet as they walked.

"Did you bring the stuff?" Theo called out as Nathan approached them. The wind had blown his hair in all sorts of directions, and he struggled to flatten it down once he was inside.

Nathan swung the bag off his shoulder. "Yeah, yeah, I brought it."

"Brought what?" Gianna asked as they rummaged through the bag.

"Our props," Theo grinned.

Nathan revealed a Canon camera and a tripod.

Gianna picked up the camera, recognizing the sticker on the side of it. "Aren't these from the yearbook club at school?"

"It's Christmas break—they won't miss it," Theo said as he rang the doorbell once.

The same old woman she'd seen in the front yard when she had dinner at Theo's stood in the doorway. Only at the time, she hadn't realized this was Magnolia Beckett.

"Hey, Mags, how are you?" Theo said casually.

Magnolia's eyes lit up. "Theo! How lovely to see you, darling. I wasn't expecting any visitors today." Her eyes fell on the camera and tripod in his hands. "Are you … making a movie with your friends?"

"Actually, my friends here are in the Yearbook Club," Theo said.

"Oh, that's nice. I had no idea you were in Yearbook."

"Sure am. Anyway, we were doing this thing for the club and were wondering if we could interview you."

"Interview me?" Magnolia's eyes widened in surprise, and then uncertainty. "Oh, I don't know, dear."

"Please?" Theo insisted. "It could be the favor you owe for repairing the engine on your car. We won't take too much of your time."

Magnolia let out a long sigh. "Alright. But give me half an hour to get myself camera ready."

Theo put a thumbs up. "You've got it, Mags."

Theo set up the camera in the living room. Nathan and Gianna sat on the couch, waiting while Magnolia fussed with the bracelets on her wrist. Her graying hair was curled at the ends, brushing against the long rope of pearls on her neck. She was wearing a layer of makeup she hadn't worn before, looking every bit like the woman she must have been twenty-one years ago. The mayor's wife.

Magnolia exhaled as she sank into the sofa, placing her hands in her lap. "Now what would cause you three lovely children to come and interview poor little old me?"

"Old?" Theo said. "You don't look a day over twenty-eight, Mags."

She let out a snort. "He's a flatterer, this one," jutted her thumb in Theo's direction.

"Oh, believe us, we know." Gianna smirked as she messed with her prepared questions.

Theo shook his head in mock disappointment. "I should have known you two would gang up against me the first moment you could."

"We can't help that you make it so easy."

Nathan let out a cough, smothering his laugh.

"I like her," Magnolia beamed. "You should bring her around more often. How long have the two of you been together?"

This time Nathan couldn't stop the laugh that ripped from his throat. Gianna felt the flush rising from her neck to her cheeks.

"We're not—" they both exclaimed, cutting off their protest with a glance before Gianna added, "Just friends."

"Yeah," Theo echoed, his voice surprisingly void of its teasing tone. "Friends."

"Good friends," Nathan supplied leisurely, and Gianna narrowed her gaze at him. He didn't cower under her stare but smiled brightly as if he knew something she didn't. That only added to Gianna's aggravation. Her gaze flicked to Theo, who was fiddling with the camera he'd brought for the yearbook ruse. Nothing either of them said was untrue, so why was it that Gianna couldn't place the disappointed feeling when Theo agreed with her?

She shook her head. They were in Paul's house talking to his mother. She needed to focus.

"To answer your first question, we heard that your late husband funded several programs at Echo Falls High School. Yearbook happens to be one of them," Gianna said. At least that part was true. She came across this information while digging into Richard's sordid past.

"Yes," Magnolia said. "Richard was very involved with the school. He used to be the mayor and wanted to give back to the community. He grew up in this town and wanted to improve it. And that was what he accomplished."

"Is it true that the gymnasium was named after him?" Nathan asked. Gianna's eyes widened. She hadn't made the connection between the Beckett Gymnasium and the former mayor.

Magnolia nodded. "It is. My husband was a star football player when he was younger." After a heartbeat, she added, "My son was fond of the sport as well. That's him right there."

Gianna's eyes flickered to the photo of three Becketts on the wall. "Does he still play?" she asked.

"No," she whispered. "He passed away years ago before he ever got the chance to go pro."

"I'm sorry," Gianna said softly.

"It was years ago, dear. Nothing you need to apologize for."

"But he was your son. Pain like that never goes away."

A sad smile tugged on her lips. "No, it doesn't."

"You must miss them."

"I do, every day. It's different being here in Echo Falls without them. Lonelier. You see, I'm originally from Georgia. It's where I met Richard—he was on a business trip with his father at the time, and we ran into each other one day. The next thing I know, I'm getting married and moving to a small town in New Hampshire. I regret that I didn't take Paul back to Georgia more often. All of my family is down there."

She pointed to the frames on the wall, telling them the names of each of her family members, which ones were living and which were dead, who were criminals and who ended up having good lives. The last family members Magnolia had yet to introduce were two blonde-haired girls sitting at a picnic table, eating their ice cream. If Gianna hadn't been looking too closely, she would have mistaken the girls for identical twins.

Nathan must've thought the same because he asked, "Are they twins?"

"Oh, no. But they do look like it, don't they? No, they were born nine months apart. They're my nieces, Emilia and Lorraine." A sad look washed over her expression. "Emilia passed away years ago, not long after this photo was taken. My brother and his wife were heartbroken."

Gianna found it difficult to take her eyes off the girl on the right—Lorraine. It felt impossible, but she felt as if she knew her from somewhere.

"What about Lorraine?" Nathan asked.

"Oh, poor thing." Magnolia shook her head. "From what I gathered, she had a rocky childhood. Emilia's death hit the whole family hard. Once Lorraine was of age, she left and didn't speak much to my brother and his wife afterwards. Didn't even get to see them before she passed, either. It's a shame, but every family has its quarrels." She *tsk*ed. "My Paul and Richard, for example. Those two could never see eye to eye." She grabbed her cup from the table and took a long sip.

Gianna's gaze snapped away from the picture. "What didn't they see eye to eye about?"

"Oh, I suppose Paul's future, what he was going to study in school and where he was going to go. Small things like that." Magnolia set her water down. "But enough about that. That was years ago. I'm probably boring you with all this talk."

"Of course not," Gianna chimed. "Could you tell us more about Paul, maybe? How was he in school? Did he want to follow in his father's footsteps? Does he still have friends in the area?"

If Magnolia thought any of Gianna's questions were odd, she didn't comment on it.

"A lot of kids Paul went to school with are still living in Echo Falls. My Paul had a lot of friends. He was quite popular at school. Oh, how the teachers all loved him. And he was excellent at football. My husband used to host dinners for the team before big games. The house would be full of teenagers running around everywhere."

"Really?" Gianna asked, reflecting back on her conversation with Paul's former teammate, Benjamin. He'd said the mayor was late to dinner. Either his memory was messed up—which she seriously doubted—or Magnolia was lying.

"Mhm. I have to say, it's still a bit lonely from time to time. Empty house, no husband, no son. Although, Paul's godfather does come by sometimes to check on me. You've probably heard of him. Dale Goodeman. He's the sheriff. He was best friends with my husband, practically his brother. Every week he brings flowers to my Paul's grave." Magnolia shook her head. "He loved that boy as much as I did. Between us … I've always had a feeling he's blamed himself for Paul's death."

"Is that so?" Gianna asked slowly.

Magnolia nodded. "He was away at his niece's birthday party in Maine that night. He thought that if he had been there, somehow he could've prevented what happened."

Gianna and Theo exchanged glances. If Dale had an alibi for that night, he couldn't be Unknown.

"What about Paul's friends? Do you know if any of them are still in the area who might be up to giving a few words about Paul?"

"Oh, dear, you're so sweet," Magnolia gushed. "I can give you a few emails of some of his teammates. I'm not sure where Mason is these days, but as for Paul's other friend …" She trailed off, fidgeting with the pearls around her neck. "I'm sorry. I don't want to speak ill of anyone."

"It's okay," Theo reassured her. "If there's anything you don't want on the record, we can keep it off the final paper."

Magnolia took a moment to think about it. And then: "Paul did have another friend he'd gotten close to during his last year in high school. One that his father didn't approve of and, if I'm being frank, neither did I. He was a pleasant boy to our faces, but he had this look in his eye I didn't like. Plus, he always reeked of cigarette smoke. I didn't like him around my son. I told Paul so, but you know teenagers. The more you push in one direction, the more they'll push back. Oh … what was his name?" She frowned, distressed about this gap in her memory.

"I'm sorry," she whispered. "I had a stroke a few years ago, and I find myself forgetting the simplest of tasks now. I can see his face clear as day in my mind. I might have a picture somewhere."

She walked over to the entertainment center and rummaged through the cabinets.

"Was that Paul's?" Nathan asked, pointing to the miniature police car by his head.

"Yes. He used to play with it when he was younger. It was his favorite toy. When he was little, he always said how he'd become a police officer one day, just like his Uncle Dale. Once he got older, he became more serious about following in his father's footsteps and getting into law school."

Gianna wondered how Richard felt knowing his son worshipped Dale more than his own father—if that played any role in his disdain for his son.

"Ah, here it is." Magnolia walked back to the couch and set the photo album on the table. "Dale gifted Paul a camera for his fifteenth birthday. He was always running around snapping pictures, taking that goddamn camera everywhere. I have my first memory card from that year, but I never found the second one from Paul's last two years in high school. Paul must've lost it. I printed out all the photos on the camera. Here's one." She laid the book on the table for them to see. "That there is my Paul right there in the middle. To his left is Mason Ramsay, and here's the boy I was talking about."

Gianna's gaze drifted across the paper until she reached the last boy. Every bone in her body went rigid as she stared at the boy on the right.

"Ah, yes, I remember now," Magnolia was saying, but Gianna could barely hear her over her heartbeat thumping in her ears. "His name was Royce. Royce Reyes."

TWENTY-SEVEN

His name was Royce. Royce Reyes.

Magnolia's lips continued to move, but her words were lost to Gianna's ears, swirling around in the air around her head like little wisps. For a split moment, she was no longer in Magnolia Beckett's brilliant living room. She was thirteen years old again, in the back seat of a bus, staring out the window with a reddened nose and a twenty-dollar bill stuffed in the pocket of her jacket.

And then she was staring at a bald man behind a desk.

"Royce Reyes," she repeated for the third time.

The bald man shook his head, peering at her from beneath his glasses. "There's no one here by that name."

"But he's here," Gianna insisted, her voice raising an octave. "I know he is. Dad!" She ran past the man.

"Hey, you can't go in there!" the man yelled.

"Dad!" she cried. "Dad!"

"Gianna?" Theo's voice coaxed her from the memory.

Her head snapped up. Theo and Nathan were both looking at her with wide eyes. She swallowed, blinking away the images. She searched for an excuse to give them, but all that came out was a choked, "I need some air."

She didn't look at them as she hurried out the front door. She'd made it halfway across the porch before her breaths started to come out wheezy and short.

He was a pleasant boy to our faces, but he had this look in his eye I didn't like. I didn't like him around my son.

The picture of Royce flashed in her mind.

Her father.

How was any of this possible?

"Holmes."

It was Theo. She hadn't realized he followed her outside. She turned to him as he reached an arm out to her. She grasped the sleeve of his shirt as he centered her, pulling her back to Earth as she tried to even out her breaths. In the midst of all this, she wanted to laugh. Of course, Royce found a way to disrupt her life when he wasn't even in it to begin with.

Once her heart stopped trying to punch its way out of her chest, she let go.

"That man back there in the picture," Theo murmured. "That was your dad, wasn't it?"

"Yes," she said shortly, not wanting to talk anymore about it. "I'm ready to go back inside."

Who knew what was going through Magnolia's head right now? Gianna surely ruined their chances.

"No need," Theo said. "I told Mags you weren't feeling well and that I was taking you home."

Gianna whirled back to face him. "Why would you do that?"

"Because you were clearly upset and you're in no state of mind to keep doing this."

She shook his arm off of her. She had it all planned out, everything they would ask her. "I'm fine," she gritted out. "Let's just go back inside."

Theo ignored her. "You're upset. You're in no shape to talk to Mags."

The fact that what he was saying was true only made her more bitter. "Oh, because you know how I feel?" She wanted to laugh. Theo knew *nothing* of how she felt.

Gianna's dad was a sore subject that she'd never brought up with him or Nathan. The thought of him was like poking a fresh bruise. The only other person outside her family aware of what occurred on her thirteenth birthday was the one person she couldn't speak to—Valarie. Valarie would understand. But they still weren't talking. Gianna had no right to go to her now when things were still tense between the two of them.

"What did Mags mean when she said all that stuff about your dad?" he asked.

"I can imagine a few things," Gianna stated dryly.

She'd read the reports. She'd heard the way Irene and Anthony referred to her dad, as if they were tasting something sour. It went past disapproval for her dad. She couldn't blame them. The last time any of them had seen Royce was when he had stolen three hundred bucks from Irene's purse and disappeared into the night.

Her father was not a good person; this she knew. But she had never imagined him to be as close to someone like Paul Beckett. A *friend.* That was the word Mags used.

A thought occurred to her, one that made her sick to her stomach. Could he be involved in Paul's death? A part of her didn't want to consider it, but doubt gnawed at her.

She knew what had to be done. Royce could have information about Paul. He could know something that Mags didn't. She was going to have to do the one thing she had refused to do for the past five years.

She was going to go and talk to her dad.

Log #12, Dec. 20th, 2023

Transcript of Second Interview with Benjamin Taylor

Gianna: Do you recall a student by the name of Royce Reyes at Echo Falls High?
Benjamin: The name sounds familiar, but I'd have to put a face to it.
Gianna: Here, I'll send you a picture of him.
Benjamin: I just got it. Oh—that guy. Yeah, I remember him. I think he dropped out of school at some point, but I saw him around at a lot of parties.
Gianna: Was Paul at any of these parties by chance?
Benjamin: Yeah, Paul was at a lot of them.
Gianna: Did you ever see them hanging out together at the party?
Benjamin: Couple of times. But that wasn't unusual. Everybody knew Royce knew a dealer from the city. Everybody knew to go to him.
Gianna: So Royce was Paul's dealer?
Benjamin: Um … not exactly. Hey, this isn't—nobody else is going to hear about this, right? You're not, like, writing it down or anything, are you?
Gianna: No, I'm not writing anything down. You were saying?
Benjamin: Paul never took the drugs Royce gave him, at least none that I ever saw. But he did take the drugs and sell them to other people at the parties.
Gianna: Paul sold drugs? You're absolutely positive?
Benjamin: Seeing how I bought from him myself, yeah, I'm pretty fucking positive.
Gianna: And you didn't think it was a good thing to mention the last time we spoke that Paul was dealing drugs at parties?
Benjamin: Well, you never asked, and frankly, I don't see how any of this is relevant. It happened years ago.
Gianna: Why would Paul sell drugs?
Benjamin: Extra cash? How the hell am I supposed to know why people do half the shit they do?

Gianna: Mason Ramsay would know, though, right?
Benjamin: He was Paul's best friend, so I guess. Although he wasn't too happy about Paul dealing.
Gianna: What gives you that idea?
Benjamin: I overheard them talking in the locker room one day after practice. Ramsay was telling Paul that it was too risky and not worth it. That they'd figure out another way.
Gianna: Figure out another way?
Benjamin: I don't know what he meant either. But I assumed Mason's nerves were all scrambled up because that one guy just died of an overdose. Cops were locking down on that shit.
Gianna: Did this guy die at a party?
Benjamin: I think so. You know how it is, though. One kid dies, and suddenly the whole town's cranking down on drugs, police are going around questioning everybody. Mason was probably worried Paul was going to get caught at some point.
Gianna: But Paul didn't quit.
Benjamin: No, he didn't.

***

After her talk with Benjamin, Gianna searched up more about the student who died of a drug overdose. All that came up was an old news article stating that a high school student at Echo Falls unfortunately passed away and his death was believed to be caused by drugs in his system. They kept his name out of the local news, most likely for the family's sake. It was a dead end there.

However, she did find a picture online of the house where the student died. It was a corner-street view, catching the ambulance and the crowd outside watching as the paramedics rolled the body into the back of the ambulance. She zoomed in to the photo, hoping to find someone she recognized who was there that night, and she found him.

The photo was grainy, but she zoomed in as much as she could, and it was definitely Paul. Polo shirt, khakis, and his watch on his wrist. He was standing off to the side, behind the police officer keeping everyone away from the paramedics. She could make out the haunted look on his face. The only reason she could think of why he looked so horrified was A) he knew the student that overdosed, or B) he sold him the drugs that killed him.

She sighed, sitting back in her chair. Maybe she was pulling at a loose thread. Maybe Paul had never seen a dead body and was simply sick at the sight of it. She didn't know.

But what she did know was that Paul's family was one of the wealthiest in Echo Falls. So why would he be dealing drugs at house parties? It didn't make sense. Maybe Royce would be able to fill in the blanks.

She wasn't so sure about Dale being involved in Paul's death anymore. Bringing flowers to your godson's grave could easily be seen as a way to remove guilt, but continuing to do it years after his murder and his killer was put in jail? Highly unlikely. There was also the way Mags described his and Paul's relationship. It seemed that Paul looked up to Dale a lot, more than he looked up to his own father. Gianna even looked into Dale's alibi that night and sure enough, his niece's birthday fell on the same day as Paul's death. It was official—Dale couldn't have been there to cover up Paul's death.

She logged all her notes from her journal and closed her laptop. Her gaze drifted to the alarm clock on her desk. It was late.

She wasn't sure if she was ready to see Royce tomorrow. She needed to rethink what she was planning to say to him.

She needed to get some sleep.

TWENTY-EIGHT

Gianna crept down the stairs, avoiding the creaky step. She had made it as far as the front hallway when she heard Anthony's voice behind her. "Where are you sneaking off to in such a hurry?"

Caught red-handed.

Gianna turned around, summoning the most casual face she could. "To the library."

"The library?" Anthony lowered the volume on the TV and looked over his shoulder. "During break?"

Gianna gave him the story she had prepared beforehand. "I just want to get a head start on next semester's work."

"Who's driving you there?"

That was the question she was expecting. "Theo's driving."

Anthony raised an eyebrow.

"I take it the date went well then," Irene said, giving Gianna a knowing smile.

Gianna nodded and smiled, but it didn't reach her eyes as she waited for Anthony's verdict.

"He better have you home by seven. And let me know when you're on your way back."

Gianna withheld a breath of relief. "Yeah, I will. See you guys later."

"Love you too, kiddo."

She hurried down and out the front door before her nerves gave her away and the guilt threatened to smother her. *Remember what happened the last time you tried to go and see Royce?* But that was different. That was back when Gianna believed there was still a shred of goodness to be found in her father. She wasn't that naive girl anymore.

Theo's truck was parked at the end of the driveway. She got inside and closed the door with a huff. Nathan was helping out at his mom's work today, so it would be the two of them.

"Alright, Holmes," he said, messing with the GPS on his phone. "Where to?"

She gave him the name of the ice cream shop, and he typed it in. As Theo drove, she ran over all the facts she had gathered in the past night. She knew for a fact that Royce had been out of prison for a solid four years now. His longest record yet, miraculously. Perhaps he did turn over a new leaf, but Gianna highly doubted it.

With a little bit of internet sleuthing and some help from Nathan, she was able to track her father to his place of work: Coraline's Sweet Shop, an ice cream shop an hour and a half outside of Echo Falls. This entire time, he had lived only an hour and a half away. Gianna knew better than to be surprised, but the shock still hit her all the same.

Theo's fingers strummed against the wheel as he turned down the road. He'd been awfully quiet since she got in, and she could tell he was holding something back.

"I can hear your thoughts from here," she said.

He glanced at her, then back at the road. "You're Sherlock Holmes," he teased, "Not a mind reader."

So that's how he wanted to play this?

"So you don't think that me going to talk to my father, whom I haven't seen in five years, isn't a bad idea?"

"Oh, I think it's a horrible idea, but I also know you could care less for my opinions."

"That's not true," she said. She ignored his stare burning into the side of her face as she filled him in on her talk with Benjamin. "It's not much, but it's a start."

Theo pulled into the parking lot. "You don't have to do this, you know. Nathan will understand if you don't."

"Are you sure it's Nathan telling me or you?"

"Why can't it be both?" he said softly. Their eyes met for a brief moment, and that was all it took for her to see the concern in his eyes.

Little good it would do. She had decided the moment she got into the car. "I'm doing this, Theo."

"Okay, then you don't have to go in alone. I'll go with you. Together, remember?" The promise that the three of them made by the lake echoed in her head.

"No," Gianna said quickly. This she had to do alone. "I'll try not to be too long."

"Holmes." She paused, glancing back at him as he weighed his words. Coming to a decision, he said, "If you need anything, just holler."

She tilted her head once. "I will."

Unspoken words flitted through his eyes, and she turned toward the door before she could ponder over them. A couple was leaving when she reached the entrance. She stood off to the side to let them through when she spotted Royce. Her feet were rooted to the tiles. He looked older than she remembered. There were lines around his eyes since the last time she had seen him.

He glanced at her and then back at the mop in his hand. Gianna stilled, her breath halting. The hum of the coolers drowned out her heartbeat. There was zero recognition in his eyes. She didn't know why that surge of disappointment hit her and scolded herself for feeling it. He had n't seen her in years. What did she think was going to happen? That this was going to be a tearful reunion with hugs and apologies?

Royce propped the mop against the wall and rounded the counter. "What'll it be?" he asked, without looking up.

It was as if the words had been sucked right out of her. She stared, gawking like a five-year-old seeing Superman. At her silence, Royce glanced up and paused. His reaction wasn't instant. At first, he simply blinked, and then his brows furrowed. His jaw slackened, mouth opening and closing and opening again, as if he were still processing what he was seeing. She waited, fingers fidgeting with the strap of her bag, as he figured it out.

"Hey, Dad." The word felt foreign on her tongue. He'd always been Royce in her head.

"Gianna," he breathed in disbelief. "You're here." He rounded the counter, stopping right in front of her. "Why are you—how are you—"

He held up a finger and turned his back on her. "Larry! I'm taking my thirty!"

A bald man wearing an identical uniform to Royce's appeared from a door behind the counter. His gaze traveled from Royce to Gianna. He tilted his head toward her. "Who's this?"

"My daughter." Royce set his arm around her shoulder and squeezed her to his side. "And I'm going to have lunch with her."

Larry eyed Gianna as if she'd sprouted wings. "Since when do you have a daughter?"

"He doesn't," she sniffled, yanking herself out of Royce's grasp. "I'll be outside waiting."

She didn't bother waiting for a response, turning around on her heel. She was grateful for the fresh air, not realizing how badly she needed it. A minute later, Royce emerged from the shop without his hat or apron.

"There's a burger shack right next door," he said. "You like burgers, right?"

Gianna had a million retorts for that, all jabbing at something he should know about his daughter, but she came here for a reason and Royce's bad parenting was not the main one. So she said, "Yeah, I like burgers."

They ordered their food and found a picnic table nearby. A million questions that had nothing to do with the case were on the tip of her tongue. *How long have you been here? Did you know where I was? Did you care*? She bit them all back, swallowing another fry.

"Uh, so, tell me, how have you been? How's school?"

She glanced at her lap. "It's been good."

"I take it you're going to Echo Falls High unless that uncle of yours finally left town."

"Nope. We're still there."

"I take it he doesn't know you're here." He dipped a fry in his ranch—the same as her. She wished that didn't matter to her, that she didn't notice the small similarity. "How is Anthony?"

He said *Anthony* like someone would describe a foul odor.

Gianna picked at the pickles on her burger. "He's good."

"He, uh, still a detective?"

"He's a police officer now, actually." *You should know. After her mom died and you went to jail, Anthony had quit his job to do yours.*

"Huh. Really? That's interesting." Through a mouthful of fries, he asked, "How about Irene? What's she up to these days?"

"She runs a law firm in New York."

Royce chuckled. "I wish I could say I'm shocked. Irene always was the ambitious type. The kids at school used to call her a shark. Always studying, working hard."

Gianna blinked, upset with how he spoke of her, but then she processed his words. "You went to school with Irene?"

"Yeah. We were in the same year. I dropped out the moment I turned sixteen, though. Nothing you can say will make me stay in high school. Good riddance to that. She'd probably tell you something entirely different."

"She doesn't really talk about her high school years that much," Gianna said. "What was high school like for you?"

"Besides being a complete waste of my time?" he retorted. "Come on, I know you didn't come all this way to listen to your old man talk about his old high school days."

"You're right," she said, and before she could stop the words, she blurted, "I want to talk about my mother."

This was evidently not the answer Royce had been expecting. She watched with satisfaction as he slowly picked up a fry and chewed on it. He stared at the ground a long time before he said anything. "You look a lot like her, your mom."

Gianna snorted. It was a common answer, a safe one. Everyone always said she looked like Elena.

"Well?" Royce prompted, taking a deep breath. "What do you want to know?"

Gianna's breath froze with anticipation. Years and years of unanswered questions and a yearning to know, and they were all right in front of her. She didn't know what question she wanted to ask first.

"How did you two meet?"

"At a party. Dawson Jeckles' house—ah, I remember. He threw the craziest parties. Your mom was standing off to the side in the room by herself. I accidentally bumped into her. She'd been standing by the wall alone—she wasn't much of a social butterfly, your mom."

"There's nothing wrong with that," Gianna said, strangely defensive.

He chewed on another fry. "I never said there was."

So they met at a party. For some reason, Gianna hadn't pictured her mother as the party type. "What about her friends?"

"Elena didn't have many," Royce said. "She mostly kept to herself. Preferred to be alone."

"Did you exchange letters?" The image of her mother's memory box flashed through her mind. "Stuff like that?"

A wrinkle appeared between his brows. "Letters? Uh, I called her house phone sometimes, when her brothers weren't home." Her disappointment must have shown on her face because he straightened his shoulders and asked, "What else do you want to know?"

Get him to talk about Paul.

"What about your friends in high school?"

Royce chuckled. "What about them?"

"Do you still talk to any of them?"

"There wasn't anyone worth keeping contact with," he said. "But enough talking about me. I want to know how you've been holding up, kid."

"There's a memorial at school this weekend that me and some of my friends were planning," she said. "Some boy who died years ago. Um, his name was Paul, I think?"

Royce stilled. "Paul Beckett?"

"Yeah, I think that was the name. Did you know him?"

"Not really." He shook his head, scratching his jaw. "But I heard about his death. Some psycho killed him, apparently.

"Oh." Gianna feigned surprise. "He was murdered?"

"Mhm. Brutally. I heard it was so bad that the police didn't want the family to see the body." Royce shook his head as his phone buzzed on the table. He picked it up and glanced at the screen before setting it face down.

She raised her eyebrows. "Do you need to get that?"

"Nope," he said, his eyes meeting hers. Eyes that looked so much like hers. "Where were we?"

"Paul Beckett. You were talking about his murder."

Royce opened his mouth before the phone buzzed again. His jaw ticked in aggravation as he picked up the phone and this time Gianna caught a glimpse of the caller ID: *Rams*. As in Mason Ramsay?

Royce silenced his phone. Gianna cleared her throat. "Can I get some more fries?"

"Uh, sure. I'll be right back." Royce wiped his hands on a crumpled napkin and grabbed her empty tray. As soon as his back was to her, she snatched his phone off the table. There were two missed calls from *Rams* and a message. She clicked on the message, and it prompted her for a passcode. Four digits. Probably not her birthday, then, but that came as no surprise. It would have to be something simple, something Royce would remember …

She typed in 1-2-3-4 and it unlocked.

Gianna let out a small huff of breath. She went to messages, being sure to glance up every few seconds to check that Royce was still in line. The line was moving fast. She had to hurry. Her palms began to sweat. She pressed on *Rams*.

My kid just showed up at my work.

No shit, Rams texted.

Yeah, heading to lunch.

Why is she here?

No idea. About to find out.

Alright. Good luck.

She scrolled up but there were no more texts between them before today. He must have deleted them. She huffed. Why had Royce lied to her about keeping in contact with any of his friends from high school?

"A basket of fries, as requested," Royce announced.

Gianna startled, nearly dropping the phone on the ground. Royce set the basket in front of her. He glanced at the spot where his phone had been. "Where's my phone?"

"Oh, sorry," Gianna said, quickly grabbing the phone. "Birds were flying around. I didn't want them messing with anything."

"I doubt they like the taste of phone," he chuckled, holding his hand out. She placed it in his palm and he glanced at her oddly. *He knew.* Or he at least didn't believe her excuse. She had to change the subject.

"So, back to you and Paul," she began.

He sighed, wearily. "Ugh, this again? I already told you I didn't know Paul that well. I doubt I can help you much more, Gia."

She tilted her head to the side. "Really? I could've sworn you knew him well enough, seeing how you dealt drugs with him." Royce's head snapped up. "Unless I heard wrong."

His jaw tensed. "Where did you hear that?"

"So it's true. You and Paul used to deal drugs out at high school parties."

"You've been asking about Paul this entire time. Why?" He seemed to put two and two together. "Oh God. This isn't some detective thing, is it? Because I hate to break it to you, but someone beat you to it. Paul's killer is rotting in a jail cell as we speak."

Unease nagged in her chest. "What if he isn't?"

"What?"

"I said what if he isn't Paul's killer?"

He snorted. "Of course he is. They had evidence and all that stuff." He looked at her expectantly, as if waiting for her to contradict him, but she wasn't going to give away her only leverage.

"Why was Paul dealing drugs?" she asked instead.

Royce sighed again. "I don't know."

"He dealt drugs for you for how long and you have no idea why? It never occurred to you to ask?"

"As long as I had my money, I didn't care. Now I don't really feel like talking about this anymore so—"

"The kid who died of an overdose," she interrupted. "Did Paul sell him drugs?"

Royce leaned back. "Paul didn't have anything to do with that. Some kid took too much and that was it," he said. "Why don't we skip to the question you really want to ask: Did I kill Paul?"

Her fingers curled around the table. She cocked her head to the side. "Did you?"

TWENTY-NINE

"Did you?"

Her father's eyes locked with hers. "No. I was at home with my buddy all night. Did Anthony put you up to this?"

"No, he didn't—"

"Because if he did—"

"This is my investigation," she declared. "Not Anthony's."

"What's there to investigate, Gia? They found all the evidence to lock away Freddy Atwater."

"Not everything," she said. "They didn't find the watch."

He scoffed, his voice hardening. "You're more like your uncle than you think."

"Don't talk about him," she spat, her voice dangerously flat, even though her fingers clenched into the fabric of her jeans. "You have no right."

"No right?" Royce scoffed. "I'm your father."

Father. Gianna could laugh at the word. "You didn't even try to get custody of me after Mom died."

Royce sighed, running a hand over his face. "Believe me, kid, I wanted to. So badly. But things were complicated at the time. I was in a bad place."

"A place that you chose. You could've at least checked up on me. Or did they not have phones where you were?"

"That's not fair."

No, what wasn't fair was growing up without her father.

"I came to see you, you know," she said. "On my thirteenth

birthday. I stole money from Anthony and got a bus ticket to go and see you, and you weren't even there."

He glanced away. "I heard about that. I didn't know until later. I … I got out early for good behavior."

The world stopped around her. *He knew.* He knew that she came to see him, and he hadn't even bothered to see her.

"You didn't even try."

She hated how little the words made her seem. Like she was that little girl again, helpless and desperate.

He sighed. "Gia …"

"You don't have an excuse!" she yelled. "You weren't in prison. You weren't locked up in a cell."

"Fine. You want the truth?" He slapped his hand against the table. "Your uncle warned me off. Told me he would use his friends high up to make sure I never saw you again."

"You're lying," she snapped. "Anthony wouldn't do that."

He raised an eyebrow. "Are you sure about that? How well do you think you know your uncle, kid? Maybe Anthony isn't all the saint he pretends to be. I remember him and Gabriel strolling down the halls like they were kings of the world back in high school. They gave Paul a run for his money."

She shook her head. "We're not talking about him. We're talking about you! You could've called. Or sent a birthday card at least."

"What would you have me do, kid?" Royce asked. "Fight him? He's a cop."

Yes, she thought achingly. *Fight to be a good, if not at the very least a decent father. Or you could've been there where I thought you were five years ago on the one day I needed you more than anything.*

But Gianna didn't say any of this. She knew the truth now, and it left a bitter taste in her mouth. Royce didn't care. Maybe he'd feel a bit guilty, but at the end of the day, he'd still be able to sleep at night.

"Thanks for lunch, Royce, but I'm going to leave now." She stood, ignoring the small sound of her heart chipping away when he didn't go after her and she didn't look back.

She didn't know what stung worse—the fact that he didn't try to stop her or that he was as bad as Gianna thought him to be in the first place.

In that moment, she wished she had given Theo a different answer in the car. She wished she hadn't gone alone.

Theo was standing against the car when she approached. He straightened up when he saw her. "Hey," he said. "How did—"

"I don't want to talk right now," she said, not meeting his eyes. She wasn't in the mood to hear *I told you so* from him. Silently, they got in the car and drove off. Theo's gaze drifting toward her as he drove, but she ignored him, staring out the window at the blurred trees.

As Theo was pulling off to their exit, a song started playing on the radio that made him smile. "This is a great song," he said.

She glumly glanced at the name. "Hurricane" by Lord Huron.

"Do you know the band?" he asked.

"Never heard of them," she muttered.

Theo gasped. "I don't think we can work together anymore, Holmes. This is the best band in the world."

She lifted her chin. "The best?"

"Yep. And this album is their best work. Just you listen. You'll thank me after you hear the whole thing." Theo played around with his phone before a new song came on the radio.

They listened in silence—or at least Gianna did. Theo was mouthing the words and strumming his fingers to the beat, humming the tune off-beat and wonky.

"Oh God," she groaned, placing a hand on her face to stop the smile from spreading, "please stop. You cannot sing."

Theo placed a hand over his heart. "That hurts, Holmes."

He stuck to humming the rest of the songs on the way there, and despite her sour mood, Gianna found her foot tapping to the beat.

By the time they made it back into Echo Falls, night had fallen and the only light on the street came from the moon hovering over the truck, watching them below. Theo pulled onto the end of her road to let Gianna out, but her hand paused on the door as the realization sunk in. She didn't want to go back yet, alone with her thoughts about today. Theo didn't remark on it; instead, he put the truck in park and sat back in his seat.

"You know," he drawled, "out of all this time we've been chasing leads and following clues, you never told me what made you want to become a detective in the first place."

Her lips lifted. "My mom." She glanced up at him to see his face was blank. "You don't seem too surprised by my answer."

He lifted a shoulder. "I suspected it, given the way you talk about her."

Did she talk about her mother that much? Gianna never thought about it. Ever since she was little, all she wanted was to do good in the world, like her. She knew it was not the same—Elena actually saved people's lives. There were people standing on Earth because of her. But then Gianna thought about the people who were alive but not living. Families with missing relatives or mothers who couldn't grieve their children because there was no body to bury. She often thought to herself, *What about them? Don't they deserve some closure to move on with their lives and live, too?*

She wasn't breathing the air back into someone's lungs, but maybe she could make breathing a bit easier for some people.

"What happened with your dad?" he asked softly. She knew that he wouldn't ask her again if she didn't want to answer, that he'd drop it altogether, but she found herself wanting to talk to him, all the words pouring out of her like a waterfall.

"He says he has nothing to do with Paul if that's what you mean," she said.

But then again, Royce had lied to her his entire life. He could be lying about this, too.

"He did sell drugs, though. He was Paul's supplier. Which means more than likely one of them knew the kid who overdosed at that party."

"That would explain why Paul looked horrified," Theo suggested. "Maybe he knew the guy's family, knew that they'd be out for revenge."

"Could be, unless my father beat him to it. He was selling drugs at that party, too. Maybe Paul felt guilty, wanted to go to the police, and my dad made sure he could never do that."

"Okay, enough about the mystery now. How are you doing?"

She shrugged, looking away from him, uncomfortable with the sudden change of topic. "I'm fine."

He grumbled something under his breath that sounded an awful lot like *bull.* "You just saw your dad, who you haven't seen or heard from in years, and all you have to say is, 'I'm fine?'" He shook his head. "Nah, I'm not buying it."

She fought to keep the irritation out of her voice. "Okay, maybe I'm not fine, but that doesn't mean I want to talk about it. Do you tell your friends every time you're upset?"

"I wouldn't know," he admitted. "I don't have any." His gaze narrowed at her when she scoffed. "What?"

"No friends? You're kidding, right? You're one of the most popular kids at school. All anyone talks about is the basketball legend Theodore Rodriguez—"

Theo groaned. "Sure. Yeah. I'm popular the moment I get here because I can play a stupid sport. My teammates are cool and all, but they've known each other for years. Some of them since they were babies." His voice lowered. "I know it's ridiculous to feel like I don't belong. It's like I'm on a float in the middle of the ocean, drifting farther and farther away from land by the second. I felt that way for months—no, longer than that, even before we moved here. Until recently."

She looked over at him. "What changed?"

"I met you and Nathan." His eyes met hers. "That's what changed."

"Oh."

"Oh." Theo tapped his fingers against the steering wheel.

Hot shame whirled up her chest. Theo just shared what was probably the most vulnerable thing about himself. She knew he wouldn't expect her to do the same, but she wanted to. "I just don't know why I thought it would go any differently," she whispered. "Why I thought he could have possibly changed."

He looked up at her. "Our parents aren't always what we expect them to be."

Surprise flooded her. "What are you talking about? Your dad seems great."

He shrugged. "He wasn't always. When I was younger, I always thought he was more like a ghost. There but not there. Translucent. And I understood a bit. I knew it couldn't have been easy raising a child all on your own after watching your wife slowly die, working long hours to make sure there was food on the table, a roof over our heads, hardly ever home. And then suddenly, a few years ago, it was like he was just there and he had all these expectations."

The medals and trophies are in their living room. Mr. Rodriguez's adamance about Theo going pro in basketball.

She pictured Theo as a little boy home alone eating dinner without his father and felt a surge of anger. "That's still no excuse—"

"I know, Holmes," he said, amusement flickering in his eyes. "I used to be angry at him all the time. For the longest time, I held onto my anger. I used to think there wouldn't be a time when I couldn't be in the same room with him at all."

"What changed?"

"I found a letter from my mom. Technically, I wasn't supposed to read it until my eighteenth birthday, but when I found it I couldn't help myself. And I'm glad I did read it then because reading her words, reading how much she wanted to live and how she wanted me to live, made me realize that life is too short. I can spend the rest of my life angry with my dad for not being more present for a decade, or I can forgive him and leave those grudges behind and look forward to having more decades with him. The time in the past I'll never get back, but I'll lose more if I hold onto my anger."

"That's … awfully mature of you."

"I'm capable of it every now and then." A beautiful grin spread across his face, and Gianna had to force herself to tear her gaze. She glanced out the windshield.

"What was her name?" she asked.

It was a long time before he answered her. When he did, his voice was hoarse, as if he hadn't spoken for days. "Raine. Her name was Raine. You know, she's actually the reason I'm doing this. Can I show you something?" She nodded, and he pointed to the glovebox. "There's a paper in there."

She did as he said, pulling out the piece of paper, faded with age. *Raine's Bucket List,* it read. *Sky dive on a birthday. Join a band. Go to a concert. Hike the Appalachian. Solve a mystery. Surf on California Beaches.*

The list went on, almost to fifty. Gianna's gaze glued on to the fifth item listed.

"You're doing the stuff on her list," she said.

Theo nodded. "Everything she was never able to do."

"Well, based on what you've told me about her, I think she would want you to tell your dad the truth about basketball."

He laughed, shaking his head. "Not a chance, Holmes."

"Why not?"

"I mean … What else am I going to do? Build robots for the rest of my life?"

"Why not? If it makes you happy?"

He smiled. "That's one of the things I love about you, Holmes. You're not afraid to be yourself. To go for it."

Her hand that had been previously resting on the armrest brushed against his, and every nerve in her body came to life at that small contact. Neither of them moved their hands.

Gianna shifted in her seat, her neck warm. "So is this your way of telling me to let go of my anger and forgive my dad?"

"Well, that's up to you. Do I think the guy deserves your forgiveness after today? Definitely not. Not in a hundred years. But I'm less worried for him than I am about you. You don't have to forgive him, but you don't have to give him any more of your anger either."

A somber silence passed over them, nothing but the low hum of the radio and the croon of Ben Schneider's voice.

"Theo?" she whispered as the introduction to "The Night We Met" began playing.

"Yeah?" His eyes turned to her, tracing her outline in the silhouette of the moon. His hand was still on hers, fingers tracing the lines of her palm. Everything she had been bottling up since she started the case was on the tip of her tongue. *Tell your friends before it's too late.* She didn't want to ruin this moment by worrying.

"Thank you." She didn't say thank you for the songs, for bringing breakfast to her house, or all the times he made her smile with his ridiculous jokes. She didn't have a way with words—not like Valarie when it came to Liam or Irene when she was passionate about something—but she hoped he heard it all the same.

"Anytime, Holmes."

He walked her to the front door. She waited until his truck drove off before closing the door behind her. She followed the light of the lamp to the living room where Anthony was passed out asleep on the couch, the TV still playing loudly. She grabbed the blanket from the other couch and draped it over him before flicking off the lamp and heading to her room. Irene's door was closed and the lights were off. She was probably already asleep as well.

The moment Gianna stepped into her room, cold air washed over her.

She paused.

The only thing she could hear was the TV in the living room and her own breathing. She moved deeper into the room.

Her shoes stepped on something as she flicked the light on. That's when she saw them—papers scattered on the floor of her room everywhere, her desk and its contents upturned.

Her laptop was flipped open. Her notes—torn. Everything had been ruined.

The watch.

She ran to her bed, feeling beneath the mattress. *Please be there, please be there.* She pulled the watch from its hiding place and sagged against the mattress in relief. Her eyes traveled to the papers on the ground. She bent down and, with shaky hands, picked one of them up.

THIS IS YOUR LAST WARNING, GIANNA. STOP LOOKING.

They all said the same thing. Gianna released a shuddering breath. Before she could begin to wonder how this happened, something moved from the corner of her eye. She turned to the window, just in time to see a dark figure dash away.

A scream caught in her throat.

She ran over to the window but couldn't make anything out in the dark. She was just seeing things. Nobody was on the roof.

She leaned on the windowsill, and her fingers brushed against something soft. A piece of black fabric, as if someone's shirt had gotten stuck while they tried to escape.

Her stalker had been in her room.

THIRTY

She didn't sleep.

She didn't so much as tear her eyes away from the window all night, a helpless feeling deep inside her bones that rattled her to her core. In case they came back.

They were in my room.

A cold settled in her bones, one she hadn't been able to banish for hours. The dark shadows in her room resembled human-like figures, their eyes following her from every corner of the room. She clutched the watch in her pocket. There was no way she was letting it out of her sight now. Her stalker—Unknown—had been waiting for her to get back. They wanted her to panic, to get the watch so they knew where it would be. She couldn't let them get it.

A knock at her door startled her. Anthony's face filled the doorway. "Whoa," he chuckled at her jumpiness. "Didn't mean to startle you there, kiddo. Good, you're awake. You have a visitor."

The last person she expected it to be was her former math teacher.

"Hey there, Gianna." Mrs. Delgado's smile was too wide to be genuine, her eyes darting away as she spoke. "I know it's break, but I wanted to stop by and give this to you." She held up the pink folder in her hands and set it on the edge of the bed. "The homework syllabus you wanted for your friend."

Homework syllabus? There was no homework syllabus. No, this was something else.

Anthony hovered by the doorway. "Aw, that's sweet of you, Christine. You didn't have to do that."

"Yeah," Gianna echoed. "Why did you do that?"

"I just wanted to do the right thing." Mrs. Delgado cleared her throat. "I better get back. Andrew and I are going up to see his family in Maine for the holidays."

"'Course," Anthony said. "I'll walk you to your car."

Before she left, Mrs. Delgado looked over her shoulder. "Merry Christmas, Gianna."

Gianna waited until they were gone to reach over to her bed and rip the folder off it. Inside was a single paper with writing on it. It took her a moment to realize that the words and numbers were an address.

Mason Ramsay's address.

She picked up her phone, about to message Theo and Nathan, when her eyes stopped at her desk. It was Sunday. Nathan had tutoring lessons. As for Theo … She'd been researching all night while sleep evaded her. A rush of guilt passed through—she hadn't meant to discover what she had. But then she remembered what she found and, more importantly, that Theo hadn't been entirely truthful to her or Nathan.

Theo? Thank you.

Anytime, Holmes, he'd said, his eyes twinkling in the moonlight.

Had that been a lie, too?

Her fingers curled around the paper with Mason's address. No, she would do this alone.

She got dressed and hurried downstairs. As her foot hit the last step, she heard Anthony's stern voice, "No. For the last time, Irene, it's not happening."

"But if you'd just consider—"

"What is there to consider?" The plates clattered, echoing throughout the room. "This house is our home. Echo Falls is our home—Gianna's home. I'm not taking her away from here in the middle of her last year of high school."

"I've been trying to get you to move out of this place for years, Tony. This place isn't healthy for either of you. Don't think I don't see how it affects her. She has one friend. She doesn't care about prom."

"So what, she doesn't want to go to a dance? You know she's not crazy about all that stuff."

"Her?" Irene countered. "Or you?"

"I don't care about that stuff," Anthony said. "You know I don't."

"That's exactly my point. Gianna looks up to you. She follows what you do. She wants to make you proud."

Anthony sighed. "Irene …"

"I'm just saying that the fresh scenery would do her some good. A fresh start—for both of you," Irene whispered.

"Elena asked me to look after her little girl," Anthony said, in a tone Gianna had never heard him use before. "And that's what I'm doing. What I've been doing for thirteen years. My work is here in Echo Falls. Gianna's home is here in this town. Besides, there's no point in moving right before she graduates. She's almost done with school. And as for all the other stuff, she's almost an adult. She can choose to do whatever she wants to do in her spare time. As long as it's not illegal."

"So if she chooses to go to school to become a criminal investigator, you'll support it?"

Gianna's breath caught in her throat.

"I'm done talking about this, Irene," Anthony said. She listened to his footsteps' fading and Irene's sigh. Gianna clutched her bag tighter to her chest and slipped out the front door, reminding herself why she was doing this in the first place.

***

She followed the sound of wood chopping to the side of the cabin.

"Mason Ramsay?" Gianna asked, although there was no need to. Despite the photos she'd seen in the paper from over a decade ago, Mason looked nearly identical, with only a few lines around his eyes that weren't there before and the beard around his face. Her mind was barely processing it.

This was Mason Ramsay.

The man Mrs. Delgado had an affair with five years before.

Paul Beckett's best friend.

"Can I help you?" he asked gruffly, switching the ax into his left hand.

Gianna swallowed. "I'm—"

"I don't care to talk to reporters," he snapped, before she could get another word out, glaring at the notebook in her hands. He went to swing the ax again. *Whoosh.* Another block of wood fell to the ground. "Go get your news somewhere else."

He thinks I'm a journalist. She took a step forward, clearing her throat. "I'm not a reporter."

Whoosh. Another block fell. "You look like one."

A prickle of irritation rushed through Gianna. "I'm a student at Echo Falls High," she stated. "I just wanted to ask you a few questions."

"Can't imagine why," he huffed.

"Twenty-one years ago, near an abandoned farmhouse on Topsfield Road, Paul Beckett, your best friend, was murdered." Mason halted the ax mid-swing. "A man named Freddy Atwater was found guilty of his murder. They got the wrong guy."

Mason turned to look at her—*to fully look at her*—and whatever he saw had him narrowing his eyes. "Who are you?"

She gave him the fake name she came up with: "Gwen Smith."

He kept in contact with Royce and she couldn't let him make the connection.

"Okay, Gwen Smith." His fist clenched around the handle of the ax. "What is it that you want from me?"

"Five minutes."

He shook his head. "I don't talk about that anymore."

"Don't?" she said. "Or won't?"

Mason's tongue poked the inside of his cheek. "What's it to you anyway, kid? It happened way before your time, and lord knows reporters were all over the case then. There's nothing left to say."

"They put an innocent man in jail."

Mason let out a loud laugh that had no warmth. "Innocent wouldn't be the word I'd use to describe old Freddy. What, are you part of this fan club or something?"

"Freddy Atwater didn't kill Paul," she stated.

"Oh, yeah?" Mason's eyes glinted. "Where's your proof?"

Stuffed in the bottom of my backpack. But Gianna couldn't tell him yet. "Let's just say that the proof I have is enough to possibly reopen Paul's case."

Mason snorted. "Sure, kid."

She huffed, crossing her arms. "It doesn't matter whether you believe me or not."

He seemed to think about this for a moment before reluctantly saying, "Okay, kid. I hear you. I'll answer your questions, but first I'm going to need a drink." He slammed the ax into the tree he'd been cutting and headed off in the direction of the cabin. Gianna stood, stunned, before scurrying behind him. By the time they made it up the porch steps, Mason had already exited the cabin with a cold beer in his hands.

"Want some?" He tilted the bottle in her direction.

Gianna raised an eyebrow.

An amused grin spread across his lips as he brought the bottle to them. He propped his legs on the stool in front of him. "Alright, then. Let's hear these questions."

But there was a more pressing thought on her mind. "Why the sudden change of heart?" He had been adamant about not talking to her. She found it awfully suspicious that he had suddenly agreed to talk to her.

"You caught me on a good day." Mason shrugged, taking another swig of his drink. "Is that your only question?"

"No." She straightened her shoulders. "Where were you the night Paul died?"

He laughed. Took another swig of his bottle. "I went to his house with him after school, but I left around seven-thirty."

"Where did you go after that?"

"Home." He met her gaze. "Do you want my home address and social security number while you're at it?"

Unfettered, she said, "Did Paul have any enemies?"

That wiped the smirk off his face. "Enemies?"

"Anyone who held a grudge against him or wanted to hurt him."

Mason thought about this, tapping his knee. "I mean, we weren't exactly the most well-behaved kids, if that's what you mean. I can think of a neighbor or two who'd been fed up with us kicking the ball over into their yard. We did cause some ruckus back then. Did things that I'm ashamed to think about today. We were kids, but we were old enough to know what we were doing. Paul liked to mess with some of the other guys in our class, get on their bad side. So to answer your question, yes, there were a lot of people who did not like Paul and despised his father even more, but I wouldn't go as far as to call any of them enemies."

"We're talking about something bad," Gianna said. "Something Paul would've done that was unforgivable. For someone to hurt him as they did. Can you think of a time that could've been?"

Mason sighed, shaking his head. "It was a long time ago. We were kids … we did a bunch of stupid things. It could be any number of them."

"What about Paul's dad?"

"Richard?" Mason's eyes narrowed. "What about him?"

"What was their relationship like?"

Mason sat back against the wall, seemingly battling between telling her and his loyalty to his best friend's memory. Gianna reached over to her tape recorder and clicked pause. Mason glanced up, eyebrow raised.

"Everything will be off the record."

She set her notebook and pen down for good measure. This seemed good enough for Mason because he continued.

"They weren't your typical father-and-son relationship. Paul and his dad … they didn't see eye to eye much. Caused a rift between them. But Paul always wanted to impress him. He did everything his dad expected out of him. Football. Applied for the same colleges Mr. Beckett went to. Got into studying law. He'd even stand up for the bastard at school when kids would start talking about him in front of Paul." Mason sighed wearily. "Although, no matter how much Paul tried, it was never enough for Richard."

Gianna shifted in her seat. "Did the mayor ever seem abusive toward Paul?"

"Where in God's name did you hear that?" Mason asked.

"I've heard rumors," she said.

Mason ran a hand down his face. "I forgot how small this town is."

"So was he abusive toward Paul or not?"

Mason took another sip of his beer. "I suspected it. Paul was wincing, blaming it on taking too many hits at practice, but he was like that even out of football season. I asked him about it many times. Each time I confronted Paul about it, he denied it. I never had concrete proof until one night Paul showed up at my front door, his jaw black and blue."

Mason glanced down at his hands. In a low voice, he said, "That was the first time he ever came to my house after a beating."

"What changed?"

"The circumstances. From my understanding, it all started out with Paul's grades and college. His dad was pressuring him about not needing to apply to all these secondary schools, something petty like that. And then, at some point, the conversation took a turn to Lina, whom Paul's dad didn't approve of. Then again, Richard never approved of any of Paul's girlfriends. But this one—this girl was different."

"Girlfriend?" she gasped. "Paul had a girlfriend?"

Mason nodded. "Lina. They started dating a few months before Paul died."

"Mags—I mean, I've never heard anything about a girlfriend until now."

"That's probably because she and Paul's relationship was a secret. Paul knew his dad wouldn't approve of her and he was afraid that he'd try to make them break up. And her family wasn't exactly all that approving of Paul either. It was easier to keep it quiet, at least until Paul was at college. He even had a secret phone so they could talk to each other without his dad catching. 'Course, that didn't last long."

"Was Lina ever a suspect in Paul's murder?" Gianna asked.

Mason shook his head insistently. "She had an airtight alibi that night. All her family vouched for her. Besides, I saw her the first day when we heard the news that Paul was missing. She was a wreck. Besides, Lina wouldn't do anything like that. Her and Paul … they were years in the making. Paul had a thing for her since we were kids. It was hilarious, the way she rejected him all the time. Even when we were kids Paul wasn't used to being told no—but Lina never gave in. Until suddenly that year something changed and she finally said yes.

"Paul was over the moon. He talked nonstop about Lina, how the two of them were going to move in together after she graduated, how he was going to marry her someday."

Gianna's eyes widened at the words *love* and *marry*. This wasn't just some girl Paul dated on a whim as an act of teenage rebellion against his father. This was a girl he saw a future with. And yet, Gianna was only hearing about her now.

"Paul's dad caught them together one day at the grocery store, and not long after, the argument happened," Mason said. "He didn't think Lina was right for Paul for all the same reasons he didn't think any of the girlfriends before her were. They weren't rich, or their parents didn't have connections, or they were distractions, but Lina, Lina was a different story."

She tilted her head to the side. "How so?"

Mason's finger swirled around the rim of the bottle, as he was lost in thought. "Lina made Paul happy. Hell, if I could see it then everyone could see it, including him. And that bastard saw how happy she made Paul, and he wanted to make Paul just as miserable as he was. Only this time, he hadn't counted on Paul disobeying him. Richard froze his bank accounts. Since Paul was still a minor, he was able to control all his money, cutting him off from his trust fund."

"Was that when he started selling drugs?" she asked.

Mason looked up, startled. "How did you—"

"A witness saw Paul selling on several occasions."

He slowly sank back in his chair. "A witness, huh?"

She didn't break his gaze. "They also said you weren't too happy with the idea."

"Did they now?"

"Mhm. You know, I couldn't figure it out until now—why one of the wealthiest kids in all of Echo Falls would stoop as low as selling drugs. But I think I figured it out now."

Mason had been the last piece of the puzzle. Now that she knew for certain Richard was abusive towards his son, and about Paul's girlfriend, it was all so obvious she wanted to smack herself for not seeing it before.

"Paul was planning to run away, wasn't he?" she said.

Mason sighed. The action made him seem ten years older. "I told him it was a horrible idea. Repeatedly. After that day he showed up on my doorstep, things had changed. He always talked of getting out of town one day, but it became more serious after that. Before, I didn't get it. Paul had everything. Nice big house, a car, a trust fund. It wasn't until he showed up all bruised and broken—saw with my own eyes what Richard did to him—that I understood. So I tried to help. He wanted to leave town with Lina. I got him to all the parties and introduced him to some people I knew who bought regularly.

"At first, it was small stuff. Marijuana, painkillers, stuff like that," he said quietly. "But the worse things got at home, the more desperate Paul became. He started selling opioids, fentanyl, some stuff he didn't even know what it was, but he sold it anyway. Then someone died, and it—that's when I told him I couldn't stand around anymore and watch him destroy himself."

"There's just one thing I don't understand," Gianna said. "Why didn't Paul report to the police what his dad was doing to him? Wasn't Paul's godfather the deputy? Couldn't he have done something? Arrest Richard?"

Mason laughed dryly. "I told Paul the same thing. Dale didn't have a clue what Richard did to Paul and Miss Maggie. Richard was good at putting on an act—no one would have voted for him if they knew how he really was. He fooled everyone, even his own best friend. Paul wasn't sure Dale would believe him, or worse, that Dale would side with his father. Besides, even if Dale was an option, Richard had friends in higher places. No judge in the state would take on a case against him. And there was also the case of Miss Maggie."

"What about her?" Gianna said.

"She wouldn't go against Richard. She … she was afraid to go up against him, and that made it more difficult for Paul. Because if she sided with Richard, then Paul wouldn't stand a chance. So Paul kept selling drugs."

"The student who died," she said, eyes flicking up. "Was Paul the one who sold it to him?"

"No." Mason shook his head. "Paul didn't have anything to do with what happened to him."

"You knew him? The student who died?"

He nodded. "He was in the same year as us. We knew him."

"Who was he?"

Mason waved a hand. "It doesn't matter now. His death has nothing to do with Paul."

"But could someone have thought he did?" she asked. "A friend or the family of the victim?"

"No." Mason shook his head, brows furrowing. "That'd be impossible."

"What about Lina, then?"

"What about her?"

"Were her feelings the same for Paul? Did she want to run away with him as much as he wanted to?"

"Yeah, I always thought it was. At first, I was a bit hesitant, but I found it safe to say that she fell for Paul just as hard as he fell for her."

"Where can I find her?"

Mason's expression froze on his face. He leaned forward, running a hand over his face, as if thinking over his next words. "I … erm, listen kid—"

He was cut off by a phone ringing. His phone. He picked it up, frowning at the screen. When it rang again, he swore. "Sorry, but I'm afraid the questions are going to have to end there. I've got to go."

Gianna jumped to her feet. "Wait. Lina—where can I find her?"

But Mason had already disappeared inside the house, leaving her on the front step.

Log #13, Dec. 23rd, 2023

Suspect List (revised)

Richard Beckett

Abusive toward his family

Was "at the office" during his son's murder, but no witnesses to give him that

Rerunning for mayor = sympathy votes

Royce Reyes

Violent past

Drug dealer that was seen often at parties with Paul

Short temper

Mason Ramsay

Motive = jealousy

One of the last people to see Paul before his death

Friends with Royce

Lina

Secret girlfriend

Possibly knows something about Paul's death?

Drug overdose victim

Revenge?

THIRTY-ONE

SIX WEEKS LATER

She slid a hand over her eyes, forcing them to remain open. The bright hue of her laptop screen glowed back at her, the words beginning to blur together. *Paul Beckett … anonymous tip.*

"Who gave the anonymous tip?" she murmured to no one, adding it to her chart.

It had only been a few hours since she started doing more research, organizing all her work. She left the lamp on and the curtains closed—windows locked always. She didn't sleep. This had been her routine for nearly the past month and a half. Between cramming for exams and spending all her time on the case, Gianna had little time for anything else.

She hadn't spoken much with Nathan or Theo lately. She still saw them at school, of course, but somehow always managed to come up with an excuse to leave. She couldn't stand to see the hope dimming in Nathan's eyes as the case took longer, or the questioning in Theo's gaze whenever it was directed at her.

She had been distant since the night they went to see Royce. She kept telling herself it was because she needed to focus on finding Ollie, but really it was because Theo would see straight through her. There were so many moments she came close to telling him about the notes. He would tell her to stop with the case, and she wouldn't let that happen.

She hadn't heard from Unknown since that day he was in her room. She didn't know if she should be relieved or worried that he left her alone. Maybe he was watching her and saw she was nowhere near the truth. Or maybe he was biding his time, waiting for the right moment to strike.

She was so absorbed in her work that she didn't hear the knock at her door at first.

"Hey," Theo greeted, poking his head through the open door. The hallway light filled her room. "Your aunt said I'd find you holed up in here."

"What are you doing here so early in the morning?" Her eyes blinked rapidly, adjusting to the light.

Raising his eyebrows, Theo strolled over to her window and threw open the curtains, revealing the afternoon sun. "It's almost one o'clock."

She looked at the corner of her computer and saw it was 12:59.

"Sorry." She sighed, running a hand over her face. She must've looked a mess—hair askew from restless sleep and most likely dark circles hovering under her eyes. "I've been doing some research and I lost a little track of time."

"Only a little?" Theo mused, helping himself to the ground beside her bed. He grabbed a pen that she had knocked to the ground hours before and twirled it in his fingers. "Out of curiosity, how long has it been since you last slept?"

"That's irrelevant." She turned back to her computer, shoving the stacks of papers to the side. Every part of her screamed to tell Theo about what happened the night they went to see Royce. But she knew he would want her to stop with the investigation. "We're so close, Theo. I can feel it in my bones."

"Holmes," Theo said softly, and when she didn't look away from the screen, he reached over and shut her laptop.

"Hey!" she protested, standing to her feet. "What was that for?"

"I think you've done enough research for one day." Concern lined his brow. "This isn't healthy, Holmes. I want to find Ollie too, but not like this."

"But we're so close. I've narrowed down Paul's killer to several suspects. One of them has to be our guy." She grabbed the papers off her desk to show him. "All we have to do is find evidence or get them to confess." She hesitated. "I … I also spoke to Mason Ramsay."

"You did what? When?" Theo's head snapped up to hers. "Why didn't you get me?"

"Weeks ago. It was a last-minute thing," she lied. "Anyway, he told me everything about Paul and Richard. Mrs. Delgado was right—Richard was abusive towards his family. Which puts him at number one on my list."

"Mason told you everything? Just like that?"

"Yeah, so?"

"It's a little odd, don't you think? That he'd tell a random girl he'd never met personal things about his best friend's life?"

The same thought had crossed her mind, but she didn't want to think about that now. She reached under her bed to pull out her murder board. She had to fix it after Unknown had broken into her room, although it hadn't turned out as it had the first time.

"Why he told me doesn't matter. We have more information now. Paul had a secret girlfriend, and he was in the same class as the boy who overdosed. A lot of the kids that attended that party were from Echo Falls High—word could've gotten around that Paul dealt drugs, and that it was his dealings that got that kid killed. His friends or family could have blamed Paul and wanted revenge. I don't exactly have a motive for the girlfriend. Few people knew she and Paul were involved, and those who did say the two were head over heels for each other. She'd be the last person they'd suspect."

The only issue with the girlfriend was that Paul's face had been beaten before he died of an injury to his head.

She looked over the pictures of her suspects. They were so close to solving this. Once they had their person, they could give the evidence to Anthony, and then Ollie would no longer be a suspect in Grant's murder, and he could come home. Nathan would have his brother back. Grant's real killer would be put behind bars, and the case would be closed. Anthony would see she had what it took to be a detective.

"I told Nathan we would go by the ruins." She turned to Theo. "He wants to check the place out, scope it for clues."

She didn't have the heart to tell Nathan they wouldn't find anything. It was almost five years since Ollie went missing, and any evidence would have long washed away, but it was the least she could do to appease him.

She expected Theo to be enlightened about this, but he looked uncertain. "Why the frown? This is good news." She tilted her head to the side. *What was his problem?*

"It's just … you've known this all for weeks and you're just now telling me?"

"Do I need to update you on every single thing I do in my life?" she asked defensively. "I told you the talk with Mason was a last-minute thing."

"I know what you said." He looked at her, jaw tense, as if trying to figure it out. "I'm just not sure you're telling the truth. And I'm not sure why you'd lie. Or why you've been avoiding me and Nathan for the past few weeks."

"I haven't … I haven't been avoiding you." She lowered her gaze to her papers. "I've been busy with the case."

"You were busy with the case before, but even then you had time for us."

She lowered her gaze. Theo swallowed, and she watched the lump go down his throat. "Are you sure this is still about Ollie?" Theo asked. "Or is this you trying not to be like your dad?"

The papers felt light in her hands. "Don't you dare," she said coldly. "Do you think I'm that selfish? I want to find Ollie."

"I know you do," Theo whispered. "But ever since you visited your dad, you've been acting differently. Burying yourself in research and obsessing over the case."

"Obsessing?" she scoffed. "If I recall correctly, you begged me to let you in on the case. You want to find Grant's murderer just as much as I do. And maybe not for the reasons you say you do."

His shoulders stiffened. "What's that supposed to mean?"

"Nothing. I …" She faltered. Her skull pounded, her throat dry. She shouldn't have said that. This was Theo. She could trust him. She was just shaken with Unknown; that was all. "I'm sorry."

His jaw ticked. "Have you spoken to Valarie lately?"

The change of subject caught her off guard. "Uh, no. What does that have to do with the case?"

"It doesn't. That's my point. Finding Ollie isn't going to make you any more like your dad, the same way it won't make you the picture you paint of your mom in your head," he said. "If you let this case consume you, you'll only be proving your uncle right and hurting yourself in the process."

She forced herself to listen to his words, to process them. She knew they came from his heart, that he wasn't saying these words out of spite. "Okay," she whispered. "I'll … I'll take a break for now. The ruins … they can wait."

His lips tugged upward, relief shining in his eyes. They were the words he desperately wanted to hear.

She couldn't meet his eyes as she asked, "So, what was it that you came here for?"

Theo looked sheepish. "It's, uh, not a big deal, but our next robotics competition is coming up in a few weeks. And good news: it's at Echo Falls this time, so no one will have to drive far for it. And I was wondering …"

"You were wondering?" She raised an eyebrow.

"I was wondering if you wanted to come and watch. It's pretty boring and all, but you know if you're free … You know it would make Nathan really happy to see you there, too. He misses you."

"I spoke with him yesterday."

"Okay, maybe I miss you."

Her eyes flicked up to him. Theo slid his hands into his pockets, gaze darting over her books, cheeks pink at the soft admission. He wasn't the only one flushing red.

"Theodore Rodriguez," she said in a light voice, "are you saying that you miss me? You know there's such a thing as texting."

"I did. Several times, in fact, if you deigned to look at your phone in the past century." He grinned, standing to his feet. "I've got to go before I'm late for practice. Text you later?"

"Yeah."

He left and she was still on the ground. His words echoed in her head. *Finding Ollie isn't going to make you any more like your dad, the same way it won't make you the picture you paint of your mom in your head.*

She forced his words out of her head. Theo was wrong. She picked up her phone and called Nathan. "Meet me at the ruins in fifteen minutes."

THIRTY-TWO

Unknown had taken her tape recorder.

Gianna hadn't realized it until she was already out of the car, her hand drifting to her coat pocket to find it empty. Her chest tightened. Anthony had given her the tape recorder for her tenth birthday. She'd taken care of it ever since, and now it was gone, most likely forever.

She spotted Nathan leaning against one of the stone walls and briefly forgot about her sudden sadness.

"Hey." Cold air swirled around them as he spoke, pushing off the stone wall. "Uh, what exactly is this place?"

"The locals call it Hollow Hill. Why they call it that is a mystery."

"I'm a local," he said. "I don't see anything mysterious about a bunch of rocks."

A smile tugged on Gianna's lips. "The mystery is that no one knows who built it or what the ruins originally were. Only guesses."

He stopped by a peculiar looking rock, running his hands over the grooves and dips. "What did they guess this was?"

"A sacrificial stone."

Nathan ripped his hand away from the stone.

She laughed, the sound echoing through the ruins. "I'm kidding. That's just a rock."

"Hilarious," he deadpanned. While he ran his scrutinizing gaze over the ruins, Gianna unfolded the map they'd originally marked in Theo's house.

"Paul's body was discovered not far from here," she murmured, body twisting so she was facing the woods. "And Grant was found a few miles down the road that way."

They came upon a hill and kept walking. She frowned. In the distance was a farmhouse. Vines crept over the house, twisting through the dislodged planks and dirty windows. She recalled reading an ad years ago for this land to sell, but it was clear they had no luck finding a buyer for it.

A chill ran down her spine as they grew closer. Something bad happened here. She didn't know how to explain the feeling.

"Doesn't look like anyone's lived here for decades," Nathan said. He tried the door, but it was locked. He pressed his hands against the window, squinting to see inside. "Agh. The window's too dirty to see anything. No wait—I think I see—is that a cooler?"

Gianna moved to stand next to him when she stepped on something loud. She bent down to retrieve the crushed beer can.

"I think some of the kids from the school come down here," she said. "According to the map there's a barn just over the hill. We could check it out."

Nathan tossed one long glance at the house before following her down the steps.

The barn looked in even worse condition than the farmhouse. The large red doors groaned as she and Nathan pushed them open. Patches of grass and wildflowers sprouted through the dirt floor. A stack of hay sat in the corner, molded planks of wood leaning against the side of the left wall. Streams of sunlight poured through the gaps in the roof.

Gianna glanced over the rusted farming tools on the old table. Her eyes snagged on the coil of rope at the end of the table. It looked brand new compared to the rest of the tools. Had someone else been in there?

Something snapped somewhere in front of them. She whirled around. This time it was closer; someone was coming.

Nathan stilled, hearing the sound as well. Gianna put a finger to her lips and pointed at the stack of hay right beside the door. He nodded, tiptoeing over in that direction.

"Someone's out there," he whispered. "Who do you think it is?"

She didn't have time to answer. The shadow emerged from the woods, the silhouette of something in his hand. Gianna sucked in a breath, scared of giving herself or Nathan away. Her heart pounded ferociously as she peered over the hay, trying to get a good look at the stranger. At first, the sun blocked her view of the person, but when he stepped closer, enough for her to make out the features of his face, recognition flared in her eyes.

It wasn't a stranger at all. It was Mason Ramsay.

And he was holding a gun.

Out of all the places he could be, he was at the same place Paul died. Why? *And why did he have a gun?*

"Gianna," Nathan whispered. A note of horror filled his voice, and that had her whipping around. Nathan's face was drained of all color as he stared at something out of her peripheral, toward the woods where Mason had come from. She followed his gaze, blinking away the spots in her eyes as if to make sense of what she was seeing. Something dark red, the color of blood. No, not just the color. It *was* blood.

Gianna shuddered, turning away from the red trail, and her eyes fell on something right by Nathan's shoe. Slowly, she crawled closer toward the hay and plucked it from the stack. A bubblegum wrapper. Just like the one they'd found in Ollie's desk.

Beside her, Nathan stilled. "That's his," he whispered. "It has to be. He used to chew that gum all the time."

Gianna didn't know how to tell him the wrapper looked brand new and would have easily been dropped by anyone, perhaps Mason. Luckily, she didn't have to. Mason disappeared over the hill, out of sight, and they had their chance.

"He's gone. We should go," she whispered.

Nathan wasn't paying attention. "Ollie could be here. What if the cooler in the farmhouse is his?" Desperation clouded his eyes. "The blood—what if it's Mason? What if he's been holding Ollie all this time? You said you spoke to him right? He's a possible suspect."

Was he? Gianna thought back to her conversation with Mason. The soft way he spoke of his friend, the look in his eyes—the one you only got when you lost someone important to you. The confidence in his tone when he claimed Freddy was guilty. Uncertainty poked at her like a needle.

"It doesn't matter what I think now. We've got to get out here before he comes back."

"Then go if you want." He stepped back. "I'm not leaving without my brother."

"We'll take the bubblegum wrapper to the police and all the evidence I've found," she promised. "If Ollie's being held against his will, they'll—"

"What evidence?" Nathan hissed. "We don't have anything against Mason, or anyone for that matter. They won't do anything because they all think Ollie left. I don't care about them anyway—all I care about is getting back my brother."

"Nate, think about it." She moved in front of him, drawing his gaze to her. "He has a gun. If Ollie's here, how do you expect us all to get away when he can shoot us anytime in the back?" Nathan looked down at his shoes. "We'll come back another night, prepared and with proper backup. But if we go right now, we could lose Ollie for good."

Nathan seemed to be fighting against himself. "Okay." He let out an angry breath. "Okay."

Gianna didn't look back as they raced to the car. Not when she started the engine or pulled out into the road, far away from Hollow Hill. She didn't look back once.

When they were halfway back to their neighborhood, her phone rang. Nathan glanced at the screen. "It's Valarie."

"Answer it," she said. A moment later, she heard a sniffle on the other end. "Gianna?"

"Valarie," Gianna breathed. Another sniffle—as if she'd been crying. "What's wrong?"

"We—don't freak out, but I'm at the hospital right now. I was in an accident and Vivian was in the car and I just … I want to talk to you. Do you think—"

"I'll be right there," Gianna said, without hesitation.

***

Gianna sat beside Valarie on the hospital bed as she recounted what had happened. Valarie was still shaken from the whole ordeal, but she managed to pull herself together to string along the story. "Mom got held up at work, so she asked me to pick up Vivian from daycare.

Everything was fine up until we left the daycare. I got on the main road and started driving but when I tried slowing down, the brakes wouldn't work. Liam managed to pull the car off to the side but we wrecked another car. Vivian could've been hurt."

"But she wasn't," Gianna reassured her, rubbing soothing circles on her back. "None of you were really hurt."

"But it could've happened. All because of me." She buried her face in her hands, tears streaming down her face.

"Hey." She moved closer so she could rub circles on her back. "This isn't your fault. It was an accident."

"I mess everything up. My parents' marriage. Tons of my relationships." She sniffled. "Even us."

"You didn't mess anything up with us," Gianna stated firmly. "That was all me. You were right about everything. I shouldn't have accused Liam like that. I should've gone to you when I first suspected him. I'm sorry."

She snorted. "I'm sorry, too. I forgave you eons ago. I just … I guess I couldn't get over my pride. And … and I was jealous."

Gianna frowned. "Jealous? Of what?"

"You and Nathan I suppose."

"Nathan?" she exclaimed.

"It's silly, but you and him were always off doing your mystery solving. I knew it was because you were looking for his brother, but a part of me was worried that you preferred spending time with him than me and that was the reason." She sniffled. "It's stupid, I know."

"It's not stupid," she said. Gianna told Valarie everything she'd been holding inside. How down she was feeling about the dance, her odd behavior, and even the letters she found in the box Irene gave her.

"A letter to you?" Valarie exclaimed. "What does it mean?"

"I don't know," Gianna admitted as one of the nurses walked in.

"You can come see your sister now," she told Valarie.

Valarie darted up, and in her hurry, knocked over her bag. The contents of the bag scattered over the floor.

"I've got it," Gianna said. "Go check on Vivian."

Valarie gave her a smile and followed after the nurse. Gianna slipped off of the bed and began picking up everything off the ground. A handful of coins, half-used lip-balms, unused plastic straws and an expired coupon to Bath & Body Works. Gianna let out a little snort as she picked up the trash—

She froze, every bone in her body turning to ice. The red ink flashed its teeth tauntingly at her. The same red ink in her bag and in her room. *No.* She picked it up and flipped it over. On the back there were no words. Only a number scribbled. With trembling hands Gianna pulled out her phone and dialed it.

"Hello, Gianna. This is your last warning," the voice said. "Stop looking for Oliver Kipman."

They were using a voice changer, so she couldn't tell if she knew the man or not. Darn it.

"Who are you?" she demanded. "Why are you doing this?"

They didn't bother with an answer. "Destroy the evidence. All your tapes. Get rid of the watch. I'll know if you won't."

"You were in my room the other night. Why didn't you do it then?"

"Because I wanted you to take me more seriously. You've seen what I can do, Gianna. How is your friend doing, by the way?"

Her fingers trembled around the phone. "Valarie had nothing to do with this," she seethed.

"I agree. But you brought her into it when you didn't heed my warnings the first time around. Destroy the evidence, Gianna. And if you even think of going to the police, the next breaks I'll cut will be that lovely aunt and uncle's of yours. Or maybe your boyfriend with the blue truck. I haven't decided yet. And there's always Oliver Kipman's baby brother to think about. I wonder how he'd feel about your boyfriend. They spend so much time together. It would be a shame for him to lose another brother in his life."

"Don't touch them," Gianna pleaded. "They're not a part of this. They had nothing—"

The voice cut her off. "Then do as I say. Destroy it all tonight."

The line went silent. Gianna grasped the wall to keep herself from falling. She grew dizzy for a moment before she pulled herself together. Her fingers trembled as she sent a quick text to Valarie and Nathan and left.

She knew what she had to do.

THIRTY-THREE

Take your computer and the watch to the lake by Topsfield Road. Throw it in and walk away. No more questions about Paul or Ollie. This is over.

Her heart sank into the pit of her stomach as she watched all her work drown. Tears ran down her face, and she wiped them away with her sleeve. All that was left was the watch.

Her fingers ran over the initials carved there. Paul's face flashed through her mind, then Mags and Ollie's. If she threw it in that lake with the rest of her stuff, Carrie would lose any chance of proving her father's innocence. Nathan wouldn't find his brother. Mags wouldn't know her son's true killer.

But everyone would be safe. The danger would be gone.

A twig snapped from somewhere around her. Her head snapped up, eyes scanning the woods, but all she saw was the trees. It could just be an animal passing through.

Or she was being followed.

Her grip around the watch tightened. She stood still for several long moments. She didn't hear any more movement, but it didn't mean they weren't there.

"I'm sorry, Mom," she whispered before tossing the watch into the water.

She wasn't like her mom after all. She was no detective; she was not brave. She wasn't breathing the air back into anyone's lungs—she was watching them drown.

***

Theo and Nathan came to see her later that night.

She noticed the headlights of Theo's truck outside her window. Watched as Irene went out to greet them. She cracked the window silently and caught the last part of the conversation.

"… maybe you can talk some sense into her," Irene said.

So Irene had called them. She should've known. When Gianna had returned from the lake, she walked straight past her aunt and uncle and upstairs to her room. They had knocked on her door a few minutes later, probing her with questions and failed attempts to get her to eat until she asked them to leave.

She saw the worry in Anthony's gaze, but her bones felt too heavy to fix it. The irony was that Anthony was right after all. She didn't have what it took to be a detective. She knew that now.

She had already planned on what to say when the knock came at her door.

"Come in," she said, her voice hoarse. The two of them walked in slowly, a wary look on their faces.

"I'm sorry for leaving you behind at the hospital," she said to Nathan. "How's Vivian and Liam?"

"Not a single hair on Vivian's head was touched," Theo announced. "Liam, on the other hand, was a bit bruised up, but nothing serious. They sent him home, but June insisted he stay over at her house for the night."

Gianna's shoulders sagged with relief, but it was short-lived.

"What happened? Why did you leave?" Nathan asked.

"Nothing. Everything's fine," she said flatly.

Theo's eyebrows pinched, and she tore her gaze from his. *He knows.*

Nathan, however, was oblivious to Gianna's inner turmoil. "I've been thinking more about what you said. There's only so many places he can be keeping Ollie. I think we should go to Mason's cabin. We'll wait until he leaves and search the place. He might be keeping Ollie there. That, or somewhere else."

"No," she said.

Nathan spluttered to a stop. "No?" He frowned. "No, as in not today or no, as in no, it's a bad idea?"

"No, as in I'm not doing any more of it at all."

"I don't understand," he said. "What do you mean you're not doing any more of it?"

Gianna swallowed, forcing herself to meet his gaze. "It's simple. I'm done with all of this. I'm done chasing leads that go nowhere."

"But you can't just give up."

"Holmes," Theo said softly. She didn't return his gaze. He would see it in her eyes that something was wrong, and if he called her out on it, she was afraid she might confess everything. She had to do this, no matter how much it hurt her to.

"Someone has to say it," she continued. "I mean, even if we find a way to prove Ollie's innocence, it won't be enough to point the finger at the real culprit. It's a lost cause."

"You know that's not true! That's my brother you're talking about," Nathan seethed. "What happened to wanting to find the boy who saved your life all those years ago? How did he go from that to being a lost cause?"

"The people closest to us aren't always what they appear to be. Sometimes we see the things we want to see, not what's actually there. I wish," her voice cracked, "that things were different. That Ollie wasn't a killer."

"What do you mean by *wasn't*?"

"He's not coming back, Nathan," she said, in the most unemotional voice she could muster. "It's time you accept that. If he were, he'd be back by now."

"That's bullshit!" He stepped forward. "You know, I thought out of everyone in this town I could trust you. But I see it now. You're just as bad as the rest of them, unwilling to look past someone's face and see the person beneath."

Nathan turned to leave.

"Nate." Theo reached out an arm to stop him, but Nathan trudged past him, and in his haste bumped into her dresser, knocking the picture frame of her mother onto the floor. The glass shattered into pieces, scattering across the floor.

"Just let him go," Gianna whispered, her eyes still on the shards around her desk.

Theo turned to her. "What happened?" When she didn't answer, he cupped her chin, turning her toward him. "Holmes, look at me. Gianna, look at me, please. What happened?"

"Nothing happened," she insisted. "It's like Nathan said. I gave up."

"That's a lie. I know it is, and I know you. Something happened for you to say all that to Nathan." His eyes searched her face for an answer. "What aren't you telling me?"

She squeezed her eyes shut. *If I do this, he'll be safe.*

"I should be asking you the same question." The words came out cold and harsh.

Theo stilled.

"When were you planning on telling us?" she asked. "Or the question I should be asking is whether you were ever planning on telling us at all?" She looked at Theo now, realizing how easily she had been fooled. "The real reason why you wanted to join this investigation—

"Gianna—" he began.

"—is because you're related to Paul Beckett."

After the visit with Mags, Gianna couldn't stop thinking about the girl on the wall, how familiar she had looked. *So eerily familiar.* So that same night that Unknown had been in her room, when she couldn't sleep, she started to do her own digging into Mag's family. She found herself back at Paul's obituary, where they listed his deceased family members. His cousin, Emilia, the blonde-haired girl on the right, had passed years before. But she had a sister. *Once Lorraine was of age, she left and didn't speak much to my brother and his wife afterwards. Didn't even get to see them before she passed, either. It's a shame, but every family has their quarrels.*

What was it that Theo had told her? *Apparently she didn't get along with her side of the family, so I never knew them either.*

Little popped up when you typed *Lorraine Hall* into the search engine, and the first link was an obituary. There wasn't much written, but it mentioned Lorraine's fiancé and three-year-old son, Theodore. She nearly fell off the bed reading it.

Gianna waited for Theo to deny it. To tell her she was wrong, but she knew he wouldn't. He couldn't deny what was right in front of her eyes. *They had the same crinkle in their eyes when they smiled.*

"How long have you known?" he asked.

"Not long after we spoke to Mags." She was embarrassed to admit to herself and to him that she waited that long for him to tell her. For some ridiculous reason, she had placed her faith in Theo. Of course, now she saw that she had been wrong, and he had no intentions of telling her anything.

Theo nodded.

"Is that all you have to say to me?" she asked. "Your mother was Paul's cousin. Mags is your great-aunt. You've been hiding this from me all along and—"

"You're right," Theo said, his eyes pleading. "I hid it from you and I shouldn't have, I know. I'll tell you everything you want to know, but first, you have to tell me what's going on. I know something is wrong."

"What's wrong is that you've been lying this entire time—"

He shook his head. "No, this isn't about me. This is something else."

"How are you so sure?"

"Because I know you."

She tilted her head to the side. "Do you? How can you know me when you don't truly know yourself? *Theodore Hugo Rodriguez*—" Theo flinched at the cold way she said his name. "Team leader of Robotics Club. Future valedictorian. Basketball star. Part-time mechanic. For all your talk of living life like every day is your last, it seems you've been doing that for everyone but yourself. Always being the person someone needs to be when you're around. The dutiful stepson. The star jock. The sub-in older brother. A *sidekick*." Her voice cracked but she kept on going. "Face it, the real reason you even agreed to go along with this was because you were just as eager as me to prove yourself that you were more than what others labeled you as."

She looked at him, blinking back the tears in her eyes. "You're just as lost as I am."

"Is that really what you think of me?" he asked in a low voice.

She swallowed. "It's the truth, isn't it?"

"Okay, Holmes," he said, not quite looking at her. "I hear you. Loud and clear. If you want me to leave, look me in the eye and tell me."

She met his eyes—eyes that had come to be familiar to her, almost like home. "I want you to leave."

Her heart cried in agony as the hope slowly drained from his face. As the mask he put on for everyone—everyone but her—slid into place. And as promised, he left. It was only when she heard his truck pulling out of the driveway that she let the tears fall.

THIRTY-FOUR

Gianna didn't get out of bed for the rest of the morning. She didn't think she had the strength to. Every time she closed her eyes, she saw Nathan storming away and the hurt on Theo's face from her cruel words.

But she'd made her choice. She may be a horrible person in their eyes, but at least they were safe.

She scrolled through her phone, hoping to keep her mind distracted when a message from Valarie popped up on the screen. It was a picture of Valarie and Vivian standing in front of the hospital, holding a thumbs-up. The photo was meant to be relieving, but the effect was the opposite. Guilt coursed through her veins, like a second pulse. Neither of them would be wearing that hospital bracelet if it weren't for her.

She turned off her phone and lay on her side, banishing the horrors and what-ifs from her mind.

Finally, around noon she got sick of lying around and wandered into the kitchen to find a note taped to the fridge in Irene's delicate handwriting. *Bingo at Christie's house. I'll be back at 4! - Irene.*

She glanced out the window. The driveway was empty. Anthony must have picked up a shift. At the thought of her uncle, her chest tightened. Anthony was right all along. She didn't have what it took to be a detective.

She didn't even bother with the mint ice cream and trudged back up to her room. Her mother's picture frame was still in pieces near her desk. Cautiously, Gianna gathered the glass pieces and threw them in the dustbin. She broke away any remaining pieces of glass from the frame and pulled the picture out when something else slipped onto her lap. Frowning, she picked up the second picture. It must have been hidden behind her mom's photo all this time.

It was slightly blurred from the flash, as if the camera was knocked askew as the photo was being taken. The boy and the girl in the photo were close to Gianna's age. The girl's head was resting on the boy's shoulder, his arm slung around hers. She was looking at the camera, but his eyes were on her, as if she were the only thing in the world. The girl was her mom. And beside her was—

Her gaze settled on the boy. That couldn't have been Royce. She'd seen pictures of her dad when he was in high school. His hair was dark and he had facial hair. The boy in this picture had a lighter shade of hair and paler skin. She flipped the photo around. In the corner of the photo were two initials: L + R.

Gianna's breath left her. She darted to her closet, pushing aside her things to pull out the box of her mother's things that Irene had given her. She pulled out the letters from her father to her mother, the ones that Elena had kept.

Dear E,

I love you.

–R

She glanced at the photo again, but this time her gaze snagged on the boy's wrist around the shoulder—or more particularly, the gold watch. All of it added up. Her father's confusion when she brought up letters. Her conversation with Mason.

"Were her feelings the same for Paul? Did she want to run away with him as much as he wanted to?"

"Yeah, I always thought it was. At first, I was a bit hesitant, but I found it safe to say that she fell for Paul just as hard as he fell for her."

"Do you have a way to contact her?"

Mason's expression froze on his face. He leaned forward, running a hand over his face, as if thinking over his next words. "I… erm, listen kid—"

Mason's phone had rung, and he never finished his sentence. But now she knew what he was going to say.

She glanced back at the photo as the heavy truth weighed down on her.

R was never for Royce. Gianna's father never wrote any of those letters.

R stood for Rowan: Paul Rowan Beckett.

And Lina—his girlfriend—was her mother.

THIRTY-FIVE

According to Mason, Paul and Lina were so much in love that they kept it a secret from their families because they couldn't bear the thought of being apart.

Dear Gianna, I'm sorry. Her mother's words echoed in her mind. When she first read the letter, she didn't understand what it meant. What did her mother have to apologize for? She didn't know she was going to die … unless she did.

Was it because of Paul? Did the pain of living without him outweigh anything else, that she couldn't take it anymore? *Elena was quiet. Sensitive. When one of us was in pain, she felt it ten times more.*

Gianna gripped the picture in her hand with a newfound determination. She didn't have any answers right now, but she was going to find them.

The sun was beginning to set by the time she made it to Theo's street. She raised her fist and knocked. When no one answered after ten seconds, she knocked again and again until—

Theo appeared in the doorway, just as surprised to see her as she was to see him. Or maybe it was the tangled state of her hair or the redness flushing her face that had his jaw dropping.

"Holmes," he began.

"I'm sorry for everything I said to you and Nathan," she blurted before he could get another word out, pushing past him and into the house. She turned around as he shut the door behind them. "You were right. Something was wrong and I was pushing you guys away and I will explain it all to you, I swear, but first I need to tell you guys something. Where is Nathan? Is he here?"

Theo was still gawking at her.

"You can talk now," she said.

"Right. I have something to tell you, too."

"Well, I—"

"It's important," Theo assured her. "Your uncle Gabriel—how did he die?"

She frowned. "Why does that matter?"

"You said it was a heart attack, right?"

"Uh, yeah. It had something to do with his heart." She peered up at him. "Why?"

"I overheard my dad and June talking yesterday. I was coming back from your place when I heard them talking about June's childhood here. At some point, she mentioned the boy at her school who died of a drug overdose." He looked at Gianna. "She called him Gabriel."

Gianna shook her head. No, that couldn't be right. Gabriel had died of heart disease. "You must be thinking of a different Gabriel."

"Your uncle's last name isn't Pescelli, is it?" Theo asked.

Gianna froze. "It can't be him," she said, but Theo had just said it was. "Unless Anthony and Irene lied to me. But I don't understand why they would lie about something like that."

"Maybe it was harder to admit that he was an addict," he said.

"Gabriel wasn't an addict, though." She never knew him, but she knew this. "He was top of his class, next to …"

Her mind flashed back to Paul's obituary in the newspaper. The photo of him and Mason standing on the podium, holding up their awards, and the other boy looking off to the side. The boy whose face she couldn't see.

"It was Gabriel who stood next to Paul," she said breathlessly.

The other student was Gabriel. Mason's words flooded her brain. *I mean, we weren't exactly the most well-behaved kids, if that's what you mean. We did cause some ruckus back then. Did things that I'm ashamed to think about today. We were kids, but we were old enough to know what we were doing. Paul liked to mess with some of the other guys in our class and get on their bad side.*

Paul was competitive in school—he competed to impress his father. By Mason's own admission, he and Paul used to play cruel pranks on some of the other students.

Theo tilted his head. "Uh oh. You have that face. What happened? What just went through your head?"

"I was thinking about what Mason had said. Lina's family didn't approve of Paul, and neither did his. They kept it a secret." *Her and Paul's relationship was a secret. Paul knew his dad wouldn't approve of her, and he was afraid that he'd try to make them break up. And her family wasn't exactly all that approving of Paul either. It was easier to keep it quiet, at least until Paul was at college.* "Neither of their families approved. Richard Beckett didn't like the idea of his son marrying a girl from a low-class family, and Gabriel wouldn't want his sister fraternizing with his academic rival."

"Wait, his sister?" Theo sputtered. "Irene?"

Gianna shook her head. "Not Irene. My mother."

Theo's eyes widened as she explained what she found. "The letters were never from my dad. R stood for Rowan. Paul Rowan Beckett."

"P.R.B.," Theo murmured.

"Paul wanted to run away." She paced the room. "My mom wanted to go with him. Gabriel never would have allowed it. Mason knew about their relationship and covered for the two of them. But there was one more person who knew about their relationship."

Theo looked up at her. "Your dad."

Royce Reyes, who didn't have an alibi that night, who worked with Paul and knew about the secret phone, who was jealous of Paul dating Lina, who shared a mutual dislike for Lina's brothers. He would never be able to be with Lina, not with Gabriel or Paul in the picture. So he made sure they weren't in the picture anymore.

Everything about Royce checked out. Violent background. History with drugs. He killed Gabriel and then he went after Paul, her mother none the wiser. Her family had no idea that Gabriel's death was at the hands of the man they despised most. But one part didn't add up in the story.

She tucked a hair behind her ear. "Nathan and I saw Mason at the ruins. We found rope in the barn, and there was a cooler inside the house. Nathan thinks they might be keeping Ollie in the area there, but …"

"You don't think so?" Theo said.

"It doesn't make sense. Why would Mason help Royce out, befriend him, if he were the one who killed Paul?"

"What if he doesn't know? Royce could've given him a story, and for all we know, Mason has no idea where Ollie really is. If Royce is Paul's murderer, then he's had everyone fooled for years."

"He's not the only fool," she stated bitterly. "All along, he was right there, right in front of me."

She had been so desperate that she was blinded by her father once more.

"Hey," Theo murmured. "You can't blame yourself for that. None of us saw it."

Because none of them knew him. But Gianna did. Her father had many years of disappointment, but this outranked them all.

Ollie's face flashed in her mind. He and Grant had no idea who they were dealing with. But Gianna did.

"We can't let him get away with this," she decided.

Theo shook his head. "He won't."

She whirled around to face him. "You don't know that! We don't have any proof except for speculation."

"Then we'll find proof." Theo sounded so confident that she almost believed him.

"We should tell Nathan," she said finally. "I'll call him."

As she pulled out her phone, Theo's hand shot out to stop her. "Uh, not to be rude or anything, but he might be more inclined to answer me at this moment."

She couldn't argue with him there. Gianna paced the small area of his porch as he pressed the phone to his ear. After a few seconds, he pulled the phone from his ear, a strange expression on his face.

"It went straight to voicemail," he said. "We should stop by his house."

Gianna shook her head. "I already did. He wasn't there."

A worried look crossed his face. "I haven't seen him since he stormed out of your house yesterday."

Wariness rose in her gut. "Where could he be?"

"I don't know." Theo frowned. "Hold on. I can track him."

"How do you have his location?"

"After our talk with Emmaline about her blackmailer, I thought it would be best if we shared each other's locations, just to be safe. Nathan swiped your phone when you weren't looking and turned it on so that only we could see it."

Theo pulled up the app and clicked on Nathan's name, but it was blank. "Shit. He turned it off." He refreshed it again, but it was no use. "Why would he do that?"

Realization crept over her. "Because he doesn't want us following where he's going." Her and Theo's eyes met. "He's going to Hollow Hill."

THIRTY-SIX

The headlights of Theo's truck cut through the darkness of the woods.

"Nate!" Theo yelled.

"Nathan!" Gianna shouted alongside him.

Nothing but the wind answered their calls. *Oh, Nathan*, Gianna thought. *Where are you?* Terror crept into her bones.

"We should start walking," Theo said, and Gianna agreed. He handed her a spare flashlight from the truck, and she pointed it at the ground as they trudged through the woods. They walked for what felt like hours, calling his name until their throats were hoarse and begging for water.

If something happened to him …

Gianna pushed away the thought. It wasn't the time to start thinking negatively, but being out there, it was impossible not to.

Something snapped beneath her feet, startling her. She lifted her foot to see a pair of glasses beneath the leaves. She picked them up and recognized the blue metal. One of the lenses was cracked. "Theo," she whispered, and the urgency in her voice had him by her side in an instant.

"Those are Nate's. He has to be close by." He gripped the glasses in his hand, shouting from the top of his lungs. "Nathan!"

A faint groan came from their left, followed by rustling. Gianna turned to the clearing in the woods, toward the hill. The leaves crunched beneath her feet as she made her way up, not stopping until she reached part of the ruins. She heard a cough and pointed her light in front of her. A familiar head peeked from behind the stones.

Nathan.

"Theo! I found him!" she cried. "He's over here!"

She ran to Nathan, cradling his head in her lap. His skin was cold to the touch and his lips were blue. Dirt and grass spotted his cheeks, but that was the least of her concerns. She was more worried about the goose egg on the back of his head and the line of blood trickling at his temple.

Her eyes fell on the rock by his head, marked with blood.

"I'm here," Theo panted, appearing by her side. His gaze went from Nathan to the bloody rock, eyes widening with horror. He moved next to Gianna, shaking Nathan's shoulders.

"Hey, Nate, buddy. Can you hear me? It's Gianna and Theo."

Nathan's eyelids fluttered open, but only for a second. "Ollie …" he groaned. "Not … not alone."

"What does he mean?" Theo asked. "Hey, Nate."

"I don't know," Gianna confessed. Theo pulled one of Nathan's arms around his neck and began raising him up. "I'm going to carry him back to the truck." As Theo lifted him up, Nathan's eyes shot wide open.

"Ollie—"

"Not Ollie, it's Theo. Can you walk?"

"Oh … Theo … I thought …" Nathan shook his head before groaning in pain. "Ow, my head hurts."

Theo laughed. "You don't say. What did you do, Nate buddy? Trip over and fall on that stone?"

Theo lifted one of Nate's arms around his shoulder as he hoisted his body up. Nathan groaned loudly in pain.

"The car's just down the hill," Gianna reassured him. As she turned to grab the flashlight off the ground, she caught a glimpse of movement from the corner of her eye. She turned the flashlight, but there was nothing there but the moon staring down at them, outlining the silhouette of the farmhouse in the distance. But she did see *something.*

"Gianna," Theo whispered when he noticed her pause. "I think he might have a concussion. We should get him to the hospital."

She turned to help him carry him when that same flash reached her eyes again.

She whirled around, certain that she had seen something. But like before, there was nothing.

Her head told her to listen to Theo. It was dark and below freezing, and they needed to get Nathan back home before his mom began to worry. But her eyes kept drifting back to the farmhouse in the distance.

Ollie, Nathan had said. What if he was trying to tell them that Ollie was in there?

When it came to it, the decision was easy. The moment Theo's back was to her, she took off in the direction of the hill. She had to check. She had to be sure.

If Theo cried out after her, she didn't hear it. Everything was lost to her but the thudding of her footsteps and the short breaths that left her as she pushed her legs further. The night blurred around her until she was standing in front of the house. The wooden planks moaned beneath her weight as she ascended the stairs. No wind blew, yet a chill ran down her bones.

She turned the doorknob, and unlike last time, it turned all the way. The door creaked as she pushed it open, flashing the light into the darkness.

"Hello?" she whispered.

The living room was empty save for a tattered mattress in the corner and a round table near the window. She shined the light on the table. Beef jerky sticks, empty water bottles, and napkins. Someone had been here. The place seemed empty now.

Smothering disappointment, Gianna turned to leave.

Thump.

She paused. Was she hearing things now? *Thump.* There it was again.

"Ollie?" she whispered into the darkness.

Gianna rushed through the living room. "Ollie?" She looked around the room for the source of the sound. *Thud.* She whirled around to face the closet.

Her hand closed around the handle. She could picture the brother's reunion in her mind. Nathan wouldn't blame himself anymore. Ollie would be declared innocent. Nathan would have his brother back and they would all be safe.

She threw the door wide open, expecting to see the soft brown eyes and smile of the boy she'd been searching for. The last face she expected to see was one similar to her own.

Confusion hit her like a train. She stepped back, her breath catching. "Anthony?"

Shock kept her body still. She took in his state. His hands were bound by rope, and blood trickled down in a line by his temple. He was trying to tell her something, but the gag tied around his mouth prevented him. The sight of it snapped her out of her stunned stupor and into action.

"It's okay," she breathed, setting down the flashlight so she could pull the gag down his neck. "What happened? Why—how are you here?"

"Gianna," he gasped, once he caught his breath. "Listen—listen to me. You need to go. Get out of here now."

Gianna's face creased in confusion at his words. "What? No, I'm not leaving you."

"This is not the time to argue. You need to go. Now, before he—"

Footsteps erupted behind her. The hope in Anthony's eyes snuffed out like a doused flame.

"Well, isn't this a pleasant surprise." Every nerve in her body froze at the sound of his voice. "Although, it wouldn't be a family affair without you, Gia."

She stood up and turned, coming face to face with her father.

THIRTY-SEVEN

Royce stood in the doorway of the farmhouse, the light from the lantern casting his face in an eerie green glow. Before she could register what her body was doing, her arm reached out to the table, and she swiped the butter knife from it.

Amusement flickered in his eyes.

"Put the knife down, Gia," Royce said. "It isn't like you're going to do much damage with it anyway. You're not going to hurt me."

Her knuckles whitened around the silver as she cocked her head to the side. "Are you sure about that?"

She shouldn't taunt him. She was staring at a cold-blooded killer. *Her father.* "I won't let you hurt him," she said. "I won't let you do to him what you did to the others."

"Gianna, get out of here!" Anthony cried.

Royce barreled past Gianna before she had time to react, pushing Anthony back into the closet and shutting the door, muffling his shouts.

"Let him go," she demanded. "There's no use in lying. I know it was you. And I'm not the only one who knows. So if you even think about hurting us—"

"I have no idea who you're talking about—"

"Gabriel. Paul. Grant. You killed them all."

"I didn't kill anyone." Royce let out a laugh. "Who told you that I did? Him?" He pivoted toward the closet door.

"You've got it all wrong." Gianna's neck prickled at the sound of the voice. "Royce didn't have anything to do with those deaths."

"There you are," Royce said as Mason stepped inside the house. "Where the hell have you been?"

"I was dealing with our problem when he suddenly disappeared."

Nathan. He didn't trip—Mason had knocked him out. If it weren't for his lack of reaction to her being here, Gianna would've paid him back for what he did to Nathan. There wasn't an ounce of surprise in his eyes at seeing her.

Mason turned his gaze toward her. He looked almost sorry for her, but she couldn't figure out why. "You shouldn't be here, kid."

"You knew who I was that day I came to your cabin to interview you."

"I knew the name Gwen Smith was a bullshit name, but no, that's not how I knew." His eyes turned sad all of a sudden, his voice softening. "You look just like Lina. I'd either have to be a fool or blind not to see it."

Gianna leveled her stare. Mason knew about Elena and Paul's relationship. Which meant, at the least, Paul trusted him enough to keep it a secret, something only the three of them were privy to. Elena knew him. They were most likely friends. Here was someone who knew what her mother was like.

She could work with that.

"I don't know what story he fed to you, but he's lying." She stepped forward. "He doesn't have an alibi for Gabriel or Paul's death. And he had the perfect motive—"

"And what motive would that be?" Mason asked, the epitome of calm.

"My mother." She frowned. Shouldn't he know this? "She and Paul were planning to run away together. Royce didn't want that, so he killed Gabriel and then he killed Paul and framed it all on Freddy Atwater. When Ollie and Grant tried to get him to confess, Royce killed Grant. And Ollie …"

Her sentence trailed off. Where *was* Ollie?

Her gaze slowly dragged up to Mason. The memory of the blood they found near the barn pushed its way to the front of her mind.

"I know he's here," she said. "We saw the blood by the barn. We saw *you*."

Royce laughed, but there was no warmth to it. Mason strolled over to the cooler near the table and popped it open. Bags of bloody meat stared back at her and the realization dawned on her.

"Venison," Mason cut to the answer before she could.

The gun had been a hunting rifle. The blood belonged to the deer. That's why the cooler was here.

Her fists clenched beside her. "This still doesn't change anything," she turned to face them. "I know what you did."

Royce sputtered a noise of disbelief. "Is that what you think happened? How long did it take you to come up with this story? Jesus, kid, I didn't kill nobody."

"On May 19th, 2003, a college student hosted a party at his house while his parents were out of town. Half of the town was invited, including all the high school seniors, and Gabriel went to the party. The same party where you and Paul were selling." She shook her head, scoffing beneath her breath.

"Did he know that you killed Gabriel?" she demanded. "Before you killed him?"

"No, he didn't," Royce said. "Paul didn't know a damned thing about the exchange. And as for Gabriel, nobody made him take those drugs. He wanted to buy them, and I sold them to him."

Mason's head slowly turned to him. "What?" he said viciously. "You told me you didn't have anything to do with Gabriel's death. You swore to me you didn't have a hand in it."

Royce glanced at the wall beside him. "No, I didn't. I swore to you that I didn't kill him. If I had forced the pills down his throat, it would be a different story. Pescelli needed something to get him through exam season. I told him to be careful and told him the exact amount to take. If he took a larger dose than he was supposed to, that's not my fault. That's not murder."

Disgust shone on Mason's face. "How could you, Royce?"

"Oh, don't get all high and mighty on me now. You had no issue with Paul dealing back then. After all, it was why you two hung around at those parties back then, right?"

"I didn't get involved in any of that," Mason spat. "That was Paul's thing, not mine."

"Ah, yes. The prodigious athlete. I forget myself sometimes." Royce smiled wryly.

"Goddamn it, Royce!" Mason shouted, pointing a finger in Royce's face. "How could you?"

"What does it matter anyway? The last time I checked, you didn't shed a tear for Gabriel."

"Because your carelessness is what got Paul killed, you asshole!" Mason seethed. "Can't you see that? He went after him because of what you did."

"Who?" Gianna said. "Who went after Paul?"

"Ah, yes, Ramsay," Royce drawled, with a smile on his face. "You haven't once asked why I brought your uncle here, Gia."

"Because you're a maniac?" she retorted.

Royce laughed loudly. A smile pulled at his lips as he pointed a finger at her. "There she is. You know I was worried you had picked up all your mother's habits after you paid me that visit. I'm glad to say I was wrong for once."

"I'm nothing like you," she said.

"You're a Reyes, and you should be proud to be." His eyes slid to Mason. "Unlike others, we do what it takes to bring justice."

It was Gianna's turn to laugh. "How is this justice?"

Royce sauntered over to the closet, reached in, and grabbed Anthony by the ropes around the wrists. He threw him down onto the carpet and tore off the gag, kneeling down beside him. "What'll it be, Pescelli?" he sneered. "Should you tell her, or should I?"

Mason looked thoroughly unamused with the whole thing. "Royce," he said.

"Shut up, Mason! It's my turn to talk." Royce grabbed Anthony by the face, forcing him to look at her. "You've been searching all this time for Paul's killer. You want to know who really killed Paul, Gia? You've been living under his roof all this time."

"You're lying," she spat. "Anthony wouldn't do that."

She turned to Anthony, waiting for him to deny what Royce was saying. But Anthony wasn't looking at her; he was looking down at the ground, shame written all over his face.

"Anthony?" Her voice was small, childlike, like she was four years old again and her mother had just died. "Tell me that he's lying."

Finally, Anthony spoke, his voice barely above a whisper. "I can't."

The butter knife slipped from her fingers; the sound of it hitting the floor echoed throughout the room.

"I—I never meant to kill him," Anthony stammered. "I only wanted him to confess what he did to Gabriel. When I realized I'd gone too far … it was already too late."

"To confess," Mason repeated flatly, "for something he didn't do."

"I thought it was him!" Anthony cried. "You know how he hated us. He'd pulled crap before, sabotaging us, dosing our drinks before a game so we were so sick that we couldn't play."

Paul liked to mess with some of the other guys in our class, get on their bad side. The other guys were her uncles. Gianna was right. The overdose victim's family did want revenge—*her* family.

The pieces were coming together. "So you lured him to the woods," she said.

Anthony nodded. "I found your mother's phone that Paul had given her. I lured him to the ruins, hoping to get him to confess, but he wouldn't."

"You killed him," she said. "And then you made it look like a robbery."

"After I realized what I had done, I knew the police would suspect me. Everyone knew of our history with Paul, so I took his wallet and watch to make the motive different. When I heard they had arrested a suspect, I used the chance to plant the wallet in his car so they wouldn't doubt his guilt."

"*You* called in an anonymous tip. You killed him, and you let an innocent man suffer in jail." Carrie's face flashed through her mind. "He had a family. And then you killed Grant and blackmailed Emmaline so that she wouldn't talk, and you sent me all those notes."

A wrinkle appeared in his brow before he looked away. "I—I lost control of my anger," he said. "I was scared. I didn't want to go to jail. I'm sorry, Gianna. I'm so sorry."

This was the man who took her in and raised her as his own, who played Cops and Robbers in the front yard, and held her without knowing the real reason why she was crying. The whole truth was right in front of her, and she hadn't even seen it. The man she trusted more than anyone in her life. She erected a wall, blocking it all out, and steeled herself to continue the story.

Gianna stood. She now knew the whole, horrible truth of what happened on Hollow Hill all those years ago. But a part of the story was still missing.

"Where's Ollie?" she demanded. "Where is he?"

Anthony shook his head. "You have to understand. I couldn't let them tell anyone. I couldn't let them go. It was too risky."

"Anthony," she repeated. "Where … is he?"

He trembled before looking away. "There's a lake not five miles from here. There are two giant rocks on one side of the lake. He's—he's buried there."

Gianna strained to hear over the whooshing in her mind.

Ollie was dead.

He hadn't killed Grant. He hadn't run away.

And he wasn't coming back.

"He tried to run—after I shot his friend. I tracked him down to the lake. By the time I got there he was already floating in the water. It was dark outside and he was running so fast. I don't think he saw the ledge until it was too late. I knew I had to be quick, so I took his keys and drove his car to the station. I went back and dragged his body out of the lake and buried him. I took Grant's belongings and hid them in the ditch by the road. The sun was starting to rise and I had a shift soon. It wasn't a busy road—I thought I'd have time to bury him, but then he was reported missing and I couldn't get away."

She looked away, unable to meet his eyes. This wasn't her uncle—this was Paul and Ollie's murderer.

"Good ole righteous Anthony," Royce drawled. "And all this time you carried out the worst deeds of all. And it's all thanks to you, Gia." Royce smiled and her stomach twisted. "If you had never given Mason the idea that Gabriel's family might have wanted revenge on Paul, he never would've thought otherwise."

Mason looked at Anthony. "Who told you that Paul gave Gabriel the pills?"

"No one had to," Anthony replied. "Like I said, Paul hated us."

"Not all of you," Mason breathed. Gianna knew he was thinking of her mom. Mason cursed beneath his breath, pinching the bridge of his nose. He turned to Royce. "We can't go through with it, Royce."

"What would you have me do, Rams? Let him go? Call the cops? Oh wait, we can't do that, because we kidnapped him and brought him here." Mason was silent as Royce spoke. "This was your idea, Rams. She said that Gabriel's family was out for revenge and they went after Paul. As far as I can see, there's only one thing we can do, and that's dispense a little justice ourselves."

"I don't think you have a right to do that."

"Oh, for the love of God. For the last time—I didn't *make* Gabriel take those pills. He asked for them. It's not my fault that the guy took twice the dosage."

"Well, Paul got blamed for that." Mason's fists clenched. "Someone *killed* him for it."

"And who was the one who killed him?" Royce pulled a pocket knife from his pants and snapped it open.

Gianna took a step in front of Anthony. He might have lost her trust forever, but he didn't deserve whatever "justice" Royce had planned.

"Royce," Mason repeated.

"Oh, don't try playing the guilty one now, Ramsay." He lowered his voice. "You knew what you were getting into when you called me."

"Your kid's here," Mason pointed out. "Are you really going to do this in front of her?"

Yes, Gianna answered in her head at the same time Royce declared, "Yes."

Mason scoffed in disbelief.

"Fine." Royce took a step back, holding up his hands. "Paul was your friend, too." He handed him the knife, the handle in Mason's direction. They all stared silently as he held it between them.

And then Mason took it.

"No!" Gianna cried. In the blink of an eye, Royce hauled her over to the side of the room, holding her back by the arms, forcing her to watch in horror as Mason took a step forward. His knuckles were white as he gripped the handle. He lifted his arm and—

"No!"

—the rope around Anthony's wrists fell to the ground.

Both men stared at each other, chests heaving.

After what felt like an eternity, Mason gritted out, "I'm not a killer."

"What the hell are you doing?" Royce seethed. He released his bruising grip on Gianna and stepped forward. Mason ignored him and kept walking until Royce pulled him back, hissing, "We had a plan."

Mason jerked his arm out of his grip. "Not like this."

But Royce wasn't done. "You're just going to let him get away with this? What would Paul say?"

"He's dead," Mason said. "Paul's been dead for twenty years and nothing we will do will change that." He gave Royce a knowing look. "Don't do anything stupid, Royce."

Royce scoffed. "Should've known," he muttered. "Gone fucking soft. I'll handle this myself."

He ripped the knife from Mason's hands and turned back to them, but Anthony had already made it to his feet.

"You son of a bitch. You killed my brother!" Anthony snarled, and the next thing she knew, he was throwing himself at Royce on the ground.

The two of them fought, arms swinging, legs kicking. Glass shattered, and the table broke.

Royce's arm brought down the knife. "No!" she shouted, throwing herself into the crossfire. She pushed Royce's arm, flinging the knife out of his reach. He retaliated by pushing her away. She hit the ground. Hard.

"Gianna!" Anthony cried, eyes darting over to her. It was only for a moment, but that was all that Royce needed. His fist clipped Anthony in the jaw. He collapsed to the ground, wheezing as Royce kicked him in the stomach.

She didn't know how many times she pleaded with him to stop. Someone was screaming. It was her.

She dashed toward them, but someone pulled her back.

"Stay out of the way, kid," Mason said. He pulled Royce back, putting himself between him and Anthony on the floor. "That's enough!"

Royce wasn't listening. He punched him, too, and Mason pushed him back. While the two of them were distracted, Anthony hobbled over to Gianna. "You need to get out of here," he breathed, running his eyes over the bruise forming on the side of her head. He helped her up, wincing as his hand went to his side. She hated herself for not shuddering at his touch. Anthony was a killer. He had blood on his hands.

But he was also the man who raised her.

"Come on," he said, limping as they made their way out of the room. The moment they reached the door, it swung open, and lights were pointed at them.

"Echo Falls Police Department! Put your hands in the air!"

"Andrew? It's Pescelli!" Anthony yelled, and the light disappeared.

Mr. Delgado's eyes widened, taking in the state of Gianna and Anthony. "Pescelli? What the hell—"

"There's no time for that," Anthony snapped. "They're back there."

Royce tried to make a run for the back door, but one of the officers tackled him to the ground. Mason was nowhere to be seen. Mr. Delgado put his gun back in the holster on his belt and helped Gianna and Anthony to their feet.

"You're safe now," Mr. Delgado reassured her. "Royce won't see the light of day except for a prison cell from now on. You hear that, Tony?"

"He won't be the only one," Anthony croaked.

Mr. Delgado gave him an odd look.

She could hear the crack of her heart breaking as Anthony met her gaze and didn't break it. "Delgado, I wish to confess to the murders of Paul Beckett, Oliver Kipman, and Grant Hayes."

Mr. Delgado frowned. "Tony?" he said, as if he didn't think he had heard him correctly.

"You heard me, Andrew." Anthony held his wrists up. "Take me in."

"I don't understand."

Anthony gave him a sad look. "You've always been a good man, Andrew, and a good friend. I'll never forget that. I know I don't deserve it, but please take care of them for me."

When Mr. Delgado wouldn't move, one of the other officers did it for him. She watched numbly as the police escorted Anthony to the back of a car and Royce to another. The world dimmed around her when a voice broke through.

"Please, I need to see her." Theo was trying to push past an officer into the farmhouse, but they wouldn't let him through. "Is she in there?"

"I'm right here," she whispered, and Theo's eyes fell on her. He pushed past the officer and made his way toward her, hands cupping her face.

"Are you okay?" The warmth of his hands sank into her skin. "What happened?"

She distantly heard someone say she was in shock. She didn't fight it when Theo pulled her into his arms. Theo's voice was in her ear. "It's okay, Holmes," he whispered. "It's alright. It's over."

"He's dead," she whispered the words into his sweater. "Ollie's dead."

Theo pulled back, face paling. "Shit—I'm … I'm sorry."

She shook her head. She was alive, but Ollie wasn't. If anyone should be sorry, it was for him. "I should tell Nathan. Where is he?"

"I took him to my car once I realized you were gone. I called the police, and an ambulance came. The paramedics and Mrs. Kipman are with him now."

"I have to tell him," she repeated.

Theo took his hand in hers, holding her steady. "We'll tell him together."

***

I'm sorry.

She hated how it was all she could say. Hated how she stood there helpless, as Angela let out a heart-wrenching cry. Hated how Nathan's lip trembled, as he shook his head in denial. "No. I—" his voice cracked. "He can't be—he was supposed to—we were supposed to find him. He's supposed to come back. He—he was supposed to—"

A sob broke through his lips. He covered his face with his hand, shoulders racking with sobs. Tears streamed down Angela's cheeks as she held onto her youngest son and cried silently with him.

Feeling like she was invading something private, Gianna stepped away from the ambulance. Theo stood beside her, hand still holding onto hers as they watched the red-and-blue lights reflect off the trees.

She took a deep breath and closed her eyes.

It was over.

THIRTY-EIGHT

TWO WEEKS LATER

Gianna should've thrown it out. The murder board taunted her from where it hung in her closet. It wasn't like she needed it anymore. She had already thrown away some stuff on it, yet she couldn't find it in herself to throw it away entirely.

It had been two weeks since the farmhouse. Two weeks since her father was arrested for trying to kill Anthony. Two weeks since Mason Ramsay disappeared into the wind without a trace. Two weeks since Anthony confessed to the three most tragic deaths to ever occur in their town. Two weeks since the search for Ollie's remains began.

It was amazing how much one's entire world could shift in just two weeks.

The doorbell rang downstairs. She tore herself away from her closet to answer it, but by the time her feet hit the last step, Irene was there.

"Hello, Irene," Mr. Delgado's voice boomed through the hallway. By the formality in his tone, he wasn't here for a social call.

"Andrew." Irene opened the door wider. Gianna peeked around the corner and saw that Mr. Delgado was still wearing his uniform. "What is it? Do you have any more updates?"

Mr. Delgado sighed heavily. "We found the Kipman boy's phone at the bottom of the lake. We've been searching the area that he told us he buried the boy, but there hasn't been anything in there for years. I doubt his body was ever there in the first place." He paused, leaning closer. "I was hoping you could come down to the station and talk some sense into him."

Ollie. They were talking about Ollie.

Before Irene could reply, Gianna blurted, "I want to talk to him." Irene's head snapped to where Gianna appeared in the doorway.

She looked at Mr. Delgado pleadingly. "Please," she croaked. "I need to see him."

Irene glanced at Mr. Delgado, who scratched the back of his neck. "I'm not sure that's such a good idea, Gianna."

"You just said you wanted someone to go and talk sense into him."

"I meant an adult."

"But I was there that night. I'm the reason they're looking for Ollie's body right now," she protested.

"Which is precisely the reason you shouldn't be talking to Anthony. It's an ongoing investigation, Gianna, and right now things are messy. Very messy. And now one of our own is responsible for three of the town's biggest murders and all eyes are on Anthony." He sighed. "I think it's best if you just … give it some time."

Gianna opened her mouth to protest, but Irene held up a hand. "I will talk to my brother, Andrew," she said, patting his shoulder. "Whatever you need."

"Okay. I can bring you down to the station right now, and you can come and see him." Irene nodded, and while she went to grab her purse, Mr. Delgado turned to Gianna.

"I know this is hard for you right now"—Gianna scoffed—"but believe me, the best chance of Anthony getting through this is his cooperation and keeping the press from breathing down all our necks." He patted her shoulder. "Hang in there, Gianna. Okay?"

Irene returned with her purse in hand. "I'll be back in time for the wedding. Is Valarie still picking you up?"

Gianna nodded, thinking of the light blue dress hanging in her closet.

"Things will turn out alright," Irene tilted her chin upward to meet her eyes. "You'll see."

She turned to leave, but, unable to let her go without knowing the truth first, Gianna blurted, "He's lying, isn't he?"

Irene paused in the doorway.

"Mr. Delgado—about why I can't see Anthony." Gianna didn't look away from her, wanting to see the truth in her face. "It's because he doesn't want to see me."

Irene's gaze softened. She paced back to Gianna, cradling her face with her hands. "Anthony loves you so much," she whispered. "He's ashamed of what he's done. He doesn't want you to see him in the state he is right now, behind bars with all his friends turned against him. He doesn't want you associated with any of that— with him."

"He should've thought about that before he decided to kill three innocent people," Gianna said, stepping back out of Irene's reach. She wrapped her arms around herself, numb.

Irene sighed and, for the first time in two weeks, Gianna could peer beneath all the layers of makeup and see the exhaustion tainting her face. "I'll see you at the wedding."

The door closed with a soft *click* behind her.

***

Valarie arrived an hour later to pick up Gianna, and Gianna was grateful for her presence. Because for a little while, she could forget about her troubles and just get ready with her best friend for a wedding.

She went to grab her dress from her closet when Valarie *tsk*ed from behind her.

"Don't you even think of touching that. You're not wearing it," she stated, disappearing from the room with a sly smile. She returned a minute later holding a tall white dress bag and unzipped it.

Gianna gasped at the green ruffles that peeked out of the bag. "You bought me the dress?"

Valarie grinned. "No offense to your mom's dress, but this occasion calls for something … more."

Gianna ran her hands over the soft green fabric, like cotton on her hands. "How did you know?" She had tried on at least five dresses that day.

"I saw you eyeing it at the mall. I get that I talk a lot, but I do tend to notice things, you know. Especially about the people I care about." Valarie shoved the dress into Gianna's hands and started pushing her into the bathroom. "Now stop stalling and try it on!"

Gianna emerged from the bathroom five minutes later. Despite the weight in her heart, she felt a little thrill as Valarie made her twirl, the green ruffles parading around her ankles.

Valarie grinned triumphantly. "Theo is going to lose his freaking brain."

Gianna shot her a disapproving look and Valarie laughed, hooking her arm through hers. "Oh, by the way, did you ever find out who the killer was in that podcast episode? You remember the one with the girl who was found murdered in her apartment? Was it the boyfriend?"

"No," she said, glancing at the floor. "It was the sister all along."

***

The venue was covered in flowers of every shade of purple. The wedding music began to play throughout the room, and everyone stood as June made her way down the aisle. As the bride and groom recited their vows, Gianna felt eyes on her and turned her head slightly to catch Theo's gaze. *Hey*, he mouthed from where he stood off to the side of his father, beside Liam.

She raised her hand to wave, but it faltered when his gaze drifted to the empty seat to her right, where Nathan was supposed to be. She sent an apologetic look in his direction. Theo shrugged as if to say *It's okay*. Deep down he was probably a little disappointed, but he understood. They all did—why Nathan was a no-show.

"I do," June declared, and Valarie sniffled loudly beside her, eyes welling up with unshed tears.

"I now pronounce you husband and wife. You may kiss the bride."

That was the exact moment Valarie started bawling beside her.

***

"Feeling better?" Gianna asked later at the reception dinner.

"Oh, for the last time—it was only a few tears!" Valarie exclaimed. "I can't help that I get emotional at weddings."

"Only a few?" Gianna teased.

While they were teasing, Liam had walked up to them. "Hey."

Gianna recalled seeing him off to June's side, wiping something off his face with the back of his hand as she and Mitch exchanged their vows. She had to admit it was an anomaly, seeing him display any emotion besides arrogance.

Neither of them said anything, glancing off to the side or to the dance floor. This was the first time since the Chinese restaurant that she and Liam had been in the same room. Judging by the way Liam was scrutinizing the tiles on the floor, he must have reached the same conclusion.

Gianna glanced at Valarie standing between them. Her eyes darted back and forth between them, an uncertain expression on her face, something out of place for Gianna to see on her usually confident friend.

She didn't want to be the cause of that anymore.

She took a deep breath and turned to face Liam. "I'm sorry, by the way." It occurred to her that she hadn't properly apologized to Liam for what she had said on their double date. "For you know … accusing you of murder and stuff. I jumped to conclusions, and I was wrong."

His eyebrows pulled together in surprise before he jerked his head once. Gianna resumed getting her punch. Well, that was that. Valarie nudged him and he hissed. He reluctantly turned to Gianna. "You're not the only one who was in the wrong. I owe you an apology, Nancy Drew. You turned out to be the real deal." He paused, probably remembering the two crucial words that make an apology, and said, "I'm sorry."

Gianna stared at him before nodding her head. She doubted she and Liam would ever truly be friends, but the small conversation was the closest acknowledgment that they were both in Valarie's life and would have to deal with each other for the foreseeable future. So long as Valarie was happy, she could live with that.

Liam let out a breath. "Well, I'm going to go and grab some food. You want me to grab you something, Val?"

"I'll come with you." She turned back to Gianna, a smile on her face. "Did you want to come with us?"

Gianna waved them off. "I'm not hungry. You guys go."

"We'll be right back," Valarie promised, following Liam to the buffet.

Gianna swayed to the music as the newlywed couple danced in the center of the diner. Her eyes were pulled to the side. For a moment, her heart fluttered at the sight of Theo. He was talking animatedly to some of the wedding guests, making exaggerated gestures with his hands.

As if his gaze were pulled, it flitted to her and stayed there. She waved and his smile grew wider. He said something to the couple before making his way over to her. Before he could get to her, though, he was intervened by one of the coaches from school.

"Rodriguez!" Coach Brown declared loudly. "This is quite the party. I've been meaning to talk to you about some of the college scouts. I spoke to them, but they told me you weren't interested in going pro at any of the schools. I wondered if there had been some mistake."

"It's not a mistake, coach," Theo said.

A wrinkle appeared on his forehead. "But this is what you've been training for all year. How do you expect to get into school without getting on a team?"

"Simple. I won't be playing basketball in college."

Gianna nearly spat out her drink. Were her ears deceiving her? Did she hear that right?

"I found I didn't enjoy it as much." Theo's eyes slid in her direction, and her heart skipped a beat. "Or rather, someone made me see that I didn't."

Her throat felt dry.

Coach Brown scratched his chin, clearly disappointed with this news. "That's a shame. You had real talent. But if that's what you want …" He sighed. "Oh, I see your father. I'll be right back. If you'll excuse me."

He left, and then it was just the two of them.

"You quit basketball," she said, dazed.

"Well, you see, when a murder-obsessed weirdo snaps at you, it's kind of an eye-opener," he said, lips lifting into a smile.

She didn't deserve that smile.

"Theo …" she began, thinking of all the ways to explain, but Theo didn't let her finish her sentence.

"Can I go first?" he asked. Gianna pressed her lips together as he continued. "You were right."

She scoffed. "No, I wasn't. What I said to you that day—"

"You did it to protect us," he finished, and she looked up at him, surprised. "I do have a brain in this head, you know. And I have a tendency to use it once in a while. I'll admit I was angry at first and didn't see it. But the next day, I thought about it, and I came to my own conclusions. I was planning on driving to your house when you showed up at my door." He sucked in a breath. "But that's not all I wanted to talk to you about. I also needed to apologize for not telling you and Nate that I was related to Paul."

"You don't have to," she said quickly. "It wasn't any of our business. I never should have even looked up—"

"Yes, you should have and I'm glad you did." Her mouth snapped shut as she gazed up at Theo, stunned. "In the beginning, it was about finding Ollie. I meant that part—I wanted to help. But then you pulled out that watch in Michael Price's house. That's when I realized my family was connected to Ollie's disappearance."

"When did you figure out you were related to Paul?"

"Not long after we moved here," he confessed. "One afternoon, I went outside and saw Mags messing with her car. I told her I knew about cars and offered to help. She invited me in afterward for a glass of lemonade and showed me the wall with all her family on it. She told me about her son who died when he was younger, and pointed out his picture, and that's when I saw my mother's picture on the wall. She was only a kid in the picture, but she had the same birthmark on her cheek. I vaguely remember asking her who she was when Mags told me it was her niece. That's when I knew."

It was impossible to believe. She turned to him. "And your father—"

"Had no idea that we moved right next door to my mom's aunt?" Theo smiled. "He had no clue. And neither did Mags. She hadn't seen nor spoken to my mom since she was a kid, and didn't really keep in contact with her after Raine severed ties with her parents. She didn't even know Raine had a son. I almost told her right there in her living room who I was."

"What stopped you?"

"Well, I figured since my mom cut ties with her family, there was a chance Mags might harbor some bad feelings toward her. I wasn't sure how she'd react to finding out who I was, so I didn't tell her or my dad at first, but they took it surprisingly well."

She followed his gaze to the corner of the room where Mags and Mitch were talking.

"But that's not all I wanted to talk to you about." He turned to her. "You weren't wrong about everything you said. I do try to be everything for everyone else without realizing it. Most of my memories I have up until a few years ago with my dad were him being sad and closed off. I remember how amazing I felt when I could do something that made him proud, that made him happy—and working in the garage and playing basketball did that. Moving here in the beginning of my senior year made June happy, therefore making my dad happy even though I wasn't one hundred percent okay about it. But do you know what the irony is about all this?"

Gianna didn't dare breathe. She didn't think she could. "What?" she asked, her voice barely above a hoarse whisper.

"I didn't realize it until you brought it up. How I wasn't being myself with everyone else. But with you, Holmes, it's not like that; it's never been. The only time I ever truly feel like me is when I am with you."

It felt like a thousand fireworks in her stomach were about to go off. A hundred words to match them were on the tip of her tongue, but she held them all back and offered her hand out inside. "Do you want to dance?"

"With you?" Theo slid his hands into hers, smiling softly. "Always."

THIRTY-NINE

Save me the next dance!" Theo shouted, running toward the table to grab them drinks.

Gianna tapped her foot to the rhythm of the song, trying her best to ignore the stares burning into the side of her face. One of the bridesmaids and her friends were looking over at her, recognition flashing in their eyes. They leaned into each other, murmuring hushed words behind their hands.

It didn't take a genius to know what they were saying. Their hushed whispers and stares pierced her like little daggers.

Eager to get out of everyone's eyesight, Gianna moved off toward the tables when she felt a tap on her shoulder.

She turned around and gasped before throwing her arms around his shoulders. Nathan stumbled back, awkwardly patting her on the back, chuckling into the side of her neck. "Well, this certainly is a warm welcome."

"You made it," she breathed, as they pulled away. The bruise on the right side of his face had begun to turn a yellowish color. Her hand stopped inches away from her face. "Oh, Nathan."

He shrugged. "It looks worse than it feels."

"Hey, man." Theo came up to them, pulling Nathan into a manly embrace. "You didn't have to come, you know. June understood."

"Well, I felt bad about missing the wedding," Nathan said. "And I figured I could do something other than wallow around the house waiting for news."

His eyes burned with hope. Gianna hated to be the one to

extinguish the flames. "I'm sorry." The words thick like sludge in her throat. "I haven't heard anything. I'm still waiting for Irene to get back from the station."

She didn't know why Anthony would lie.

"It's okay," Nathan said.

Gianna put a hand on his shoulder. He smiled at her and held up the wrapped box in his hand. "Well, enough depressing talk about that. I brought something for the happy couple. You guys haven't gotten to opening wedding presents yet, have you?"

Gianna gasped in realization. She'd forgotten her present for June and Mr. Rodriguez. It had been on her desk upstairs. "Crap. I forgot the present on my desk."

"It's fine," Theo reassured her. "We can always grab it tomorrow. You know, give me an excuse to come over to your house and see you."

She knew he was teasing her, but she also really wanted to bring their gift. It was a brand-new mystery novel that she and June had discussed. "No, I can grab it real quick."

Theo took her hand in his. "I'll go with you."

"Well, well, well." Nathan's eyes twinkled with amusement as he took in their clasped hands. "I guess it's a good thing I didn't miss this after all."

"Oh, yeah?" Theo retorted, letting go of Gianna's hand to pull Nathan into a headlock, ruffling his hair with his fist.

Gianna laughed as Theo's name was called at the other end of the room. June and Mitch were waiting near the photographer. Theo hesitated, glancing from where his father was beckoning him to where Gianna was gathering her coat.

"Go ahead. I should be back soon," Gianna said, already searching for Valarie in the crowd.

"I'll go with you," Nathan offered. "I should go and check on my mom. She wasn't in the best shape when I left earlier."

"Okay." Theo stilled, as if he weren't ready to let her go. After a moment, he went to where his father and June were waiting. Gianna pulled her coat on and headed toward the crowd.

"I don't see Valarie," she said.

"Maybe she's outside," Nathan suggested.

They made their way to the glass doors. The moment they reached them, Irene stepped through, a faint sheen of sweat on her forehead. "Ah, there you are. Where are you off in such a rush?"

"I forgot the wedding present on my desk," Gianna explained. "I need to find Valarie to drive me back."

"No need." Irene held up her keys. "I'll drive you. Is your friend coming?"

"I just need to check on my mom real quick," Nathan said. "If that's okay."

"Of course it is." Irene's smile didn't reach her eyes. *The talk with Anthony didn't go well,* Gianna thought as they got into the car. Irene tossed Gianna a water bottle once they were inside. "You look like you've been dancing for a while. I don't need you passing out from dehydration the moment we get to the house."

"Thanks," Gianna replied dryly. "Did you want some, Nathan?"

"I've got one for him, too." She passed the water bottle back to him.

Earlier in the week, their street had been lined with news vans and reporters eager to talk to them. When it became clear that neither Irene nor Gianna was going to talk, they slowly left, thankfully taking their cameras and questions with them. At least she wouldn't have to worry about darting out behind a bush to avoid overeager journalists.

"I'll meet you back here in five minutes," Nathan promised, cutting through the neighbor's yard to get to his house.

Gianna gave him the thumbs-up and headed inside. The Agatha Christie novel was still on her desk, wrapped in purple wrapping paper. As she went to grab it, her eyes fell on the bin beneath her desk.

There's nothing left to solve. Anthony killed Paul and the rest of them. It's all over. Just grab the present and go.

Downstairs, she heard Irene's heels clicking against the floor, followed by the bathroom door closing. Gianna snatched the gift off the desk, but her feet didn't move toward the door where she should've gone. No, she went to her desk and pulled out the murder board. She traced the red line of yarn from Ollie's picture to Paul's.

There had been a nagging feeling all night. That she had overlooked something. She blinked away the sleep pulling at her eyes, upturned all the contents of the trash bin onto the floor. Angela's interview that first day. The notes from Anthony. The polaroid of Emmaline in Ollie's bag. She looked over all of it, rereading for some clue, some connection she missed, until she stumbled upon Freddy Atwater's confession tapes. She grabbed her radio and entered the tape, pressing play.

OFFICER 1: Then how do you explain Paul's wallet we found in your car?

FA: I don't know how that got there—I didn't put it there.

OFFICER 2: If you didn't, then who did?

FA: [whispers something unintelligible]

OFFICER 1: Speak up.

FA: Voices. I heard—there were voices that night.

OFFICER 1: Were these voices in your head, Freddy? Were they telling you to kill Paul? Are these the same voices that told you to kill your father?

FA: No! That was an accident. I didn't—I didn't kill him. You're not listening.

OFFICER 2: We're listening, Freddy.

FA: The voices.

OFFICER 1: But you didn't hear voices. Admit it, Freddy: there were no voices. There was no one else that night but you and Paul, who you confessed to murdering and stealing his wallet. His wallet was found in *your* car at the shop. The evidence is there.

Gianna paused the tape. She grabbed her computer off her desk and opened it up, searching for the nearest mechanic shop. The only one that popped up was Rodriguez's Auto Garage, formerly known as Ryder Automatics. Why did that name sound so familiar? She clicked on images and saw the same building Theo's dad now owned and froze.

She had seen this building before.

Her heart pounding in her chest, she ran to her closet and pulled out her mother's box. Dumping the contents of the box on the ground, Gianna spread the photos out, searching for a particular one. "Come on," she muttered as she searched the scattered photos. When she found it, she picked it up, holding it next to her computer. The wall her mother and Irene were standing in front of—it was the same color as the side of *Ryder Automatics.*

"No," she whispered, shaking her head. *No.*

Her mind was swirling as she stood. Every step she took thudded in her ears until she reached the first room downstairs. She flicked on the light.

When Unknown had been in her room, he had taken her tape recorder. But there had been no sign of it in any of Anthony's belongings after the police went through everything. She assumed that Anthony had tossed it away.

But what if she was wrong?

When we were younger, your mother and I kept photo boxes like these where we kept important stuff.

The closet door creaked as it opened. The box was sitting there, right in the open, barely concealed. She removed the lid.

And found her tape recorder inside. And shoved along with it was a jacket with a piece of the sleeve missing.

The piece she found on her windowsill.

The world, coming undone around her, stilled at the sound of a sigh. "I really hoped you wouldn't find that."

FORTY

Gianna's gaze trailed up from the black heels to the violet ruffles of her dress, to the clinking jewelry on her wrists, up all the way to her face. There was no fear there. No surprise or panic. Only disappointment.

"I really hoped you wouldn't find that," Irene sighed heavily, throwing her clutch onto the bed. "Although I suppose it was only a matter of time until you figured it out. You were always too clever for your own good, you know?"

"It was you," Gianna choked out the words. "You killed Ollie and Grant."

Irene didn't bother denying it. "Yes."

A memory crept forward from the farmhouse when Gianna confronted Anthony about the threatening notes he left. The flash of confusion on his face that came afterward. She had chalked it up to shame, but she was wrong. Anthony was genuinely confused because he had no idea, because he wasn't Unknown.

Irene was.

Her aunt was behind the notes that tormented her for months. She was Emmaline's blackmailer. She was responsible for Ollie and Grant's deaths. But she did more than that.

"You cut the brakes on Valarie's car," she breathed. "You were the person on the phone. Vivian was in that car. She could have died! Both of them could have!"

"I needed to get your attention. My other methods weren't working and I needed you to take me seriously, but you are so stubborn." She shook her head. "I shouldn't be surprised. After all, Pescelli blood does run through your veins. But I'm curious as to how you figured it out."

"I kept asking myself why Anthony would give himself up now," Gianna said. "And then I started looking back at Freddy Atwater's confessions. There was a moment when Freddy changed his story, saying he heard voices that night. The police didn't believe him and dismissed it as him trying to weasel his way out of the blame or that he was crazy, but he wasn't lying. There were other people there that night. He did hear voices."

"Yes, Anthony was there—" Irene began.

"Only he wasn't the only one there," Gianna interrupted. "Was he?"

Irene was silent for a beat. And then, "I think you know the answer to that."

She pictured that night: Paul parking his car along the side of the road and walking in the direction of the ruins, with no idea what was waiting in the shadows. She looked at Irene. "You were there, too, that night. That's why Anthony confessed he did it alone. So you wouldn't get arrested either. But it wasn't just you he was protecting."

Gianna closed her eyes as the harsh truth made its way toward her. There had been one part of Anthony's story she couldn't get, and that was how he was able to lure Paul to the ruins without anyone realizing.

"Someone had to draw Paul all the way there. For him to get out of the car without alerting anyone to where he was going."

He even had a secret phone so they could talk to each other without his father finding out.

The truth settled over her like a cold breeze. "My mother."

Irene's face said it all.

"But she loved Paul," Gianna said. "How could she do that to him? How could she be an accomplice to murder?"

"You underestimate Elena. Gabriel was her brother, too. And despite what Anthony told you about Elena, she wasn't the angel he made her out to be. She didn't marry Royce out of guilt, but because she needed to be sure the cops wouldn't trace it back to her. All of this could've been prevented if she had thrown out that damn watch all those years ago."

Irene sighed wearily, leaning against the doorframe.

"We had it all planned out, you know. After we found out that Paul was responsible for selling the drugs that killed Gabriel, we planned on how to get justice. At the time, I suspected Elena was seeing someone. She'd been acting weird for months at this point. Sneaking out in the middle of the night. Being gone for hours after school. I went into her room one night when she was out, found the letters and put two and two together.

"When she found out what Paul had done, she agreed to help. She called Paul on the phone he had given her, asking him to meet her out by the farmhouse. She told him she'd gotten into an argument with Anthony and he had left her there in the middle of the night. Elena had him wrapped around her finger." She smirked. "Paul came right away.

"When Elena wouldn't come with him into the car, he was confused. But then he saw Anthony and me and realized he had been tricked. He was angry. He started shouting, and one thing led to another." A haunted look clouded Irene's eyes. "It got out of hand. One moment my brother and Paul were yelling at each other, and the next the two were tackling each other to the ground when we heard a crack."

Irene's voice tightened. "Paul's body started to shake. His eyes rolled to the back of his head and foam started coming out of his mouth. I still—I still remember how Elena had started yelling, turning him over onto his side. Shouting something about a seizure. But it was too late."

"He was dead," Gianna said.

Irene nodded. "Anthony was in shock, unable to tear his eyes from Paul's body. His hands were soaked in Paul's blood. He'd tried to stop the bleeding. He just sat there, not responding to anything I said. So I did what I had to do. What I always did. I took care of it.

"I took Paul's wallet from his pants and told Elena to grab his watch to make it look like he'd been robbed. She refused at first, sputtering about how we needed to call the police, but I snapped some sense into her. If the police were involved, Anthony would be arrested for murder and we'd be accomplices. I remembered that Paul had driven his car, so I ran to it. Handling it wasn't too difficult. I'd seen tears in tires at my boyfriend's shop. It wasn't too difficult to find a nail in the road and make it look accidental.

"Anthony wanted to turn himself in but I wasn't going to let him do that. I'd already lost one brother. I wasn't about to lose another. When we heard about Freddy Atwater being a suspect, I recognized the name. His car was at my boyfriend's shop. I went over there the next day and hid the wallet inside his glove compartment. We called and put in an anonymous tip. Luck did the rest for us. I thought we'd gotten away with it, that Anthony was safe."

Irene scoffed at the idea. "But then one day I got a phone call from my brother, asking for my help. He said two teenagers had broken into his car and stolen the watch. The watch," Irene gritted out, "that Elena was supposed to throw in the lake on her way to school the next morning. But she hadn't. She confessed to Anthony that she had hidden it only a few days before she died. I would've thought that was the end of it, only Anthony couldn't find the heart to throw it away.

"He never stopped feeling guilty for Paul's death. Especially what it did to poor Elena. She was never the same afterwards." Irene laughed coldly. "Years of hiding away evidence, keeping my siblings out of jail, only to be ruined by my sister's stupid sentimentality."

"It wasn't sentimentality," Gianna said. "Elena loved Paul."

"Clearly not enough to betray him."

Gianna wanted to argue, but she bit her tongue. She still needed more information. "Anthony didn't kill Grant, did he? He only said that to protect you, but really, you're the one who should be in jail."

"Do you think I wanted to kill them?" Irene shrilled. "It was an accident. I'd planned on giving them money in exchange for the watch. I told them to meet me near the ruins so we could do the exchange. They agreed. But then they tried to see my face. It was a stupid plan." She shook her head. "Ollie dropped the gun near us when he attacked. I wasn't planning on using it, but then Grant moved so quickly …" She closed her eyes. "I can still hear his friend's screams when I close my eyes."

Even though a part of her didn't think she could bear it, she asked, "What happened then?"

"He ran. I chased after him. It was dark and he was shaken. He didn't see the lake, not until it was too late. By the time I found him, he was already dead." She huffed. "The watch wasn't on either of them."

Gianna could picture what happened next. She would've called Anthony to help her. Ollie had never gotten on that bus. "Anthony drove the car to the bus station," Gianna said, piecing together the events of that night. It would've taken some time to bury Ollie and frame it all on him. Angela had woken up in the middle of the night, when she thought she heard something.

"You snuck into the Kipmans' house, thinking the watch was there, and when it wasn't, you left. You got rid of their phones so they couldn't track the messages and have no doubt about Ollie's guilt."

Irene nodded. "We promised not to talk about it ever. To protect Elena's memory and you."

"You didn't do it to protect me," Gianna seethed. "You did it to protect yourselves. You're not even sorry you killed two innocent boys in cold blood—"

"They had a choice!" Gianna flinched at Irene's raised tone. "As did I. Don't ask me if I regret everything because all of it was for this family." She laughed, shaking her head. "But then again, when has anything ever been that simple for me? I practically raised my siblings. My parents certainly didn't. I gave them a luxury I never could afford as a kid. What other choice do you have when your brother comes to you in tears because he's so lost without his other half? What else can you do but agree to help ease his pain? When your sister calls you in the middle of the night, terrified because her deadbeat husband just drowned the dog in the bathtub and her toddler saw the whole thing? When you're in the middle of a serious conversation with your fiancé and you get a call saying that the one piece of evidence that could destroy everything you worked for is out of your hands? The answer is you don't."

Gianna willed herself to look at Irene and see it from her point of view. To see the woman who spent all her life protecting her family, and she did see it. But she also saw Ollie's contagious smile. She saw Nathan's sadness over his brother, Angela's tears in the low-lit room of The Retro, and a younger version of her mother crying over Paul Beckett's body. Grant's picture on their high school walls. Their deaths never should have happened.

It wasn't a question of what came next. Gianna had already made the decision. But when she lunged toward the door that led to the living room, she found her legs falling slowly behind her. She reached out for the wall, steadying herself against it. She felt off. Everything felt wrong.

She pushed herself against the wall, sliding down the hallway until she came to the counter. Irene's heels clicked on the floor behind her.

She faced her, her tongue heavy as she spoke. "What … what did you do?"

"What needed to be done."

Her eyes gazed over the counter, and she spotted it—the orange prescription bottle shoved behind the utensils.

Irene's voice was distant, coming in and out of her ears. "After Paul's death, Anthony had a hard time sleeping. He'd taken everything they had over the counter to help him escape the nightmares. I thought he'd stopped taking them years ago, but imagine my shock when I discovered these on the top of the fridge." She gave the small bottle a shake, the pills rattling inside, echoing in her ears.

Her stomach twisted. Gianna always assumed that Anthony took the pills because of the haunting terrors other people committed. It hadn't occurred to her that his sleeplessness was due to the one murder he was responsible for.

"But … I didn't drink anything," she rasped.

And then she remembered—the water bottle in the car.

"Don't worry," Irene said. "I only put a dose small enough that they wouldn't kick in for a little while, just for you to fall asleep for a few hours until we get to New York."

She shook her head. *I don't want to go to New York. I don't want to go anywhere with you.*

She must've spoken the words out loud, because Irene said, "I know, but we can't stay here. People are already looking too closely at us and I can't risk anyone finding out the truth. I was planning on taking you tomorrow morning, but I had a feeling something like this would happen. You were always too smart for your own good, Gianna.

"I promised Anthony I would look after you." Irene's voice came to Gianna as a shriek, switching from ear to ear until her breath was right next to her. "I'm the only family you have left, Gianna, and you're mine."

This wasn't right. Family didn't drug other family members' drinks. Family didn't ask each other to keep secrets like this. Gianna tried to say this, but the words came out sluggish. She needed to go. She needed to call the police.

Her phone. Gianna felt nothing but the skirts of her dress. She left her purse upstairs, her phone still inside. A part of her wanted to cry, but she bit it back. *Nathan.* If she cut through the lawn across the street, she'd make it to the Kipmans' house. They would help her. They would call the police.

Irene's back was to her as she went through the cupboards, grabbing food. She was still talking, but Gianna couldn't hear any of it over the pounding of her heartbeat in her ears. Using the wall for support and guidance, she took small steps toward the door until her fingers grasped it.

Cool air hit her face as she staggered down the steps, holding herself up only by the railing. Her ears rang loudly; her head throbbed.

One step.

Two.

A cold hand gripped her arm like a vine. *"Gianna."*

She closed her eyes, and when they opened again, she was staring at the open car door and at an empty back seat.

"No!" she cried, hurling back from the icy grip on her arm. Her fingers lost their purchase, and she stumbled down the driveway. The house across the street was fading in and out of her vision.

Almost, her head screamed. She was almost there.

And then Irene was in front of her again, coaxing her into the car. "—you'll feel different about this in the morning. You'll see this was all for the best."

"No," she grumbled weakly. She couldn't get into that car.

Summoning all the strength she had left, she pushed past Irene and sprinted across the street. Colors blurred past her, blending and twisting into one colossal painting. Ten more feet and she'd be there. Almost—

Hands shoved her down to the grass, a weight pinning her knees and arms.

"No!" she sobbed, trying to push herself up, but she was too weak, mind addled by the pills. Irene was speaking sentences she couldn't dissect; her fingernails biting down into her skin.

Get off, get off, get off.

Her throat cried for air. She was dying. She was going to die here, just like Paul Beckett, like Ollie and Grant.

"Gianna!" A voice that didn't belong to Irene called out her name. The biting pressure on her arms vanished and was replaced with warmth, like sunlight on a summer afternoon. She curled into that warmth, grateful for it.

"It's okay, Holmes," Theo said, pushing hair back from her face. The stars and moon blended together behind him. Her head was propped on his lap, his eyes rapidly searching her for wounds she knew he wouldn't find. You couldn't see a bleeding heart torn to pieces. "What's wrong? Tell me how to fix this, Holmes."

"Theo!" Nathan appeared above them, panting hard. "You found her."

"Something's wrong," she heard him tell Nathan. Her eyes opened slightly, and she saw he hadn't taken his eyes off her. "She's not … something's wrong."

"Theodore." Mitch was here, too? Who else was here to see her final moments? "Did you call the police?"

"Gianna, can you understand me?"

Gianna tried to nod, looking at Theo, as his face swirled in with the other colors in the background. She registered Theo saying something and other voices, but she couldn't see them. Her vision was clouded with a series of images: Irene holding a gun pointed at her, Anthony's hands covered in blood, and her mother mouthing the two words she'd written in that letter all those years ago, but it wasn't her voice saying it. It was Gianna's. *I'm sorry. I'm sorry.*

I'm …

EPILOGUE

SIX WEEKS LATER

Gianna's muscles screamed as she heaved the last box onto the ground, pushing it along with the others. She straightened, wiping an arm across her forehead. She had cracked all the windows, allowing a faint breeze to flow through the room, but the spring heat had taken its toll inside the house.

"That's the last for this room," she declared, setting her hands on her hips.

Only two rooms were left to be finished before the movers came. She should've packed all of it away weeks ago, before she left for the criminology program, before she walked the stage at graduation with Theo and Valarie, but she couldn't bring herself to do it then. Now, she had little choice. As it turned out, solving a decades-old murder case did wonders for a résumé. After summer ended, she would be leaving.

Leaving Echo Falls. And she couldn't leave this empty house and all its ghosts to collect dust.

Thunk. Gianna turned to see a box of all her books from her room by her feet. Theo's face was red from exhaustion as he stood. "Where do you want these, Holmes?"

She pointed toward the pile of boxes that all had the words GIANNA'S BEDROOM written in bold black Sharpie on the side. He shoved the box into the pile and grabbed the tape from the floor. Before he could start taping it together, she held a hand out.

"I'll do it," she said.

Theo raised an eyebrow but said nothing. He handed her the tape and stepped to the side as she sealed away all her mystery books. She was done with mysteries. For good.

The tape still clutched in her hand, her eyes drifted to the other section of boxes with Irene's name scribbled on it. That night still lingered in the forefront of her mind, no matter how hard she tried to forget it. One moment she was in the present, and the next she was back on the grass, Irene's fingers digging into her skin, unable to do anything as the drugs stole control of her body.

She supposed she should be grateful that was all she saw. She had faint memories of what came after she passed out. Flashes of the paramedics pumping the drugs from her body, waking up in the hospital to find her friends surrounding her, and then the police coming in, asking questions. Resting for a few days in a hospital bed, feeling sorry for herself as her whole world shattered around her. No one in her life had been as she thought they were. Not even her own mother.

And then, a week later, was Ollie's funeral.

It turned out that Anthony wasn't lying when he told them where Ollie was buried. Irene had gone back at some point to move his body to a different location in the same area without telling him. It wouldn't have been the first thing she hid from Anthony.

Ollie's remains were put to rest a week later at the Echo Falls Cemetery, where the Kipmans held a private funeral. Gianna and Theo were the only ones who weren't related to Ollie that were invited. The sky was clear that day, the sun bearing down on all of them, with a slight breeze in the air. It reminded her of the day she first met Ollie.

"For five years I've mourned my brother," Nathan had said, a slight wobble in his voice. "Ollie was the best big brother anyone could ask for. He was there when you needed him, even if you didn't want him to be. He had a laugh that could put a smile on the coldest of faces. But most importantly, Ollie cared. It didn't matter if you were strangers or old or young—Ollie would be there. He had the biggest heart of us all, and I can't help but feel that if he were here, he'd tell us some joke to make us laugh." A few laughs scattered across the crowd. Nathan looked from his paper to his brother's grave, his face solemn. "I miss you, Ollie."

Nathan stepped from the center, walking towards Gianna and Theo. "Do you want to say something?" Nathan asked her. "After all, you're the reason any of us are here."

"I don't know," she hesitated, grasping the letter she had written to Ollie. She had planned on reading it at his grave once everyone left.

"That's okay," Nathan said.

He turned to face the crowd, but something made Gianna step forward. "I'll do it."

She stepped up to the front, facing Ollie's family. "I don't think there's a way for me to top that," she joked, her voice raspy. "The first time I met Ollie, he saved my life. I wouldn't be here today if it weren't for him. When I began this investigation, it wasn't because I wanted to solve a mystery or even get fame. I just couldn't picture him as the killer everyone made him out to be. Which was why, when I heard he was missing, my first instinct was to find him. Not to turn him in for murder, but because there were people out there who didn't know the real Ollie, didn't know about the people who cared about him. People who looked up to him."

Her eyes found Nathan's in the crowd. He gave her a sad smile.

"I only wish that I could have repaid the debt before he went," she continued. "I'll always remember him as the boy a block over with the skateboard with a smiley face sticker on the bottom of his board. Who taught me how to skate and inspired me to be a better person. A happier one despite all the cards life dealt us."

A shuddered breath left her. "He was killed trying to prove a man's innocence. Ollie was good until the end. And I will live by his example for the rest of my life."

Despite the sad reason they all came together, the day felt lighter, like a heavy cloud had been lifted from their town.

"I know it sounds kind of crazy," Nathan had said afterward, as they walked back to the Kipmans', "but it feels like he's here with us. That he made this day so perfect."

Gianna took Nathan's hand in hers and squeezed. "I don't think that sounds crazy at all."

The same day Ollie's body was put to rest, Freddy was released from prison. She had watched from the television as daughter and son were reunited with their father. Carrie had stopped by to thank her, even inviting Gianna to meet her father, but Gianna didn't think it would be right, considering it was her family that separated theirs for decades.

What *was* crazy was the letter the Kipmans received later that week in the mail. A formal apology from Kyle Jenkins personally, for everything he said about their family. He even went online to apologize, no doubt from all the criticism he was receiving after Grant's true murderer was revealed. Gianna got a letter, too, although it was less flowery than the one Nathan got.

It's not often I find myself wrong, but this one time would be the exception. I can't say that I won't look forward to our future talks.

Sincerely,

K. Jenkins.

Gianna snorted, remembering how she tore the letter to pieces and flushed it down the toilet right after. Kyle might have been convinced their story was still unfinished, but that didn't mean she had to.

"What are you smiling about?" Theo was leaning against a box, a gleam in his eye as he looked at her. "Not that I'm complaining. It's good to see you smile, Holmes."

An uninvited flutter made its way into her stomach. Speaking of unfinished stories …

She shrugged. "I was just thinking about what I'm going to order at Lori's when we finally finish up here."

"Hmm." Theo tapped the box. "I think I know what we need to motivate you."

He pulled his phone out and music started playing. She slapped a hand over her mouth to keep from laughing as he danced his way across the room, closing the space between them until he was standing right in front of her.

"You know we never did get to finish that second dance," he said, his voice low. A giddy smile crossed her lips as he took her hand in his and pulled her to her feet, twirling her around. After a second spin, she changed her mind. She didn't want to forget everything about that night.

As they danced, Gianna caught a glimpse of one of the framed pictures that hadn't been packed away. Her mother and her siblings smiled back at her. Gianna's body went cold. *You're no different than them,* the voice in her head echoed.

She stiffened in Theo's arms and he stepped back, eyebrows pulling into a line. "Are you—"

The doorbell echoed throughout the house, cutting off whatever he was going to say.

"I'll get it," Gianna said, breathless as she pulled away. Her face felt warm as she opened the door to find Valarie on the other side. "Val! Theo and I have already started …" Her words cut off at the sight of her friend's puffy eyes. "Val? What's wrong? What happened?"

Tears littered Valarie's beautiful face. "It's Liam." Her voice cracked. "I think … I think he's missing."

Interested in seeing more of Gianna and the gang? Keep up to date by signing up for Keona's newsletter:

What's included:

The Disappearance of Oliver Kipman Official Playlist
The Disappearance of Oliver Kipman Pinterest Boards
Bonus scenes
and more!

keonamistisshen.com

ACKNOWLEDGEMENTS

First off: Mom, Dad, Christian, Keilani and Layla—thank you for the endless encouragement and motivation. And by motivation, I mean the constant question: *"When are we going to get to read it?"* Seriously though, I could not have done it without you. Thank you, Mom and Dad, for your utmost patience for this book to come out; Keilani for listening to me ramble about my books for hours; and Leah for listening to my updates as I finished the book.

A ginormous thank you to my editors Michelle and Rue for all your hard work on turning this messy manuscript into a polished book. No number of words can express how grateful I am.

Thank you to my beta readers, who were the first to set eyes on this book!

And last but not least, thank you to all the readers (YOU) who picked up this book and decided to give it a shot. I hope you fell in love with Gianna, Theo, and Nathan as much as I did while bringing this story to life.

ABOUT THE AUTHOR

Keona Mistisshen fell in love with reading at a young age and has been falling ever since. After multiple attempts at writing a book at fifteen years old, she finally managed to pull together the world of her debut novel, *The Disappearance of Oliver Kipman*. When she's not writing or getting lost in a book, you can find her crocheting, strolling through bookstores, or spending time with her family.

www.ingramcontent.com/pod-product-compliance
Lightning Source LLC
Chambersburg PA
CBHW020930310726
48980CB00007B/707/J

* 9 7 9 8 9 9 9 3 9 0 7 1 4 *